THE POSTMISTRESS OF NONG KHAI

THE POSTMISTRESS OF NONG KHAI

FRANK HURST

Matador
9 Priory Business Park,
Wistow Road, Kibworth Beauchamp,
Leicestershire. LE8 0RX
Tel: 0116 279 2299
Email: books@troubador.co.uk
Web: www.troubador.co.uk/matador
Twitter: @matadorbooks

ISBN 978 1785890 574
British Library Cataloguing in Publication Data.
A catalogue record for this book is available from the British Library.

Printed and bound by CPI Group (UK) Ltd, Croydon, CR0 4YY
Typeset in 11pt Minion Pro by Troubador Publishing Ltd, Leicester, UK

Matador is an imprint of Troubador Publishing Ltd

For my wife Kate, who has stoically endured my many weaknesses.

"There is a condition worse than blindness, and that is, seeing something that isn't there."

Thomas Hardy

"Men outlive their love, but they don't outlive the consequences of their recklessness."

George Eliot (Middlemarch)

"Everything you look at can be turned into a story, you can make a tale out of everything you touch."

Hans Christian Andersen (The Elder Tree Mother)

Any work of fiction based on the classified activities of a secretly minded government service will inevitably contain a substantial facet of make-believe, as a true to life account would, in all probability, contravene some section of some official secrets act. This book is a work of fantasy. Names, characters, places, events and incidents are the product of the author's imagination and any character resemblance to real persons, living or dead, is purely coincidental.

PART ONE

CHAPTER ONE

Bangkok, Thailand – 14 April 1988

'Are you quite sure you can trust your informant, Mike?' Head of Station enquired languidly. He had asked me the same question the day before and it irritated me.

Pompous prat.

'No problems, Jim – it's all A1 and verifiable,' I replied wearing my best smile.

'OK, it's just that it seems to us that you are the only one with a handle on the intelligence.' He fixed me with a cold, oily stare; his face reminded me of a long dead codfish. I knew he expected me to elaborate but I resisted and just stared benignly back. After a few moments of awkward silence, he cleared his throat uneasily and said, 'Just checking. Nothing meant by it. Understand fully.'

It was uncalled-for and he knew it. It was a deliberately nasty prod, motivated by petty jealousy. He knew, only too well, that I had to do things by the book; there could be no careless shortcuts now, no sloppy tradecraft. If I had not been sure of my source, we would not be congregating now – I would not be wasting everyone's time.

Although I liked to pretend otherwise, there was a limit to what I could do single-handedly. The business of intelligence is often a solitary one, but with selective support from a few proven colleagues, I could control my cases up to a point. In my heart, I knew that working alone could only take me so far and that sooner or later I would have to involve others. That's where the trust came in. This had been such a long-running investigation already, winding its curious and unpredictable course over ten

3

years. Parcels of time filled by collecting scraps, listening to fragmented conversations, and watching – endless watching. There had been other cases, of course, but this one had become special.

Recently, the early wake-up calls; the late nights in noisy, smoke-filled bars and tedious airport concourses; the monotonous legwork spiked with intermittent, adrenaline-rush moments had cost me. My mind was deadened and my body creaking. So, I smiled a lot in a struggle to mask my disintegrating appearance, but the truth was that I was not looking my best. Embassy colleagues had begun to notice; a few of the closer ones had observed politely that I looked a little tired. I had brushed things off valiantly, but I felt exposed and psychologically debilitated, unable any longer to camouflage my puffy and lined features, caused by lack of sleep and too much alcohol. I did not look well. And there had been the assignations and the anxiety – the emotion-sapping interludes – the passion.

But I could see the end now. The briefing had been the penultimate scene in the last act – only the finale remained and I welcomed it; I wanted closure. The time for scheming was over. The embassy had not been helpful, constantly reminding me that I was a guest in the country with limited official powers to act. Her Britannic Majesty's Foreign and Commonwealth Office could support me only so far and did not welcome unpleasant surprises. It had been the FCO that had coerced me into assembling this mixed bag, most of whom had been invited just to satisfy protocol. Thankfully, there were a few key players in attendance; ones I knew and felt I could count on, locals mostly. They deserved the facts and I had done my best to impart my knowledge to them as fully as I dared. I would require their expertise and home-grown wisdom to help me deliver a workable plan.

There could be few secrets now. Like a gambler playing a decisive hand, I had put nearly all my intelligence chips on the table. The ones in my pocket were for self-preservation – to keep me in the game if my fortunes went awry. The two Thai specialists in the audience understood this. They accepted that I would conceal a few choice morsels from them – maybe the particulars of some clandestine methodology or the identity of my most coveted source. Officially, making such economies with the facts amongst allies was frowned upon. But everyone did it; they kept secrets from me and I did from them. It was a game – we knew that and we consented to it.

I chewed my lip and responded pleasantly to the diverse questions the small group had dreamed up. Most of their enquiries had been wearisomely brainless, asked only to justify their attendance. But slowly, their reservations had turned into support and even the Head of Chancery, a naturally cynical human being and very much one of the protocol invitees, was now upbeat.

'Looks spot on to me, Mike,' he puffed.

When the probing finally finished, those with any private doubts about the quality of my intelligence chose to remain silent and I took this as a green light to proceed. The Thais left quietly and the others returned to their air-conditioned offices, presumably confident that the operation was in good hands and mentally drafting the cables they would send to their various departments in London and Canberra, claiming all the credit when it was over. If the case collapsed, most of them would scuttle into the long grass and it would mean conspiratorial whispers and sideways glances at the Ambassador's weekly meeting for months.

As I tidied my papers and watched the others trundle contentedly out of the room, my Aussie colleague, Sonny, had shuffled up alongside to tell me he would catch the six thirty flight down to Phuket and we agreed to meet at the hotel later that evening. I had a more pressing engagement, however, and had booked an earlier aircraft. There remained some final fragments of information I had to collect; tiny facts which only my informant could provide. It was to be our final contact and I was already experiencing an overpowering sense of loss.

En route to Don Muang Airport, I reflected that the next twenty-four hours would be a major turning point, not just for the investigation, but for me also. I knew that the operational master plan would, almost certainly, be chucked in the bin within an hour or two – it pretty much always happened that way. We couldn't plan for a whole host of imponderables, but I found myself concerned less about the case than about my own personal demons. They worried me the most; the thought of them made me retch. There was no doubt – I was scared.

The hour-long flight south was annoyingly delayed to wait for a couple of connecting passengers from Copenhagen. I glared at them as they bumped down the aisle, overloaded with hand baggage, but they were clearly in holiday mood and showed no signs of remorse. I refused the coffee and cake proffered and called for a cold *Singha* beer instead. As we descended over the northeast coast of Phuket Island, I could see the tiny, sand-fringed, volcanic outcrops that sprouted out of the blue of Phang Nga Bay like a scattering of fallen petals from a frangipani bloom. The aircraft slid further downwards and the specks of billowing yachts and other small, littoral craft became increasingly visible as they left tell-tale white trails in their wakes, noiselessly plying the dappled shoreline.

That is where it's all going to play out. That expanse of dark water with its sprinkling of islands will be a witness to my fortune over the next few hours.

A car had been arranged for me and had been waiting for twenty minutes by the time I scurried out of domestic arrivals. I threw my small bag into the back seat and did some mental arithmetic, calculating with relief that I would just be a few minutes late for my rendezvous. Then we hit the first bottleneck and it dawned on me that there was something that I had not factored in – I had forgotten that it was *Songkran*, the Thai New Year.

As we approached the Kamala Beach Road the heat was only just beginning to slacken. The sun hovered low in the western sky, appearing to hesitate like an unwilling diver perched on a swollen cloud, before the inevitable fall towards the orange expanse of iridescent ocean. Brightly-painted long-tail boats swayed easily at their moorings. Silhouetted against the diminishing light, they appeared as charcoal cut-outs, sharply defined, touching the sky. Bathers yawned and stretched their cherry-oiled bodies out of their water's edge loungers, wearily shaking down sand-encrusted towels in readiness for the barefoot march along the shoreline towards one of the welcoming beach bars, perhaps to watch the sunset with an iced mai tai.

Songkran is a Buddhist festival designed for quiet reflection, prayer and the gift of food to monks; in practice, it's all about throwing water at people. Drunken locals roam the city streets armed with water pistols and buckets and if you are not careful you will get a soaking. I was definitely in no mood for a drenching, especially as my instinct told me that the next hour was going to be draining in the extreme – all because I craved the sight and scent of her just one more time.

We came across the first festival roadblock as we drew near to the outskirts of Patong. A young traffic policeman in a tight-fitting, brown uniform waved us down a side street. The cars obeyed and ground to a halt as a result. I glanced distractedly at my watch and all my private worries intensified. Even the *tuc tucs* were at a standstill.

Unexpectedly, the cab driver managed to break free and we ducked down an alley and back onto a major thoroughfare; he zigzagged through the crowds and cars, evading the next two roadblocks and most of the water projectiles. He took me down backstreets I never knew existed, around the sides of markets and shopping centres and even stole a shortcut through a hotel car park, which gave him access to a *soi*, or road, and minute by minute we jolted ever closer to my destination.

Clearly, the gods of Songkran were doing their worst and could control the weather, for there was an almighty clap of thunder and the heavens opened, releasing hot torrents of vertical rain that thumped onto the steel bonnet of the taxi. Stray tourists were suddenly everywhere, stepping off pavements unexpectedly, darting through traffic. Some were still in their sodden swimsuits as they hurried towards the shelter of their hotels. I opened the passenger window an inch and peered along the ever-bright shop-front lights of the beach road. The blue and red neon sign for the *Happy Endings* bar, about twenty yards up the street, greeted my squinting eyes.

'It's OK,' I shouted, 'you can stop here. I know where I am. I can walk from here.' As I levered myself out of the back seat, I pushed four blue fifty-baht notes into his outstretched hand.

I covered my face with fanned fingers, splashed my way across the street towards Bang La Road and hurried past the *Happy Endings*. Soon, I was wading along the pavement, trying my best to feel for the underwater potholes, now invisible through the muddy, red water. After a few minutes, I stumbled, sodden, across the open threshold of the *Blue Lotus*.

So much for trying to avoid a bucketing at Songkran!

The *Blue Lotus* was one of the many Patong bars that welcomed customers on the Bang La Road, but it tried to set itself above the others. Its pretensions meant that a cold *Kloster* cost twenty baht more than in any other place within a quarter of a mile. The bar staff, or Lotus Ladies, as they preferred to be called, were renowned for their good looks – or, at least, for what passed as beauty in the eyes of Steve Swann, the retired, American chief petty officer, who owned the bar. The rumour that he had personally selected each of them was probably true and judging by their appearance,

I suspected that recruitment must have been one of the business chores he enjoyed most. All his ladies wore a standard issue, tight-fitting, black cotton dress and no jewellery – an effort, apparently, to bring a sense of decorum to the establishment.

Steve was a big man with a disarming smile and a symbiotic relationship with the Patong police chief. The latter held the true key to his success. Some of his regulars thought the *Blue Lotus* was sophisticated, which given the primordial nature of most of its near competitors was perhaps not too surprising. But at six thirty in the evening, before the rush, it was at least quiet, cool and subtly lit, and unquestionably an ideal place to have my meeting.

She was waiting for me at a tall table at the shadowy rear of the bar, under a set of mounted photographs of old US warships. Her slim legs were wrapped around the frame of a metal bar stool. A single empty seat stood beside her. In the background, a familiar Thai ballad played softly. '*Sa baai, sa baai,*' the vocalist crooned, which means relaxed, comfortable. I felt quite the opposite, but the gentle melody was pleasant all the same.

'I'm late,' I said simply, fixing my eyes on the remnants of the lemon soda in her hands. 'I'm sorry, Lek.'

'*Mai pen rai* – no worries, Khun Mike, I can wait.' Even now, she still insisted on using the polite form, *Khun* Mike, meaning Mr. or Mrs.

I shook the corners of my dripping shirt. One of the ladies hovered. 'A *Singha*, please. *Yen yen,* cold please.'

'You want big one or small?' she chirped.

'Small is OK,' I smiled back.

'What about your friend – she want more drink?'

Lek shook her head and pointed to her half-full glass, '*Mai ka, kop khun ka.*'

We sat in silence for a few seconds, knowing the routine well by now; our official exchanges were usually functional and brief. But this time I had a desolate urge to linger in her company. I looked at her now and marvelled again at her flawless complexion.

Before I could speak, she pursed her lips and started to open her mouth as if she was making a supreme effort to overcome a sudden attack of dumbness.

'I have what you want…'

I said nothing and just looked at her.

'Bart has got the place. He wants me to take something to Kevin. He does not want to go himself and he does not trust the phone. He has marked it here.' She reached into her handbag and pulled out a shiny tourist map.

My god, a bloody holiday map! Unbelievable. I must have been giving them too much credit.

She passed me the folded sheet, which I unwrapped, sliding my bottle of beer away in the process. Between the advertisements for restaurants, hire car services and elephant trekking there was a glossy picture of Phuket Island framed in a rectangle, about twenty-four inches by twelve. Lek pointed to the top right-hand corner where a small, black biro "x" had been drawn in the middle of the electric blue bay of Phang Nga, about three miles to the right of Koh Yao Yai, a long, thin, double-headed island off the east coast of Phuket. The tiny cross in the sea was directly east from a low-lying isthmus that connected the two larger "heads" of the island.

Perhaps this map is not as "Mickey Mouse" as I thought.

'What has he said to you? Tell me again.'

'He wants me to give this to Kevin tonight at the *On On* – and give him a message.'

'Yes?'

'At eight, I will see him in the lobby.'

'And then what?'

'I have to give him some numbers.' She put her hand into her silk blouse and drew a small piece of paper from inside the left cup of her bra. 'These.' She handed the scrap to me.

I opened the paper and my heart bumped against my ribcage.

535543955855609

You beauty,' I croaked to myself as the significance of the fifteen numbers hit me. No difficult codebreaking was needed – they were transposed, of course, but that was easy to unravel. Astonishing! I tried to appear calm, but if this was authentic, it would be gold ingots. 'Did Bart say anything else?'

'Only that we would go away together afterwards and all would be fine – to trust him.'

The irony was not lost on me and I was sure she felt the same. *Where's the trust here?*

'Did he say where he will be when the boats arrive – where he will meet you?'

'If everything is OK, he will go to Kuala Lumpur the next day. I have to go to meet him in KL. He will not go to meet the boats when they come – he says it is not safe – Kevin will go. He will stay nearby and wait for Kevin to tell him everything is OK. If Kevin gives him bad news, he has a friend who will take him to Langkawi in a speedboat. When he gets there, he will call me and we can meet in KL next week.'

'This is new,' I said. 'Who is this friend?'

'He did not say, but I think he is a Thai man.'

'Do you know about this speedboat?'

'No, but he has a Thai friend in Rawai who has a big speedboat. We went out together to Coral Island last month. You remember, Khun Mike, I told you about it.'

I recalled her saying she had been out on a pleasure boat trip with Bart a few weeks earlier, but had thought no more of it at the time – merely a day's jaunt, I had fancied.

'Do you know who this man is, Lek?'

'His name is Khun Bee. I think it is him. I think Bart will go with him to Langkawi.'

'Let me copy this, Lek.' I pulled out a pen and scribbled the numbers on a paper napkin. 'Don't worry about the map, I can remember the picture.'

I should have felt elated but my gut ached and my throat was dry, despite the now drained bottle of *Singha*. I called the girl over and ordered another. Lek was still sipping her juice and waved her hand to show she wanted no more.

We sat perfectly still. We seemed physically closer than five minutes ago. The bar was quieter or maybe it was my imagination. I really did not know what I should say. Thank you, perhaps?

'Will you go to Amsterdam when all this is over?'

'Yes, it is what he wants. I will go. You know I have to try. It is best for me and my family. I can work in Holland and send money back to my father and son in Nong Khai. Bart is kind to me.' She paused and looked at me. 'Will it be cold, Khun Mike? I hate the cold.'

'Yes, I am afraid so, Lek,' I said softly. She put her hand close to mine on the table and our fingers touched.

'I will miss you, *teelak,*' she said. It was one of my favourite Thai words, *teelak*: darling.

'You could stay, you know – maybe I can help you find a business in Patong or Nong Khai. You could stay here and help your family that way.'

She tried to smile but her eyes betrayed her. 'I must go to Netherlands Embassy in Bangkok next week for Holland visa. He has booked a flight for me. Then I will meet him in KL. After that, everything will be OK, all clear; we will have money and we can start a new life.'

She paused and her little finger gripped mine. Around her wrist was the gold bangle that I had unwisely given her as a birthday present. It took my mind elsewhere for a moment.

'This is the last one he will do, Khun Mike. He has promised me.'

'I know,' I said. We sat without speaking for a few minutes.

The waitress returned with the cold beer. I gazed out across the empty bar onto the street. The rain had let up and I sensed a whiff of fresh jasmine on my face. A battered motorbike stopped outside. Its small sidecar supported a blue striped awning and was loaded with pots, pans and dishes of fresh fruit. An elderly woman climbed out of the saddle, deftly avoiding the puddles, stretched her groaning limbs and started to set up a stall in the street. Soon we would detect the comforting bouquet of fresh pancakes and cooked bananas.

'I must go soon; I must talk to my friends,' I said. 'Don't worry, I will make sure Bart is safe. I won't tell them about the speedboat and Langkawi or KL. I'll find something else to say.'

'Why do you do this for me?' She had asked this many times in the last few weeks and my response had always been the same.

'Because I love you, Lek, and I want you to be happy. I think about you every day and worry so much that you are safe. But you and I cannot work out – you know that. This is the best thing to do now, for both of us. Bart is a lucky man.'

She scrutinised me again and her lips nudged at her lemon soda. Her wide eyes moistened but she said nothing.

'I must go now,' I whispered.

Our fingers touched again but this time she gripped my hand and squeezed. I knocked over my half-empty bottle of beer. The mood lightened – I was wet enough already. Seizing the opportunity, I stood up to leave, awkwardly blotching my trousers with a stray napkin.

'If you need me – an emergency – you know where to find me,' I said. 'I will be there to help you. I promise.'

She nodded. A line of moisture fell from the corner of her eye.

As she wiped it away her lip trembled. She struggled to frame a smile, but she knew this was the end and there was no point in pretending.

'*Chohk dee, teelak,*' I said. 'Good luck, *teelak.*'

She stepped off her stool and her legs folded, unable even to withstand her petite figure. As she struggled for balance, she threw her arms around me and looked up into my face.

'Thank you for everything, Khun Mike. I will never forget – I love you always. I cry now.'

I kissed her forehead, held her slim shoulders in my hands and gazed at her long, dark eyelashes. An unbearable few seconds passed and I released her.

'Goodbye, Lek,' I said and walked away, out into the Bang La night.

My apartment and the encrypted phone were just a short distance away by car. My shirt was sticking to my back, still damp from the earlier downpour and from the emotions that now simmered inside me. I had never felt so drained, so dejected. I needed to find a cool sanctuary to compose myself. It was going to be a busy night and I had to think straight. The friendless back seat of a cab seemed the perfect place and in a few moments I had stopped one of the many that plied the beach road. The traffic was jammed, of course, and we started a time-consuming creep towards the intersection into Rat U Thit Road. The inevitable rise in blood pressure failed to materialise – for once I was in no mood to brood about the snarled congestion – the truth was, I embraced it.

PART TWO

CHAPTER ONE

A course set by my father's colonial government career and the changing face of national priorities were the curious reasons why I was now living and working in Bangkok; the seeds of my destiny had been sown in 1940 as I took my first clumsy steps in a Singapore playpen with my mother fussing and the Japanese pressing in from all sides. My love affair with the Orient became unstoppable when my father was posted overseas again after the war – this time to Hong Kong.

Back home in suburban Britain, the dreams I had nurtured of finding my own job in the Far East took an almighty setback – or so I thought at the time – when, aged twenty-one, I accepted a position in the home civil service and learned that my allocated department, HM Customs and Excise, had no international representation and, worse, they had no plans for it either. The work was dull, but I learned to curb my disappointment; for excitement, I married the curvaceous Maureen, whom I had met at an office Christmas party. A daughter, Caroline, soon followed and my life was quickly absorbed by nappies, lawnmowers and Radio 2.

But as my world advanced unvaryingly into the 70s a new war began to occupy the energies of governments – the war on drugs. I had showed some talent for "sleuthing", as it was quaintly described, and as departmental dead men's shoes became available I had filled them. After a few tedious years of this relatively stress-free and ordered existence, things suddenly changed. One day, pretty much out of the blue, I received a call that would revolutionise my existence. The department's elite Investigation Branch had invited me to join their hallowed numbers. Apart from the accolade the appointment conferred, the new job promised extra money and the prospect of a considerably more fulfilling and exciting career.

The Investigation Branch was perceived, by anyone who counted, as the zenith of the department's many-fingered law enforcement arm. It attracted the most resourceful officers and I pinched myself as I realised that I was about to become one of their splendid number. Despite my excitement, I had a definite feeling of unease as I made my way into their rather ordinary-looking offices in New Fetter Lane on my first day. Given the glamorous and powerful reputation of The Branch, as it was commonly called, and the reverence it was held in by most, I had been wondering for many weeks what cosmic events must have combined to offer up this opportunity for me. But as I presented myself to the uniformed Revenue Constable at the front desk, I was still none the wiser. So I signed in solemnly and made my way upstairs to the second floor, where a meeting with Mervyn Nugent awaited.

Mervyn was the Senior Investigation Officer of Customs Team C and my new boss. He was completely different from anyone I had encountered in my short, provincial career. A pit-bull of a man – squat, stout and grim-faced – he had played as hooker for Bridgend Rugby Club in his youth. He was not a man with whom to be messed.

'Sit down, Mike,' he said without a hint of benevolence, his valleys accent unaffected by his years in London. 'You have come to us from Bill Gough – how is he?'

'Very well, Mr. Nugent. He sends his regards.'

'Good man – Bill. A little quiet for my taste, but does his stuff, all the same. No need to call me Mr. Nugent – it's all first names here. Just call me Merv.' He smiled weakly.

'I hope you don't disappoint. You will find it different

here – you'll earn your corn, for sure – long hours and lots of pressure. We do things right, here at the IB, and we take no prisoners.'

He tried another smile. This time, the attempt produced something bordering on cheery. 'What I mean to say is, we take no *passengers* – we take as many prisoners as we can.' He grinned expectantly and I beamed back. He had made a joke and the ice was broken. 'We have a saying here: we work hard and we play hard. We don't mix the two. I hope you understand what I mean.'

'Yes,' I replied, 'of course I…'

'Good, it's important that you know the distinction. Follow the rest and you won't go far wrong.'

I nodded and in that moment I grasped that it was best to let him do the talking.

'Now, there is something I need to brief you on,' he said darkly. 'Have you heard of OTW?'

'No, I can't say I have.'

'In order to collect the best intelligence against the most serious criminals, we here at the IB have authority to intercept and record telephone conversations. Did you know that?'

'No.'

'Righto – now you need to forget it. You must never discuss this with colleagues. Do you understand? Especially with those outside the IB – they do not need to know and it's not in our interest that they *do* know. If the subject is raised, even by your colleagues in the IB, you will say nothing and tell me about it immediately. This is important. You have signed the Official Secrets Act, so you know the implications. When the time comes for you to learn more about intercepts, you will be told. Is that clear?'

I nodded again and ventured a question. 'What does OTW stand for, Merv?'

He scrutinised me and said unaffectedly, 'Over The Way…

OK, now I think it's time for you to meet the team.' He stood up and asked me to follow him along the corridor.

Customs Team C was London-based and had a direct mandate to tackle the largest general smuggling cases that surfaced in Southern and Eastern England. The patch was large: it included Heathrow Airport to the west and the ports of Dover and Felixstowe to the east, plus everything south of these lines in between. But in effect, the team was a national operation and its officers could travel anywhere in the country, if the need arose. London-based smugglers did their dirty work throughout the land and it was our duty to track their movements and catch them in the act, if we could.

The staff under Merv's command consisted of seven officers and a junior clerk. I was now the proud possessor of the call sign "India Charlie Eight". There was a strict pecking order when it came to the allocation of call signs and at number eight, I was right at the bottom. Despite the newness of my surroundings and the intimidating nature of my workmates, I soon found myself enjoying the banter, even though at the beginning I was treated with disdain – much like a boy from the remove mixing it with the sixth form. The IB was a well-organised and properly resourced outfit – its professional standards were high and it wanted to preserve a reputation for hard-nosed but fair case building and investigation.

I was taught to mistrust the police, especially the officers at New Scotland Yard, the Met. We called them the "Oscar Bravo" (Old Bill) and they called us the "Church" (C&E) – neither agency was particularly imaginative with their epithets. We avoided including the police in our cases whenever possible and, as a result, frictions built up between us. We perpetually cited the threat from corruption, of intelligence getting into the wrong hands, and played our cards close to our chest, giving nothing away unless absolutely necessary. And anyway, we said to ourselves, we were self-sufficient and didn't need them. We had a raft of customs laws to underpin us and the skills and resources to conduct even the most sophisticated investigations. We also had substantial powers – some greater than theirs. We could arrest and prosecute, that was a given, but there was one ancient power which we had retained over the centuries and it created real envy. We had the ability to enter premises without a search warrant.

An ancient charter, a legacy from the time of Charles II, provided us with a Writ of Assistance, valid during the lifetime of the reigning monarch and for six months beyond, which allowed us to cross the threshold and search any property in the kingdom if we had reason to believe it contained seizable goods. Not for us, the frenzied trips to find a magistrate in the middle of a wintry night, on the hunt for a search warrant! We just went to the boss, who issued a writ straight from his office security cupboard. The formidable document was usually secreted behind the Glenmorangie. The IB had at least a dozen of these prized parchments handily available if the need arose and we flaunted them provocatively in police stations whenever the opportunity presented itself.

As competition for the best cases increased, so did the turf warfare and our relationship with the police bordered on the downright hostile at times – it was unhealthy, no doubt, but it did provide an extra layer of frisson to our working week.

As a team, we made a lot of cases and were regular attendees on the London law court circuit. In the process, I learned to respect the courts but be wary of lawyers, even the ones assigned to prosecute on our behalf.

The hours were long and I found myself away from home for extensive periods – just as well Maureen could hold the fort.

After about a year, I was called in to see Merv. His demeanour towards me had remained largely unchanged. He looked at me ominously when I took a seat in his office.

'I have just read the witness statement you took last week from John Foster. He is an import agent in Dover, I believe. Haven't you heard of *hearsay*, Mike?' he said gloomily.

'Er, yes, of course – have I drafted it badly?' He read from the paper in front of him. '"On 14 June, I met a port worker called Peter Fishwick in the dock bar at Tilbury. Peter told me that he knew a man called Fred who was bringing drugs into the port on the back of… et cetera, et cetera…" Anything wrong with that, Mike?'

I flushed. It was a schoolboy error. The reference to Fishwick telling Foster about someone bringing in drugs was clearly hearsay and, as such, it was inadmissible evidence. While it was not critical and the mistake could easily be rectified by obtaining a statement from Fishwick, it was an embarrassing blunder.

'I'm sorry, Merv. It's my mistake. I don't know what I was thinking. I'll get back down there and sort it out.'

'Yes, you had better do that. And take young George with you – he needs to know how to take a proper statement.'

As I got up to leave he called me back.

'Before you go, Mike, you should know that you have passed your probation. Well done. You are properly one of us now. I'll be allocating a case to you next week.' He put out his hand, while his staged smile fought a losing battle with the melancholy expression in his eyes.

'Thank you, Merv, and er… I'm sorry about the statement.'

'Never again, please,' he said, still without a hint of an encouraging expression. *I* was smiling, though – from ear to ear. As I hurried to leave his office he called me back for the second time. 'Ah, Mike, I need you to ask the others about this. A name has cropped up in a new enquiry and I think some of the lads may know this guy – rings a bell, for some reason.' He handed me a slip of paper. The name "Isaac Hunt" was scribbled in his tiny handwriting.

'Ask the chaps if they know this fellow, would you, and come back to me straight away with their answer – quick now – it's important.'

I hurried off, gathered the team together and asked the question. 'Do any of you know Isaac Hunt?' The answer came ringing back to me in a rehearsed chorus of shouts.

'Yes, Mike, we know you are!'

I gawked blankly; they hooted and roared. And then the embarrassing comprehension of what I had said suddenly hit me. I looked up and saw Merv standing at the door, his florid face distorted by a huge grin.

'What was that you asked, Mike?' he said, laughing. 'I didn't quite catch it.'

Despite the humiliation, I knew I had arrived. I was part of the team and had been properly accepted. It was an excuse to go to the pub to celebrate – so we did.

CHAPTER TWO

The cases came and went and my experience grew further. My first investigation as the officer in charge was exhilarating. It involved a hundred kilos of ganja smuggled in from Montego Bay in a fifty-foot ketch, a midnight beach landing on a remote corner of Anglesey and a car chase along a dark coast road. The case was reminiscent of an earlier time conjured up by Rudyard Kipling's romantic depictions of deserted, moonlit beaches, hidden caves, flashing lights on clifftops, creaking ships and stalwart ponies heavily laden with tea, gin and brandy clattering over cobbled streets. In this twentieth century version, we had deployed a large group of officers, some borrowed from other parts of the IB, and also enlisted the services of the department's Marine Branch, which dispatched two revenue cutters into the Irish Sea. At its conclusion, we had managed to capture the whole crew and its shore party, surprising them as they unloaded the drugs onto the beach in the early hours. All five of the gang were later convicted at Mold Crown Court and when the jury brought in their verdicts, I was ecstatic.

By the mid-70s, the Investigation Branch had expanded both its manpower and projection, so much so that it was renamed the Investigation Division, or ID. A new recruitment drive meant that its numbers had more than trebled since I joined. After five short but lively years as "Charlie Eight", I was transferred onto my first specialist drugs team – Team D – the Deltas, and with my new call sign of "India Delta Four" my star began to rise.

The head of Drugs Team Delta was a studious, moustachioed, stylish man called Bob Hibbard. He spoke in a hoarse whisper and it was easy to underestimate him. He was as physically different from Mervyn Nugent as it was possible to be, but they shared a common trait – both were hard-nosed investigators from the old school. They just went about their business in different ways and I soon realised that Bob was no pushover, despite his scholarly outward appearance.

As my youthful ambition for an international career had long been forgotten, I concentrated on improving my investigation skills and doing what I could to help with the family. The latter at times seemed precious little. The work, however, was fabulous. The next few years provided an equal mixture of hard graft and never-to-be-forgotten, breath-taking moments; then a magical thing happened. Just as we were recovering from our Queen's Silver Jubilee hangovers, I had another career-transforming piece of news. We had been investigating a case involving tea imported from the Indian subcontinent; cannabis had been cleverly concealed in tea chests destined for the London auction market. It was proving to be a fascinating enquiry involving the Amsterdam drugs trade, crooked foreign officials and corrupt tea brokers. And then the call came – prosecuting counsel required witness statements from overseas officers to bolster the case and I was dispatched to take them. I was on the hunt for the missing Dutch drug supplier and Bob Hibbard was sure that the answer lay overseas with the foreign authorities who, according to him, were bound to have some valuable information.

As Bob handed me a bright red airline ticket, he said, 'I want you to chase up the *cloggy* angle. This supplier guy could lead us to something big and he may be worth targeting. But first, you need to find out where the hell he is.'

My journey was not a mere excursion to Holland, either. I had been directed to travel much further east – to an island in the remote Indian Ocean. The destination imprinted in exciting, bold ink on the ticket was Colombo.

The "Tea Chest Case", as it became known, was certainly as intriguing as it was perplexing. It had kicked off in the Felixstowe docks with a seizure of three hundred kilos of compressed, herbal cannabis concealed cleverly in plywood boxes of tea from Sri Lanka. A secret box had been constructed on a pedestal inside the authentic tea chest and then covered in tea. Any cursory examination of the first few layers would reveal nothing abnormal – just loose tea leaves. It was a bit like the lucky-dip at a village summer fête. Only if you dug your hands in deep enough, would the hidden box be revealed. Search officers regularly used iron barbs to penetrate bags and boxes. When the spike was withdrawn, a small sample of the contents would come out with it. This canny concealment was designed to confuse this search technique, as unless the barb was driven right into the centre of the box, only tea leaves would spill out.

It was also highly unusual for tea shipments to receive anything more than a cursory paperwork examination. Vast quantities of tea were imported into Britain every year and the regular loads received little or no attention from port customs. Most of the consignments left their ports of origin unsold and were offered up for purchase as the cargo ship carrying them navigated across the world's oceans – to be bought, in bulk, over the phone by the major tea houses. Any tea that was not procured on the high seas by the big conglomerates was consigned to the London Tea Auction. This was an institution steeped in history, set up by the East India Company in 1679; it was situated in Mincing Lane and made London the world centre for the international tea trade.

Credit for the discovery of the drugs belonged to an eager black Labrador. On a routine inspection of pallets in one of the landing warehouses, Jason had bounded towards the Colombo consignment, sniffed noisily, wagged his tail and then looked expectantly at his handler. At first, his master called him away, not trusting the young dog's judgment. After all, experience told him that tea chests never had anything in them other than tea. But the dog was persistent. Driven by the desire for a tasty morsel or tummy-rubbing praise from his handler, he would not budge. His whole rear end wobbled with excitement and his dripping tongue slathered the boxes with goo. The handler diffidently called a search officer over; a spike was inserted and after penetrating for about eight inches, it thudded against something hard.

The lid was removed, a lucky-dip fumble ensued and the discovery was made. A search of the rest of the boxes revealed that all sixty of them had been corrupted – each had five kilos of cannabis buried at the centre.

But the really clever part of the smuggle was not the shrewd concealment; it was the way the delivery phase of the consignment had been planned. The problem for us was that, as things stood, no one *owned* the tea. It had not yet been purchased, so we had no consignee – no one to whom we could deliver the shipment. The export paperwork revealed a Sri Lankan company as the shipper, but we had no way to check their credentials. Even if we could have picked up the phone to Colombo customs, we wouldn't have done so. We could not and would not trust anyone, and as things unfurled, our caution proved to be well founded. There was only one way to progress the case. The tea was destined for the London auction in another four weeks. We would just have to wait and see what this revealed and the overseas enquiries would have to be put on hold until we had got our hands on the UK purchaser.

A month later, the tea chests, stripped of their illicit cargo (now under lock and key in the Queen's Warehouse (QW) at the London Custom House), appeared as an auction catalogue item under lot number 248 – "Sixty boxes of orange pekoe. Origin: Sri Lanka." We went to Mincing Lane in force to watch proceedings and had reluctantly brought the auction management into our confidence. It was a calculated risk – they could conceivably be involved – but on the balance of probabilities, it was one worth taking. We knew nothing about the way the sales worked and, in the end, the auction house proved to be a good ally.

The chief auctioneer was an angular man called Hargreaves. He had a handlebar moustache, a strangely-shaped bow tie and a sense of theatre – like all good auctioneers, he was a frustrated thespian.

'Glad to help, old chap,' he had roared, and then suddenly realising the sensitivity of the whole affair, he reduced all his subsequent interventions to a kind of gravelly stage whisper.

'Does anything strike you as strange about today's auction?' I enquired.

Hargreaves cast his eye over the catalogue and settled his finger almost immediately on lot 248.

'That's intriguing,' he said. 'You see, it's so small – merely sixty boxes. A *very* small lot, if you ask me. We mostly deal in thousands of boxes, certainly hundreds, so sixty is rather uncommon.'

'What about the buyers? I suppose they are all regulars.'

'Precisely!' he mouthed almost silently, his eyebrows trembling. 'And what's more, they are all registered with us – that's a rule. But today we appear to have a new buyer on the list, someone I have never seen here before.'

He scrabbled for some papers. 'Here it is: a Mr. Manik Dissanayake has registered with us for today's sale. Not someone we know at all.'

This was interesting indeed.

The auction started precisely as an ancient wall clock chimed ten. I was surprised how few attendees there were and did my best to look inconspicuous. The auction management had provided some of us with brown porters' coats to aid our effort to blend in. I had decided not to wear one, for fear of being diverted by a buyer who thought I could help with something. So I sat quietly in the back row, pretending to be important.

After about two hours, as lot number 248 loomed ever closer,

I noticed a dumpy, Asian man settle into a seat towards the front of the auction room. His oiled black mop gave the appearance of being painted onto his large round scalp. He was fortyish, possessed of a generous waistline and had a cherubic face, blemished only by heavy charcoal rings under his eyes. He was clutching a catalogue as he scanned the room. A slightly built, older, distinguished-looking man joined him after a few minutes. He had a shock of grey hair and wore an ill-fitting corduroy jacket that accentuated his narrow, bony shoulders. A pair of half-moon spectacles sat on the end of his pointed nose as he leafed aimlessly through the catalogue. The two engaged in quiet conversation, both looking up from time to time to absorb their surroundings. The second man drew heavily on a thin roll-up cigarette, coughing from time to time. I wondered if he was ill or whether it was nerves that made his chest heave.

'Lot 248,' Hargreaves boomed, his voice restored to all its reverberating glory, 'is sixty boxes of Sri Lankan OP. What am I bid for it?'

He then resumed the unintelligible babble that had accompanied the previous lots and which only the regulars fully understood. The garbled sentences lasted just a few seconds and then, with hardly a pause, his gavel banged down abruptly and he pointed at our two new friends in the third row.

'Sold!' he declared grandiosely. Without a flicker of emotion, he moved on seamlessly. 'Lot 249 is five hundred boxes of Zhejiang Gunpowder.'

The two men in row three hesitated a moment, glanced at one another and then stood up together. They gathered their papers and walked to the side exit of the auction room, towards the cash desk in the anteroom beyond. Two porters followed at a discreet distance. I tracked them to the threshold of the side door and watched. The Asian man appeared to lead the way. There was a small queue at the cash desk; a man was settling an account for Lipton's and it was taking time. The two waited their turn without talking, just looking straight ahead into the cashier's booth. After a few minutes, the Lipton's representative had completed his business and the pair advanced to the desk. A brief conversation took place and the cashier looked bemused. I needed to hear what was being said, so I quietly joined the line behind them.

'It's not normal, you know; everyone has an account,' said the cashier. She looked irritated and turned her head in the direction of the back office. 'Mr. Cooper, these men want to pay in cash. They are registered, but don't have an account yet. Is that OK? It's seven hundred and eighty pounds.'

I did not hear the reply nor could I see Mr. Cooper, but after a few seconds she turned her head back to the Asian man, who now looked decidedly flustered.

'All right, he says it's OK – it's not normal, but as it's the first time, it's OK. Do you want to open an account now?' She waited while the two men looked at one another uncertainly. 'So it will be easier next time,' she added. 'We just need your bank details and a reference.'

'That won't be necessary today,' the cherub said in a heavy subcontinent accent. His head rocked gently, almost imperceptibly, from side to side. 'You see, we have no time now. We can come back later for that. I have the cash here – you can count it.' He stuffed a bulging envelope under the grill. The cashier tallied the notes, which appeared to be all brand new twenties, and pushed a sheet of paper back through the hatch.

'Sign here. Thank you.' She tore off a copy. 'If you take this to the warehouse in Dagenham – the address is on there – they will release the goods to you.' As he took the paper, she gave him a feeble smile, but he took no notice and turned on his heels.

I followed as both men walked through the exit into the car park. As the bespectacled, older man unlocked the driver's door of a silver Mercedes, the sun came out from behind a cloud and shone down onto its roof, dazzling him for a second. He pulled his arm up to shield his eyes and as he did so, a burly porter in a brown coat tapped him on the other shoulder. Opposite, on the passenger side, another porter had approached his stocky friend. In fact, the car park was now full of brown-coated porters.

We bundled the men separately into the back of official Vauxhalls and drove them, handcuffed, to our offices in New Fetter Lane, just a short distance away. It made a pleasant change; it was rare to make daytime drug arrests within the walls of the City of London. The Mercedes was rummaged and both men were frisked – the contents of their pockets quickly filling plastic bags. From the documents recovered, two separate North London addresses were established and I dispatched officers to make house searches – or, as we charmingly put it, "to spin their drums". As the officer in charge, it was my job to question the main suspect and it was clear to me that this had to be the chubby, Indian-looking man. He appeared indignant and resentful as I sat before him and went through the formalities, reading him his rights and introducing myself in the process.

'You are Mr. Manik Dissanayake, I take it.'

'Yes, of course.'

'You have been arrested today on suspicion of importing a large amount of illegal drugs into the United Kingdom. Do you understand?'

'Yes – but I know nothing about this thing – I don't think I can help you.' He glared at me.

During the next few hours of ducking and diving, Manik Dissanayake offered up an explanation for recent events which I found more implausible than most I had ever heard. The story that unfolded was one of complete innocence on his part – he was a man duped – a guiltless citizen trapped by circumstance.

'I was asked to purchase the tea as a favour to a man I met.'

'I see, and what is his name?'

'He is a businessman from Holland. I met him through friends at the *Colombo Club* earlier this year. He was back visiting his family.'

'That is most interesting – but can you give me his name, please.'

'He is Dutch.'

'Yes, you told me that already.'

'He told me he was not going to be in England at the time of the auction, but wanted to buy this special blend for the London market. He asked me to store the boxes until he arrived in Britain. He is coming next week.'

'Did you know that drugs were in the tea chests, Mr. Dissanayake?'

'Goodness gracious no!'

He wittered on, shaking his head from side to side, explaining that his slender companion at the auction was just a friend, a man whom he had met through his business. Both of them were documentary filmmakers. His friend had simply come along for the ride.

I let him talk and did more listening than questioning. He told me about his life – how and why he first came to England, his work in the film business, his disgust at the trade in drugs, his ignorance and innocence of this terrible business. Why had he trusted this mysterious Dutchman? He was just doing a service – he seemed a nice guy at the time.

I repeated the question. 'Do you know his name?'

Dissanayake pulled at his lank hair and looked at my notebook. 'No, sorry, not his full name – I just know him as Bartholomew.'

'Is that his first or second name?'

'I don't know – not sure.'

'What did he look like?'

'Normal, really – average height, youngish, blond hair. How stupid I was to have had faith in him!'

As he spoke, his confidence seemed to grow and his story became more bizarre by the minute. It was as if he was in a world of his own, unaware of the inevitability of his imminent downfall. His personal denial gave me the impression that his story was beginning to seem real to him, however ludicrous it sounded to others.

But I knew he was lying. I already had a raft of information that stacked up against him, obtained during the four weeks before the auction – facts that linked him inextricably to the consignment, truths that would counter his fairy tale. I decided to bide my time and let him paint himself into a corner.

After the first two hours of the interview, I left Dissanayake with a cup of tea – Darjeeling, as it happened – and went to review the evidence and to get an update on the interview with his accomplice. The teams that had been sent off to search the houses had returned with bundles of papers. These had a valuable story to tell, as did the wads of fresh twenty-pound notes found under the water tank in Dissanayake's loft – £25,000 in all.

In contrast, Dissanayake's friend turned out to be a revelation. He was a fifty-three-year-old man called Gerard Martin Flood. Our checks showed he had a criminal record, having been arrested by the Met in 1975 for *possession with intent to supply* of a weight (a pound) of cannabis resin. He had served two years in Wandsworth Gaol for the offence. After a few minutes of gentle questions, he surprised his interviewers by quietly taking off his glasses and wiping his forehead with the back of his hand. Then he spread his bony fingers flat on the table and said, 'Look, guys, let me level with you.'

He must have appreciated that things looked bleak for him; customs officers did not pull people off the streets for nothing. Maybe his previous experience with the Met had softened him up. He announced that he really wanted to cooperate but that he had been involved on the periphery. He had once been a respectable music teacher from Edinburgh, he had taught guitar, but the swinging 60s had got to him in the end and by the time he was forty-five he had developed a serious drug habit. Over the years, he had become a regular traveller to Amsterdam, frequenting the infamous coffee shops, where he consumed and traded in all forms of illicit substances. He had been arrested once. On a return trip from Europe, his car was struck down with an unwelcome flat tyre on the outskirts of Dover. A police patrol car had come to his rescue and the officer had found the cannabis in the boot when they both searched for the car jack. A prison term followed, which Flood had found insufferable.

He had met Dissanayake six months ago in the *Black Sun* coffee shop on Prinsengracht. Dissanayake was there to research a movie about the Dutch drugs culture. They struck up a marijuana-induced friendship and Flood was able to help with Dissanayake's academic research, filling in the details of how street deals worked and where bulk shipments originated. Dissanayake became increasingly interested in the huge profits that could be made. If risks were managed properly, he told Flood, a clever scheme could make them both a lot of money. Dissanayake was persuasive. Flood felt that for far too long he had been scrambling around at the bottom end of the drug business and the film project idea gave way to the new venture. They started planning something that promised to be significantly more exciting and profitable.

Did he know anyone who could procure the drugs in Sri Lanka? Dissanayake had asked Flood. He had worked out a good scheme but he needed someone with connections to buy the drugs at source.

That's where the London Tea Auction plan came in. Dissanayake was on familiar terms with some corrupt tea brokers in Sri Lanka – old school friends of his – who could put together a special, one-off shipment, which could be consigned direct to the

Mincing Lane sales room. Flood told him that he knew a young and ambitious local financier who had some contacts in the Far East from whom he obtained regular supplies into Amsterdam. Perhaps *he* could put the deal together.

He confided that the young man's name was Bartholomew Vanderpool. A meeting was set up, Vanderpool had been suitably impressed and a scheme was hatched. Vanderpool's fledgling Asian drugs network, combined with Dissanayake's knowledge of the tea trade, formed the basis of their perfect plan.

When questioned further about his own role, Flood reiterated that it had been minor. Once he had put the two together, he had been sidelined. He stood to profit nothing out of it, except some cannabis for personal consumption. Needless to say, he did not mention that he had the street-level contacts essential for the profitable disposal of the consignment. He didn't need to – he had said enough already. The jury would make its mind up, in due course.

The paperwork retrieved from the houses was damning: a copy of the shipper's bill of lading, Dissanayake's passport showing regular trips to Amsterdam, an entry stamp proving that he had been in Sri Lanka at the exact time the goods had been exported, and a business card from Bartholomew Vanderpool presenting himself as an "Importer of Oriental Furniture". And most incriminating of all – a colour photograph showing Dissanayake and a young, blond-haired man standing triumphantly in front of a pile of tea chests in the blazing sun, palm trees embedded in the jungle background. The boxes bore the estate markings of the drug-laden load and were emblazoned with the words *Ceylon Tea*. The circle had been squared. There seemed hardly any point in interviewing Dissanayake further, but the evidence had to be put to him.

'I want to see a lawyer,' he said when I showed him the photograph.

From then on he said not one word and after showing him

our UK evidence, I closed the interview. I had heard enough. It was time to start making enquiries abroad.

* * *

As the wings of the Boeing 747 lifted me blissfully away from a leaden and drizzly London into clear blue skies, my thoughts drifted to my early life in the East. It felt as if I was heading back towards a spiritual homeland and the thought that in some way I was retracing my father's footsteps gave me a warm glow. I also silently raised a glass to my first bosses who, fifteen years ago, had stubbornly rejected any possibility of a role for Customs and Excise or me in international work.

Two fingers to them.

Fortunately, the trust that Bob had placed in me was justified. I collected the Sri Lankan evidence without fuss and found the local customs and police to be exceedingly cooperative, especially when I told them that by making a statement they might have to come to London to give evidence, on our expense account. My research with the Colombo drug squad to pin down the Amsterdam connection was less successful, however, and I had reached a dead end. I had given them all we knew about Bartholomew Vanderpool and, although they could confirm that a Dutch national of that name had entered Sri Lanka on no fewer than six occasions in the last two years, they concluded that he was no longer in the country. Immigration records showed that he had flown to Madras a week after we had made our London seizure and he had not returned. So, the trail had gone cold. There was nothing for it but to fly home, add the information to our growing dossier and file it for another day.

Had I been more streetwise at the time and appreciated the true depths of contamination within the international drugs business, I might have concluded that there was little benefit to the resident agencies in fingering anyone involved in the native drug trade to a foreign jurisdiction, especially if the person in question provided opportunities for officials to line their pockets. The main players had enough influence, and cash, to buy silence. But at the time, I naïvely put it down to bad luck.

Despite this disappointment, I found myself enjoying a wonderful and eye-opening six days in the company of my hosts, who I found to be unreservedly attentive throughout. The High Commission had been very accommodating, also. They had booked me into one of the best hotels in Colombo, the *Galle Face*, which proved to be a delight, despite its fading colonial grandeur. A diplomatic car collected me from its sweeping front steps every morning and chauffeured me regally through my daily round of appointments, during which I sipped tea, conversed guilelessly with local officials and chatted happily to potential witnesses.

The High Commissioner asked to see me after a couple of days and seemed genuinely interested in what I had to tell him.

'First time we have seen you chaps here – hadn't realised we had a drugs problem, in fact. Do you think these visits will become a regular thing?'

'I believe so,' I said as seriously as I could. 'The world is a much smaller place than it used to be – criminals respect no boundaries and we are determined to tackle the problems of drug smuggling at source.' I hoped he would not pursue his line of thought, as I had exceeded my brief by a long way. But he just nodded sagaciously and I wondered if, through his frown, his diplomatically-trained mind was simultaneously composing a telegram to Whitehall on the subject.

In the evenings, I drank sundowners and dined on spicy fish curry in the hotel's veranda restaurant, listening to the waves breaking against the sea wall and the cicadas singing. As I quaffed my cocktails, I thought smugly of my colleagues at home.

Despite the fact that we had failed to arrest one of the main organisers, the case was judged to have been another success. Our efforts to trace Vanderpool in Amsterdam and Colombo were unproductive, but at least the Dutch Politie had been able to give us some personal information about him, confirming also that he had featured on the periphery of previous drugs investigations. We now knew that he was born in Rotterdam in 1953 and we could also put a face to him, courtesy of Dissanayake's photo. We sent a telegram to the Indian authorities asking for enquiries in Madras, but never received a reply.

By the time of the trial, we were no further forward in locating him. The last positive intelligence, that he had boarded the flight from Colombo to India, was four months old. The court case could not wait and went ahead without him. In view of the huge weight of evidence against his co-conspirators, the outcome was a formality. Both of his accomplices were convicted after ten days of courtroom wrangling, much of which had been taken up with speeches in mitigation. The jury had delivered unanimous guilty verdicts; Dissanayake was sent to prison for eight years, Flood for four.

But not everything in my existence looked bright and promising. The time I now spent at home was a mere token in the context of the working day. I began to begrudge my life outside the office and the relationship with my wife Maureen suffered as a result – it was now awkward and constrained. I neglected my fatherly duties, missing birthdays, prize days and nativity plays. My work consumed and engrossed me and I took any chance I was offered to be amongst my colleagues, often away for protracted periods in distant parts of the country.

I grew a beard. One had started to sprout after a draining mobile surveillance that took the team to Inverness and back in three days. I just let it grow and before long the team said that I looked like one of the Bee Gees – but not as good-looking, of course. Maureen said nothing when she saw it for the first time –

her eyebrows raised a little – that was comment enough, perhaps. Looking back now, I still cannot fathom whether it was the work that took me away from my marriage or my marriage that drove me to the work. Was it a subconscious feeling of domestic entrapment? Or was it naked ambition and the thrill of the job? Both, perhaps. I turned up for work, the vigour and enthusiasm of youth saw me through each case. Seizures continued to be made, investigations came and went non-stop, intelligence was collected, surveillance was conducted and arrests were made. Appearances in court, once a frightening experience, became an agreeable game of cat and mouse with defence counsel. Such were the wheels that turned in my life then.

CHAPTER THREE

Eighteen months after the dust had settled on the Tea Chest Case, Bob Hibbard phoned me just as I was thinking of nipping out to the Mucky Duck to enjoy a pie and a pint with the others.

'Can you pop up to see me? Quick as you can.' His voice grated down the phone.

I had been sorting out some surveillance photographs; I dropped them back onto my desk and headed up the short flight of stairs to his office.

'Come in, Mike. Do you know Tom McCarthy?' He waved his hand towards a slightly-built man about my age with a crop of curly red hair. I recognised him immediately.

'Tom is from Heathrow Investigations,' Bob muttered almost inaudibly.

'Yes, I know. We met last year when we were running the Qantas case – the one involving the golf bag full of gear.'

'Oh, yes,' Bob said absently. 'The guy got five years, I recall.'

'And we got a brand new set of golf clubs,' I laughed.

'I hope they are safely locked away in the QW,' he countered, looking decidedly unamused by my feeble witticism.

'Oh, er, yes. I doubt if they will ever see the light of day, let alone a golf course. They must be destined for destruction soon, no doubt.'

'Good. Tom is here today with an interesting story – one that I think deserves our full attention. Tom, perhaps you can run through the details.'

We sat down around Bob's small, polished oak coffee table.

Tom smiled uncomfortably. 'Hello, Mike,' he said in a slow Glasgow burr. 'Good to see you again. I like the new beard.'

I ignored the barbed observation. 'This all sounds very intriguing, Tom,' I said.

'Yes. We have had an unusual approach from one of the British Airways ground staff – she has been asked by someone to find a couple of bags airside in Terminal Three. She has been told they contain drugs. She thinks they came off yesterday's Bangkok flight.'

'A woman?' I asked pointlessly.

'Yes. In fact, they are both women. The BA girl's name is Rose. She has been working with the airline for a couple of years. She used to go out with one of our preventive officers in Terminal Two, but that's all finished now. The story is that she met a Greek woman called Mina at a party in Hounslow. This Mina works as a croupier in a big London casino. They got talking and Rose told her what she did – working at the airport and all that. The long and short of it is that the next time they met, Mina asked if Rose could help her find two pieces of missing luggage from a Thailand flight that she thought might be in the customs hall in T3. When Rose asked why she could not just call the airline and enquire herself, Mina offered her a grand if she would go and see if the bags were there. She had the baggage tags – it would be a simple job to check them against the luggage – all done and dusted in a few minutes and she would be a thousand pounds richer. Rose asked her why she would pay so much money and Mina then coughed that there was gear in the bags.'

'When was this?'

'Yesterday evening – they met last night.'

'What did she do?' I asked.

'Well, she is quite streetwise, is our Rose – she told Mina she would sleep on it and let her know today. And then she contacted her area controller, and both of them turned up in our office first thing this morning.'

'So we have just a few hours before she has to give her answer,' Bob intervened.

There was stillness for a few seconds as the three of us mulled over the possibilities. Then Bob raised his trim frame up from his chair and walked behind his desk. As he picked up the phone he said, 'I want to run with this one, Mike – I'd like you to grab Pete and the both of you go back to the airport with Tom to speak to Rose. Can you contact Rose and fix a time for them to meet, Tom?'

'Yes, of course. I can call her now.'

'I'll get on to the Technical Support Unit and arrange a covert mike and a bag camera. Do you think you will need anything else?' Then, without waiting for a reply, Bob added, 'You can collect it on your way out.'

I dragged Peter Tidy out of the *White Swan* just as he was downing his second pint. We collected my car from the underground car park in High Holborn. It was a burgundy red Triumph Stag which leaked horribly when it rained – but I adored it. The V8 burbled softly as we drove down through the Temple and turned right towards Westminster and the Great West Road beyond. I tried to brief him on the way, but Pete had other ideas.

'This car is damp, Mike – I'm sitting on a wet patch! Why don't you get something more sensible? It can't be good on surveillance either,' he complained. The beer was obviously fuelling his whinge.

'It works fine – I've never shown out before and you know it! No one suspects the Cussies in one of these.'

'There's always a first time and then you'll be sorry. Bob will haul you over the coals if you wreck a case. It's just too showy.'

'Shut up and let me tell you about Rose,' I chuckled.

Rose and Tom were waiting for us in the Investigation Unit office when we arrived an hour later. Tom introduced us and we found a quiet corner of the large, open-plan office to sit down and chat. Rose was in her early thirties, strawberry blonde and leggy.

She wore the simple, blue and red uniform of British Airways ground personnel, which gave her a glamorous appearance. But on closer examination, I could see that she had a look of tired severity in her eyes, a hardness of expression and a rather careworn air. It was as if she had seen a lot of life and what she had seen had largely disappointed her.

The four of us sat together and she went through her story again, talking confidently in a distinctly South London accent. There was more of Streatham about her than Sloane Square. I listened in silence and when she had finished I looked at her calmly and said, 'Do you want to take this any further, Rose – would you like to help us? I don't wish to put you under any pressure, but we would really appreciate your help.'

'What would you want me to do?'

'Well, the first thing would be to call Mina – we will listen in. You should tell her you are interested and ask her to meet you again. That way, we will get a chance to observe her and with a bit of luck we can take it from there. Just one meeting is all I ask and then we can manage things ourselves.'

'What should I tell her?' Although she looked me straight in the eyes when she asked the question, I detected a glimmer of apprehension flicker briefly across her face.

'You just tell her that you can have a look for the bags later today, but first she has to come to the airport to give you the baggage tags.'

Rose said nothing.

'It would be important to impress on Mina that after twenty-four hours the bags may get shifted to a lock-up and then you would not be able to help. So, if she wants you to do this, it has to be done today.'

She lit a cigarette and took a couple of pulls. And then she surprised us all by uttering suddenly, 'OK, I can do that – what the fuck!'

Within a few minutes, we had fitted the phone with a

recording device and given her the mouthpiece. She stamped out her cigarette, I dialled the number for her and it rang five times before it was picked up.

'Hello,' a woman's voice answered.

'Hi Mina, it's Rose. Look, I've given your idea some thought and it will be OK – I can check those things for you.'

'Great. That's good news,' came the reply.

'Only thing is, dear, I need to do it fairly quickly or the bags will be moved to lost and found. So, can you meet me in Terminal Three today? As soon as you can get here, in fact.'

'Sure, I'll be there in an hour. I'll bring the tags.'

'Meet me at the airport information desk at four.'

'OK, fine. Bye.'

And that was it – no more than thirty seconds had passed and already the first of many such subterfuges in the case was underway.

I admired Rose's coolness but regretted that she had organised the rendezvous so soon – it gave us precious little time to prepare. The first thing to do was to get a description of Mina from her and then brief her on what to say when the meeting went down. I told her that whatever happened, even if she was able to locate the dirty bags, she was to tell Mina that she could *not* find them. Then she could ask for her money and that would be it. We would do the rest. And in case Rose had not worked it out already, I broke the news that if any money did change hands, she would have to give it to us; she would get a nice HMCE receipt, naturally.

'Of course – what do you take me for?' Rose hooted.

One of the girls in the office helped Rose to fit a miniature microphone with recording attachment inside her blouse. After they had finished titivating and testing, it was impossible to detect the hidden gadget.

Even at the quietest of times, the main concourse at Heathrow's Terminal Three is a bustling place – a fact that helped us. We were practiced in blending into the background of hurrying people and mountains of luggage. I had asked Rose to delay her arrival at the information desk by ten minutes, so we could get an advance look at anyone fitting Mina's description hovering in the area. At five minutes to four, I spotted her – there could be no mistake. A slender woman of about forty with long, dark hair tied behind a gaunt neck, an olive complexion and wearing a dark blue pinstripe jacket and a white silk blouse was standing awkwardly within a few feet of the information desk, chewing her fingers. She looked around the terminal, presumably hoping to see Rose emerge from the crowd. I sauntered over to Pete, who was by a confectionery stall, munching on a Mars bar.

'That's her,' I hissed.

'Sure – she looks quite a piece of work,' Pete chomped back.

'Look,' I said, 'can you pop round the back to Rose and tell her to come out ASAP? No point in waiting. We have seen Mina now – last thing we want is for her to abandon the meeting.'

Pete swallowed the final chunk of his snack and hurried off. As he disappeared airside, I noticed that Mina was not alone. From what I could see, there were three others with her – two men and a young woman. The first man was about forty-five, large and swarthy with an unshaven face showing black stubble against a dark complexion. He looked Mediterranean. The other man was younger, tall, blond, with gold-rimmed glasses. His broad shoulders and trim waist suggested that he knew what the inside of a gym looked like. The final member was a fragile-looking young woman in her late twenties with shoulder-length golden curls and knee-high boots.

Rose appeared on the concourse after a few minutes looking directly ahead, and with an air of unblinking confidence she approached Mina. They spoke for a couple of seconds and Mina handed over some slips of paper. Then Rose turned on her not inconsiderable heels and headed back into the airside access channels.

Ten minutes elapsed as I watched the small group linger conspicuously. My radio earpiece sparked into life. 'India Delta Four – this is Delta Eight – it's a negative on the bags. We can find no trace of them here. Zulu One is returning landside now.'

'Confirm negative on the bags,' I acknowledged.

Not a big surprise; this is just a test for Rose. They want to know if she really has access.

Rose re-emerged through security from the baggage hall on cue and soon all five were engaged in animated conversation. Rose must have been breaking the bad news to them, but I detected very little disappointment in Mina's body language. In fact, the conversation dragged on for a full five minutes with Mina and Rose doing most of the talking. When they had finished, they parted without shaking hands. Rose returned into the bowels of the airport, while the other four headed towards the car park – anonymously shadowed by five of my colleagues. I left them to their work and made my way to meet up with Rose.

'How did it go, Rose?' I asked as soon as I had found her in the Customs office. 'It seemed quite a long chat you had with them.'

'Yes – and I wasn't expecting to see so many with her. When I told them that the bags were missing she got a bit edgy and her and this guy, Tony – I think he is her boyfriend – started to talk in some bloody language I didn't understand.'

'Is Tony the older guy – the heavy-set, dark-haired one?' I asked.

'Yes, that's him. Anyway, she said in the end that they needed to recoup their losses and she wanted me to help them.'

'What did you say, Rose?' I looked ominously at her.

'I said yes – why not? I thought.'

'Christ!' I muttered under my breath – it was a development that we had not planned for. This was supposed to be Rose's chance to extricate herself from the whole dodgy business, make an apology and get the hell out. But she had chosen to stick in there and the decision, which had obviously been made on the spur of the moment, startled me. I had envisaged that after this short meeting, we would be compiling our case against Mina and her associates alone, which would require the usual long hours of surveillance and painstaking evidence-building. But now, unexpectedly, and fortuitously to be frank, we still had a player in close with them. It would certainly make our job easier, but it could be dangerous for Rose.

While I was contemplating this game-changing turn of events, she added perkily, 'So we have agreed to meet again and make a plan about how I can help them. We're meeting tomorrow lunchtime in a pub on the A4.' Things were moving faster than I wanted. After all, *we* were supposed to be calling the shots.

'I'll need to think about this, Rose.' I spoke slowly choosing my words. 'This could have implications for you – we will have to tread very carefully, you know. Are you sure you want to meet them again?'

'Why not? What the fuck – someone's got to do it,' she said impulsively.

'You'll have to curb that language, Rose.' I smiled. 'Not very BA, is it?'

The next few hours were spent plotting a scenario for the assignation the next day. The surveillance team designated to follow Mina away from the airport had watched her and the others get into a silver 7 Series BMW. A quick check of the number plate led us to a large detached house in Twickenham and this had instigated a raft of further checks and background enquiries. Hopefully, we would have some results soon. Rose had agreed with Mina and her friends that she would be in the *Traveller's Friend*, where the A30 meets the A4, at one o'clock the next day, so we had to think and act fast. After we had thrown a few ideas around and ruled most of them out, we settled on a plan which Pete, Rose and I thought could work, given a following wind and sanction from the fifth-floor bosses. I telephoned Bob Hibbard, gave him the encouraging gist of what had taken place and asked if I could meet him at seven thirty that evening in his Holborn office. There was something I wanted to put by him, something that would need his consent. He readily agreed. He was used to working late – in fact, he relished it, especially when there was a good case brewing.

The London-bound traffic was dreadful, as usual, and I didn't manage to get to Bob until just before eight. So when I tapped on his half-open office door, I was pleased to distinguish his hunched figure in the gloom, pen in hand, working noiselessly under the light of his desk lamp. The proposal I had prepared was one based on maximising the unexpected opportunity that Rose's boldness had given us, while finding a way to distance her from the potentially hazardous chain of events that was likely to follow. Bob agreed quickly that a second meeting with Mina and her friends would give us an ideal opportunity to build our dossier on the group. And he took little persuading of the need for officer reinforcements so we could have a larger presence on the ground when the next meeting took place. We required enough men to be able to follow at least three of the new targets away from the RV (rendezvous), even if they left separately.

But the main reason I wanted to discuss things with Bob was that I needed his OK to allow me to make a significant step change to the investigation. I wanted him to agree to use an undercover officer to infiltrate the gang – and I wanted that officer to be me. Before I could raise the topic, Bob interrupted my flow. 'This is all looking rather dodgy for your girl Rose, isn't it? Looks to me like she has got herself in quite deep. Playing with fire, I'd call it.'

'Yes, Bob. I agree.' This was my chance. 'I'd like to replace her,' I said quickly. 'I'd like her to put me up as a bogus BA baggage handler and work the team that way – work it with me as a UC.'

My idea was that Rose should suggest to Mina that she knew a BA guy who worked airside; he was short of money and for the right reward, could smuggle out any bags from the airport Mina wanted, providing he had the flight number and tag details.

'I'd like her to do this tomorrow, Bob – and if the woman agrees, I can be fed in at a future meeting. This way, we would still have "our man" in the middle of the organisation and we should be able to control things better.'

'And Rose?' he enquired.

'Well, that's it – by introducing me, we will be limiting any future threat to Rose. She can merely drift into the background and play no further part.'

'That's all very well, Mike, but I didn't know you had any experience of UC work. Do you think you can pull it off?'

'I did a little in SI before I came into the ID – low level stuff, I admit – but I have a good feeling about this one. I have seen Mina and her cronies up close and am sure I can handle it.'

'You'd need cover from BA – some identification, in case Mina gets suspicious and wants to see it.'

'I've got that organised. I can get a BA photo-pass first thing in the morning.'

'You obviously thought I'd agree,' he said tersely.

'Well, I thought…'

He interrupted impatiently, 'OK, I'll go with it. But I want a full team briefing tomorrow morning at eight sharp in the conference room – I'll drag in half a dozen Oscars to make up the numbers. I'll speak to the head of Drugs O now. We will need your plan and dispositions at the briefing and we'll take it from there.'

Very little sleep accompanied me over the next few hours. The briefing went without any major hiccups, as did Rose's engagement at the *Traveller's Friend* at lunchtime. To my surprise, Mina went for the bait immediately it was offered up. She wanted to meet the "bent baggage handler" soon though, as she had an important shipment waiting for dispatch. I was beginning to think she was too impetuous for her own good – she was taking some big risks and did not appear to worry about the consequences. It was now clear that she was the driving force behind the gang of four. Rose reported back to me that the others had done very little talking. Her boyfriend, Tony, spoke from time to time, but even his interventions had been brushed aside. He, too, seemed to be under Mina's spell. When they had finished, it had been arranged that Rose would bring me to the next meeting. At Mina's suggestion, it would be at the *Excelsior Hotel,* on the perimeter of the airport, next time. Rose had proposed the date and time – we had agreed it ourselves in advance. It would be in two days, enough time to get our ducks in a row and complete our background research. Rose told her the timings were necessary to suit the shift pattern of the baggage handler – yours truly, in other words.

My UC role was fully sanctioned by the fifth floor a day later. It had been a formality, but it had to be done. Bob hurriedly reassigned the job of case officer. Fortunately, he gave it to one of my favourite colleagues, Harry Birdwood. Harry was old school, hailed from the middle England shires and had a distinct air of gravitas in his bearing. He had been a mentor for me in my early Deltas days and a tower of strength when things had occasionally gone pear-shaped. He knew his stuff and it was a relief to know that the case would be in good hands. The transfer of responsibilities gave me time to focus on my new acting role, as I could leave the strategising and plotting to Harry, Pete and the others. Naturally, I would still have a huge part in most of the decision-making; my insights into Mina's little band would be invaluable.

CHAPTER FOUR

It was a misty, late autumn evening as I drove alone down the Bath Road towards the *Excelsior Hotel*. It was already dark and cold droplets of water drizzled down the windscreen and side windows of the official Vauxhall Cavalier; I had reluctantly acquiesced, agreeing that my red Triumph Stag was an inappropriate form of transport for such a sensitive mission.

Fifty-five hours had passed since Mina had agreed to meet me; they had not been wasted. We had commenced surveillance on the Twickenham house and had photographed Mina and all three of her associates entering and leaving. Some of the background checks had also come back – the Criminal Records Office, the Twickenham Police Collator, the Driver and Vehicle Licensing Agency, the local utilities companies and, of course, Interpol. A better picture of our new opposition was beginning to emerge and very interesting it was, too. We opened four new target files. Harry and I went through the details late one evening with a bottle of *Famous Grouse* to chaperone us. We allocated numbers to each of our suspects, depending on our perception of their role and importance.

Tango One was clearly Mina and I was not disappointed when I read what we had collected on her. Her full name was Mina Parayi Christofe, she was a thirty-eight-year-old Cypriot national with an Interpol warning attached to her name. She was wanted by the Dutch authorities for selling heroin to an undercover police officer in a Rotterdam bar three years previously. Before her trial, she had absconded.

Tony was Antonious Sotirou Papadopolous, another Cypriot,

aged forty-three and a long-time UK resident. Papadopolous was a nightclub owner who had been bankrupted once and had a conviction for VAT fraud.

Conrad Duncan was the strongly-built, fair-haired man. He had an Irish passport and was quite a colourful character with convictions for assault, grievous and actual bodily harm.

Never make assumptions about men wearing gold-rimmed spectacles.

As for the waif of a girl seen with them at the airport, she was a twenty-six-year-old Dutch national by the name of Alicia Duykers. She had stood surety for Mina in Rotterdam after her arrest and had also gone missing recently from Dutch records.

Always better to be armed with a healthy knowledge of the opposition.

I manoeuvred the Vauxhall from the main road and drove under the *Excelsior's* neon welcome sign. The plan was to meet Rose in the lobby and then, together, we would move into the bar to await the arrival of the others. It would give us a final chance to get our stories straight. As I backed the car into a marked bay on the periphery of the hotel car park, I noticed a silver BMW close to the hotel entrance, which I recognised immediately.

So much for the quiet, pre-prandial chat with Rose.

The sight of the unmarked white transit van with darkened windows lifted my spirits – at least the Oscars had arrived, too. I unlocked the car, fingered inside my breast pocket to ensure I had my new BA identity card, just in case, and headed up the glistening hotel steps into the welcoming amber lights of the lobby. Rose and Mina were seated at a small table with their backs to an ornamental fountain in the centre of the room. As I approached, Rose stood up to greet me. Nerves fluttered into my belly, my hands were clammy.

Good. Your persona would have every reason to be nervous now – so don't worry about showing it.

As I approached, Mina sat implacably watching Rose. They appeared to be alone, but I did not want to start gawping around the lobby in search of the others, so I just smiled and sat down opposite them. Close up, I could study Mina now. She had a long narrow nose, high angular cheekbones and a thin mouth. She looked cruel, but maybe my opinion was prejudiced. Time would tell. One thing for sure – she appeared much slighter now that she was just a few feet away, almost emaciated, in fact.

'This is Derek,' Rose started helpfully. 'And this is Maria,' she added a split second later with an awkward movement of her hands. I tried to disguise my surprise at the use of a false name. Clearly, everyone was at it – you couldn't trust anyone these days! I smiled again.

'We want you to do some business for us,' Mina said suddenly.

That was two surprises in as many instants – straight for the jugular, no pleasantries, right to the point. There was only one thing for it; I had to be direct too.

'What business?' I replied.

'We would like you to change the tags on some bags and put them on the roller.'

'What do you mean, change the tags?'

'In the baggage hall, so they can be put outside.'

'Do you want me to get them off the airport without going through customs?'

'Yes, if you can do it.'

'I might be able to,' I said cagily.

And so the conversation developed. I was well into the part now, the fear factor had receded, my first night nerves were extinguished. I was running on the adrenalin of performance and quietly enjoying myself. After about ten minutes of chat, we had reached the basis of an agreement. She would give me £2,000 up front for expenses and then £20,000 if I could deliver four large suitcases that would arrive on a BA flight from Bangkok. She told me that each suitcase would contain about twenty kilos of Thai cannabis. Each case would have baggage tags indicating they were in transit through Heathrow en route to New York. She had two couriers who would be taking the four empty suitcases to Bangkok in a few days. On their arrival, they would contact the supplier, collect the drugs and return with the filled bags in a week.

'I have a contact in Bangkok who can make sure no one checks them or the bags when they are leaving. It has worked before, many times,' she assured me.

'What happens when the bags arrive at Heathrow?' I asked.

'It's so simple.' A smile flashed across her face. 'My couriers just walk through customs with their hand baggage. If they are checked – no problems. They leave the four big suitcases at the airport. And, of course, this is where you come in – you have to find them and deliver them to me.' She looked at me expectantly. 'Should be easy – yes?'

'Yes. Easy,' I said, looking calmly into her eyes. 'But I will need to see the bags first, so I know what I am dealing with. Can you show me them before your people take them to Bangkok?'

'I can arrange that. No problem. Shall we have a drink now?' she said, standing up. 'There is a bar here, I am sure.'

Why not? A few pints on Queen's business.

As I followed Mina and Rose towards the bar, I had an opportunity to glance around the lobby for the first time. I spotted Conrad Duncan immediately, lurking by the reception desk, amateurishly holding up a copy of *Country Life* to his face and trying to peer past the folds.

Who is he kidding?

Inside the bar, we approached the counter and Mina ordered a whisky, Rose, a glass of white wine. As they were talking to the barman, I noticed Tony Papadopolous, alone except for his half-full beer glass, sitting in a leather armchair and looking purposefully at the wall.

Two down, one to go.

Before I could look further for Alicia, Mina said, 'What can I get you, Derek?'

'A beer, please – a pint of lager.'

'There is someone I want you to meet before we go any further,' Mina said, as the beer was being poured. She put a finger to her lips melodramatically and waved me away from the counter. I grabbed my beer and we all moved to a table in a quiet part of the bar. Tony was still examining his wall.

'You know, we have lost two loads in the last three months – the bags disappeared at the airport. We got ripped off by someone in the airline and now I owe my supplier. The next load will be the last one he will send unless we get this right. He wants to meet you first and then, if he is OK, we can go ahead.'

'Fine by me.' I kept it simple. 'Just tell me when.'

'Tomorrow – he flies in tomorrow. Can you meet him at eight p.m.? I think the *Ariel Hotel* is good.'

'Who will be there?' I asked.

'Just you and me – same as tonight.'

Bloody liar. Same as tonight, indeed!

Conrad had wandered aimlessly into the bar and was ordering a Guinness.

'OK. No problem. Just you and me and – what's his name?'

'You can ask him when you meet him if you like.' She fixed me with a stare. 'He is coming in from Bangkok tomorrow morning. It will be fine – don't worry – he just wants to see you first.'

'No need for Rose, I take it. Just the three of us?'

'Yes, just the three of us,' she said comfortingly. But those lips looked cruel. I was sure of it now.

* * *

Maureen was waiting for me when I returned home just after midnight. I had decided to walk the two miles from the station to clear my head from the effects of the five late-night ales I had consumed with Harry as we plotted our next move. I felt more dishevelled than usual as I turned the key in the front door and sneaked into the hall. She was sitting on the sofa in front of the television, wrapped in a dressing gown. The TV was switched off and the room was dim and noiseless. A single table lamp, glimpsed from the garden path, was the only clue that someone was still awake. As I entered the small living room, the scene reminded me of one of those romantic Victorian paintings – *Woman at a Window*.

'Hello, dear,' I chirped, trying not to slur my words. 'Is everything all right?'

'I need to go home to Skibbereen. Uncle Pat has died.'

The subdued lighting made it difficult to see her face clearly, but I could tell her voice had emotion in it. This was a little surprising, as I did not recall that she and her uncle had ever been particularly close.

'Oh, I'm sorry. When was the last time you saw him? Must have been a good few years ago.'

She did not answer the question. 'I want to take Caroline with me. I assume you will be too busy to join us.' Her speech was now steady and business-like.

'Well, actually, things are a bit all over the place at the moment. I've got this big case on and it's likely that I'll be tucked up with it for the next few weeks, at least.' I tried to look cheerful, but the effort was wasted. Maureen did not raise her eyes to look at me.

'Do you know how much time you have spent at home since Christmas? I've been keeping a record. Fourteen days. Fourteen bloody days.' She was railing now. 'That's two weeks in ten months, near as damn it.'

'Well, it's the work. You know I have been busy, dear. It's the same for all of us,' I lied.

Still she didn't look at me. I hesitated. I wanted to change the subject.

'How long will you be away?'

She stood up and as she balanced against the arm of the sofa her gown fell open. I could see she was wearing nothing underneath.

'Look, Mike,' her tone softened, 'I have not said anything until now because I know you live for your work, but can't you try a little harder to be here for us? Caroline hardly talks about you, now. Can't we just try to be a family?' She looked at me pleadingly, moisture in her eyes.

So that's what this is all about.

'Of course, it's just that the work is so important at the moment. We are on to something pretty immense and I'm right up to my neck in it. Perhaps we can go away when it's over – take a holiday. The three of us. Cornwall?'

Maureen pulled the hair away from her face and looked intently at me. She gathered the ends of her dressing gown cord and pulled the material together sealing her body from view. 'Wrong answer,' she said lugubriously. As she walked past me into the hall, she started to sob. 'I am catching the train to Fishguard tomorrow at ten. Can you at least run us to the station?'

I winced. 'I have a briefing at nine – I can't miss it, Mo. I can order a taxi for you, first thing. I'm sorry, but we are really under the cosh. Call me before you come back and I'll be at the station to pick you both up. Leave a message with Control if that works better. It's just that tomorrow…' I let my voice trail off.

'I'll be sleeping in the spare room tonight. Try not to wake us. And I'll be taking the dog, too – at least he'll get fed.'

CHAPTER FIVE

The next morning, I was up at seven and out of the house by seven fifteen. I knew that it was best not to wake the girls, that deep down it was me running away, and seeing Maureen again would probably only make matters worse. Even the dog stayed in his bed as I tiptoed around the house. Clearly, he had no need for me either. I decided to grab some breakfast on my way into town, but the prospect of a hot coffee and a tasty bacon sandwich only cheered me up for a couple of seconds. By the time the train had loaded the scrum of passengers at East Croydon, my mind had drifted away from my collapsing marriage – my attentions were now firmly on Mina and our meeting later that day.

I was not sure why Mina had selected the *Ariel Hotel* for our next encounter. Something worried me. A cautionary voice resonated in my head – it might be a set-up, but I could not work out *why*. Maybe she just wanted a change of venue. I knew the hotel quite well, in fact; I had enjoyed an epic Cathay Pacific Christmas party there the previous year, including an unexpected one-night stand in one of the fourth-floor bedrooms.

The ground staff at Cathay are always so accommodating.

I smiled inwardly, as images of the evening came fleetingly back to me. But then I thought of Maureen and Caroline and any vestige of a smirk wiped from my face. Spasms of remorse flooded into my mind and I made a mental note to make it up to them as soon as I had finished this case.

At the operational briefing, we had decided it would be best if I took a cab to the RV this time; it would be anonymous and safer. Especially as it would be the ID's own black taxi for the meeting, driven by Stuart, one of my closest colleagues. We had acquired the cab a few years earlier and it had proved to be invaluable as a surveillance tool – ideal for blending in to London's hectic traffic scene and for collecting stray foot soldiers who had become detached from a tail. I had learned to drive it, too. It was not a demanding task, once you had learned how to start the thing. It had an amazing turning circle, much beloved by bona fide cabbies and mobile surveillance teams who often required a quick U-turn.

At ten minutes to eight, with me sitting comfortably in the back, Stuart parked the cab a few streets away and we listened to the chatter on the official radio. It had been agreed that I would deliberately arrive five minutes after Mina and her friend to give the impression that I was not doing the chasing. True to form, the BMW was spotted by the assembled Deltas entering the car park at five minutes to eight, and a few seconds later, Mina walked into the hotel to await my arrival. There was no sign of anyone else, except the driver of the BMW, who remained in the car. As soon as the radio traffic had settled down, Stuart drove me to the front doors of the hotel. I made a fuss of paying him the fare through the front window and exchanged a few pleasantries before mounting the steps into the lobby. Mina sighted me as soon as I put my foot onto the hotel carpet, and hurried over to greet me.

'Can we talk in the car, Derek? It's just outside – my friend is waiting there.'

'Hang on, Maria, why can't we meet here, as we arranged? I'm not sure about this.'

'My friend does not like hotel lobbies. He would like to talk with you in the car. And we have your money – the expenses.'

I had no real worries about meeting in the car park – I knew my colleagues were watching over me – but it made sense to appear cautious to Mina.

'This is not what we agreed, Maria', I persisted.

'Look, it's just this once. It will be just five minutes. Then we can come back for a drink, if you like.'

'OK,' I said, looking as troubled as I could. 'I'll follow you out.'

Mina led me outside and across the car park to the waiting BMW. I called to Mina, 'I'll sit in the back, OK?'

She opened the rear door for me and I climbed in, making sure to leave it slightly ajar, in case I needed a quick retreat. I didn't want a driver-controlled child lock to trap me either. The man behind the steering wheel was blond. He did not turn his face to me as I slid into the seat behind Mina and the only glimpse of his face I could pick up was from the rear-view mirror. I could see his vivid blue eyes, but not much more. Mina was quiet, for once, as she settled into the front passenger seat.

'You can close the door, if you want,' he said after a pause.

'No, it's OK – I could do with the air,' I responded.

'Fine. Up to you. I just wanted to say hello,' he said smoothly. 'Maria has told me about you and that you can help us.'

'Yes, I think I can.'

'Just one thing, before we start.' The man shifted his posture and in a remarkably effortless movement, he turned his body and looked over his shoulder at me.

'Can I see your airline identification? Just a precaution.'

I looked into his suntanned face for the first time and in an instant, I recognised him. My brain filled with blood.

God! I didn't expect to see you today. Keep cool, Mike.

My heart was thumping now and it was tough to disguise my surprise.

'Yes, of course,' I said as unassumingly as I could and fumbled for the laminated card in my top pocket. I handed it to him and he smiled amiably back. He was young and good-looking; he had not changed in the slightest since the photo with Dissanayake in front of the stack of sun-baked Ceylon tea chests over a year ago.

'I'm Bart, by the way.' He examined the identity card carefully and when he had finished his scrutiny, he continued to hold on to it, turning it over absently between his fingers, much as a roulette player might with a fifty-pound chip. I resisted the temptation to ask him to return it.

'I'm Derek. Maria has told me your plan, but I am short of some details. I will need to have firm dates and flight numbers and I would like to see the cases first, if that can be arranged.'

'Yes, of course. We have the suitcases in the car tonight, in fact. But first, tell me, Derek, how do you propose to do this for us?'

'Look, it should not be difficult, as long as the bags are tagged for an onward destination, as they would go into a holding area before the connecting flight. It would not be a problem for me to pick them up from there and put them into my van; I have access to a small airline van on the tarmac. At the end of my shift, I will just drive the bags through security. They know me and the van and never check for anything leaving – it's the stuff coming in they look at, sometimes.'

'I see,' he said, turning back around in his seat. His eyes studied my reflection in the driver's mirror. 'Have you done this kind of thing before?' he enquired softly.

'Yes, many times, but not drugs. We're all at it – all the baggage handlers – stuff goes missing. That's why some people call the airport "Thiefrow",' I said lightly. There was no movement or sound from the front two seats.

'I'll need my expenses up front, though. Today, if you can.'

Mina remained rooted in her position. She knew she was in the presence of a greater force than herself.

'Maria may have told you that we have lost two loads recently. If I lose another one, I will not be happy. Do you understand this, Derek? Do you understand how important this is to us?' There was no doubting the overt threat in his tone. He turned again in his seat and looked straight at me. I looked back steadily and could see his features more closely now. Below the clear blue of his eyes, a long, aquiline nose, reddened by the sun, led my gaze to a set of thin lips and a wide mouth. I knew that he was just twenty-six, but his appearance gave the impression of a much older, wiser man. I imagined, irrationally, that I could see the beginnings of a Machiavellian intensity etching remorselessly into his face. *The Picture of Dorian Gray* came to mind – a revised version in which the main character had not acquired eternal youth, but had maintained all the bad habits just the same. His skin, once ivory, no doubt, was tinted with a strong pinkish hue – an effect that was probably caused by long-term exposure to the sun and embellished by alcohol.

'This has to work this time or someone will pay. And I don't mean just money, Derek. Do you know what I am saying?' His voice was clear and unruffled and in that moment I comprehended that he had become used to dispensing menace on a regular basis. The guttural pitch of his Dutch accent made the effect even more pronounced. I nodded compliantly. He looked back at me coldly. 'OK, good. I am glad you appreciate our position.' He clapped his hands in a gesture of dramatic finality. 'Maria, give Derek the money, would you?'

Mina opened the glove box and pulled out an envelope. I reflected how the team had always joked about the police receiving brown envelopes in return for favours, but the irony stopped there, as there was no real comparison to the scene that was now unfolding. Besides, the envelope she held in her bony hand was white. She passed it to me without comment.

Bart looked away into the car park. 'Do you want to count it?'

'No, I trust you.'

'I have written the flight number on this paper. The bags will be tagged to an address in New York. The details are there also. They will be on the Thai Airways plane from Bangkok next Thursday. That is in six days. Can you be available for that?'

'Yes, no problem.'

'Good. You can call this number – it's under the flight particulars – if you have any problems.' He reached out his left arm and without turning his head, he swung his hand close to Mina's sinewy neck and offered me a slip of paper. 'It's a Bangkok number. Someone is there at all times, so don't be afraid about calling. Just leave a message and it will get to us. You must call the number once you have the bags and we will tell you where to take them. There is no need to meet us again before Thursday. Do you understand everything? Are you clear?'

'Yes, it seems fine. But when will I be paid in full?'

'As always – on delivery. Maria will have the money for you when you hand over the bags.'

'You said you have the suitcases here – I need to see them.'

'Maria, can you help Derek, please?' Bart said lazily. 'I'll say goodbye now, Derek. Please don't let us down.'

'Why should I? Twenty grand is worth having.'

'Exactly.'

Mina opened the BMW's front door and stepped into the car park, which was now wet. I had not noticed it start to rain. I took the hint and pushed my door open to follow her. She walked around to the rear and clicked open the expansive boot. Inside were four large, identical, brown, mock leather suitcases, each held closed by a substantial zip and two fat straps with metal buckles. Mina lifted one of the cases out of the boot and pointed her lean index finger at the handle, where a small, emerald green ribbon had been attached.

'All of them will have the New York tags and this ribbon,' she said.

'Good. I'd like my ID card back now, please,' I said in a loud voice so Bart could hear.

He must have anticipated my request, as his hand instantly appeared like an extended tentacle out of the driver's window. He waggled my pass indolently in small circles without turning to look. I took it from him and grimaced at Mina. She looked back implacably.

'Thanks. I will be in touch next week.'

I walked away into the dark and the sheeting rain.

The deal was now set up – money had exchanged hands and I was confident that we were very close to pulling off a nice little sting. But a lot of work still needed to be done. The appearance of Bart had unnerved and elated me in equal measures, but I knew that with a well-worked plan and a slice of luck this would be a golden chance to bring him to book for both this and the Tea Chest Case, as well.

'I just hope he stays here for the delivery,' I said to Stuart as he cabbied me back towards the office.

'My bet is, he will return to Thailand and get ready to meet the couriers,' he said, and of course I knew he was right. Guys like Bart did not hang around when the troops were going over the top. Far better to stay well behind the front line as the bullets started to fly.

Our rather pessimistic assessment proved to be correct. By the time we arrived back in New Fetter Lane to debrief the events of the evening, we had already received news from Control that the airport intelligence team had found a booking for a Bartholomew Vanderpool, travelling alone to Bangkok on the British Airways flight the following morning. We had no alternative – we would have to let him go. We had to make a seizure before we had a chance of pinning anything on him, or anyone else for that matter. But at least it gave us a chance to have a good look at him on his way out and peek inside his checked-in baggage.

A team was set up and dispatched to Heathrow early the next day. When they reported back at midday, there was good news and bad news. Bart was travelling with just cabin baggage – he had a business class ticket and no checked-in bags. The disappointment that we had no opportunity to rummage around his personal belongings was tempered with the good news. He was seen arriving in the BMW with a slim, golden-haired girl. They appeared very friendly, holding hands and kissing on the concourse, but at check-in, they had gone their separate ways – he to business class, her to economy. The really upbeat aspect, though, was that she had checked in two large, brown, strappy suitcases weighing, in total, just fourteen kilos. Obviously, they were practically empty. According to the passenger list, she was Alicia Duykers – our old friend from the first meeting with Rose. The net was closing fast. The team took photos with concealed bag cameras and watched both of them onto the aircraft. Alicia's bags were searched, but just a few bundles of clothes and cosmetics were revealed – nothing incriminating, no paperwork. Bart must have had all that in his cabin bag.

The Deltas had been conducting round-the-clock surveillance on Mina's Twickenham house, but it revealed little – just a daily night-time trip to the local pub and an unstable, inebriated walk home four hours later. But on Sunday, only one day after Bart and Alicia's departure, we got another positive hit on the BA passenger manifest. Conrad Duncan was on the move and surprise, surprise, he was on his way to Bangkok, too. A similar airport surveillance operation was mounted and Conrad, as we had expected, checked in the other two suitcases. They weighed in at just ten kilos; he was travelling even lighter that Alicia. We joked that the difference in weight was probably due to all the cosmetics she had been carrying.

So by Sunday afternoon, both the couriers had departed to meet their supplier. All we had to do now was to set up a nice reception for them when they returned in four short days. But first, I decided to test the telephone number Bart had given me. I had a good reason to want to speak with him, as I needed to tell him where we would meet with the bags. I was not happy to leave the choice of time and venue to him or Mina – we needed to control events from now on. It was important to ensure that the final phases of the action went smoothly and safely for everyone, me especially. I would be in the vanguard when things started to get interesting and I wanted to take every advantage I could get.

On Tuesday evening, less than forty-eight hours before the drop was scheduled, I rang the Thai number from a hotel room at the *Ariel*. I did not want to use an office phone, as it might have given them a chance to trace the origin of my call and if Bart decided to ring back, the hotel room cover would seem plausible. We had set up the usual recording devices and listened intently as the phone rang out. I knew it would be very early in the morning in Bangkok, but Bart had said I would get through at any time. After four single buzzes, it picked up.

'Hello.'

'Can I speak with Bart, please? I am calling from London.'

'He is not here right now. Do you want me to give him a message?' I detected a strong London accent.

'Yes. Tell him Derek called. I need to speak to him urgently. I am in the *Ariel Hotel*, room 412.' I gave him the phone number. 'I need to talk to him soon – can he call me within the hour?'

'Yes, sure. I'll let him know when he returns. Is there any other message to give him?'

'No, just tell him to call me.'

I replaced the receiver and we sat down to wait. Harry called the coffee shop for sandwiches. Stuart went out and bought some cans of beer, 'to ease the boredom,' he said. In truth, I was feeling more tense than bored – the beer would help relieve the pressure, perhaps.

'That guy I spoke to sounded English. South or East London, I reckon,' I said. We played the tape back and everyone agreed – definitely a London boy. It was an accent we knew that foreigners found very difficult to mimic – Dick Van Dyke had tried it and failed miserably.

Two beers later, the phone rang. It was exactly an hour after my call, almost to the second. Stuart started the tape and I picked up the receiver.

'Yes. Hello.'

'Is that you, Derek? It's Bart.'

I recognised the gravelled, Dutch accent. 'Yes, it's me. Look, everything is fine here – I have fixed my times so I can meet the package, but I want to talk to you about where I should deliver it.' I pressed on, deliberately giving Bart no chance to interrupt. 'I have a place in mind that will be very safe. There is a railway station near the airport called Feltham, it's just a few miles away. I will meet you there, in the car park, at seven p.m. It will be dark by then and I will have finished my shift, so I can meet you. I won't bring the airport van, it's too risky. I have hired a car. It's a white Ford Cortina with a black vinyl roof on a T registration plate.' I stopped talking and there was silence at the other end.

'Hello, Bart. Did you hear me?'

After what seemed like an eternity, I heard his clipped reply. 'Call me in eight hours – I will let you know. You say Felsham at seven p.m.'

'Yes.'

'Can you spell it?'

'F-E-L-T-H-A-M.'

'OK. Call me in eight hours and you will have my reply.' The phone went down; the call had lasted just seventy-five seconds. I realised that it would now be my turn to be available at an unearthly hour – maybe that was deliberate on his part. We kept the room for the night, ordered some more food and finished the beer. There was enough sleeping room for all four of us – it was very cosy. The sky was still black outside when I awoke to take a hasty shower. I wanted to be as alive as I could be when I spoke to Bart again and at that moment I was feeling pretty dreary – the effect of the beers had not abated with just four hours of wakeful sleep. At five fifteen, I rang again. This time, the conversation lasted just twenty seconds. 'OK, agreed – seven p.m. on Thursday at Felsham station. White Cortina, T registration.'

'Feltham,' I stupidly corrected him.

'Yes. It's fine. Make sure you are there, OK?'

We had chosen Feltham station for a good reason – it gave me a chance to escape on foot through a broken fence onto some waste ground by the railway line when the knock went down. *Knock* was the term we used to order a takedown or strike. It was unique to our service. No one quite remembered how it had come into usage – perhaps because so many of our calls were in the early hours and a knock on the door was usually the first stage in the strike. If the door was not answered quickly, we just heaved it in – we had some pretty clever tools to make the job of unhinging a front door simple. But as gentlemen investigators, we always started the process with a polite knock.

Feltham station directly adjoined the busy Hounslow Road and had just one entrance/exit, which was another advantage. We could block the escape route of a car easily – any vehicle entering the car park was effectively trapped. We had planned our tactics carefully. We presumed Mina and her team would arrive in a car, the BMW probably, but we could not be sure. They would need a second vehicle to carry away the eighty-plus kilos of drugs. We hoped that Bart would be with them, but our experience and the latest intelligence told us that this was unlikely. The idea was that when the suitcases had been loaded into Mina's car, Harry, as case officer, would call the knock and the Deltas, supported by the Oscars, would move in quickly to make the arrests and seize the drugs.

In fact, if all went well, we would already have most of the drugs in our possession – we were going to remove the cannabis from three of the bags and substitute it, or dummy up, with something to make up the weight. Stuart suggested bags of sugar. He then had the interesting job of finding someone who would sell us sixty kilos of sugar without reporting us to the Excise on suspicion of operating an illicit still. The irony of someone in another part of the department opening an enquiry file on such a purchase was not lost on us. We needed to keep one suitcase with the live drugs inside, in case Mina asked to see the cannabis resin before accepting delivery. My most important job was to remember which bag had the gear in!

When the knock was called, I would dart into the shadows and find the carefully prepared hole in the fence and run across the waste ground. The Deltas would do a lot of shouting in the car park to give the impression that they were in hot pursuit across the desolate tract of land behind the railway line. They would return five minutes later to announce that I had got away into the night. Then they would swear a lot and start blaming one another. The ruse was intended to preserve my cover for a little longer. It gave the interview teams an opportunity to harangue the gang about who I was and what had been my role. This was useful – it kept me clean, the gang thinking and I could be introduced again at a later date, if the need arose. There was no reason to let them know they had been stung, just yet.

So, the trap was set; all we needed was for the drugs to be brought to us. Our airport passenger intelligence team came up trumps again the next day: two business class bookings in the names of Duncan and Duykers, passengers on Thursday's inbound Thai International flight from Bangkok. It was due to land at seven, so it would be another exhausting, early morning start for some of us. I was excused, since I would need to be fresh for the encounter that evening. I went home to an empty house and tried to sleep in. Maureen and the family were still in Ireland. I had not heard from her. The lights were off, the dog's basket was empty and I felt lonely and unloved.

CHAPTER SIX

Just after nine o'clock, I was woken from a dreamy sleep by a call from Pete. 'It's a go, Mike – we have the bags.'

'Great news. Did everything go all right?'

'You could say so. We watched Conrad and Alicia through controls with their carry-ons – they are now safely housed in Twickenham. Are you sitting down, Mike?'

'Well, I'm in bed, if you really want to know, mate. Is there bad news?'

'No, only good.'

'Spit it out, man,' I said, my voice hoarse from slumber and midnight whisky.

'We've been had over. It's bloody smack, man! The fuckers have sent us fifty kilos of heroin.'

'Bloody hell. Christ, you must be joking.' I leaped out from under the duvet.

'No – straight up! We are all pretty gob-smacked, if you'll excuse the pun,' he gurgled. 'Look, you had better get in as soon as you can. The boss says we need a plan B. We are all decamping now to T3 for a briefing at one o'clock. And you've got to put that call into Bangkok.'

We were now in a completely different ball game. Fifty kilos of heroin was astonishing. It was a jackpot seizure for the UK. The street value could be immense – running into tens of millions of pounds, depending on the purity. Being exported out of Bangkok, it was very likely to be Golden Triangle-sourced heroin: high quality, white and extremely valuable. We needed to get it tested and fast. I said as much to Pete.

'It's at the government chemist already – we should know in the next few hours. Anyway, shake a leg, mate, and get your fat arse up to Heathrow.'

By midday, we had the results of the analysis. It was seventy-five per cent pure, which made the consignment worth at least fifteen million pounds by the time it had been cut into thirty per cent, single gram deals for the street market. The effect on the user population of such a sudden inflow of hard, addictive drugs would be huge. The heroin business depended on creating as many addicts as possible.

There is something truly sinister about a drug which generates new disciples so quickly and those who trade in it exploit their fellow human beings in a particularly cold-hearted way. Its reputation as a killer and destroyer of lives was well-earned. The profits generated by its trafficking were mind-boggling. The American Drug Enforcement Administration, the DEA, collected data on source prices in key drug-producing locations worldwide. Using their figures, we estimated that this haul had probably cost the shipper no more than one hundred and fifty thousand pounds – at about three grand a kilo. Even given the shipping and travel costs and various bribes necessary along the way, this heartless get-rich-quick scheme had no equal. It made the twenty-two grand they were going to pay me to get it through controls look risible – and I felt slightly insulted.

I parked the white Cortina in the T3 car park just before twelve and made my way across the pedestrian bridge into arrivals. I pinned my BA identification on my jacket, just in case any of Mina's group was watching, which I doubted, but it made sense to be careful. After a few minutes, I passed through security controls to airside, where I knew I was safe from prying eyes. The briefing room was really just another of Customs' nondescript offices. News of the case had spread like a virus. The ID's top boss "the Chief" (the Chief Investigation Officer) had been personally briefed by Bob Hibbard. He had asked for fifteen-minute updates, which frankly, was not helpful – we had enough on our plate without ringing him four times every hour.

So much for the "need to know" principle. Rank has its privileges.

In essence, the case had not changed and the operational demands were still pretty straightforward. Little had altered, except that now the pressure of failure was enormous. The takedown should be routine – a simple knock, the type of thing we had done time and time again. After an hour's preparation, before the briefing, we made only one change to the original plan. We decided to dummy the whole consignment – it was just too risky to let any heroin close to the gang. If we cocked up and a suitcase full of smack hit the streets, we might as well hand in our officers' commissions. If Mina asked to look inside the case, I would take a white handkerchief out of my pocket and signal the knock – no mucking about – straight in. I would still do my *Great Escape* routine, minus the motorcycle, and run for the hole in the fence.

My god!

The briefing room was chock-a-block. The Chief had ordered reinforcements for us and now, alongside the Deltas and Oscars were Foxtrots and Limas, representing the heroin target teams (wishing, no doubt, that they had been in at the start). We had a surfeit of talent on show – an *embarras de richesses*, as my mother would often say, with none of us quite knowing what she meant. It was a case of too many soldiers and not enough generals, for once. At least Bob Hibbard had persuaded the Chief that the Deltas could still lead on the case – we had been involved now for weeks and knew the targets inside out. This decision had created some tension with the heroin boys, but they had to lump it and they knew it.

After everyone had been allocated their jobs, four of us – Bob insisted on joining – made our way to the *Ariel Hotel*. I waited until mid-afternoon to call Bangkok again. Four predictable buzzes then a voice, Bart's voice.

'Hi,' I said. 'It's all good, I have the merchandise. I can deliver as planned. Is all OK at your end?'

'Don't worry about us. We will be there, as you say – seven at Felsham.'

This time, I resisted the urge to correct him. 'You will have my money, I hope.'

'For sure. It is OK.'

'Good. I'll see your people later.' And that was it. It was clear now that Bart would not be making a personal appearance. We had four hours to organise ourselves.

Ten kilos of sugar sat on a shelf in the Delta's tiny kitchen, where the tea was made and other stronger beverages were stored.

'By the time we get the other fifty back, we'll have enough for about five years, I'd say. We'll be sprinkling it on our cornflakes until 1984,' Harry said wryly.

Only three of the large, brown suitcases fitted into the Cortina's boot. We put the fourth on the back seat. By a quarter to seven, I was sitting alone in a shopping centre car park on Bedfont Lane, just minutes from the station. An official radio had been wired into the car and it now crackled with messages from all points as officers took up their positions. At five minutes to seven, Harry called for radio silence and the car became quiet.

I wound down the window an inch to let some cold air in. I was alone with my thoughts and could feel the adrenaline pumping into my arteries. We had not called for any armed police back-up, as we had no evidence that Mina's team had a track record for carrying weapons or acts of violence – apart from Conrad's GBH convictions, and we were confident we could handle him. As I sat in the dark, I began to wonder if we had done the right thing. We liked to do these cases on our own – it was a pride fixation as much as anything. But one skill we could not bring to the table was an armed response – we simply did not possess it. A silver tongue worked better than a silver bullet, or so we thought. And up to now we had always been right. But there was always a first time. My thoughts were broken as the radio sparked to life.

'All mobiles from Delta Three stand by. Tango One vehicle entering the car park now – silver BMW. Stand by. Manoeuvring now. It's a stop, stop. Lights out.'

'Delta Two, acknowledge. Can you provide sector.'

I started the engine and while closing the window with one hand, I put the car into gear with the other. My lights illuminated the exit from the shopping centre.

'Affirm sector Bravo, sector Bravo – facing out. There are three occupants.'

We had divided the car park into sectors. This information told me the BMW was parked at the eastern end, next to the railway line.

'Delta Two, Delta Four, receive,' I said into the microphone.

'Go ahead, Delta Four.'

'I am going in now – about two minutes.'

'Delta Four, Delta Two, affirm going in now. Good luck.'

There's no need for that!

It was against all radio procedures to wish someone luck. I switched off the radio and hid the mike in the glove box. The last thing I needed was it squawking during the handover.

As I drove into the car park, I saw the BMW parked as described at the far end, sitting alone with no other cars nearby. I drove slowly towards it and pulled alongside. I could see Mina and Tony in the front two seats. Conrad was behind them in the same back seat that I had occupied just six days previously. I stopped the car nose-first, facing the railway so the boot was exposed, switched off the lights, got out and walked to the rear of the Cortina. Mina and Tony joined me.

'Hello, Derek. Glad to see you. Have you everything as arranged?' Mina trilled, her thin neck silhouetted against the platform lights.

'Yes, it's all in here, but it doesn't weigh as much as eighty kilos.' I knew I was pushing my luck.

'There was a change of plan, but it makes no difference.'

'OK. Do you have my money?' I was suddenly conscious of all the unseen, watching eyes and listening ears around us. All hell would let loose soon and I was the only one in present company that was ready for it. It gave me confidence.

'Let me see the bags first,' Mina said.

'Just show me the money and I'll open the boot.'

Mina looked irritated – her narrow lips pursed. 'Don't you trust me?'

'Yes, of course, but please show me first.' There was no need for this. I was improvising now, extending the agony to watch her wriggle. I should really have just opened the boot, waved my white flag and let the cavalry charge in. But I was relishing the moment – I was in control of everything and I liked it. I stared back grimly.

'Tony, show him the money,' she said suddenly.

Tony, like a dutiful Labrador, leaned into the BMW and pulled out a small briefcase, which he opened in front of me. I could see neat rows of crisp twenty-pound notes. They looked plenty enough but it was difficult to be sure in this light. The thought crossed my mind briefly that I should ask to count them, but I resisted and flicked the boot open.

'See, there are three here. The other is in the back seat. Now can I have my money?'

'Tony, unlock the top one, please,' she said.

Tony reached into his trouser pocket and pulled out a bundle of keys. At the same time, I told myself enough was enough and took out my handkerchief to blow my nose. I don't know quite what I expected, but nothing happened. Tony was now fumbling with the top suitcase. The first key did not fit. He tried the second.

Where the hell are they?

'Look, Tony,' I said, 'before you open the case, can you let me have the money? We agreed.' It was enough for him to stop and look up for reassurance from Mina. Still no one came.

'Just do it, Tony!' she shrilled. 'Open the fucking case – we need to be sure.'

Tony looked blank and resumed his scrabble. The game of Russian roulette could not last much longer. The second key turned in the lock and the zipper was cleared. He now had to undo the two brass buckles. As his fat fingers worked on the catches, I looked up to see a car arrive in the car park, its lights shining against the front of the station. A man got out and walked into the ticket office. The car reversed and departed. I blew my nose extravagantly again. Tony was into the bag now.

'It looks OK,' he said to Mina. 'I can see it.'

As Mina peered into the case and started to lift out one of the bags of sugar, two more cars entered the car park. I recognised them and my racing heart jumped a few hurdles. Both cars drove over sedately, almost silently, to where we were standing, their tyres whirring against the asphalt. Tony and Mina were preoccupied with the cases; she had a bag of *Tate & Lyle* in her hands. A third car appeared and hovered at the car park entrance.

'Hang on!' I shouted. 'I don't like the look of this…' I bolted towards the station entrance. There were loud voices now. I scurried towards the perimeter and could hear car doors slamming. Before I scrambled through the hole in the wire fence, I had time to look back into the car park. Torch lights were flashing and through the glare I could see Mina and Tony standing transfixed next to the BMW. They had not moved a foot. Conrad appeared to be trapped in the back seat. I could see eight of my colleagues swarming all over them.

Suddenly, Tony went face first over the bonnet, his hands being handcuffed behind him. I heard a woman's voice screaming obscenities but I had no time to watch any longer. I had a rendezvous on the waste ground with India Oscar Nine.

I reached home that night feeling exhausted but euphoric. I would take no part in the interview process – my job was done, at least for the time being. I had debriefed Harry about the final conversation with Mina in the car park and then had driven quietly back to Purley to write up my notebook. I thought I would start the long process of preparing my witness statement in the morning. It would be required at a later date almost certainly, but now I needed a stiff scotch and some sleep – that was about it.

The house was quiet when I pulled the Cortina into the front drive. The landing light I had left on that morning shone dimly out of one of the upstairs windows. As I reached the front door, I noticed that the kitchen light was also on and the side gate was unlatched. I silently pushed the gate open and walked into the back garden, where I had a full view of the rear of the house. The downstairs curtains were drawn, but the living room light shone through the cracks. Someone was definitely inside – I had an intruder. I stood mutely in the garden for at least two minutes, thinking. After what seemed like an age, I came to the pretty obvious conclusion that I was not up to tackling a couple of burglars. My thought processes were agonisingly long-winded and over complex – the pros and cons wrestled one another in my jumbled brain, but eventually I decided that I needed to find help. I would have to call the police.

I retraced my steps back through the gate and tiptoed into the tree-lined avenue, where I crossed the road and crept into a neighbour's drive. I rang the doorbell of number ten. After a few seconds, the door opened and the plump figure of Stella greeted me warmly.

'Hello, Mike – long-time no see. Is everything all right? You look pooped.'

'Hi, Stella. Look, I'm sorry to disturb you, it's so late, but I need to use your phone. I have burglars in the house.'

'My god! Oh goodness! Of course, come in quickly. I'm a night bird anyway. The phone is on the hall table.'

I padded into the house and picked up the receiver.

Stella stood beside me and said, 'We have been having a spate of break-ins, you know. Mrs. Collins at number thirty-three was broken into last month. It's all drugs, you know; the youngsters are stealing to buy drugs. It's in today's *Daily Express*.'

I dialled 999.

Stella continued, 'Is Maureen with you? She looked well this morning, I must say, when I saw her with the dog. Been away to a funeral in Ireland, hasn't she?'

'Emergency services. Which service do you require?' came the urgent voice at the other end of the phone.

I gulped. 'I'm sorry, it's a mistake. Really sorry. Everything is fine,' I said and put the phone down.

'What's the matter, Mike? Aren't you going to tell them? My goodness, you really look dreadful. Shall I make some tea?'

'No, it's very kind, Stella. I have been working late and am a bit confused. I'll pop back if I need anything. I'm really sorry about this.' I walked briskly to the door and back over the road to the house. As I put the key into the lock, a dog barked inside. I stepped into the hall and Maureen was standing by the stairs watching me.

'Oh, you're back. It's really good to see you,' I said lamely. 'I wasn't expecting you.'

'We need to talk,' she said. 'Do you want a drink first?'

I wrenched off my coat and disintegrated onto the sofa. Maureen brought me a beer. We sat and talked for the next hour; well, I listened, mostly. Maybe she had intended to talk about us but instead she told me about the trip and the funeral – how everyone was sorry not to see me. It had all gone well and she thought a few more days with the family would be enjoyable for both her and Caroline, and there was so much space to walk the dog. It had done them all good, she said. I started to explain about the case, the office and the pressure I had been under but the words never came out as I wanted. I stumbled and blustered and it was pretty clear that she was not interested anyway, so I just left it. It was late. I opened a bottle of *Teacher's*. It felt as if I had dodged a bullet. I would do my notes in the morning.

CHAPTER SEVEN

A week after the pandemonium at Feltham, Bob called a team meeting to review the case. The seizure had hit the press and was being hailed as a major success in Britain's new war on drugs.

"Huge Heroin Haul!"
"Customs Drug Bust – Four Arrested"

We knew better and tried not to get carried away by the headlines and the empty rhetoric. It was true that we had made a significant seizure, by UK standards, but it was difficult not to wonder just how many shipments by-passed us. If a small group run by a twenty-six-year-old Dutchman could organise such a load, what could the other, more established international gangs do? It raised huge questions about our intelligence capability and structures. None of the heroin teams had got wind of the consignment – not even a scrap of information. We had, in effect, got lucky – a cold case informant had led us into the investigation and now we were as surprised as anyone at the apparent ability of the opposition to source fifty kilos of high-grade heroin so effortlessly – and risk it on a first-time operation. Common sense dictated that it would have been prudent to run in a few soft drug shipments first, to establish the system and iron out any glitches. But this group had apparently gone for gold straight up – or had they? Had Bart's previous imports been heroin also? Our intelligence operation was left scratching its head and clutching at straws.

The Chief and his fifth-floor management team wanted answers. Questions were asked in the House of Commons – were we sitting on a powder keg? Our lack of coherent responses made it increasingly evident that we knew precious little about how the trade in heroin really worked. What did the supply route from the source and transit countries look like? What did the operation entail? At this point, we had no means of finding out, other than by speaking to the Americans. We were wary because we knew the DEA had its own agenda. But it would be a start.

The preceding seven days had seen the case against Mina and the others run a fairly predictable course. The arrests at the railway station had gone without major incident. Conrad had locked himself in the back seat of the BMW for a while, which had amused everyone enormously. Once the Deltas had found the car's ignition key in Tony's jacket, it was a simple task to drag him out. A house search in Twickenham located Alicia – apparently in the bath, washing her flaxen hair – and she was pulled in for questioning. Of course, there was no sign of Bart. It was pretty clear he had intended to stay in Bangkok until he received the green light from Mina.

At first, all four of them denied any knowledge of the heroin shipment. This was not unusual and, in fact, it made our job easier; the more they lied, the more stupid they looked. Piece by piece, over the next forty-eight hours, the evidence was put to them. There were surveillance photographs of them meeting a bearded man in the *Excelsior* and *Ariel* hotels. There were photos taken at the railway station showing Mina with her hands in one of the suitcases and also holding a suspicious-looking bag of sugar – the same bearded stranger alongside them. They were questioned about the trips by Conrad and Alicia to Bangkok and their checked-in suitcases, identical to the ones now in our custody and dotted with their fingerprints, inside and out. The interrogators deliberately asked pointed questions about the mysterious, hirsute man – the one that fled into the night. Much to all our surprise, none of them gave me up. Either they had been taken in hook, line and sinker or they were saving me for when they got out. One way or another, it made us think about the cliché of loyalty amongst thieves. The questions were dropped after a time – it made sense to keep my identity secret if we could – no sense in pushing it if they did not want to cooperate.

Despite their gratifyingly tight lips on my behalf, they were less successful in protecting themselves and gradually they managed to incriminate one another. One by one, over two days, they all caved in. Conrad, belying his physical strength and square-jawed appearance, collapsed first, admitting he had gone to Bangkok to deliver two near-empty suitcases to a man called Farouk and then checked them back in, heavy this time, for the return trip to London. But he strenuously denied knowing anyone called Bart or that heroin was in the bags. He said repeatedly, in his brassy Irish brogue, that he thought it was hashish.

'What the fuck would I be doin' with smack? Dat's just for monkeys!'

And, maybe he was not lying. It was not unusual for co-members of drugs syndicates to withhold key information from one another and lie to their couriers to protect their interests, usually with the sole aim of eking out a better financial reward from their share in the profits. Greed was key in all things. He told his questioner that he was to get twenty-five thousand pounds for his troubles. He had some Cheltenham gambling debts that needed settling.

Alicia coughed her lungs up next, explaining that she did the run to earn enough money to pay for a fashion shop she wanted to open in Islington. Her cooperation stopped suddenly when she was shown photographs of her and Bart canoodling at the airport. She promptly clammed up and refused to answer any questions about him.

Tony blamed Mina and Mina blamed Tony, each saying the other put them up to it, but both eventually and reluctantly agreed their part.

The common theme was that they all thought they were smuggling hash which, conveniently for them, was a significantly less serious offence and carried a much smaller sentence.

After a series of failed bail applications and pre-trial hearings, Regina v Christofe et al was set for Aylesbury Crown Court in October. All four defendants had stopped applying for bail after about a month, presumably on advice from their lawyers, who must have told them that things looked bleak and lengthy custodial sentences would follow in due course. This way, they could serve at least the initial part of any gaol term on remand, where their privileges would be greater. This was a good sign for us – maybe they would all plead guilty and we would be spared a lengthy and costly trial. But we prepared the evidence meticulously all the same, leaving nothing to chance – this was still a huge case and we did not want it to fail because of a badly written witness statement or an improperly labelled exhibit.

Three weeks before the trial, we were informed that all four would indeed plead guilty and their lawyers would focus on mitigating their roles to ones of mere cannabis smugglers. If it washed with the judge, a shorter prison sentence would probably follow, but it was a risky strategy, as it was never certain what mood His Lordship might be in on the day of sentencing. I fully expected them to obtain some credit from the court by pleading. In effect, their defence was now one of damage limitation – appeal to the court, get the sentence over with, do your time and get out quicker to fight another day. We had no illusions that they would be reformed characters by the time they were released – certainly not Mina, who looked like a career criminal to us.

The real bonus for me was that my undercover identity was protected and I would not be required to attend court to give evidence. I was keeping my fingers crossed – things could change and attitudes could swing in the final hours leading up to the trial. I need not have worried, though. The trial opened with all four pleading guilty. Following two days of mitigation speeches, the judge reconvened the court to pass sentence. The maximum he could pass was fourteen years – he chose to give Mina twelve, Tony ten, Conrad eight and Alicia six. He told the hunched group in the dock that he had rejected the hashish defence for Mina and Tony but had accepted that, as couriers, Conrad and Alicia had been, in all probability, kept in the dark. Given the way custodial sentences worked, Mina could expect to be out and back in circulation in seven or eight years.

Harry reported the final scenes to me when he returned to New Fetter Lane later that day. He spoke with a sense of pride, brightly and entertainingly, as he described how the convicts looked shattered and broken as they turned in the gated dock, heads bowed, to disappear one by one down the stone steps into the bowels of the ancient court building to the cold and clammy cells below.

As he described the courtroom tableau, an unexpected thought crossed my mind. I wondered for the first time in my career whether the whole thing had been worthwhile. It had been an exhilarating ride for me personally, of course, and we had done what society had expected of us and performed the job well. But what difference had we really made? In a few short years, all four of them would be back on the streets, wiser and better-equipped to take us on again, if they chose. Was the solution to the vicious drugs trade law enforcement, after all? Perhaps it had a part to play, but as I sat nursing my celebratory beer with the rest of the team laughing and wisecracking around me, I wondered why we did not do more to educate and support the vulnerable users. If somehow society could help them resist the lure of drug dependency, the malicious, profiteering pushers and traffickers would have no market for their venomous products. We needed to do more for those susceptible. I kept my thoughts to myself – no sense in raining on everyone's parade and I'd have been laughed at anyway. Now was not the moment.

Harry topped up my glass and launched into yet another description of how he had dragged Conrad kicking and shouting out of the back of Mina's BMW and we all hooted. Any lingering doubts about the value of our work passed quickly out of my head. It would soon be time to focus on the next case and I looked forward to it with all my heart. And I now had someone firmly in my sights, a long-term target – Mr. Bartholomew Vanderpool. Clearly, he had been the force behind this attempt. His personal risks had been few. He had slipped away again and all our efforts to trace him had failed. Holland, Sri Lanka, India, Britain and now Thailand – where would he pop up next? I wondered whether, on this occasion, his own greed may have got the better of him. To have purchased fifty kilos of heroin was no mean feat. Had he taken a big financial risk with the consignment or was it just another write-off expense in a much bigger game? Time would tell, no doubt, and from now on, I'd be watching.

CHAPTER EIGHT

Despite my disappointment at missing the biggest shark in the tank, again my career was on a roll, so much so that the department decided to give me my first team to lead. And that was not all; I was to change disciplines. For over eight years, I had effectively been a foot soldier, albeit in an elite investigators club; the time had come for me to make a transition, a move towards the more obscure and shady edges of our work – into the world of intelligence.

My new job was to head up the freshly-formed Heroin Intelligence Team, a long-overdue initiative to plug the gaps in our knowledge, exposed so ruthlessly by the Feltham case. I greeted the news with a large dose of professional unease, as I knew that the forthcoming years would prove the most challenging I had yet experienced in both my career and my rapidly deteriorating married life.

Was there room for both?

This new opening would take me into the enigmatic world of information and informants, clandestine phone tapping and hush-hush, secret undercover operations. It would pit my wits, and those of my staff, against some of the best criminal minds the field could offer – characters who masterminded and financed the largest international organisations, while remaining unseen, in the shadows – the hidden men, the Marco Polos of drugs smuggling, the global drugs kingpins.

It was a big assignment and despite my nervousness, I relished it. The first priority would be for others to ensure I had a cast-iron background and the maximum level of reliability to take the new job. To this end, my security clearances would be reviewed. My name was put forward to increase my vetting to the highest level in Government: DV-TS – Developed Vetting – Top Secret. I filled in the forms, which seemed to be mostly questions about how much money I had and how I spent it. Then I attended an interview with a retired army officer, who fired embarrassing questions at me for three hours.

'Have you ever slept with a man?'

'No, not if you mean having sex with him.'

'Precisely.'

'Well, no then – never.'

'Have you ever been unfaithful to your wife?'

I had been waiting for this one and dreading it. I had resolved to tell the truth. Everyone who had been through the process told me it was the only way.

'Well, yes, as it happens.'

I sensed that my interviewer took a little vicarious pleasure from my answer. His lips curled in a suppressed smile and he launched into twenty minutes of close interrogation on the whos, whens and wheres. He did not ask me the "why" question, which I thought rather strange, at the time.

'How much do you drink?' I gave him the same answer that I gave my doctor; not exactly a lie, just a little economy with the truth.

He wanted to know if I held any extreme political views – fascist or communist. That was easy – of course not; I was far too busy to be messing with that sort of stuff. Finally, he packed up his notes, tidied his pens and solemnly told me that I would learn the result in a few weeks. He gave me no indication one way or another.

Part of his job. I'm glad I don't have to do it!

Two days after the 1981 New Year celebrations had ceased and we had all recovered from our hangovers, I received the news that my top secret vetting had come through and I was to be appointed Head of Intelligence Team M. I was now "India Mike One". Although the new job had been expected for some time, and despite the lurking anxieties, I felt a huge surge of pride. To have a full Intelligence team at my command was an awesome responsibility.

At about the same time, the ID made a significant step onto the international stage, one that would have profound personal and professional repercussions for me in the future. At last, the Chief and his merry men had persuaded Whitehall to finance the posting of our first officer abroad. Notwithstanding my personal, rather jaundiced view that the step was long overdue, the fact was that HM Customs Investigation Division was about to become the first UK agency to send a law enforcement officer beyond our most adjacent European neighbours.

I felt vindicated – my apparently adolescent notion that quality international relationship building would support our efforts had finally been accepted. The increasing need to monitor the movement of trade around the world and the necessity to track the activities of those whose aim was to break transnational rules must have been decisive factors in the bold decision. Like a huge penny dropping, it dawned on the fifth-floor senior management team that our results could be hugely enhanced by building multinational liaisons and by developing opportunities for global information sharing. I had played no part in the judgment. Despite heading a new intelligence team, I was still considered by the big bosses to be very much "swimming in the weeds" when it came to strategic decision-making. In fact, my influence was so slight that when the news was leaked, it came as a real surprise to me.

When the advertisement for the first post to Karachi was announced officially, about two months later, I sat in my office for a while, drumming my fingers against the desk, as I considered the implications. It was pointless for me to apply – I had just started a new job and was sure my new managers would not release me. Besides, I did not have the track record required or the intelligence experience. But to have a trusted colleague working in a foreign jurisdiction, in touch with trends and developing threats, could prove a boon to my own work and ambition… providing we sent the right man. Unfortunately, we had no home-spun knowledge in this area to lean on and we would have to build from scratch. I wondered what type of officer the fifth floor would appoint to this first critical position. To get it wrong would be embarrassing; to get it badly wrong could the kill the project, and any hope of further postings, stone dead. More importantly perhaps, it would open the way to other British intelligence agencies in the corridors of Whitehall to try their luck.

Would the new officer be the "win friends and influence people" diplomatic type? Or would they send a roughty-toughty gumshoe kind of investigator, used to making big cases in the UK and bullying his way to success? I hoped the selection would be sensible and we would be lucky enough to find a hybrid – an audacious facilitator, perhaps? One thing was certain, it could take a while for the office to identify which formula worked best. I did not know it at the time, but for me it would be another four years of R&D before my name was considered amongst the runners and riders for an overseas slot.

I settled myself into my new work with a sense of resolute determination. The first thing to do was to mould an effective team around me. I needed people with an inquisitive mind, a relentless attitude and an eye for detail. At the outset, however, I was given very little influence in the selection of my new staff. Names were offered up to me on my first day by my new boss, who had hand-picked every one of them.

'Tell me what you think, Mike. I hope you will be pleased. There are some good guys there and I'm sure you will be able to pull them together as a team in the next few months.' His tone implied that the list was not negotiable. I was seeing it as a courtesy only, so I spent a few thoughtful moments running my eye down the names and gave the sheet back to him.

'Yes, Joe, they look fine. There are a couple I don't know too well but the rest are all suitable blokes. And I see Rosie is on the list – she will definitely be a positive addition.'

My new leader was Joe West. He was an assistant chief investigation officer with over twenty years' experience in the IB and ID. He was one of New Fetter Lane's senior management team and had direct responsibility for the ID's intelligence collection. He commanded five distinct but interwoven intelligence units. Alongside my heroin team, there were ones for cocaine and cannabis, a combined unit for yachts, small maritime craft and general aviation and one dedicated to telephone intercepts (which had a wide functional responsibility to support and supply information to the other four intelligence teams). This was the "OTW" outfit that Mervyn Nugent had referred to so obliquely on my very first day as an IB officer ten years before.

It was difficult not to like Joe West – he was very pleasant, courteous and middle-aged, in all respects. He smiled rarely, he was too serious for that, but there was a warmth and graciousness about him. He was urbane, cultured and well-mannered – personal traits which were quite rare in our offices at that time. He did suffer from one personal frailty, however – his work ethic. It was not uncommon to find officers at their desks at seven a.m. and seven p.m. on the same day – it was part of the ID culture, engrained in us from the beginning – the work hard/play hard principle. But for Joe, it was an obsession. He would arrive before everyone and leave after them. While the rest of us were enjoying our last pint before the journey back to our families, his office lights would continue to pierce the gloom of the New Fetter Lane corridors. He would be turning the combination locks in his file store as the dawn chorus twittered in the Holborn trees outside and at the end of a long day he would gather up bits of unclassified paperwork into his battered leather briefcase to complete at home over a late dinner in faraway Beckenham. He was totally and utterly preoccupied with his administrative work. If I left an intelligence report for him to read, last thing, on my way home, it would be back on my desk at seven the next morning, pinned with slips of paper and suggestions for amendments and points for discussion later that day. He was unremitting and his micro-management would grate, at times. But we put up with it because he was on our side and wanted the best for us – we knew that and loved him for it.

Intelligence work is all about building a picture of the opposition – observe their actions, predict their movements and then plot their downfall. For the India Mikes, the focus was heroin and those who sourced it, shipped it and smuggled it. Heroin was a product of opium; opium was harvested from a particular type of poppy grown widely in South and East Asian countries. We had experienced a flood of heroin importations into Britain over the previous three years and the task now was to understand what had caused the surge and what measures we could take to stem the flow. We had all been to see *Popeye Doyle* chasing a Marseilles-based smuggling ring through the streets of New York in *The French Connection* and loved every minute of it. But while this memorable film, based on a true incident, was an enjoyable, fast action, seat-jumping thriller, we also laughed at its simplicity and its depiction of intelligence casework. The truth was much less glamorous, even though we had our moments, too.

We quickly deduced that the vast majority of the heroin delivered into the UK was from an area we called the Golden Crescent – Pakistan, Iran and Afghanistan – and of these, Pakistan was by far the biggest problem for us. Of lesser significance, but still responsible for huge amounts of opium production, was another heroin-producing region which everyone knew as the Golden Triangle – Thailand, Burma and Laos. So, it was in these vast expanses of the globe that we had to start our search and begin to build our intelligence picture. The new overseas post in Pakistan could be a breakthrough for us and much of my opening few months as India Mike One was briefing the new man selected to take up our first post at the British Deputy High Commission in Karachi.

Dick Preston was a no-nonsense, plain speaking Lancastrian with a ruddy complexion, gnarled features and curly, ginger hair. He had been working in the IB and ID for fifteen years and knew every trick in the book. He had a reputation for being hard on colleagues who had, in his view, transgressed in some way – making stupid mistakes on surveillances or speaking out of turn at briefings when he thought more senior voices, like his own, needed to be heard first.

"I wouldn't send him out for a bag of chips. The man's got the brains of a rocking horse!" was one of his favourite expressions to describe colleagues who he thought were not up to snuff. Dick had been chosen by the fifth floor because of his knowledge, experience and drive – not for his rather agricultural diplomatic skills, although he was being urged at every turn to hone the imperfect talents he possessed as a tactful interlocutor before meeting the British High Commissioner in post for the first time.

Dick and I got on very well. I liked him and his candid bluntness, even though it made me flinch sometimes. The thing about Dick was that what you saw was what you got. Perhaps he lacked subtlety, but he had no conniving ways either, and as things turned out, this would win him friends and lead to a highly successful first overseas posting for HMCE.

When I visited him in Karachi to assess the intelligence picture emerging from his first half-year in post, I found that everyone was eating out of his hand. I am not sure if the Foreign Office had ever seen a Whitehall colleague quite like Dick before – but they clearly loved him and he could do no wrong in their eyes. More importantly, the local law enforcement officials took to him too and despite their machinations and politics, their trickery and double standards, he was making real progress.

As time passed, Intelligence Team M increased its influence and within a few months we were producing cases for the operational teams to investigate. The methodology was simple – we identified the greatest threats, developed lines of intelligence on them and produced working packages for the operational teams to adopt as their own cases. We used all the usual tools in the box, which usually started with a thorough collation and analysis of existing reporting and then followed up by, as and when required, mobile and static surveillance – room-bugging and use of hidden cameras. Full-blown undercover operations and telephone intercepts would be considered, too. But by far the most productive technique we employed was agent running, or informant handling, as we preferred to call it. This could also be the most hazardous modus operandi as, by their very nature, informants, snouts and grasses were not the most reliable types of creature – most had their own hidden agendas and all were capable of unravelling a complicated and long-running investigation in a matter of minutes. Some of my officers had a particular penchant for recruiting and working informants; others were hopeless at it.

The trick, as a manager, was to match like with like – the officer with the role. The outgoing characters, the talkers and jokers, the risk-takers were usually good at handling human sources but often had no feel for long-term surveillance, which required a grim determination and a concentrated focus. Both were important. The team had to be good at each discipline and had to have an ability to sift through endless streams of intelligence reporting and pick out the plums.

I decided, after about a year, that we needed to create a hit list of our top ten targets and put a concentrated effort into maximising our chances with them. These were individuals or groups that had crossed swords with us in the past and had a proven track record of involvement in the most serious cases of heroin smuggling. Completion of the list took six months of painstaking research, sifting through hundreds of files, held not just by us, but at airports and ports and within police and security service circles, as well. When the work was complete, we had dossiers, coloured red for dramatic effect, on our top ten, plus assorted paperwork and files on at least a dozen others who had not made the scarlet hit list. I sent the papers to Joe with a request to brief him fully on our findings when it was convenient. The next morning, at seven minutes to eight, as I was hanging up my overcoat and shaking my sodden scarf, the phone rang. I reached for it, my hands still wet from the driving winter rain outside.

'Rawlin,' I said, self-importantly.

'Mike, it's Joe. I'm glad you are in, at last. I'm going to walk across to see you – about two minutes, OK?' That was typical of Joe – he must have been ringing me every three minutes for the last two hours.

'Yes, of course. I'll put some coffee on.'

I called Steve, the team's young clerk, and asked him to bring coffee for two and biscuits, if we had them, to my office and I settled back into my chair, still brushing off the London rain from my collar. On cue, Joe breezed in without knocking. He was carrying the ten intelligence dossiers and the assorted 'also-ran' files, each with copious pieces of coloured paper sticking out from the hidden pages like bristles from a porcupine. He said nothing as he plonked them down on my desk. I sighed inwardly.

Here goes – four hours of critical analysis. I hope that coffee gets here quickly. Six months of work and he has turned it round overnight.

'I wanted to go through your top ten list. I hope you have a moment or two, Mike.'

By lunchtime, he had de-selected three of my preferred targets, relegating them to the ranks of odds and sods, and promoted three new ones to take their place.

'I like the idea of selective targeting, Mike, but we have to be realistic. We do not have a snowball in hell's chance of furthering intelligence on some of these guys where we have no access. We need to concentrate on Pakistan and the routes from there where we know we have a handle, where we know Dick can help us. The Golden Triangle files may be worthy targets, but I cannot see us taking any of them forward without involving the locals and you know the problems as well as I do.'

One of the files he had culled was labelled "Bartholomew Vanderpool" and I was bitter. I protested as much as I could, but he was the boss and, in fairness, he had a point. While it was satisfying to know that I had assembled a list of suitable targets, it equally made sense that if the intelligence needed to update and develop them was lacking, we would struggle to make much progress. In the cases of Bart and the other two Far East targets I had selected, we had to accept that we had no viable access in Bangkok.

'I hear what you say, Joe, but the Bangkok stuff will come back to bite us eventually.'

'Without access there is no chance. Until the Chief appoints a liaison officer in Thailand, we cannot move a muscle. Focus on Pakistan – that is by far our best bet, Mike.' He got up to go. It was ten minutes past two and I needed a pint.

'What if I prepared a paper outlining the risks from the Golden Triangle, Joe? That would add fuel to the fire, wouldn't it?'

He stopped and turned. 'Yes, that makes sense. Why not draft a report for me, explaining that we have a Far East void in our intelligence picture. If it's good enough, I'll submit it to the Chief as a discussion topic for the next senior management meeting.'

'How would you feel if I did a short exploratory trip to Bangkok? I could ask the Septics to set up some meetings for me.' *Septics* was the rhyming slang for the US DEA: Septic Tank = Yank.

'I'm not letting you loose in Thailand, mate,' he said cheerily. 'At least, not until you have drafted that report. I won't rule it out, though, I'll give you that. My god, what would Mrs. Rawlin say? Her husband off to Bangkok on some wild goose chase! Bloody hell, Mike.' He laughed out loud and I did my best to look amused. I made a mental note, though, not to tell Maureen about our emerging plan of action.

'Oh, and another thing, Mike – get rid of those dreadful red files. What on earth were you thinking about? Far too showy; the normal buff ones will do just fine.'

The rehabilitated top ten list was re-packaged and circulated amongst the team. Each officer was given responsibility for working up the profile of one of the targets. There was one case for each officer, but everyone would muck in when surveillance was required. Two on the list merited an immediate hook-up from OTW. Both cases had significant UK angles which we felt we could advance effectively and after the Home Secretary's approval, they were wired up and the phone tapping began. Interception of telephones was a hugely valuable tool and we guarded its secrecy very closely. We never disclosed the use of the technique at court trials and we never relied on it as evidence. It was just intelligence – pure and simple. If OTW told us that one of our suspects was meeting another target to discuss a drugs shipment, we sent officers from one of the operational teams to cover the meeting, to watch, and hopefully listen, first-hand. That way, we could use the surveillance of the meeting as evidence obtained from the officers present at the time – not from the intercept. Physical corroboration on the ground was essential. Although this took time and patience, the process had a hidden advantage – it kept the opposition guessing.

Most career criminals knew the dangers of telephone intercepts and the risks they ran by talking too openly. One would say to another in guarded tones, 'My dog is sick – can we RV?' In other words, his dog (cockney rhyming slang for phone: dog and bone = phone) was being tapped, so could they meet face to face to talk things over? Despite the risks, most of them seemed to carry on, regardless. As they were never confronted with the details of their phone calls at court, they never had the bugging confirmed officially. If defence counsel asked one of us in the witness box whether we had bugged his client's phone, we just said we knew nothing about it and looked pleadingly at the judge who, knowing the score as everyone did, would intervene and demand that the barrister take another line of questioning. All the lawyers knew we had power to collect evidence this way, but none of them were able to prove that we had used the technique in any specific case. It was another game really, but the semblance of doubt remained. As long as it did, the weaker the opposition were and the more mistakes they made. It suited us – although there were times when we knew a man was cold, stonking guilty because of what he had said over the wire but we simply could not use the intelligence in court. That made things difficult and frustrating on occasions; we swallowed it and found ways round it next time. We usually got our man in the end, even if it took two or three cases and further trials.

My Golden Triangle paper was on Joe's desk in four days. A visit to the London boss of the DEA at the US Embassy in Grosvenor Square had assisted in making my argument and I was confident that a compelling and thorough report had been produced. At least *I* thought it was convincing. I had concluded the paper by recommending a fact-finding trip to Bangkok and few had been surprised by my suggestion that I was the only man who could do it. As Head of Heroin Intelligence, I was better placed than anyone to take the recommendations forward. As a sweetener, to save costs, I proposed that I could pop in and see Dick Preston in Karachi on the way home. Joe predictably made a hatful of adjustments to the twelve-page document, but to my great satisfaction, he endorsed it and approved the exploratory trip into the bargain.

'Good paper, Mike. I've crafted a couple of alterations. You have made a few too many assumptions for my liking, but on the whole, it's fine. The Chief will have it tomorrow.' It was in Joe's gift to authorise the overseas visit, but if I wanted to win the battle for a full-time liaison officer in Bangkok, I would need to persuade the Chief himself. But for now, I just wanted to become more acquainted with the Thai Airways flight schedule.

CHAPTER NINE

Bangkok is the essence of the Far East – and how much I loved it! Steamy, pungent, cacophonous, vibrant, gaudy. It is *in your face*, so much so that my first walk out of the cool marbled halls and tranquillity of the *Shangri La Hotel* into the pulsating street scene lasted just thirty minutes; I was forced to retreat back inside to recover. Like a climber on the north face of Everest, I demanded oxygen. And a cold beer did not go amiss, either. With a cooling *Kloster* lager in my hand and the tinkling of a polished grand piano in the background, I sat in the cocktail lounge and planned my first meeting.

Earlier that afternoon, the Royal Thai Police had sent a driver to pick me up at the airport and transport me – such an apt expression – to the *Shangri La,* which stood as an impressively modern edifice overlooking the Chao Phraya River which snaked its thick, russet course through the ancient capital. It was dark already – my first encounter with the brief Bangkok twilight. I would sleep well tonight, wrapped in the crisp white sheets of my immense hotel bed, but first thing in the morning, at eight o'clock sharp, a car from the Office of Narcotics Control Bureau, ONCB, would arrive to take me to my first official engagement. The British Embassy had arranged for me to meet the colonel in charge of the foreign affairs section, Maitree Sorncam.

Bangkok traffic is notorious, possibly the worst in the world, and although I knew its reputation, I was still rather surprised that the car scheduled to pick me up for a nine thirty meeting with Colonel Sorncam was waiting for me outside at eight a.m. The city map I had picked up in the lobby suggested that the journey would be just a short hop across the urban sprawl. Despite my misgivings, I made sure that I was on time and my driver from the day before greeted me like an old friend when I walked out of the lift into the lobby. As I popped my key into reception, the attractive receptionist, clad in a traditional tight-fitting, crimson sarong, smiled appealingly. She handed me a sealed envelope with a blue coat of arms on the reverse. I immediately recognised the monogram and accompanying French words that meant Britain: *Dieu et Mon Droit*.

I hesitated, studying the envelope for a moment. It didn't seem appropriate to tear it apart disrespectfully, so I took my time, gently peeling the edges away, and pulled out a short, typewritten note on official Foreign Office paper which said:

Dear Mr. Rawlin,
Sorry I could not meet you yesterday. If you can pop in to the embassy later today to see me, it would be nice to meet you. Maybe we can help. Your colleague, Dick Preston from BDHC Karachi, called yesterday. He is due in town tomorrow. It would be very good if we could all have a chinwag.

It was signed in bright blue ink "*Nigel*" with the typed words underneath, *Nigel de Courcey, First Secretary*.

Dick's imminent arrival did not come as a surprise, as I had received a call in my room from him the night before. He jokily enlightened me that London had been reconsidering the whole trip and thought it would be useful to send him along to accompany me. I wondered how much lobbying on his part had been required to get the fifth floor to dispatch him; he must have heard me thinking as he made a point of teasing.

'Look, Mike, I am Customs only officially recognised diplomat and the Chief thinks my silky skills will be useful to you!'

But I actually welcomed his intervention – together we would present a much stronger team and I knew we could work together harmoniously. I planned to meet him at the airport the next day, if only I could find someone to take me there. Nigel, perhaps?

I grasped that the police driver was called Khun Dong but learned very quickly that he spoke no English apart from "Good morning. Have a nice day." So I sat back in the car and watched the rush hour traffic and the tide of people as we snailed our way through the endless torrent of moving vehicles, inching our way ever closer to our destination. The ONCB offices were close to the Victory Monument, which looked a bit like Nelson's Column without Nelson on it. It tapered into a spike instead and was erected in June 1941 to commemorate the Thai victory in the Franco-Thai War, a brief conflict waged at the turn of the nineteenth century against the French colonial authorities in Indo-China.

As the car pulled to a stop outside the rather grand entrance and atrium, I noticed a small entourage of smiling, uniformed policemen and the comprehension hit me suddenly that they were waiting for me. The tight-packed group escorted me into the building. We entered a lift and on the second floor the doors opened to yet another gaggle of waiting officials who ushered me the few remaining yards directly into Colonel Sorncam's generous office. He looked up from his desk as we walked in and I put out my hand to greet him. He did not reciprocate – instead he smiled and made a little nod of his head, putting his hands together, as if in prayer.

Sorncam was a small, neat-looking man, who clearly kept himself fit. I suspected he was about my age but he looked a lot trimmer; his body shape was compact and well-defined and his eyes had a distinct brightness about them. I thought he had the look of an inquisitive squirrel. There were a lot of deft hand movements and I quickly saw that he possessed an effortless ability to move his svelte frame to precisely where he wanted it to be, at any given moment, without any fuss. We sat down on some embroidered chairs and he said in excellent English, 'Khun Mike, we are very pleased to meet you. I hope you are not tired from your long journey.'

Before I could respond, he stood up again and clicked his fingers at some junior officers who had been lurking at the back of the room. For an instant, I thought the interview had come to an abrupt conclusion. I looked around wondering who I had offended, but he quickly waved me to stand up.

'Would you be pleased to follow me?'

'Yes, of course,' I replied, slightly uneasily.

'We will go to see General now.'

He led me out into the corridor with the others trailing behind. I clutched my leather briefcase and tried to straighten my choking tie with a free hand. I was feeling the heat now and sweat was pouring down my back and under the lining of the smart, wool suit trousers I had foolishly bought at *Burton's* for the trip.

'It's so good of you to come. I trust the hotel is to your liking.' He chatted away amiably as we walked; I managed to grunt a few single syllables in response. We rounded a corner and entered a small anteroom from where I glimpsed, through another open door, a gilt-painted sign indicating loudly, "*The Office of the Head of the ONCB*".

If Colonel Sorncam's workplace had been smart, the one occupied by General Suthep Sawang was positively ostentatious. A huge, teak desk sat under an enormous portrait of King Bhumibol and the large red, white and blue flag of Thailand. The walls were adorned with coloured, wooden plaques from every conceivable worldwide law enforcement organisation and there were glass cases full of silverware and other valuable-looking objects, including a preponderance of ornate knives, which had me thinking for a moment. The room was empty, aside from its glittering treasures and a glamorous young woman in uniform, who I assumed was the General's secretary. Colonel Sorncam pointed to a white sofa and indicated precisely where I should sit. He took his place on my left. To my right was a vast, vacant, ebony armchair.

The entourage left the room in single file and closed the door. Colonel Sorncam kept up his chatter and we waited. After a few minutes, jasmine tea arrived. Now the Colonel was telling me about his visit to Scotland Yard the previous year and how much he liked the British. I managed to find my tongue and soon I was telling him vacuously how wonderful Thailand was and how my fifteen hours in his country had been such a delightful experience already.

Another four or five uncomfortable minutes elapsed, then suddenly a discreet side door swung open and General Sawang made his entrance. His full uniform was a blaze of gold and red; badges, medals and insignia swamped his chest – the marks of rank for all to see. He was a good-looking, wiry man of about sixty. His uniform gave the impression of being too big for him and the burden of its metalwork must have hurt, as he appeared gloomy and discontented. He looked me up and down with a deadpan face. Not wishing to make the same mistake that I had made in the Colonel's office, I performed a little head curtsy and brought my hands together under my chin, with my fingers pointing upwards. The General responded with the briefest of brief bows and we sat down. He muttered some words in Thai and looked at his beautiful assistant.

'The General wishes to welcome you and asks why you are here,' she said in what sounded like a tutored, home-counties accent.

I felt a bit like Captain Cook greeting a grand chieftain on a remote Pacific island for the first time. 'I am from British Customs – the British Government has given my department the responsibility to investigate serious cases of international drugs crime and I am here to work with your organisation and to share information and resources. There are some wicked British people who are involved in transporting drugs in and out of Thailand and we want to work with you to fight them.'

I tried to keep my sentences simple and thought I had made a pretty good fist of things. Feeling quietly pleased, I was surprised, therefore, to see General Sawang looking blankly at me as his sexy translator burbled away into his right ear. Colonel Sorncam continued to sit wordlessly next to me.

The General said something in reply and his secretary translated. 'The General wants to know if you are a policeman or not.'

'Well, no, I am not a policeman, but in England the Customs is the organisation that investigates international drugs crime. Parliament has given us primary responsibility in that area. The police in Britain have different concerns and different matters to deal with.'

He grunted unhappily when he heard the answer and said something to Colonel Sorncam, who replied at length. I just hoped he knew what he was talking about, but as I understood absolutely nothing of the exchange that followed, I just sucked my teeth. It was as if I was an unwelcome invitee now – rather like a Tory MP might feel at a trade union committee meeting – the business was being carried on around me and I had no part in it. After about two minutes of trading impossible Thai words, the General looked more content. Sorncam smiled at me with a trace of mischief and I realised the interview was coming to an end. The General waved his hand and his lovely secretary went to a cabinet next to his desk and brought back three neatly gift-wrapped parcels, which he then pressed onto me. As he did, he put out his hand to shake mine.

'Sank you for coming. Have a nice day. See Colonel, please.'

He smiled genially and I kicked myself for not bringing my own version of the football club emblem to swap with him – there was space for a British Customs plaque on his wall, I felt sure. Next time, I would not make the same mistake.

Outside the General's lavish office, I followed Sorncam back to his room, which now seemed quite meagre.

'General Sawang is happy for you and me to do business now,' the Colonel declared. 'It was important to let him meet you first.'

'Thank you, Colonel, but I did not understand a word of your conversation with him – he looked a bit disgruntled at first.'

'Yes, he wanted to know why Customs in England does the big drugs cases. He did not understand – here in Thailand, the Customs are all corrupt and he was worried about it. But I told him I could trust you.'

'How do you know you can, Colonel? We only just met about half an hour ago.'

He responded in a torrent of words, only faltering slightly with his grammar. I was mightily impressed. 'I have done my research – I know British Customs is a fine service – not like Customs here. I study for my engineering degree in London in the 60s, so I think I know the English quite well,' he said modestly. 'The DEA and BKA and RCMP also tell me they work only with HM Customs on their big drugs cases – mostly smuggling, of course. When I go to London last year for my Scotland Yard senior manager training course, I take time to speak to the Metropolitan Police about my narcotics cases in Thailand.

The dreaded Met. My god, what did they say about us?

The Colonel continued. Clearly, he had not interpreted the disapproving frown that had appeared on my brow. 'They were very helpful but they said to me that they could not do the big smuggling cases – only British Customs could – and they said you were very trusty and good people, so I was happy.'

Wow! An accolade from the Old Bill? – surely not!

It was pleasing that the BKA (the German police) and the RCMP (the Canadian Mounties) also rated us, especially as our dialogue was mostly via Interpol messaging and some sporadic agency to agency telex exchanges. The next hour or so was spent in animated and highly productive conversation. Colonel Sorncam proved to be a revelation and we started to piece together strands of enquiries which offered us hope of some real progress. It was not long before I raised the subject of Bartholomew Vanderpool and his response was immediate.

'Yes, we know him. He lives now in Chiang Mai – in the north – near to the Burma border. We were watching him last year, but now we have stopped, as he does nothing except make love to his girlfriend – very dull for us – *nabulah* – boring.' My mind was galloping over hedgerows as if in pursuit of a recovered scent.

Fucking hell! I have got you on my radar at last, Mr. Bartholomew Vanderpool, you bastard.

The Colonel and I agreed to meet again in two days – he promised to show me the intelligence they had gathered on Bart and to give me a tour of the ONCB telephone intercept suite. Importantly, he said he would help if I needed a phone tapped. No Home Secretary's warrant and signature was needed here – just the Colonel's say-so.

The opportunities here are fantastic.

I tried not to get too carried away. I had other meetings to arrange and Dick was coming in tomorrow – he would bring me back down to earth, I was sure. Before then, though, I had an appointment with Her Majesty's First Secretary for Politics, Mr. Nigel de Courcey at the British Embassy on Wireless Road.

It felt like I was walking into a Sussex garden when I first arrived inside the British Embassy compound later that day. The Gurkha guards on the gate had been all meticulous, military precision as they searched my briefcase and turned out my pockets with respectful professionalism. My HM Customs identity card held no sway here, even though I seemed to be entering a mini version of Britain in bloom. The trimmed hedges, neat borders and clipped pathways led me by stages into the wonderful coolness of a reception area that would not have been out of place in New Bond Street.

A middle-aged lady in a pastel twinset adjusted her perm as

she looked up from her desk. 'Nigel won't be long. He is with the Ambassador at the moment. If you'd like to wait over there – there are some magazines, if you are interested.'

I flicked through the pages of a six-month-old edition of *British Birds* and then found a more up-to-date version of *The Lady*. There was no signs of *Private Eye* or *Autocar* anywhere.

'Well, hello, Mike – or is it Michael?' A slim, fair-haired man in his late thirties, wearing a cream-coloured linen suit and a pale blue silk tie, strolled down the wide staircase into the lobby and greeted me with a bluster and flourish that I later learned was all part of the FCO pretence. He reminded me of the gardens I had just walked through – fragrant and well-manicured. 'Lovely to see you – sorry about the wait; I was with the Ambo, you know. He needed a briefing on the Thai-Cambodia situation and it took rather longer that I thought. Would you like to come up? We have been expecting you.' Then he stopped for a moment and looked earnestly around the lobby, as if he was trying to spot a trespasser. 'Can I just confirm one thing, Mike? I hope you don't mind.' He looked at me conspiratorially. 'Just to check about your vetting – all up to date, I hope?'

'Yes, Nigel, I am fully DV cleared – all current and up to date. The renewal came through last month, as it happens.'

'Jolly good. Let's see if we can get some tea.'

An hour later, after three cups of Earl Grey, Nigel and I were the best of friends. I realised rapidly that my rather negative initial perceptions of him as an over-effusive, blundering *Carlton-Browne of the FO*-type were off the mark. His outwardly raffish appearance belied a much more interesting and cool-blooded character underneath. It took him no time at all to grasp what my mission entailed – we even seemed to speak much the same language – and before long, he had provided me with a list of potential interlocutors. He also offered to arrange meetings for me – a proposal that I readily accepted. Of course, his moniker, *First*

Secretary Political, did not accurately describe the full range of his duties. Nigel confirmed that he was part of "Station" – he was an officer of SIS, the Secret Intelligence Service, otherwise known as MI6. I had met and worked with officers from MI5 many times before in London and had appreciated quite early on that the two sister services enjoyed an intense rivalry. The depth of antipathy between MI5 and their overseas intelligence counterparts in MI6 was striking to an outsider.

So, this is what James Bond really looks like.

'I would like to meet the Royal Thai Customs, if possible,' I said. 'Colonel Sorncam tells me they are all corrupt, but I cannot leave without touching base, at least.'

'Seek and ye shall find!' came Nigel's singing reply. 'There is corruption here for sure, but there are a lot of good people too. The inter-agency rivalry is a major factor – the customs people will also tell you the police are dishonest, the army will try to undermine the navy. The fact is they all hate one another. But I think you are right – you do need to see the customs – they have a key role. I can organise a meeting with the Collector at the airport, if you like. Maybe you can kill two birds when you meet Mr. Preston tomorrow. You can both go in to see him – a baptism of fire for your friend!'

'Sounds good to me,' I said. Minutes later, Nigel's secretary, Audrey, had booked us for a seven p.m. meeting at the airport the following day.

'Don't worry about the timing,' said Nigel, 'they work funny hours here and he has invited you both to dinner at the airport hotel afterwards. Lucky you!'

I spent the evening writing up my notes and calling London. Another full day lay ahead and I wanted an early night. Nigel had prepared a lengthy visiting programme for me and most of the next day would be spent at the embassy talking to department heads. I was scheduled to see Nigel again at four and then meet

Dick off his Pakistan flight at five thirty. I was looking forward to telling him that he had to start work immediately – no night out in Bangkok for him. I chuckled as I anticipated his reaction. He'd put on a face like a bulldog chewing a wasp, no doubt!

As things turned out, I couldn't have been more wrong…

CHAPTER TEN

Dick greeted me jovially outside the Don Muang customs hall and shook my hand with stout-fisted enthusiasm. When I told him we were going straight off to meet the Collector, Paiboon Somchainuk, the bulldog face was pulled, as expected – but it soon passed. The prospect of a free dinner cheered him up enormously.

'After all, Mike – we have another eight days here – plenty of time to see the sights!' How right he was.

We dumped Dick's luggage in the embassy car and gave instructions for the official driver to take it directly to the *Shangri La* and get Dick checked in. Customs had kindly offered to drive us back into the city after our meeting, so we had no further need for him that night. The Thai Customs HQ at Don Muang was much like most large official buildings around the world – architecturally dull but resilient and functional. We presented ourselves just before seven and were told in broken English that our meeting had been rescheduled. We greeted the news with a low groan, but our initial irritation was short-lived, as a car soon arrived and we were bundled into it. Apparently, the Collector was waiting for us at the airport hotel, where he was hosting a lavish dinner for customs and immigration officials. We were to be the honoured guests. On arrival, we were shown to a large circular dining table in the spacious *Leelawadi Restaurant* and drinks were ordered for us.

'This is convivial,' I said to Dick. 'We should have more meetings like this at home. Do they do this for you in Pakistan?'

'They don't bloody drink there – not officially, at any rate,' he grunted.

There was no sign of the Collector, so we ordered another couple of *Singha* beers and gossiped about colleagues at home. After an hour, we were beginning to feel a little uncomfortable, resentful even. The alcohol had softened our disappointment somewhat, but there was no escaping the fact that Khun Somchainuk was discourteously late. A menu was brought and we helped ourselves to food. The spicy prawn soup, a dish called *tom yang goong*, caught in my throat and more cooling liquids were applied to relieve the burning. Just before nine o'clock, a small group of officials approached us and sat down at our table.

'Dear sirs, I am so sorry about the lateness of the meeting. Khun Somchainuk will be here in a few minutes – he has been busy with some problems he had to sort out.' A young, clean-cut man wearing a sharp, double-breasted, blue blazer spoke for the rest of the party, which comprised two ladies and another man. 'In the meantime, please help yourself to anything and let me know if there is anything I can do. I am Khun Sanit, the Collector's personal assistant.'

'No problems. Thank you for the hospitality,' I said. I introduced Dick as our man in Pakistan and we chatted amiably about our respective customs services for a few minutes. Dick started to describe his work in Karachi and Sanit and his friend looked interested. I leaned over to the young lady seated next to me and asked, 'How long have you been in customs?'

She pulled a face and wrinkled her nose – very prettily, I thought – but said nothing. Clearly, she spoke no English. I did my best with sign language and some awkward charade-type gestures, but she still looked rather bemused – and anyway the Collector had just arrived, so I stood up to greet him. Collector Somchainuk wore an expensive-looking, white suit and had large chunks of gold wrapped around his fingers and wrists. He was in his mid-forties and exuded both menacing brashness and practiced urbanity in equal measure, something I had not noticed in any of the other Thai officials I had encountered up to now.

'I am so sorry about this, Mr. Rawlin. Can we reschedule again? Would tomorrow be too much trouble, gentlemen?' he said in perfect English. 'The thing is, I have to attend a rather important meeting now. We have some industrial problems and I must sort them out tonight. Shall we say three tomorrow afternoon?' He looked at us coolly.

I was bitterly disappointed – we had come all this way for nothing. 'No, that should be all right,' Dick said quickly, pre-empting what would have been my more unconstructive response.

'Good,' the Collector said decisively. The surrounding entourage appeared to be hanging on his every word. 'Sanit, make the arrangements, would you? Until then, my car is at your disposal, gentlemen, to take you to your hotel and please help yourself to anything you want.' He hurried off with half a dozen executives tripping along in his wake. Sanit rose to his feet and told us he would see us the next day at three. He made a signal to a man in uniform loitering at the entrance to the restaurant.

'What is your hotel?' Sanit said genially.

'*Shangri La.*'

'I will make all the arrangements. Do not worry, this man will take you there. You can leave when you are ready.'

'I think we will go now,' I said hurriedly. 'We could do with an early night.'

'That's fine. I'll see you both tomorrow. Enjoy the evening and please – everything is organised – I will speak to the hotel personally.'

We got up to leave and the two customs ladies stood up with us. We said our goodbyes and followed the man in uniform through the lobby onto the elevated hotel entrance outside, where a large, white Mercedes Benz with a Thai Customs pennant flapping gently on the bonnet, waited. Dick climbed into the front seat and I opened the back door.

How nice, the two customs ladies have come to see us off.

They were right behind me. As I swung my legs into the rear of the Mercedes the ladies motioned me to slide over to the far side. They then stepped into the back seat alongside me. I noticed for the first time that they were both wearing very short, tight-fitting skirts, which rode up as they climbed into the car. I looked at Dick; he looked back. The penny dropped. We were in Bangkok and this was a professional courtesy afforded by one of the Royal Thai Customs' most senior officials. I had wondered what Sanit had meant when he had talked about making hotel arrangements – the mist of ignorance was beginning clear.

'Lie back and think of England, Michael,' said Dick from the front seat in mock Churchillian tones. He had obviously worked out what was going on much earlier than I – his recently acquired overseas experience was beginning to pay off.

'*Quum Romae fueris,*' my flippant reply leapt out rather too quickly – the *Singha* was speaking now. I looked for a reaction from my fellow backseat passengers but none came, except a sort of vacant smile; it was abundantly clear that neither of the girls spoke a word of English – or Latin, for that matter. As the car pulled away, the two ignored me completely. Instead, they seemed to be having a fit of giggles as they nattered contentedly with one another in Thai. We reached the intersection and the driver took the car onto the dual carriageway heading back into the city.

'What do you reckon, Dick – what should we do?' The girls were laughing and joking. They looked very cheerful.

'Let's see what happens when we get to the hotel. Best not to be too hasty – after all, we don't want to offend the Collector – his driver will surely dob us in if we chuck them out now. I think we just have to go with the flow. England expects —'

'I agree,' I said simply as I gazed over again at our two

stowaways. The recent dinner was making me feel quite mellow and the naked leg touching my knee became ever more fascinating as the journey progressed. I tried to make conversation again. This time, the girl next to me just squealed and squeezed my thigh.

'WHAT – IS – YOUR – NAME?' I ventured. I pointed at her as I spoke.

'Han Som Man,' she said in a heavy accent and twittered enchantingly. Apparently, they were the only English words she knew.

'Do you think we should at least invite them in for coffee?' I suggested.

Dick turned his head towards me. 'Yes, a good plan, Mike. You are learning this international game bloody quickly, I must say. Let's do just that.' And that is exactly what we did.

The following morning, I awoke to find that my charming night visitor had crept away unnoticed in the early hours and I was relieved to find my passport and wallet intact. I had sensibly put everything of value, including my official paperwork, into the room safe immediately on my return from the abortive airport meeting – which in itself was a surprising victory for clear thinking! But finding all my possessions untouched the next day still felt like a minor liberation.

I pulled back the bedroom curtains. It was still dark outside and the lights of Bangkok shone brightly for as far as I could see. My body clock was still adjusting to the seven-hour time difference. My watch read five forty-five and somehow I resisted the temptation to ring Dick. I took a shower instead, to clear my mind and wash off the smell of the cheap perfume that cloyed on my skin. By eight a.m., I had re-read my notes and rehearsed the morning meeting with Colonel Sorncam over and over in my head. I decided to be bold and ask for his help with all three of the Far East cases I had on my top ten hit list.

There was a tap on the door and I heard the muffled sound of a man who was apparently in some discomfort. Dick fell into the room looking dishevelled, bloated and redder than ever. 'My god, Mike, that was some night. I feel like shit!'

'So do I, Dick, but the car is coming in twenty minutes. Will you be OK?'

'Of course, onwards and upwards. I'll meet you in the lobby in a quarter of an hour.'

It's amazing what some hot water, a handful of shaving foam and a splurge of deodorant can do. Dick looked totally transformed when he greeted me again at eight thirty – a crisp white shirt, a patterned tie, the crease lines on his trousers sitting neatly on highly-polished black shoes and a jacket slung nonchalantly over his shoulder.

'What a fine pair we make, don't we, Mike? Just look at us – officers of the ID in the tropics. The Chief would be proud of us!'

I was not sure what the Chief would think and in truth I didn't really care that much – not at that moment, at any rate. My time with him and his fifth-floor cronies would come when our business in Bangkok had finished. For now, my focus was to give them all something positive to chew on.

The next seven days were intense in the extreme. Never before had the sage words from Mervyn Nugent all those years ago about the hazards of mixing business with pleasure been more fitting – and I was sure that if he had been able to see us, he would have been gratified that we had taken things to a whole new level. The jet lag was forgotten – we worked a combination of London and Bangkok hours all at the same time. The pattern of our days could best be illustrated by the timings of our showers – we took the first at seven when we woke up to meet the sunrise and the last at about three the following morning when we went to bed.

Nigel's embassy visiting list got longer as more folk realised we were in town. The Americans, Germans, French, Dutch,

Australians and Canadians all wanted to meet us. Happily, the consensus was that you could do business in Bangkok if you had energy and enough common sense to understand that dealing with Thai law enforcement and intelligence officers was not entirely straightforward – it was all about deciding who you could trust. Each foreign agency had different local allegiances, supporting some and decrying others. They all boasted of their spectacular successes, but were bitter about their occasional woeful failures, which they blamed squarely on local incompetence or, more ominously, on host agency venality. We gleaned from this that in order to make cases work in Thailand, a very fine line had to be walked. To be successful, the foreign forces of law and order were required to walk a tightrope over a chasm of catastrophe, where nightmarish scenarios awaited on either side, should they slip. The stakes were high, but the rewards were great.

Our catalogue of daytime meetings was followed by a succession of night-time entertaining or "bonding", as we preferred to call it – not the James type, either. As we only had seven nights at our disposal, we made sure we made the best use of them and all were packed. Generally, we were the ones being shown the hospitality, but on our last night we hosted Colonel Sorncam and his small management team, courtesy of "Auntie Betty's" generous handbag! If there was a place on the planet to entertain red-blooded men, Bangkok's nocturnal haunts must surely have no equal: a cocktail mix of fine dining, copious liquor, frenetic partying and sheer pizzazz. By the time we boarded our flights home, we were undeniably shattered but wore wide grins on both our faces.

The business had gone well, too. Colonel Sorncam had agreed to work on two of my cases and we had set up an information sharing system and arranged a weekly long-distance telephone call to discuss developments. Critically for me, we saw eye to eye on Bart and he offered to trace him again for us. If we wanted to, he told us the ONCB could hook him up again and monitor his activities.

'No problem, Khun Mike, maybe he is sick now of making love – maybe he is back working again. We can try for you.'

Our postponed meeting with Collector Somchainuk had gone surprising well, too. The Americans had warned me that he was perhaps the most corrupt man in customs, but they also said that his sphere of activity appeared to be restricted just to extorting money from local businesses; in international matters, he was perceived to be an ally, albeit one to watch. I was certain that as Head of Airport Customs he offered us a series of opportunities, so I made sure to emphasise the positives in my report back to London. We had met again only once, at the rearranged time. Sanit had attended too, but there was no sign of the others who had so generously shared their time with us on that memorable occasion – nor was there any mention of them. We did not ask either; it seemed inappropriate while we were discussing such important matters of transnational liaison...

CHAPTER ELEVEN

Back in London, I wasted no time in finalising my report, which came with a persuasive recommendation to make Bangkok the ID's second overseas post. A few eyebrows were raised and close colleagues joked that the job description and the officer competencies proposed for the new post, which I had helpfully added as an annex, seemed uncannily to put my name well into the frame.

'It's almost as if the job is purpose-designed for someone with your background and experience, Mike; it's spooky,' they quipped sardonically.

'If I read between the lines correctly,' Harry told me over his glass of Guinness one lunchtime, 'it looks like the only person fit for the post must have had at least ten years' operational drugs experience, recent heroin intelligence know-how, relevant management skills, be in their mid-forties, live in north Surrey with a wife called Maureen and have the initials M.R. – who can we find like that?' he mocked. I had no counter except an innocent expression and a shrug of the shoulders, so we had another pint and chuckled together.

The regular ONCB liaison reporting into Intelligence Team M and the weekly calls to Colonel Sorncam proved to be hugely helpful. I made sure that I handled the verbal exchanges personally; a decision spawned by pure selfishness. I was not prepared to let anyone else into my little Thai secret or to share my newly-won contacts within the Thai authorities. The routine telex transmissions flowed in and out and gradually grew in number and significance. I had assigned one of my senior officers to handle the traffic, but the weekly calls were my domain and even when I was on leave, I rearranged my diary to ensure I was available to make them as scheduled.

In the summer of 1983, Sorncam and his team made a breakthrough – they had located Bart, not in the northern city of Chiang Mai, but on the sun-drenched island of Phuket in the southwest corner of the country, which was described in the holiday brochures as *a little pearl on the edge of the Andaman Sea*. Popular with tourists, it had glorious beaches, rolling golf courses, magnificent restaurants and a teeming nightlife. It was also a significant sailing destination, with yachtsmen from all over the world attracted by its clear, blue waters and the countless small islands that dotted its coastline.

Sorncam agreed to run an intercept line into Bart's rented villa and listen for a few weeks, but he fell short of agreeing to an out and out surveillance operation – Phuket was a long way from Bangkok and he needed more grist to the mill before taking on such a resource-intensive activity. I accepted his strategy, but it convinced me even more that we needed our own man on the ground to coordinate this and future enquiries. I knew it was essential to get alongside the locals and develop our influence. But for now we would have to just listen and wait.

The intervening period after my return from Thailand had seen no movement on my recommendation for a full-time Bangkok posting – nine months had passed and still nothing from the fifth floor. Joe West had been supportive, but he continually laboured the point about costs and value for money. He had sent the Far East file up to the Chief, who was apparently considering my recommendations alongside some other overseas candidates – Miami, Nicosia, Kingston, New Delhi and Bogota were also under review. The news that Vanderpool had been tracked down, for the time being at least, was the lever I needed to raise the matter again and I prepared an updated report for Joe. To my surprise, he called me into his office a week later and before I could sit down he said, 'We are going to see the Chief. He wants your opinion on the latest Thai material.'

I was unprepared for such an off the cuff briefing with the head of the ID but felt quietly confident, as I had been practically living and breathing Thai drugs intelligence for the last twelve months. I thought of my sudden encounter with General Sawang and it gave me courage.

At least the Chief speaks English.

I gloomily considered the downsides of that reality as I shuffled up the stairs after Joe to the fifth floor.

The Chief Investigation Officer was Ralph (he liked it to be pronounced Raiph) Skinner. He was a career investigator like the rest of us – he had just been at it longer than most. Skinner had a schoolmasterly air about him and since he had become Chief, about a year previously, the teacher manifestation in him had hardened. He was now most definitely our headmaster and he made sure we knew it. His secretary, Grace, ushered us silently into his spacious, carpeted office which had views over Fleet Street from its southern window.

'Come in,' he said without looking up, his polished head bowed over a bulging file, a fountain pen curving sprawling, wavy blue lines across the paper. 'I'll be with you in a moment – a note for the Chancellor, I'm afraid. It can't wait.'

But we have to!

I looked at Joe, who was obviously used to this performance and sat quietly, legs crossed, arms folded, prepared for the duration. A clock ticked noisily in the room and echoed around the empty corners. Skinner's pen scratched deafeningly into the parchment. I looked around and took in the browns and creams – the old, painted radiator under the window; a small portrait of the Queen; an oak conference table, nicely polished, I thought; his bland raincoat, solitary on its peg. My mind went back to General Sawang's office. *That would put this place to shame. I bet the Chief has never been in an office like that.*

My reverie was interrupted by the sound of Skinner's thin voice. 'Right – I think that gives him the information he needs. Damn silly question, if you ask me.' He picked up the phone. 'Grace, can you come in please?'

Still, he did not look at us, amusing himself with the red fabric ties on the file instead, making a nice neat bow. Grace pottered in. 'This file – it needs to get across to Number Eleven pronto. Can you arrange that? My driver can take it if the messenger is unavailable.'

She took it from him, nodded and left without saying a word.

'Now, gentlemen!' He looked up at last and frowned at Joe. The Chief was in his late fifties, a tall, lean man with very little hair and long white fingers, which constantly fiddled with a pair of wire-rimmed reading glasses. He wore a tailored, blue pinstripe, which looked sadly like it might have come from *Marks & Spencer's* high-end range. From the top pocket of his jacket, a pink silk handkerchief sprouted, carefully positioned to be just the right length for display – not too long, otherwise one might look eccentric, too short and no one would notice.

'Yes, Chief,' Joe said deferentially. 'You wanted to talk about Bangkok. Mike is here to fill in the gaps.'

'Ah yes, of course.' The air in his lungs made a deliberate escaping noise as it released through his pursed lips.

How much longer will this pretence continue? He knows exactly why we are here.

'As I recall, you think there is a case for a new post in Bangkok. I've read the reporting and I have to say that I am not as sanguine. Perhaps, Mike, you can enlighten us?'

I rattled off the statistics – the rise in Bangkok heroin and cannabis seizures, the increased number of investigations we had encountered in the last two years with Golden Triangle links, the burgeoning list of Far East flights landing in the UK, the multiplying figure of British nationals with criminal connections now living in Thailand. I quoted the Americans and the Australians and pointed to their experience. 'The DEA has an office of twenty-plus agents in Thailand alone,' I said, trying to make the news sound positive.

'They would, of course,' the Chief retorted impatiently. 'Why does everyone always make the same mistake – we are not America – we have a completely different set of values.'

'I agree, of course, but they make a lot of heroin seizures.'

Skinner went silent. I looked over at Joe and he just stared back at me, giving me no visual clue what to do or say next.

'Well, go on, Mike – what else?' Skinner removed his spectacles and scowled at me.

'There is the case of Bartholomew Vanderpool. He was responsible for one of our biggest ever heroin seizures and we have just tracked him down in southern Thailand.'

'Yes, I remember that case. Two years ago, wasn't it?' His voice softened, 'You were UC, weren't you?

'Nearly three years ago now, Chief,' I corrected him.

The Chief leaned towards us. 'Look, we have to consider all the options.' His voice grew louder, as if he was reading the first lesson at sung Eucharist in the college chapel. 'The Treasury is not a bottomless pit, you know, and we have to be very careful where we spend our money. Do you think the Thais can be trusted?'

'Not all of them,' I said honestly, 'but I think the right man can find a way to collaborate with the best of them.'

'And I suppose you think that man is you – do you, Mike?'

I assumed that the suddenness of his question was intended to make me blink. Instead, I looked brazenly back at him. 'Well, I would not presuppose anything, but I *have* been studying the situation for a while now. I think the case is getting stronger by the day and I already have some useful contacts there – a base from which to grow. So yes, I suppose I think I could do the job – yes, certainly.'

Joe shuffled uncomfortably in his seat. I was conscious that he had not said a word for the last fifteen minutes.

The Chief balanced his glasses back onto the end of his long nose. For a fleeting instant the image of a pampered Dachshund came into my thoughts. 'Would you leave us for a moment, Mike,' he said. 'Joe and I need to discuss something. Grace will make you some tea. Just wait outside, if you would.'

I got up to leave.

'Shut the door behind you, thank you.'

Outside in the small ante office, I sat down pensively. Grace asked me if I wanted a drink.

'I don't imagine you have a gin and tonic, do you, Grace?'

'My goodness, no, Mr. Rawlin – those days are gone! The last two chiefs drank a bottle of gin a day – it was all part of the job, or so I thought. In fact, we used to say that the chiefs' daily expenses allowance was based on the price of gin at *Augustus Barnet.*' Grace pointed at the door I had just come through. 'He drinks nothing – just tea. No milk, even. It used to be much more fun in the old days – what larks we all had!' She looked wistfully into the corridor, clearly absorbed by the ghosts of yesteryear. If there had been a window in her little domain, I'm sure she would have gazed out of it, but her tiny cell had no such trapping, so she settled for the passageway instead.

After about ten minutes, the door to the Chief's office opened and Joe West walked out. 'You had best come with me, Mike.' I followed him back down the corridors into his office. He said nothing as we walked.

He motioned for me to enter his room ahead of him and then closed the door behind him. 'You had better sit down, I think,' Joe said, looking a little befuddled. He slapped his papers onto his desk. 'The Chief has decided to open the post in Bangkok and he wants you to do it,' he said abruptly. 'Think you can manage it?'

CHAPTER TWELVE

Opening a new overseas post was not like opening a bottle of rum – it did not happen instantaneously. A lot of ground work was necessary and a variety of other government departments wanted to heave an oar or two into the debate. For the time being, while the wheels of Whitehall rotated in ever decreasing circles, it was decided that I should pay another visit to Bangkok – alone this time. The main purpose of the mission was to sound out the locals, to see if we were really welcome and to reinforce our liaison positions. I was pretty sure I knew the answer to the first question already, but it had to be asked officially and anyway, there was no reason to turn down a spot more business class travel – I was getting used to it, after all.

The subplot would be to take forward our existing joint investigations, if possible, and it was this facet that motivated me the most. I needed to make some real progress in the Vanderpool case. For some reason, a vision of the back of his neck as he spoke to me in those condescending, guttural Dutch tones in the rear of Mina's BMW had been occupying my thoughts for the last few months.

One cool and bright morning, weeks after the English summer had drawn its final breath, garden lawnmowers had long fallen silent and the dark days had started their gradual creep towards Christmas, I climbed aboard a Thai Airways Jumbo and turned left into the accommodating arms of the first class cabin crew. I had been upgraded – what joy! As I nestled into the soft comfort of the plush armchair, befittingly numbered 1A, and sipped my first glass of champagne, I tried to blank over the sombre scene that I had just left on Oakleaf Avenue, Purley.

The news that I was to be appointed to the British Embassy in Bangkok had not gone down well at home and Maureen and I had been at loggerheads over it for the last three months. Quite rightly, she had wanted to know why I had not consulted her before accepting a job which would have a huge impact on all our lives. I agreed that it had been a mistake to keep her in the dark and apologised for it, but had argued, with a great deal of personal honesty I thought, that the benefits would outweigh the detriments – and by a long margin too. I really believed this would be a positive move and a fantastic opportunity for the whole family. Maureen disagreed and we had quarrelled almost continuously since I had told her my plans.

At least we are on speaking terms again.

Caroline was now seventeen and she sided with her mother. She had a happy circle of school friends and told me that the last thing she wanted was to be parted from them; the very thought of going halfway across the world to a place she had never heard of was just too dreadful to contemplate. It would be the worst thing that could ever happen to her – ever, ever, ever.

As I wheeled my suitcase towards the waiting taxi, Caroline had come running down the garden path and grabbed me by the elbow. She looked like she had been crying.

'Come here, darling. Let your Dad give you a big hug,' I said and wrapped my arms around her.

'Please don't go, Dad – stay here. It's here you need to be.'

'Look, poppet, I have to go. It's only two weeks. I'll be back for Bonfire Night and we can all talk about it again then. This is important to me – you must understand that.' I imagined that my little speech had sounded pretty reasonable, if not compelling. Obviously not. The mood changed swiftly. 'Well go, then – and see if we miss you.' She turned and scuttled back into the house, a stream of curls trailing behind her.

My heart ached like never before. Had I lost her as well? I

stood alone with my thoughts for a few seconds, tightly clutching the handle of my gleaming new *Samsonite*. The front door of the house closed on me and I became a solitary figure standing self-consciously next to the fading roses. Then I noticed that the black cab was waiting with its diesel engine thumping noisily. The driver looked at me disdainfully, as if I had just run over a puppy. Maybe I had. I ducked my head and flopped into the rear compartment. He knew where he was taking me, so I decided that there was no need for me to break the mood by saying anything, which was just as well, as words at that moment felt like a complete impossibility. Fortunately, he chose silence also. He fiddled with the meter and we set off sedately towards the M25.

Nigel de Courcey had booked me into the *Oriental* this time, which was a shame – in view of my very tender memories of the *Shangri La*. Happily, any downbeat reflections about the change of accommodation were dispelled shortly after the embassy car pulled up outside the imposing entrance. As I approached a huge, polished wood front desk, I gaped into the sumptuous lobby. This was a serious hotel. It rested on the banks of the river, sophisticated, elegant, lavish and expensive. I imagined that it would be only a matter of time before I spotted a tropical-suited Alan Whicker, helping himself to a pink gin from a silver salver of assorted cocktails held stiffly upright by one of the army of attendants in crisp white livery.

A message from Nigel was waiting for me; I had been invited to dinner. He would pick me up in an hour. I took a luxurious shower, trimmed my facial hair, changed my shirt and was waiting in the lobby five minutes before he arrived.

'Great to see you again, Mike. Good flight, I hope?' He was looking as breezy and confident as ever. 'Now listen, there has been a change of plan. Hope you don't mind. The DA will be joining us and we thought a trip to Soi Cowboy would be just the ticket. Have you been there before?'

I shook my head innocently.

'Jolly good – then this will be fun, I'm sure,' he chirped.

The Defence Advisor, Trevor Ramstead, was waiting for us in the back of the car. He was a broad, dark-haired man in his mid-forties who held the rank of captain in the Royal Navy. I slid along beside him and we exchanged pleasantries as the embassy driver wove us through the brightly lit streets of the city. I started to tell him about my work and how much I was looking forward to renewing acquaintances, but it was clear that his mind was on other things.

'First time out East, Mike?' He brusquely interrupted. He didn't wait for my answer. Instead, he poked the driver on the shoulder and barked, 'Good. Excellent. Stop here, can you, Tong? Yes, just here will do nicely.' The car came to a sudden halt in the middle of the busy road at a dangerous-looking intersection. Traffic hurried past the car doors on both sides. 'We'll find our own way back in a cab, so you can stand down now,' he added. And with that he levered himself into the hot air and we followed. 'Over here – this way!' He pointed at a huge, blue neon sign. Suddenly, we were running as if in a war zone, dodging *tuc tucs* and motorbikes as we made for the relative safety of the pavement. 'Bloody hell, Trevor, that was a bit hairy,' Nigel shouted above the din of cars.

'No worries, we're here now,' he yelled back, snorting and the three of us turned a corner and trooped into a bar which had the interesting name of *Pink Panther.*

A show was in progress and a waitress wearing not much more than a scarlet G-string ushered us towards some low seats which looked up towards a makeshift, island-like stage forming the centre of the club. It was rather like being in the first row of a tiny Roman coliseum, with the audience jammed in on all sides. It was incredibly dark. Nigel said something to the scantily-clad girl and within a few seconds, drinks arrived. I did my best to absorb the stirring scene in front of me. Nigel and Trevor were now in conversation, shouting to hear one another above the loud beats of the heavy metal music. The show was an interesting one – and of a type I had never witnessed before. A bubble bath with shower attachments appeared to be central to the panorama and female communal bathing was clearly the theme. I tried to look nonchalant, but it was difficult.

Lucky it's so dark.

About five feet away, half a dozen young nymphs were cavorting naked in soap and water. It was a tableau of writhing bodies, slithering hands and pouting lips. I became aware that I was taking longer than usual to finish my beer. My comrades appeared to have no such problems and kept ordering more. After about half an hour, I had caught up with them, downing my fourth cold one. As the alcohol kicked in, the noise seemed to subside and I started to relax into the moment, minute by minute, soap sud by soap sud. It dawned on me that any chance of discussing our important affairs of state that evening had evaporated. That would have to wait until the morning; now it was all about male bonding.

The lather and bubbles show gave way after a while to one which consisted mostly of ping pong balls and bananas, and then to another which had as its star a large snake, but by this time I was well past caring. Watching, yes – but caring, definitely not. Trevor and Nigel looked over in my direction from time to time. Dialogue was impossible, so a series of hand signals and gawky facial expressions passed for conversation. After our sixth *Singha* beer, Nigel pointed at the door in an expressive gesture and we all got up to leave. In the street I gulped in the air and tried to look calm.

'Where to now?' Trevor asked. 'I hear the *Cat Suit* bar up there is very good. OK?'

I nodded and we followed. The evening went on like that for the next four hours – a new bar, a few beers, a short walk and then another new venue. It was, in effect, a pub crawl – Thai-style. By midnight, we found ourselves in a place called *BJ's* bar. We had grabbed some hawker's food from a street stall to soak up the beer and I sensed we were now finally on the homeward trail.

Surely these places must close sometime.

As I was coming to the end of our first drink in *BJ's*, I felt a slight tugging of my trousers, just below the waistline. I was seated at the back of the bar on a high stool and looked down between the legs of my table into the semi-darkness to see that someone was trying to open my flies. In fact, they had made pretty fast work of it, as a hand was now grabbing my nether regions which, despite the oceans of beer I had consumed, appeared to be waking from slumber. I stared down and signalled my mock displeasure, shaking my head from side to side to indicate sham horror at what was happening. A pair of wide, dark eyes gazed back up at me and a small hand pointed along the line of bar stools to my right.

'Look, see – no problem – is OK – no problem.'

I turned my head and gawked down the course of silhouetted bar stools. In the gloom, I could see two other customers in similar predicaments and I suddenly realised the significance of the bar's short name. *BJ* was not Brian Johnston or Bob Jones. *BJ* was not a person, at all. And as the meaning sunk in, I recognised, through the murk, that the two neighbouring forms were my erstwhile drinking pals.

When in Rome...

I unwound to let her get on with the business in hand.

The following two weeks passed quickly as I made a long round of official engagements. The Thais took me into the wild border region of the northeast, where opium and heroin crossed over from Burma. The police chief of the Chiang Mai drugs squad took me to Chiang Rai and beyond, to the Burmese border at Mae Sae. I was slightly unnerved, as he gave me a long explanation about why the heroin trafficking across the frontier was not his fault. I listened to him obediently, rather like a new pupil would to an elderly schoolmaster on his first day of Latin grammar. At the time, I was completely innocent of the very active role that some policemen played in the trade – that kind of intelligence was to come later – but his hand-washing monologue rang a few early alarm bells. Back in Bangkok, the welcoming serenity of my room at the *Oriental* became something I actively looked forward to; it was a little oasis of calm reflection and I loved the pampering and the smiling attention.

A long way from South Croydon!

Colonel Sorncam and his staff had seemed very happy to see me too: delighted, in fact. They confirmed that approvals had been given by the Thai Government for HMCE Investigation Division to open an office at the British Embassy and start liaising with the local agencies. The good news was that, in theory, there would be no restrictions regarding those with whom we could conduct our liaison. But there was a sting in the tail: a new drugs investigation corps was to be set up by the Thai authorities, specifically to handle foreign agency liaison and I got a strong signal from Sorncam that this was where the real work in the future would be conducted. The Bangkok Narcotics Unit, BNU, would open for business in January the following year and he told me that it would be there that I would need to make my first official contacts and advance my initial casework.

The BNU would have a staff of forty and would be fully equipped with genuine surveillance capacity, an intelligence cell and a modern eavesdropping capability. The head of the new BNU had not yet been announced. I asked Colonel Sorncam hopefully if his name was one under consideration. His reply was to "wait and see" but he added, rather guardedly, that he thought that another challenge now lay before him. He was not specific and I decided not to press him. Khun Maew, his coquettish new PA, told me happily that her name had already been accepted as part of the new outfit and she looked forward to working with me next year.

The operational casework news was less encouraging, though. The investigation against Bart had gone cold again. After a mere two weeks of monitoring Bart's line in Phuket at the rented villa in Patong, Bart and his girlfriend had suddenly left the country on a flight to Manila. The immigration records showed they had not yet returned. That was three months ago. Sorncam told me that the line had revealed very little, not much more than idle chit-chat, apparently, but I asked him if I could review the tapes all the same.

'Perhaps I can put a different slant on things,' I said.

I spent the following two days going through the conversations in detail, trying to pick up some clues that would build a picture of Bart's activities, interests, associates and movements – anything that could help us anticipate his next move. By the end of my labours, I was pleased that I had taken the trouble. There was certainly no earth-shattering dialogue that told us about an imminent shipment or movement of money; Sorncam was right about that. But my experience told me that the devil was in the detail, and I had not been expecting any huge revelations. Instead, I uncovered a host of small facts that would keep my London team busy checking and counter-checking for weeks.

Bart, it turned out, had a live-in lover – we knew that from his days in Chiang Mai, of course – but I was pleasantly surprised to find that she was none other than our old friend Alicia, Mina's right-hand girl, now released from Her Majesty's embrace and locked into another clinch – this time with Bart. Hindsight is a wonderful thing and it is easy now to say I had suspected as much – the covert photos taken at Heathrow all those years ago as they canoodled together before flying out their separate ways spoke volumes. But it also looked like Bart was a loyal boyfriend too; he had waited for her. Away from the bedroom, Bart's other activities proved to be rather more enlightening. He had an interest in a small, local Patong business – a massage parlour called Élan – and he had an English partner in the venture named Kevin Silverstream.

Passenger arrival records showed that Kevin was thirty-six and had been a long-time resident in Thailand, for over eight years, in fact. His major business was import/export – he shipped fresh flowers to Europe. My eyebrows rose a few inches when I read that. The back and forth chat also revealed that Bart was a keen golfer; he and Kevin were constantly comparing notes about their recent rounds at the *Phuket Country Club* and boring one another by describing in detail a magical shot one of them had played at a critical point. As a golfer myself, taught by my father from the age of eight, this fact both interested and surprised me.

A Dutchman playing golf... can't be many of those.

Background checks in London revealed nothing of real consequence about Silverstream. It turned out that he was a Hackney boy with a conviction for petty larceny when he was the tender age of sixteen. Apart from that, he had not appeared on anyone's radar screen. A clean skin, almost.

So the dots were beginning to join. It was early days – there was nothing on the tapes that suggested Bart was active anymore, but as long as I had the time and was prepared to be dogged, I reckoned something would turn up sooner or later. I could wait and watch. I would be back next year and somehow I expected he would too. We could start in earnest then.

But for now, I agreed that we should cut the line and let Bart stew in the Philippines.

What was he doing there?

Back in London, my new appointment was confirmed and I set about preparing myself for four or five years in the tropics. I had requested that I should start work in Bangkok in early September the following year, allowing some time for special training with the security services. This was carried out at Fort Waverley near Studland in Dorset, which was the Secret Intelligence Service's field operations training centre, where both basic and advanced field training is given to MI6 personnel. My course focussed mostly on refreshing my tradecraft techniques, polishing up some counter-surveillance procedures and learning how to evade a pursuing car by executing a handbrake turn in a speeding vehicle. I fervently hoped things would not come to that. I had similar reservations about being taught how to handle and fire an automatic pistol, which was a compulsory part of the training, and I kept quiet about this when I reported back at home. Thai language lessons were squeezed in too.

The autumn start date would also dovetail with the beginning of a new school year and allow Caroline and Maureen the summer holidays with their friends. But as spring turned into summer, it became clearer and clearer that I was fighting a losing battle. Neither of the two women in my life wanted to move home, let alone integrate into a new country and adopt a fresh, albeit alien, regime. The fact was that both Maureen and Caroline were totally unenthusiastic about joining me on my voyage of discovery. In my heart, I knew it was *my* adventure – just that – mine, not theirs.

After a lot of soul-searching and agonising, we came to the decision that I would start alone. We would reunite in Bangkok for the Christmas holidays and take it from there. I could not help thinking that my imminent departure from their lives was, for them, a type of hushed benefit, a sort of unspoken boon. The money would still come in, they could run the house the way they preferred and live, unhindered, in the safe world they wanted, free from any rebuke or criticism from me.

Maybe absence will make their hearts grow fonder.

Then I thought about the dog and felt even more miserable.

The office was not amused.

'This is supposed to be an accompanied post, Mike,' Joe West told me, clearly irritated.

'The Chief is not best pleased – especially as you are going to a place like Bangkok! He has heard all about it, you know.' I reasoned back that Foreign Office staff often went abroad unaccompanied and the news seemed to calm him slightly.

'And think of all the money the Department will save on school fees and housing at post. All I'll need is a small flat.' Money, as always, spoke volumes – and the budget was already stretched. He knew it and so did I.

'Well, let's see how the first year goes,' he said. 'A year to make your mark. Sound OK to you?'

'Yes, Joe – fine by me,' I said.

Just get me on that fucking plane.

CHAPTER THIRTEEN

September in Bangkok is just another sweltering month and as good a time as any to find one's feet. The embassy had set me up in a nice two-bedroom apartment about a hundred yards from the central part of Sukhumvit Road. It was well-appointed and comfortable, but certainly not the *Oriental*.

The Ambassador called for me on my second day. Bernard Norman-Smith was an old-school career diplomat on his last posting. The fact that he was British Ambassador to Thailand at this stage in his profession meant that he had not made it right to the very top – a close third, perhaps. Any signs of disappointment or resentment at the relative lack of glittering prizes were not evident in his convivial demeanour and his firm handshake.

'It's a pleasure to meet you, Mike. Do sit down.' After we had lowered ourselves in unison onto some expensive, cushioned upholstery, he brought his suntanned hands together with a crisp clapping sound, pointed his interlocked fingers towards the ceiling fan, put his fingertips under his chin and crossed his long legs. I now had a close view of his highly-polished, black brogues. The Ambassador looked me up and down over the top of his two index fingers, which now rested on his taught mouth, and said candidly, 'We've not come across your kind overseas before – bit of a first for us, in fact. But I am sure we will all see eye to eye. We have the same objectives, of course.'

I remained silent.

'Britain,' he announced loudly, 'Britain is our keystone. We all want what's best for Britain. I'm sure you agree.'

'Yes, Ambassador. I hope I can help in the common cause. My job is to protect Britain, I suppose.'

'Goodness!' he thundered. 'That's what Station tells me all the time and I don't mind admitting to you that sometimes our paths have crossed, so to speak. But we have found that with good communication we can prevent any sudden surprises. That's the main thing – no surprises. I really do not like unforeseen bombshells. Can you promise me that, Mike? If something is looming on your horizon – best to speak to us in Chancery ASAP. Especially,' he leaned towards me ominously, 'if there is an embarrassment factor for HMG. I expect your job is quite *cloak and dagger* by our rather mundane standards. Most of the embassy will not understand your type of work and they don't need to, but if something you are involved in looks like it could backfire on us – best to let me know. Agreed?'

I nodded politely.

'And on the subject of your work, I have been briefed by Station that you will be recruiting information sources – agents, I think you call them.'

'We call them informants, Ambassador,' I said evenly.

'I see. Sounds rather lowbrow to me, but much the same thing, I suppose. The issue here is that you must disclose your agents – er, informants – to Station. Do you understand how important it is to ensure that your work and theirs is fully coordinated?'

I had expected this topic to be raised and had prepared my response. I was not in a mood to lie down. 'Yes, of course, sir,' I countered, 'but it's not our policy to identify our sources to anyone who does not need to know, and I suspect that although the work of Station is similar, we are unlikely to be investigating the same matters. I shall be collecting intelligence on drug smuggling and criminal money laundering and I will be keeping strictly to my brief. I give you my word that if I think Station needs to know I'll inform them immediately.'

'Just so.' His reply was thoughtful and his fingertips flicked against his lower lip again. 'But Station has asked me to tell you that they will need to hold the details of all your agents – your informants, as you call them.'

'I will certainly consider it,' I replied steadily. 'If Station is prepared to provide me with the data on all their agents, I will reciprocate with mine – a *quid pro quo,* perhaps?'

There was an awkward silence. That was not the answer he wanted or expected and he shifted uneasily in his seat.

'Well, maybe this is a matter for you both to sort out. Have you met Jim yet – our new Station Head?'

'Yes, I met him yesterday. He asked me the same thing, actually, and I gave him a similar reply.'

Norman-Smith looked tense. 'OK – well, best to keep up the dialogue, don't you think? I understand you knew the previous incumbent, Nigel de Courcey.'

'Yes, I think we had a pretty good understanding,' I replied.

'Nasty business, that – quite a shock to all of us. I may have mentioned that I do not like surprises; his fall from grace was one we could all have done without. And the DA to boot – really quite damaging all round.'

'Yes, I heard what happened.'

The Ambassador bent forwards and offered me his hand, indicating that the discussion was over. 'Well, that's about it, Mike. Good luck in your new post. I am here to help, so please keep in touch. I'll be seeing you at morning prayers, of course. You need to know that I am interested in your work, so keep the lines clear. My door is always open.'

We shook hands again and I retreated down to my new office. As I navigated my way back along the corridor of the embassy's confidential fourth floor, I found myself thinking about my wild, drunken night with Nigel and Trevor in *BJ's* bar. I had heard that their late-night jaunts had become an escalating habit and that they had been compromised in one of Soi Cowboy's notorious nightclubs with their trousers down – quite literally. Naturally, things had been hushed up, but within forty-eight hours they had been ordered to leave their posts and head back to Blighty with their families in tow. Their careers were in tatters. A shame, as I had rather warmed to Nigel; he was a man with whom I could have done business – and fun, too. His precipitous demise had been all the more upsetting as my initial swordplay with his successor, James Gallow, had been somewhat unpromising.

Jim, as he preferred to be called, had been dispatched at short notice to Bangkok as Nigel's replacement by his MI6 bosses and at our first encounter he gave me the impression that he would rather have been tending his garden in Oxfordshire. He was an older man and much less flamboyant than his fallen predecessor, dull even. He had informed me coldly, within the first few minutes of our meeting, that he would be overseeing my work; I made it crystal clear, in return, that I was not going to let that happen. I made my point politely and clearly – I did not want any misunderstandings so early in my tenure. The only person I was responsible to was my boss in London, and Jim and the rest of MI6 needed to know that.

He had then made another audacious play by asking me to send him the details of any informants I recruited and when I flatly refused he looked affronted and changed the subject. He had plainly taken it up with the Ambassador behind my back. He must have known he was being mischievous in the extreme and, although I admired his chutzpah, I was certain there was no way he would hand me his list of sources as an honest trade. I would play the game, of course, and ensure that my interactions with him and his small team were as cordial as possible and I would seek his advice from time to time to make him feel important. But there was a limit to how much I was prepared to divulge about my cases. He was cut from the same cloth, after all, and I hoped he respected me for my bluntness.

Only time would tell.

In the initial weeks, I quickly found my way from the embassy to the newly-formed BNU's offices and then to and from Don Muang International Airport. The occasional journey to the container port added some variety, but the time it took made the trip seem hardly worth the effort, as the BNU had their own contacts there and could achieve much more than I could with my broken Thai and best English smile. At least it was good to put faces to the names and it meant I could talk more confidently with the BNU when I needed something done.

Maureen and Caroline visited at Christmas as planned and appeared to enjoy themselves at first, but it was not long before I heard them complaining about the heat and the fetid aroma of Bangkok's heaving streets. When they received news that it had been snowing back home, they were mortified and became homesick and irritable.

'Why, oh why,' they wailed, 'have we missed the first white Christmas in Surrey for ten years?'

Then Caroline got sick. She put it down to a prawn curry in the *Shangri La* and that marked the end of any nascent affection either of them might have harboured for the exotic and, in particular, for the City of Angels. I just kept my counsel and after a week I found myself counting the days to their departure. I had begun to get used to my self-contained existence; I had more time for my work and a maid to do my shopping, washing and cleaning. My favourite ex-pat bar was just around the corner. I imagined that I could not have been much happier. But as we loaded their luggage onto the weighing scales at the airport, there were tears all round. On reflection, this was just the beginning of an emotional roller coaster ride, one for which I was totally unprepared.

After they had returned to the security and predictability of suburban Purley, I flew back up to Chiang Mai to renew connections and take another look at the border. A month later, I took a plane down to Phuket. For some reason, I wanted to see for myself the villa that Bart and Alicia had been using before their untimely disappearance to Manila; there was no logic to it, really. There had been no further sightings of either of them and I began to wonder if something had spooked him. Maybe his intelligence was better than mine and he knew a British agent was on his tail. Possibly, he had decided to go straight and was now living a quiet life off his previous drugs earnings. I passionately hoped not. I wanted so much to have another crack at him – it was somehow becoming personal.

I also spent an hour at the Élan massage parlour, just off the Bangla Road in Patong – for purely professional reasons, of course – even though I already knew it had changed hands and Bart and Kevin were no longer the owners. I just wanted to get a feel for the place and that was pretty much what I got, so to speak. Shortly after Bart had vanished, the establishment had acquired a new owner – a gigantic, bronzed Norwegian with a handlebar moustache called Vidar. As I looked around inside, I was fairly sure that the place still ran along much the same lines as before, as there was no evidence of a recent refurbishment. It had not taken much courage to go in either – I had been dragged forcibly, albeit willingly, from the road by one of the better-looking masseuses with a shrill, 'Hello! Welcome – you come for massae!'

Once she had pulled me safely inside, the beautiful, front-of-house siren turned on her heels and returned to her post on the street corner, presumably to lure further wavering souls into the establishment. Another, considerably less attractive lady now showed me a menu card. There was a range of options: Thai massage, oil massage, foot massage, head and shoulder massage, oil massage with coconut…

I wonder where the coconut comes in.

I chose Thai massage – it sounded the most authentic and it was the cheapest, too. 'You want Thai massase – one hour?' Girl Number Two asked, trying to interpret where my finger was pointing at her card.

'Yes, thank you, er, *kop khun crub.*' Whenever I had the chance, I did my pitiful best to speak some of the tiny vocabulary of Thai words that I had retained.

'Take off shoes, please,' she barked. I felt like a schoolboy about to meet Matron for the first time. Then a third woman appeared – this one was noticeably more homely than the second and a far cry from the bombshell that had grabbed me off the street. I noticed that Number Three had strong shoulders and impressive forearms.

'This way, mister.'

She led me down a narrow corridor and into a roomy chamber, in which were a dozen raised booths, each surrounded by lightly flapping curtains. There were six cubicles on either side of the room. It was shadowy and I stumbled as I tried to work my way, shoeless, down the middle track to a vacant booth near the end with open curtains. They rustled each time the revolving corner fan pointed in their direction. Number Three prodded me into the cubicle, pointed at a pair of strange-looking fabric trousers and motioned me to put them on.

'Take clothes off, mister.' She pulled the curtains tight and left me there feeling awkward. Balancing on the bed, I took my socks off, then my shirt and lastly my undergarments. For a few seconds, I was completely naked and as I fumbled with the unusual item that I had been instructed to wear, I became conscious that the fan might at any second breathe on the curtains and reveal my embarrassment. I hurriedly pulled on the gold-coloured, Thai pyjama bottoms and lay down on my back to await Lady Macbeth. After a few minutes of restless silence, the curtains parted again and she appeared. The booth seemed to wobble as she climbed up alongside me. I was mightily relieved to see her again – mostly because she had not been replaced by Number Four. My imagination struggled to form an impression of what *she* might look like – if indeed she existed.

'Please turn over,' she said, all business.

The following sixty minutes were a mixture of pain and pleasure – in about equal amounts. Number Three squeezed, thumped, stretched, cracked and pummelled me. At the end of it, I lay back and waited for the happy ending that I had heard so much about, although I was fully aware that I was not in any fit state to enjoy it. But nothing happened.

'Get up, mister. Finiss,' said Number Three, as she muscled her way out through the curtains to leave me alone with the whirring fan and my thoughts.

So this was Bart's little sideline. An excellent way to launder his cash.

I wondered if his regular customers got some special kind of therapy. Then the paranoid thought crossed my mind that I had been sussed, my cover had been blown and I had been singled out for the pain treatment by the new management, who were still in cahoots with Bart. But I felt quite mellow, all the same. My bones ached a little, my limbs were limp and for some reason my mouth was dry – a cold *Kloster* would cure that.

Back in Bangkok, I revisited my files and considered my options. Kevin Silverstream had been traced entering and leaving Thailand four times in the last twelve months – three times to Kuala Lumpur and once to Manila. But that was it. All our combined efforts to house him had failed. His flower export business had folded owing money; maybe that meant there were others on his trail. My best guess was that he was in Bangkok somewhere because he always flew in and out from Don Muang, but it was just that – a guess. Despite the lull in proceedings, I still felt confident that one of the three of them would poke their noses over the wire soon and we could resume our little game. I just needed a breakthrough – something or someone to tell me where Bart was.

During my evenings after work, I usually left the car at home and ventured out on foot. I swiftly found my local bearings via the intricate network of bars, cafes and clubs that dotted the streets within a quarter of a mile of my apartment. I never felt any threat walking alone in the city, which was just as well, as some evenings I struggled to manoeuvre my way home, especially once I had discovered the taste of the local Thai whisky. Much of the rest of Bangkok continued to be a mystery for months – the Royal Palace, the Temple of Dawn and the floating markets all remained images on a postcard for me.

I would find time sooner or later. But not just now.

I became a self-sufficient creature in my own square mile world. To relieve the incipient uniformity that was creeping into my routine, I shaved off my beard.

It's just too boiling in Bangkok, after all. And now I look five years younger!

And then another glance in the mirror.

You are deluded, Mike – you know that, don't you?

Any fears about the effectiveness of the BNU were quickly dispelled and I rapidly made some headway on a series of cases which would have been impossible to progress from a desk in New Fetter Lane. The success made Joe West and the fifth floor relax a little. As predicted, Colonel Sorncam had not been appointed as the new boss, but I found the new man in charge, Colonel Surachai, to be an excellent, if rather eccentric, contact point. The Royal Thai Customs also proved to be positive allies and listened patiently to my many requests for assistance. Khun Putsorn, the new Collector, acceded to most of them, including a couple of controlled delivery operations, which certainly made

London sit up and look. After my first twelve months and bang on schedule, as was his way, I received a visit from Joe. Three days of meticulous examination of my records and a close scrutiny of my travel expenses followed, which I withstood steadfastly.

'Remind me again why you flew all the way down to Phuket, Mike.'

We did a round of official meetings together and I chose the personnel we met very carefully.

No sense in him meeting someone who might rock the boat.

He wanted a one-to-one with the Ambassador, who apparently thought the sun shone out of my nethermost regions. Then he asked to see Jim Gallow at Station alone. I briefed him in advance about our first-day spat and the ongoing cold war, but when he returned he looked very sombre. He put his battered briefcase on my desk and said simply, 'Don't like the man much, I must admit. And what is he thinking? Wanting to pore over our files! You did right, Mike, by refusing – what an affront!'

When the inspection was over, I offered to take Joe out for a few beers and he readily accepted. I made sure we visited one of the more salubrious establishments, one which was a little more up-market than the venues with which I had become so familiar. It was a calculated risk, but I just wanted to give him a flavour of what the city had to offer – just a taste, certainly not more, and a mouthful was out of the question!

The gamble paid off and I sent him home a contented man after his week in the tropics. He believed, I'm sure, that he had ferreted out every last detail of what made things tick at post. Within days, the Chief had confirmed my appointment for a further three years, with an option of four. The new post's results were good, seizures were up and Joe phoned me to say that London was even contemplating letting me have an assistant.

One morning, a few months after my extension had been approved, I was dropped off outside the embassy at around eight o'clock, as usual. I glimpsed the slim frame of a tall, dark-haired man standing in reception. He was looking a little lost and was constantly eyeing his watch.

That was me a year ago.

There was something about the figure that made me look again and when I passed him, heading towards the stairs up to my office, I stopped and turned.

'My god, is that you, John?' I called out.

The lanky man looked round and a broad smile appeared on his familiar face. It was John Morris, an old colleague from my very earliest days in the Department. We had gone our separate ways when I had joined the ID but he looked just the same – a few grey flecks and a line or two under his chin, but he had kept his shape and looked good in his new, tropical suit. It was undoubtedly a gift from Auntie Betty – one she proffered to all her staff travelling overseas to non-temperate destinations. It was a bit like a WWII demob suit and just as recognisable.

'Bloody hell, Mike! What on earth are you doing here?'

'I could ask the same of you! I work here. My god, how long is it? Must be fifteen years, at least.'

'I work here too,' he replied. 'Well, I will be very soon if things go OK today. I'm with the Department for Trade and Industry now – been with them for nearly ten years. I thought Customs was going nowhere for me, especially after you left for the ID. I was made an offer by the DTI and so I transferred – I've done OK, too.'

'Well, you look very well on it! Are you here to meet anyone, John? Can I steer you anywhere? Do you have time for a coffee?'

'Well, I'm about to see Mr. Norman-Smith in ten minutes, but I'll give you a call and tell you all about everything later – a lot to tell.'

'Best of luck with him.' I put my hand over my face to part-cover a theatrical yawn. 'I hope you don't have to cut your throat in there.' I yawned again.

We met that evening in the embassy bar, over an early gin and tonic. John told me that his meeting with HMA had started with the words, 'We've not seen your kind overseas before...' We both rolled our eyes and sniggered over our drinks.

John explained that the DTI had been trying to open some overseas posts for the last two years in areas where they could boost British business and commercial opportunities. Bangkok was seen as central to the emerging Asian tiger economies and had been selected as an ideal place to post an officer. Final approval had come through and he was planning to start in three months – no additional, specialist training was required for him, apparently.

So, after all these years, our tracks had crossed again and I found myself blinking at the coincidence and marvelling at how small the world had become. John was to be accompanied by his spouse, Sarah, and their two children. He had married late and now found himself with a beautiful, young wife and two small boys, aged eight and ten. We spent a lot of the next week in one another's company, reminiscing and swinging the lamp. I took him to some of my favourite spots and his response was reminiscent of my own first encounter with the metropolis, two years previously. He reminded me of a young spaniel, let loose for the first time amongst the mixed-breed dogs in the park – full of eager anticipation but completely unaware of the dangers that lay hidden in the tempting bushes. When he saw first-hand the range of activities and hedonistic pursuits that were available on Sukhumvit Road, he simply inhaled deeply and gawked at me.

I was relieved to find that we still had so much in common, even though his current portfolio sounded rather dreary to me. Our mutual, historic ties with Customs bound us together and I sensed I could talk to him privately about aspects of my cases that I kept from others. Despite his current situation – he was no longer even in the Department – I felt he was probably the only one in the embassy that really understood the nuances and challenges of my work and the thought provided me with a warm sense of inner release. However, his arrival had also made me acutely aware of my own companionless existence and I realised that I had been deceiving myself and inwardly burying the uncomfortable truth about my increasingly lonely and self-centred lifestyle. The first pangs of envy started to filter into the corners of my mind. I was trapped alone in an alien environment with a host of acquaintances and no true friends. And no family to love. At least now I would have someone in whom I could confide some of my professional confidences, but more importantly, I hoped that I might be able to unburden some of my personal troubles as well.

When he left for home, I bid him farewell at the airport with a lot of reciprocated backslapping and then returned alone to my deserted apartment, consoling myself that he would be back again soon. But then, of course, he would be with his family and our relationship would be altered somewhat. No doubt I'd get used to it and we would still be able to find some time together and sneak away for a chat and a noggin or three. Until then, life had to go on. I had my cases to make, my intelligence to collect and I swiftly got back into the thick of things.

PART THREE

CHAPTER ONE

It had all been agreed. Colonel Surachai had given his authority, at last. I would be given access to the woman they called Lek. I had wanted to talk to her for ages and although she did not officially know of my existence, I suspected she was aware that it would only be a matter of time before she would have to meet a *farang*, a foreigner, from one of the embassies. And she would have to *talk*. But Surachai wanted to meet with me first; a typewritten message had come through from the BNU that morning which Gill had left on the desk for me. It looked chillingly official.

Colonel Surachai Tinthalang of the Royal Thai Police, Bangkok Narcotics Unit would be pleased if Khun Mike Rawlin, First Secretary, could call on him as soon as convenient to discuss the Harrier case.

Had he changed his mind?

I decided to ring him first and fix a time to meet. I looked up from my desk and gazed out of the window across the neatly trimmed embassy lawns, crammed with water sprinklers, and over the metal-spiked perimeter wall towards Wireless Road. Beyond, the city was in full afternoon tilt in all its cacophony, colour and heat. Three years had passed since I had started my sojourn in Thailand and I wondered where the time had gone. From the cool cocoon of my office, the noise of the city was inaudible; all I could hear was the whir of the air conditioner and the faint tread of footsteps in the corridor outside. Gill arrived into the room fresh from her lunch and gossip in the staff restaurant.

'Oh, you're back, Mike. I thought you were going to be at the airport all day,' she said cheerily.

'I got lucky. The meeting with Customs went well, Putsorn is happy to assist with another CD and the highway traffic was lighter than usual.'

Gill had been working with me for just over two years, which in the way of things at the British Embassy, was a long time for a personal assistant in the confidential area. She was the wife of a major in the Defence Section who was coming to the end of a three-year posting. At thirty-seven, she was nearly ten years younger than me and had a strong look about her – a no-nonsense, sensible shoes look – but with a sports mistress's appeal. Her family was from Grantham in Lincolnshire and she shared many of the characteristics of the town's most famous daughter, whose star was now riding high at home and around the world.

I would soon have to recruit Gill's replacement. I dreaded the thought. It was an overdue piece of administration that I would not relish. It would be time-consuming and a serious challenge, given the very small pool from which I was permitted to choose. She was damn good at her job. She knew all the cases, the names and the contacts – well, most of them; some I was required to protect, even from her. She organised my working life and sometimes it seemed she sorted out the rest of it, too. Her knowledge of my brief had grown steadily over the years and she could now educate visiting officials about trafficking routes and smuggling methods and quote the latest opium production figures in the Golden Triangle as well as I could, perhaps better. She arranged my travel and hotels, reminded me when the car needed a service and, most importantly, she nagged me to be careful when I was out on operational assignments. I would miss her.

Gill's successor would take months to train and I had limited time before I also succumbed to London's call to move on myself.

'Good for your career, old chap. Four years is quite enough, don't you think?'

While I was toying with the idea of asking Gill to run the recruitment campaign for her own replacement, she piped up again.

'It's good you're back,' she said. 'Did you see the note from the BNU?'

'Yes. It's long overdue. I just wish they had agreed in October when we had that CD seizure at Station 25.'

The controlled delivery case two months earlier had been codenamed "Harrier". It had involved an aircraft container that had transited through Don Muang Airport from Chiang Mai en route to London Heathrow's cargo area, which HM Customs called Station 25. The case had started when the Thais found two hundred kilos of compressed herbal cannabis inside eight boxes labelled dried papaya, which had been temporarily warehoused while awaiting the Thai Airways London flight. The drugs were a type of locally produced marijuana, which the global drugs fraternity called Thai sticks. There had been no officially documented pre-intelligence or information from routine profiling. It was apparently a chance discovery by the locals, a rare event these days, and it had all the alarm bells ringing in London. No one had a clue who was behind it.

I had hastily arranged a CD with the Royal Thai Customs (RTC). This required their full cooperation and involved emptying the drugs from the concealment and replacing them with something innocuous, in this case bags of sand, to make up the weight. All had gone remarkably smoothly; cooperation at all levels between the BNU and the Thai Customs had been excellent. The unpacking and repacking had been done in record time in a covert location on the edge of the airport cargo area and the newly-packaged dummy consignment met its target flight to London with ease. In fact, I had been surprised how stress-free it had all been. To get agreement for the CD so quickly and to have turned the container around so fast had been almost too good to be true.

Of course, the real work had only just begun. I was under pressure to find the origin of the shipment and the identities of the shippers, but my local informants could tell me nothing and for once I believed them, as blank stares greeted my questions, instead of secretive grins. My paperwork trails had also gone cold. Nearly all the names and addresses were false and the others unproductive. The London airway bill and manifests had shown bogus company and destination details. Ordinarily, this should not have been a major obstacle – all would be revealed as soon as someone collected the shipment. In order not to attract the attention of the rank and file at Heathrow, the trick now was to process the consignment as if it had been any other. It was important to do everything by the book and as normally as possible. Only a few trusted airport workers were taken into confidence.

On arrival in London, the dried mango boxes had been off-loaded into an airport warehouse and kept under close surveillance. The ID had assigned the Harrier operation to my old team – Drugs Team D, the Deltas – and they started a long vigil of concealed observation which was to drag on for weeks. During this time, the goods did not budge once – they remained obstinately in their stack, amongst other shifting cargoes that came and went around them in the normal course of daily deliveries and dispatches. Not one enquiry to the cargo agents had been received, no one called into their offices to request any information about the load and no suspicious vehicles had been seen patrolling the area.

The case had gone completely dead.

It did not need the brains of an archbishop to deduce that the London opposition had either been tipped off or had smelled a rat and backed off.

Senior management wrung their hands for a while and then pulled the plug on the operation. Nothing to show after nearly a month, during which the Deltas' full surveillance team had been plotted up around the airport perimeter road, clogging their arteries with cheeseburgers and sausage rolls, waiting in vain for the consignee to turn up.

Needless to say, the whole debacle had not done me any favours with the foot soldiers in New Fetter Lane. The Deltas went into customary mocking mode and put it down to "more duff gen from Rawlin in Bangkok". They had a point, but I was not going to agree with them openly. I had a post to defend. At least a large seizure had been made and, with a little good fortune, I would be able to kick through the traces in Bangkok and come up with something to lead us to the culprit sooner or later.

Despite the bantering and brickbats from the officers of Drugs Team D, I had taken some credit for the work from the fifth-floor management. They knew that a few months earlier, I had briefed the RTC on the latest intelligence regarding cross-border traffic from Burma into the northern areas of Thailand, where we knew increasing numbers of Brits, Dutch nationals and assorted international travellers were now beginning to settle. Some of them had "interesting backgrounds" and there was a sporting chance that not all of these new ex-pats were there just to improve their health or sample the local lifestyle and culture – fascinating as it was.

But the Thais knew this already and did not need me to lecture them. They had smiled their famous Thai smile and taken the time to ask some searching questions, which I cynically thought were really intended to see if I knew my stuff rather too much. That might have given them something to ponder, especially if my expertise had the potential to make their lives more uncomfortable. For some, there was money to be made, after all.

There had been one person who I thought could have given me some useful leads with the load of dried mango. I knew of her existence only because she had been mentioned casually to me one day by the likeable and elegant Major Pongpat, Head of the Covert Intelligence Cell at the BNU.

Pongpat was a career policeman and at thirty-three was destined for one of the top jobs. Narcotics was an assignment where officers could make their name and cultivate some useful foreign contacts. These could help as promotion beckoned and international positions became available. So Pongpat was lucky, or more likely, he had an influential sponsor in the service. Investigating drugs was also an occupation where serious money could be made by the unscrupulous and there may have been a few who had taken their chances and gone this route. My best guess was that both the BNU and Pongpat were straight, but my judgment on these things was based on only three years in country – hardly any time at all to really understand what made things tick.

Of course, the DEA had marked my card. They had warned me about certain Thai officials, but I did not trust the Americans either – less, in fact. So it was an incessant mind game – a continual mental jousting and elbowing for the best angles. Who to trust? Who to avoid? Who to lay false trails for?

Pongpat first mentioned his source a year earlier when I was investigating a small concealment of heroin in packages of lemongrass paste that had arrived at Heathrow. The dog in the freight shed had indicated positively, despite the pungent cover load – I never cease to marvel at their aptitude – and two kilos had been retrieved from twenty packets. I had been trying to track the shipment back from its origin in Don Muang and he said carelessly that he had a good informant at the airport who might be able to help. He could make some discreet enquiries for me. Nothing more than that. True to his word, he had come back a few days later with some useful shipping details which took me forward another stage. But it had ended ultimately in a dead end.

'Fantastic, Major!' I had said at the time. 'This will help, for sure. Your contact must be good.'

'Oh yes,' he laughed, 'very good, work with us long time. He can do many things for me.'

I later learned that the "he" was, in fact, a woman who went by the nickname of *Lek*, which means *small* in Thai, and apparently the name fitted her well. She had been working for the BNU for about two years and had been a very reliable inside source at Don Muang's busy cargo terminal. Few knew her real name or even her job – probably the only ones who did were Pongpat and Surachai. The sum of my knowledge was sparse, to say the least. I knew that she excited quite a lot of man talk in the office, especially from the boys in the surveillance team who joked that she was "very nice, very sexy" even though it was perfectly clear that none of them had ever met her. All the same, they had formed a sort of fantasy picture of her. One thing they were certain of – she was definitely out of their league, both professionally and socially. More importantly though, it was clear that she was close to someone or some system at the airport which gave her access to the inner workings of at least one important narcotics group. As a result, she was a valuable and closely-guarded asset to the BNU and could only be used sparingly.

When I had broached the subject with Pongpat, suggesting hopefully that it might be possible for me to meet her, he pretended not to hear and looked awkwardly into the sticky rice and mango that one of the office girls had just brought us. I left it a moment, munched on my mango and said, 'It could be useful, Major. I know she is your source; I don't want to take her on full-time. Just a few questions?'

They liked me, maybe even trusted me, a little, perhaps. But this was a big ask.

'*Mae diy*,' he said simply – 'Cannot.'

He had looked up and smiled, though – something all Thais do easily to cover a range of differing emotions. So it was not easy to fathom if his response was an encouraging maybe or a flat refusal. I decided not to press, but the short exchange had started the juices flowing. Had I touched a nerve? I realised that this was something I would need to come back to when the time was right.

Now, months after Pongpat's polite rejection, the way ahead appeared to be clear. Colonel Surachai's unexpected approval seemed to set things up nicely. A connection at the airport would be enormously valuable and if I was lucky, I could task her to do some digging on the unresolved two hundred-kilo Harrier shipment. But I would need to take things easy, no rush, softly, softly...

The main thing was that Colonel Surachai, Head of the BNU, had given the green light and had told me as much at our last meeting, less than twenty-four hours ago. I hoped he now just wanted to go through some final details before the contact could be arranged.

'Can you get Surachai on the phone please, Gill? I hope we'll be able to catch him – he does like to spend some midweek afternoons with Wife Number Three.'

Gill banged out a few digits on the phone.

'I have Mr. Rawlin from the British Embassy on the line. He would like to speak to Colonel Surachai. Thank you. Putting you through.' She pressed another button and I was now connected to Surachai's secretary.

'Can I help you, Khun Mike?' Maew said brightly.

All this telephone protocol was wearisome. It just made the whole thing more drawn-out and time-consuming – so much easier if I could just ring him direct. But I accepted that etiquette was necessary and I knew that a political awareness of mutual status was an important factor in UK/Thai diplomatic relations.

Colonel Surachai was a square-shaped, solid man in his late forties who had an affable smile and a most respectful *wai* when greeting *farangs*. His salutation consisted of a pronounced bow of the head that always appeared more scrupulous than the version most other Thais proffered; his palms, pressed together as if in prayer, were straighter and higher and somehow less casual than the rest. His courtesies extended beyond formal introductions and in conversation with me he was unfailingly charming at all times, even when he was disagreeing or refusing my requests for help, which fortunately were relatively rare. Underneath this cloak of geniality, however, was a man of considerable durability and resolve.

I already knew that Surachai possessed a number of personal shortcomings. His private life was colourful, to say the least. But despite his lusty predilections, he did his utmost to encourage the highest standards possible amongst his staff who, despite his recognised failings, widely respected him – and not just for his rank. On occasion, I had witnessed him delivering some severe dressings-down to his Thai subordinates. If he considered them to be deficient, either in their work or their private lives, he could be intolerant and harsh. The previous year, an aspiring, young, married captain under his command had been found fraternising once too often with one of the girls in the admin team and was transferred summarily, in two short days, to Hatyai, a posting well off the HQ radar in the southern reaches of Thailand, not far from the Malaysian border. His meagre office belongings were packed off to him a week later. The fact that Colonel Surachai had a wife and two children at home and two professed mistresses elsewhere did not seem to matter. He ran his office the way he wanted; he was the boss.

Through the prism of his management style, I could see a hard and ambitious man. He did not worry if his staff liked him or not and he did not court popularity unless there was reason for it. And this was the key to his leadership. He gauged each of his team's worth by their individual ability to make him look good to his own superiors; the calculation of this included whether they possessed access to the patronage of the highest police force ranks through family or marriage ties. The son or cousin of a commissioner would be protected at all costs. Although the rank of colonel made him powerful within the confines of the BNU, he had one clear, driving force. He had an unremitting and naked ambition to make general before he was fifty. It was his holy grail and he would do anything to grasp it. But for a *farang* official like me, Surachai was unrelentingly polite, bordering on the obsequious.

'Oh, hello, Khun Maew. Can you put me through to the Colonel, please? He has asked me to visit him and I want to fix a time.'

'No problem, Khun Mike. He is in office. Just wait a minute.'

Colonel Surachai spoke English very well, albeit in a strange, staccato style. Most medium to high-ranking government officials did the same. That was fortunate for me; I had laboured lethargically through my compulsory Thai lessons and emersion training, the net result of which was that I could engage in a lot of unimportant small talk, which included ordering a cold beer, flattering a waitress and thanking a taxi driver. I could not tackle anything meaningful when it came to the subtleties and technicalities of our work together, so we spoke in English, which was an immense relief.

'Good afternoon, Khun Mike,' Colonel Surachai opened. I could envisage him nodding his head towards me down the phone as he spoke.

'Hello, Colonel. I got your message – do you want me to pop round?'

'No, I prefer if we can meet tonight. Can you have dinner with me? Just you and me, OK?'

This made me think. I had known Surachai for a long time and although we had eaten together on many occasions, he had always brought company with him, usually in the form of a couple of junior officers. Safety in numbers, perhaps. He had even introduced me to each of his three "wives" over dinner. He was sensible enough to do this one at a time, although it was clear that each knew of the others' existence and the whole arrangement seemed perfectly harmonious. This was one of the idiosyncrasies of the Thais that no longer surprised me. Some of the New Fetter Lane senior management team, who were now finding various excuses to come to inspect my post, adopted a more puritanical view when I told them about Surachai's energetic private life. When I stuck up for him and said the practice was quite normal in these parts, they insinuated that I was "going native".

'No problem, Colonel. I can meet you tonight, if you like. Where did you have in mind?'

'There is a place on Chao Phraya River called *Bua* near to French Embassy. It means lotus, in English,' he added unnecessarily. 'Can you be there at eight o'clock?'

'Yes, I'll find it. So you want me to come on my own?'

'Good idea. Best if it's just you – we can talk better.'

Just like him to credit me with the idea that we should meet alone.

I put the receiver down and looked over to see Gill tidying her desk and clearing the files into the cupboards.

'I have to go early today, Mike. I have a rehearsal for the staff pantomime in five minutes and I have not even had time to practise my lines.'

The embassy put on a pantomime each Christmas and there was pressure for everyone to take a part. Even the Ambassador had been roped in and, leading by example, he was playing the evil vizier in this year's performance of *Ali Baba*, which had been suitably rewritten to poke gentle fun at selected members of the British diplomatic community. The self-appointed director of the production, an irritating, frenetic man called Brandon Hooper, Head of the Consular Section, had buttonholed me a few weeks earlier. I had made my excuses, citing pressure of work and I had been spared. The truth was that while I might be able to turn up for rehearsals, I could not guarantee being available for the actual performances. If something cropped up unexpectedly, I would have to drop everything to go to work, which it did more often than I cared to think about. Such a friendless existence sometimes…

'Oh, of course. I forgot. How is it going?'

'Fine, I suppose. Brandon is being a pain, as usual. His latest idea is that we should have more songs and has got Felicity to write another and I can't sing. But I expect it will be all right on the night.'

'No worries,' I said absently. 'One thing, Gill, just so you are aware – I'm meeting Surachai at the *Bua* in Silom, near the French Embassy, tonight for dinner. Do you know it, by any chance?'

'Sorry, no,' she said breezily. 'Have fun!' She hurried away down the corridor, clutching her script.

At six, I emptied my desk and locked all my papers away into the combination-sealed cabinets. There was a strict policy to leave nothing stray around and the security officer was annoyingly vigilant with his late-night checks of the desks and drawers in the confidential area. I had been caught out twice in the last three years, once just for leaving a discarded note in my waste bin. I had received written warnings, which were known as "breaches" by all of us, and one more would see me in front of the Ambo. So I made sure everything was spotless and made my way down to the staff bar. It was empty; presumably everyone else was gallantly rehearsing their new panto song. I sat alone with my thoughts and a double *Black Label* and soda.

It was strange, but I felt unusually apprehensive about

the rendezvous in a couple of hours. It was highly unusual for Surachai to want to see me alone – what could it be that demanded this secrecy? Perhaps my uneasiness was all mixed up with the approaching encounter with Lek. It would be straightforward, I had been telling myself. I had met and run countless informants and agents over the years, but for some reason I had a buried and uncomfortable anxiety about this one. Maybe it was her reputation, or the fact that she had been kept from me so deliberately and for so long. Was there a hidden agenda, a subplot? I put down my now drained scotch glass, walked to the phone at the corner of the vacant bar and dialled the drivers' room.

Wut had better come with me on this one, I think.

CHAPTER TWO

Khun Wut had been my driver for eighteen months. Soon after my arrival, I had asked London if I could engage a local assistant, someone to primarily tackle the appalling Bangkok traffic, but also to run errands, collect packages and meet visitors. After a long deliberation and, no doubt, a close examination of their budgets, they had been persuaded. The clincher had been when the Head of Drugs Investigations paid me an official visit and spent most of his time in traffic en route to the long list of meetings I had arranged for him.

Wut had proved to be a real asset and had become much more than just my driver. Not only did he know all the shortcuts around the city, but he had an easy-going charm that served to calm my feverish agitation when I tried to squeeze more into the day than was sensible. Wut was an unmarried man in his mid-twenties, quite striking in his own way, with a flashing smile – for the ladies, especially. His English had been rather scratchy at first, but had gradually improved enough to be able to keep me informed about his latest girlfriend and his mother's heart condition. Above all, he was reliable and I had begun to feel safe in his company. I kidded myself that he only had a vague idea about what I did. He had reasoned that I was a sort of policeman – that must have been pretty obvious, as we visited so many Thai police offices.

Routinely, he would drive me across the city, while I caught up on the reading for my various meetings from the front seat of the Land Rover Discovery, our allocated official car. If parking was a problem, he would drop me as close as he could to my target and then find a place to lurk nearby. The diplomatic number plates on the car made this task easier and helped to fend off any unwanted attention from overzealous traffic police. During my meetings at the BNU, he would wait in the congested car park and over time he became a familiar figure with the staff and on sociable, chatting terms with some of the junior officers. There was little doubt that he learned a lot from them. But he never asked any questions about my work and that was important.

Wut popped his head into the embassy bar at seven fifteen and soon we were in the Discovery on our way to Silom, fighting the congestion. I told Wut to make for the French Embassy and at ten minutes to eight we had pulled into *Bua's* car park.

There was no sign of Surachai's car or driver, so I made my way past the bubbling tanks of swimming fish and live lobsters into the bar area. I ordered a bottle of *Kloster* and waited. My first impression was that the place looked like a typical tourist trap, so I was pleasantly surprised to see that most of the diners appeared to be Thais. The restaurant was largely open to the air and quite substantial – there was seating for at least a hundred. Lines of candlelit tables extended down from the bar towards the river; the closer they got to the Chao Phraya, the more populated they were. Only one tiny table at the water's edge remained empty; the candles illuminated a "reserved" sign. Around *Bua's* boundary verges were flaming tapers, placed between tidily-clipped bushes and fairy-light clad palm trees. A whiff of breeze moved along the river and gave some welcome relief to another clammy night. As I absorbed the scene, breathing in the scent of lemongrass and the faint waft of citrus, the Colonel arrived. He greeted me with his legendary *wai* and prayer hands and I responded in kind.

'Good evening, Colonel. Can I get you a drink?'

'Khun Mike, so happy to see you. I would like some white wine, please,' he said coolly.

Wine was not a drink I savoured much in Thailand. By the glass, it was typically warm and vile. By the bottle, it was generally not much better and always horrendously expensive. For the Thais, though, it was a status symbol; to be seen drinking wine was a sign of affluence and authority, even if it tasted dreadful. Judging by Surachai's confident reply, he had presumed that Auntie Betty would be picking up the tab for tonight's meal. But as he was about to give me access to his star stool pigeon, it seemed a small price to pay. So I ordered a bottle of *Pouilly Fuissé* 1986. The waiter led us to the remaining riverside table, removed the sign and hastened off to search the stores for the wine. As he withdrew out of earshot, Surachai looked at me solidly.

'Khun Mike, I want to speak about Lek.'

A promising start. Let's cut to the chase.

'I am all ears, Colonel, and very much looking forward to meeting her.'

'Major Pongpat has told you some things, but there is more information you should have before you meet. I am happy for you to see Lek,' he added after a pause and then hesitated again. 'I want you to know that I gave my approval personally because I trust you.'

Now I was worried. He had never been so open with me – so why now? It was unlike him to be candid; always terribly polite, of course, I had got used to that, but this apparent sincerity made me edgy. I said nothing and let him carry on. The wine had still not arrived and my mouth was sticky, despite the recent beer. I needed a refresher.

'Lek has worked for us for nearly two years. She has been good for us, but there have been problems.' He paused again, as if reluctant to continue. In unison, we looked over towards the bar – still no sign of the drinks! The menu arrived and we spent a few awkward moments casting our eyes down its pages.

'Would you choose for me, Colonel? The fish should be good here.'

Surachai nodded knowingly and muttered a few sentences in Thai to the waiter, who then lingered a moment. After a brief silence, he added some more words, spoken as if they were an absent-minded afterthought and waved his hand carelessly. The waiter retreated and we were alone again.

'You say you have had problems with Lek,' I said gently.

'Yes, but not much now, I think.' He looked me full in the eyes. 'She knows a lot about the airport and a lot about the monkey business going on there.' He leaned forwards, putting both elbows on the table. 'Her brother, his name is Bhang, works at Don Muang as a cargo handler for Thai Airways. He has many friends; he knows many *farangs* and meets many times with them. Recently, one of them has become Lek's boyfriend. He is a *farang* man and he has spent a long time here in Thailand. We have known about him for many years. He now has a house in Phuket, where he lives sometimes.'

He looked down at his empty wine glass.

'The problem is that this *farang* – he is in the monkey business, too. He was the man who sent the shipment to London last time – the dried mangoes one, which no one collected.'

There was an uncomfortable silence, as I struggled to find the diplomatic language to respond. The news that Surachai had known the supplier of the mango consignment all along came as a professional shock.

The *Pouilly Fuiseé* finally arrived and was uncorked at the table. The moment gave us a chance to lighten the mood. Surachai suggested I try the wine, which tasted remarkably good, considering the conditions in which it had probably been kept. The waiter poured two glasses and withdrew. I had questions now, heaps of them. I started with the easiest.

'Can I ask how you recruited Lek? Where did she come from? Why does she want to help you?'

Colonel Surachai's face brightened, as if he had been let off school detention. He explained that the BNU had received intelligence that Bhang was involved in moving heroin and cannabis through the airport in freight shipments for export. He was, in effect, acting as a pseudo criminals' agent. He was prepared to move consignments of anything for anyone to anywhere, as long as they would pay handsomely for the service.

His job was to guarantee that the prohibited packages would not get checked. He manipulated the paperwork, arranged the shift patterns and organised the packing onto outbound aircraft to ensure that any illicit items were loaded at the very last minute, so they come off first at the port of destination, presumably to be removed by another group of corrupt baggage handlers.

This news made me sit up and listen. An opportunity to crack two corrupt airport syndicates at Heathrow and Don Muang was rare indeed.

Colonel Surachai pressed on. 'What happened was this. One day, the Crime Department arrested one of Bhang's friends fighting in a bar in Soi 33. He worked with Bhang at the airport, in the Thai freight office, and he knew him very well.'

The arrest had triggered a huge flow of new human intelligence. The arrested man, who Surachai described as an obnoxious, thuggish lout called Ma, had been captured after knifing a man in a drunken bar brawl over money.

'The local police found big money in his pocket. He had a bloodstained knife from Nepal, also.'

'A kukri?' I asked.

'Yes, a cookie,' he agreed.

The combination of large amounts of cash and an airport connection rang alarm bells and the BNU was invited to interview Ma. Major Pongpat took a personal interest and conducted the questioning.

'We thought – how can a cargo worker have nine hundred and fifty thousand baht in his pocket?' Surachai grinned, looking a lot more relaxed now, as he spun his story. 'Maybe he saved – one hundred baht a week?' He laughed mockingly.

It was certainly a big sum, more than any cargo worker could earn legitimately in three years.

'Major Pongpat interrogated him but he did not talk, at first,' said Surachai.

But gradually Pongpat had put the squeeze on him. I imagined him doing this in his inimitable, impeccable but unfeeling way – rather like a doctor, amputating a limb and smiling as he did it. Pongpat had promised Ma that he could reduce the attempted murder charge he faced, but only if he cooperated... maybe they could even return the money, he had hinted.

Pongpat's capricious offer proved too much for Ma and the story of Bhang's illicit activity and airport scams started to pour out. He portrayed Bhang as a brutal, cold-hearted man who would stop at nothing to make money. He talked of Bhang's attractive, younger sister, who, although not involved in the actual smuggling, did perform some important tasks for him. She acted as a go-between, carrying messages around the city and sometimes beyond.

'If you want to know about Bhang, you should speak to her – speak to Khun Lek. She will help you for sure,' Ma had suggested to Pongpat.

He claimed Lek played the role of postmistress under duress. Bhang exploited his sister and she deeply resented it. He was paranoid about using the telephone, hence the need for the postmistress service. Bhang would show himself very rarely and only when money was being discussed or exchanged. His sister was his single means of communication – she was family and would not betray him. He had an unshakable belief in this and, according to Ma, it was his blind spot, the weak link in his chainmail.

For good measure, Bhang reinforced the familial bonds with a combination of violence and blackmail. At first, Lek had refused to help him, so he had beaten her cruelly, threatening to shame her in front of the whole family. After all, they were supposed to be rebuilding their ancestral fortune; profiteering through drugs was the best and quickest way to do it. She was ensnared and her hatred for her brother increased day on day, deal by deal, message by message.

'For sure – she will help you – *loy* per cent – one hundred percent,' Ma had sniggered at Pongpat.

Surachai sat back in his chair and gazed out at the river. The lights of passing restaurant barges shone onto the black water of the Chao Phraya as the throaty engine exhausts of long-tail boats broke the silence of the tranquil embankment scene.

'So what did Major Pongpat do next?' I asked as another long-tail boat thudded by, taking its time to move out of earshot.

Surachai resumed his monologue. Pongpat had realised that he was on to something good, so he gave orders to trace Lek and pull her in for a chat. If it did not work out – no harm done. If she cooperated, a gold seam of new casework could be exposed.

'One thing also,' Surachai's eyes brightened, 'it is very funny. When Major Pongpat left the Crime Department, he thanked the officer in charge of the bar investigation and told him to charge Ma for the attempted murder.' He chuckled.

'What happened to the money?' I asked carelessly.

'It went to the court and was seized. Khun Ma went to prison for twelve years for attempted murder. Ha, ha!'

I wondered how much bloodstained cash had ended up in police back pockets. But at least it was reassuring to know that Ma's incarceration in Klong Prem, otherwise known as the notorious Bangkok Hilton, would keep him out of the game for a while.

'So, it was Major Pongpat who first recruited her?' I said.

'Yes, and he took control of the information she gave. He did not like anyone else to see her.' Surachai looked thoughtful – the earlier smiles had disappeared. Did I sense a trace of bitterness?

'Was the information from Khun Lek helpful, Colonel?'

'Yes, for sure! When he took her for questioning she denied everything, at first. But then Pongpat told her that her brother was a bad man and if she did not assist them, he would arrange to sack her from Thai Airways. She knew he could do this, if he chose, and so she agreed to work with him. She said that she did not like her brother either, that she was sick of all the things she was forced to do for him. She wanted to stop him. After that, it was easy. She wants us to catch him and now she worries that we are taking too long. She wants to end her problems quickly.'

'OK, Colonel, that is very interesting. You have clearly cultivated a very good informant. But why did you not tell me about the supplier of the London shipment before?' I asked as amiably as I could.

Surachai looked at me stiffly. A nearby brazier danced its red glow against his face, emphasising the lines that creased between his eyes. 'Khun Mike, that is why I have to talk with you tonight,' he said in a low voice. 'This is the problem we have: we want to protect Lek because she has been giving us so much information. She has helped us to make some big cases at Don Muang. The Americans and Germans have already caught six people this year – so it's excellent for us.'

'So what has changed? Why do you want to help the British now?'

'Things have changed because Lek's boyfriend is trying to do another big case for England and we cannot allow it this time – we need you to be involved. It's better if Lek meets you now. I do not want any secrets this time. And anyway, we can share the information. You can help us. We can work together with Lek,' he beamed.

Despite his forced smile, his reply sounded too ambiguous for my taste. Bowls of rice appeared, followed by a plate of Thai fish cakes and sauces, a specialty which I knew Surachai particularly liked. He continued chatting good-naturedly. I did my best to appear relaxed and tried to focus on the possibilities for the future rather than the betrayals of the past. For Surachai to tell me that he had deliberately withheld intelligence which had a direct bearing on the UK narcotics criminal community was as startling a confession as it was refreshing.

I knew, of course, that partner agencies had their own agendas and it would have been childlike of me to expect full disclosure of sensitive information. It was not the perfidy that shocked me – it was the fresh air admission that was so astonishing.

So I could not help thinking there must be more to the story than he was giving me. But for now, it seemed sensible to listen and calmly ask some more questions. The last thing I wanted was to jeopardise my introduction to Lek. We had not agreed the whens and wheres of that yet, and this was my clear priority. If she could set me up with the next UK-bound consignment, the Deltas would have to find someone else to taunt.

'So, what do you suggest, Colonel?' I said quietly.

'You can meet Lek tomorrow. I will arrange.'

'I would want to meet her alone.'

'OK – no problem – can do. I can fix it for you.'

'What else can you tell me about her? It's important I know her background.'

'Of course, I will tell you all we know.'

As the waiter tipped some more wine into our glasses, Surachai divulged that Lek had been working for Thai Airways at Don Muang for about three years. She had been born into a respected, land-owning family who farmed in Nong Khai in the northeastern province of Isan. They had once been rich but her father and Bhang had speculated unwisely and had lost all their money. But Bhang was a resourceful and confident brother. Despite their quarrels, they resolved to pull the family back from the brink. He had some friends working for the airlines in Bangkok and he secured positions for both of them to work at Don Muang. Soon they were working for Thai Airways – she as a junior ground hostess and he as a novice baggage handler in the cargo area. Through Bhang's network at the airport, Lek had met her *farang* boyfriend.

'This boyfriend – is he English, Colonel? Do you think he wants to become a big player?'

Surachai put his glass down on the table and looked at me ruefully. 'I think he is already, Khun Mike. He is called Bart Vanderpool.'

I sank abruptly back into my seat as I tried to absorb this staggering news. How many more revelations would I have to endure? I must have paled, as Surachai looked at me curiously. He knew that his words had made an impact – they were meant to, perhaps. Was this the bait, I wondered?

I let the silence hang in the air. There was no point in trying to play games with Surachai. He knew the background; he knew the form.

'So, Bart is back in Phuket now,' I said.

'Yes, he has been there for over a year. He is in Patong again.' He said it as if it was good news.

I spluttered and felt some of my saliva drop onto my hand. 'You know, Colonel, that Bart Vanderpool is one of our major targets. You know that I have been trying to track him down for over ten years. He has been running cannabis and heroin into Britain and we have been very close to trapping him on more than one occasion. I was there when we missed him last time. He would be a huge catch for us.'

'Yes, I know he is big fish for you. You must decide what you want to do, Khun Mike. When you meet Lek, you can ask her anything you want – she will help you, for sure. But there is something that you need to know.'

He waited for me to say something. I remained silent and tilted my head in expectation.

'She wants to protect him, if she can. It's up to you if you agree,' he added hurriedly, 'but she will ask you, for sure.'

'She wants to protect this man Vanderpool! Why?'

'She says she loves him.'

'You know we cannot make any deals.' I was indignant now.

'Yes, I know that, Khun Mike, and you know that – but she doesn't.'

'I am confused slightly.' This was a colossal understatement. The truth was that I was totally bewildered. 'Why is she giving you information about Bart when she says she loves him? It doesn't make sense.'

He shook his head vigorously. 'No, you don't understand; she does not give us information about Bart.' He emphasised the word "Bart", and as he did, his throat made a gurgling noise and his voice raised a pitch. He leaned towards me and hissed, 'She gives us intelligence she gets from her brother, Khun Bhang. She passes us the messages he sends. He controls the cargo operation and he has been doing monkey business with many *farangs* who take drugs out from Don Muang. Bart wants to work again with Bhang – he has a consignment to send to London soon. We know this from intercept.'

'How long have you known Bart's whereabouts?'

'A long time – about a month after he moved back to Phuket.'

'How long have you been tapping his phone?'

'Not so long. Only since we found out about the mangoes.'

My indignation turned to anger but I contained my emotions; it was the only way to do effective business in Thailand. Any obvious displays of rage went down very badly – it was a matter of loss of face. But Surachai must have detected that I was looking more agitated by the second, as I could see that he too was beginning to look a little unnerved.

'Why did you not involve me earlier, so we could build a case against him together?' I asked coldly.

'Because Lek had been giving us such good intelligence from Bhang and we had caught a lot of smugglers here and abroad – it made the DEA very happy. We decided we would not arrest him for the time being. We wanted him to do some more shipments.

It was like we had a duck giving us golden eggs every few months – so we did not want to kill the duck.'

I could detect small beads of sweat appearing on the Colonel's upper lip. He must have felt them too because he wiped his mouth hurriedly with a napkin.

'So, you delayed taking action against Bhang and his team because Lek was providing you with information about other drugs groups operating out of Don Muang?'

'Yes, Khun Mike. We knew if we arrested him, Lek would be no use to us anymore. But then last year, by good luck, Customs found the shipment of dried mangoes with the drugs all packed ready for London and we informed you, as we wanted to do a case for the British, for you. It was easy for us because Lek was not the one who told us about it. It was a customs officer that found it, in fact. So we informed you and you started your investigation. We started a controlled delivery – you remember?'

'Yes, Colonel.' I shook my head unhappily. 'I remember the case only too well. It went nowhere – my team waited at the airport in London and no one came to collect.'

Colonel Surachai looked across the moonlit river for a few moments and then resumed his story. His mood looked darker now.

'The reason why no one came to collect in England was that three hours after the mangoes left for London we heard from a wiretap that Bart was the shipper. He made a call to England to say that some fruit had just left. We put two and two together, as you say, and we realised he was behind it. Then we had a big problem – we worried that if you made arrests in London you would link them back to Bart and you would then ask us to arrest him. If we did that, Lek would refuse to help us in the future.'

'I take it that you told Lek to warn Bart that we were interested in him?' I said, feeling very uneasy.

'Yes,' he said bluntly. 'It is true. Major Pongpat spoke to her. Look, I feel very sorry, Khun Mike, but please understand that at the time we had some other very big cases we needed Lek's help with and we did not want to spoil them. Major Pongpat told her to alert Bart that it would be dangerous for his friends to pick up the mangoes in London because the British Customs was waiting.' He scrutinised me again. A sudden thought must have entered his mind, as he added brightly, 'But at least you got a seizure!'

'Colonel,' I said, as calmly as I could, 'this makes me quite unhappy – don't you think you could have said something to me at the time? I am sure we would have been able to work together instead of wasting all our efforts on a pointless, dead-end case.'

He just looked back at me and said nothing.

'Does Bart know that Lek is working for the police?' I asked.

'No. Definitely not. We told Lek to tell Bart that Bhang had to pay money to the Customs to get the consignments out and one of them had tipped her off that the drugs had been found. Lek was happy because she wants to protect Bart, but she does not want him to know that she gives us information from time to time.'

'Why would Bhang not tell Bart himself?'

He laughed and looked at me as if I was a naïve greenhorn. 'Khun Mike, Bhang is only interested in his money – he will send out drugs for anyone who pays. If Bart has paid him and he sends out the drugs, he has done his job. He does not worry about what happens in London.'

He had a point. There was another pause as the waiter fussed with some water for us and clinked some fresh ice cubes into our glasses.

'Do you have a plan to arrest Bhang at any time in the future? I asked optimistically.

'Yes, we have a very good case, for sure. Bart and Bhang have a new consignment ready for London. Don't forget, Khun Mike, that Bart's English friends lost money when he told them to keep away from the mangoes last time, so he has a debt to them. Now is the right time to close the case once and for all and we want to work with you to end it. And you can help us by meeting with Lek.'

Things were beginning to make sense, but I had more questions.

'I'm sorry, Colonel – I still don't understand why you want me to meet Lek. Surely, it would be better if Major Pongpat continued to work her, as before.'

After a long pause, he scratched his ear and said, 'Now is a good time for us to work together. General wants us to work together. No more monkey business, he says.' He had not answered the question and we both knew it.

Why is he being so cagey? He could be selling me another pig in a poke.

For the time being, I thought it best to change the subject. I would come back to the main question later. 'How long has Major Pongpat been seeing her?' I asked.

'Maybe two years. He did a lot of good work to recruit her and now she gives him all the messages that Bhang tells her to collect and deliver. She has helped us a lot. It has been good for Pongpat's career, too.' And then, almost as an afterthought, he absently added, 'General Sawang said he should be promoted, but I advised against it – not now – too young.' He blinked at me, realising perhaps that he had shared something he shouldn't.

'But why do you think I should take her on, Colonel?' I came back to the burning question.

'We are worried about our future cooperation from Lek because she thinks we are too slow at catching her brother. And this next shipment is for London, so it makes sense for you to talk to her.'

And yet something was still nagging at me. This was an act of surprising generosity by Surachai and knowing the raw ambition than ran through his veins, I could not help feeling sceptical. Maybe he really did feel some guilt about the previous treachery and wanted to balance the books – but I roundly doubted it. Surachai never gave out presents like this without an expectation of a reward down the line. But the bait dangling at the end of the BNU rod was undeniably substantial. London would love it. I decided it was worth a gamble. I'd watch my back and take things steadily.

'What about Major Pongpat – is he OK about this?'

'No problem – he must do as I say. He is fine. No problem, Khun Mike.'

'I can call him, if you like. Maybe he can help with some more information about his previous meetings with Lek.'

'No, Khun Mike. I do not want this,' the Colonel said firmly. 'I am in charge of this case now. Please… I do not want you to talk to Major about Khun Lek. If you need anything, you can ask me.'

'Of course,' I said lightly. 'No need, I suppose. A clean break is fine for me.' But what caused this angst? Was jealousy at play? Had Pongpat over-stepped the mark in some way? Was his success now too much for his boss to bear?

'I will need to see your file on Bart. I hope that will not be a problem.'

'No, of course – we have plenty of intelligence which can help you, for sure. We have photographs and wiretaps and –'

'OK, it all sounds good,' I interrupted. 'You said I can meet Lek tomorrow?'

'Yes, no problem.'

'I want to meet her alone.'

Another nod of assent from Surachai.

'One more thing – you did not tell me how she met Bart.'

'Her brother asked her to take a message to him one day,' he replied simply. 'He liked her and later when she gave him *our* message that the drugs in the mangoes had been discovered, they became even closer. After a week she asked Thai Airways for a transfer to Phuket, so now she lives there with him. Maybe he loves her, but maybe he just needs her for her contacts and the inside information she gives. One thing is guaranteed, she has had enough of all this business. She just wants her brother to be arrested as soon as possible. She hates him. I think she believes that Bart can give her a new life when all this is over. That is why she wants us to protect him.'

'Is she in Bangkok at the moment?' I asked.

'Yes, she came to see Bhang today.'

'Can you ask her to meet me in the lobby of the *President Hotel* on Sukhumvit tomorrow at three p.m.?'

'No problem, Khun Mike.'

'How will I recognise her?'

He smiled. 'I think you will see her OK.' He reached over and pressed a small, full-length photo of a young, slim woman into my palm. He gave me a "Long John Silver" wink. 'This was taken a few years ago, but she still looks the same. Very sexy.' He laughed and we smiled together as only men can. Obviously, he knew what his surveillance team had told me about her and was having a modest jibe at my expense. 'I'll tell her to carry a black handbag, just in case,' he grinned.

'Just ask her to come alone and sit in the lobby. I'll wait for her.'

CHAPTER THREE

She stepped out of the *tuc tuc*, leant into the cockpit, slipped the driver one green twenty-baht note and walked unhurriedly up the steps into the lobby of the *President* and towards a red leather sofa. She sat down with her back to the wall. With a full view of the hotel entrance, the tourists in cotton dresses and coloured shorts that seemed a size too small, amongst the stack of recently-packed luggage, she waited.

She fitted the description Surachai had given me, but the photograph had done her no justice. Aged about thirty-five, she wore crisp, cream slacks that worked closely against her slight figure. Her clothing exhibited no evidence of the dirt from the city. Neither did she. Her raven hair was cut neatly in a bob, the precisely-trimmed fringe rested on her forehead just above her eyebrows which framed her face above a slender neck which was encircled by a single gold necklace. A miniature Buddha pendant dropped from the chain against her amber skin. She wore a black silk blouse which shimmered as she breathed; her small breasts, hidden but discreetly evident through the fabric, moved silently as she inhaled. It was Lek, for sure, and I was transfixed.

I observed her from a distance as she opened a neat, black handbag and dropped in her sunglasses. The bag and glasses looked expensive and for some reason it occurred to me that they were probably gifts from a rich admirer.

Just a thought – could be wrong. Maybe the handbag was a prop from Surachai.

She crossed her legs, looked around the room again and put

the palm of her hand behind her slender neck. I wondered if she had seen me. She had moved her head and eyes in my direction more than once, but had she registered? Had she seen me? The lobby was busy, noisy and confusing. I needed to wait and watch a little longer. Was she really alone or was one of Surachai's men discreetly placed to observe the meeting? Or worse, was there an unknown presence watching us? I hoped that Surachai would keep his promise that our first encounter would be private, but if not, it was not a deal-breaker. It wouldn't be the first time he had broken his promises.

One of the receptionists, a pretty girl wearing a smart, emerald green skirt, left her counter and approached the sofa. The two women spoke for a few seconds and then Lek followed her to the lobby phone, where she took a call. She was only a few yards from me.

Here we go. Now, let's see what happens.

A few moments later, Lek looked up again. Her delicate countenance turned in my direction but she seemed to see through me. Calm and poised, she put down the phone and started to retrace hers steps back into the miasma and steam of Sukhumvit Road. As she passed, no more than four feet from me, I glimpsed her elliptical eyebrows and broad cheekbones, the aroma of an indeterminate but costly French scent flickered into my nostrils. In that moment, my life was changed. Forever.

She was not a classical Asian beauty. Her face was longer than most, especially for a Thai, but her nose seemed to sit perfectly between her large eyes and full lips. I imagined that her legs were slim and elegant, although perhaps a smidgen too short for the catwalk. What did I know, anyway? I took a longer, gratuitous look as she glided towards the lobby entrance and was struck by her apparent composure. She was graceful, petite and beguiling. I wondered absently if her appearance, her impact, this visibility, much desired by so many, could be, for her, an unwanted endowment, a hindrance in fact, given the shadowy world she inhabited.

She took the steps down into the road and I followed. She stopped briefly, felt in her bag and put on her sunglasses. The abrupt brightness made me squeeze my eyes. I fumbled for my own glasses and looked back into the road, hoping to pick up a telling movement from her retreating figure. Some pedestrians passed with umbrellas raised against the sun, a truck chuntered past, spewing acrid, black soot and, despite my squinting, I realised that I could see her no more; she had simply evaporated into the heat. I shielded my forehead with my hand and stared carefully again into the traffic, my eyes tracking from side to side, but I could not spot her. I was beginning to sweat and beads of moisture trickled down behind my ear.

Damn – I'll just have to go straight to the RV.

I scanned around again one more time, doing my best to extract something from the chaotic landscape, a revealing glimpse of movement, perhaps. But this time I was not looking for her. I wanted to see if she was alone. Or did she have protectors? Was she being followed? It was a fruitless effort, as I instinctively knew it would be. Without Lek in my sights, the task of spotting her tail was hopeless.

I turned left onto Sukhumvit Road. Despite her vanishing trick, I knew where I could find her. The call she had taken in reception had been pre-planned. I had given instructions to Gill to ring the hotel at ten past three and ask them to locate Lek in the lobby and tell her she had a call. Gill had given them a name and a brief description – I'd left Lek's photo with her, which I thought might help. I had no need for it now; her image was lodged in my psyche. Gill had then told Lek to walk five minutes along Sukhumvit and into Soi 5, where I would meet her in *Filomena's Coffee Shop*, a modest but fashionable little café.

A bright red *tuc tuc* appeared and I jumped in. Quicker and cooler this way and perhaps I would catch a glimpse of her enroute. But after a brief and uncomfortable lunge through the stream of traffic, I arrived outside the coffee shop without a sighting. I decided to go in – perhaps she had taken a *tuc tuc* too and would be there before me.

The place was nearly empty – just a few perspiring tourists in for their fix of cappuccino and amaretto biscuits. There was no sign of Lek, so I took a table at the back of the café with a view of the entrance and ordered an espresso. After ten minutes, there was still no sign of her. Concerns started to surface, so to keep me from fretting, I ordered another coffee. Had she understood Gill's message? Had she got cold feet? Had she been intercepted on the way?

Then the street door opened and she appeared. She hovered uncertainly in the entrance for a second or two, which must have seemed longer to her, and then she made her way towards me, her posture poised and confident. I stood to greet her, gave a welcoming smile, a small bow and *wai,* and did my best to look squarely into her eyes.

I said cautiously, '*Swadi krup* – hello. I'm Mike. Thank you for meeting me.'

She returned the smile. '*Swadi ka* – hello. I am Lek. Good to see you.'

'Please sit down. Er, would you like a coffee?'

'No, tea is better, I think – green tea.'

We sat without speaking for a few moments. These first meetings were always awkward, especially when I did not have the advantage of custody over a prospective informant. She knew this. I would have to make the first move and I had no real hold on her. It gave her an air of cool assurance.

'I'm sorry about the phone call at the *President*,' I said cheerfully. 'I hope you don't mind the change of venue. I thought it would be safer to meet here instead.'

'*Mai pen rai* – no worry. Better here, I think,' she said.

I glanced restlessly towards the waitress as we waited for the tea to arrive and decided to press on.

'Colonel Surachai has told me a little about you, but if it's OK, I would like to ask you some questions. I think you can help me.'

'Colonel is good man, I think. But before, I saw mostly Khun Pongpat. He say I have to meet with you, now.'

'Yes, I know.'

'How can I help you?' she said abruptly, putting me off balance. 'You are from England, *na*?'

And so it started. I explained that I was a first secretary, working at the British Embassy. I flattered myself horribly. I told her that I was a force for good, using all my righteous energies to catch wicked drug smugglers. I was collaborating with her fellow Thai citizens, locked in a dedicated struggle against the common enemy, etc., etc. We were brothers in arms in the war on narcotics, the evil trade, the modern scourge of humanity.

I had made this speech, or versions of it, on numerous occasions before, but each time I repeated the well-worn clichés I believed them less. The sermon sounded even more ridiculous as I sat opposite Lek and craved her sympathetic audience. In my heart, I knew I was no crusader for the cause. I was just another pushy foreigner sticking his nose in another country's business – a man feeling his age, possessed of tired limbs and a growing paunch, bent on climbing as far up the greasy pole as he could towards a self-righteous retirement and a timbered cottage in a Kentish meadow. I was just doing my job – no better than the rest – no worse than some drugs smugglers, perhaps.

In that moment, it occurred to me that I might, in fact, have fewer qualities than the man I was now hunting so vigorously – at least he did not suffer from my hypocrisies. Did I really care a fig if the London street price of cannabis fell or rose? As I spouted, I sensed that she did not appear too impressed by my attempt at earnest rhetoric, either. Her expression had not changed, not in the slightest. There was not a flicker of encouragement or a ghost of antipathy. She took in the words with a steady patience, and as I set out my stall, she watched me fixedly. At the end of my effusive introduction, I paused for breath.

'So, what do you want of me?'

'I need to know more about you first,' I replied quietly after a second's hesitation.

'What do you want to know?'

'Well, it would help to know where you are from and something about your background. You could tell me about your work with the airline and why you give intelligence to the Royal Thai Police,' I said gently. 'If you can talk about this, I think we can help one another. I can give you money for information, you know.'

She then gave me her first visual clue – her eyes narrowed and her lips pouted thoughtfully. She looked distinctly unimpressed at the mention of money.

'OK, I will tell you, but I need you to help me.' I waited for more. None came.

'What can I do for you?'

Now she looked faintly apprehensive. 'I have *farang* boyfriend. He say he can take me to Europe to start new life. I want to go with him – it is my big chance. If I tell you about the airport drugs business, can you protect him?'

I wondered if the Thais had told her that I knew all about Bart. In any event, her request was preposterous. It went without saying that the power to offer such a deal was way above my pay grade and anyway, it would never have been granted. It was simply unthinkable. In fact, it was unethical. London would never entertain such an idea. The Thais might consider it, for a while; they tended to be rather more imaginative. But after exploring all the angles, I was sure that even *they* would refuse in the end. It was doubly impossible to agree to such terms, as it affected one of

HMCE's major targets – my *specific* target, to make matters more acute. The rules were as clear as the Crystal Palace. I could never agree or even hint at it.

But as my mind started to stack up all the reasons why her proposal was impossible, I found myself saying, 'It depends, of course. I'll need all the information, but I'm sure we can arrange something that will work for both of us. I cannot see why we should not be able to do some kind of a deal, if this is important to you. You say that you are worried about your boyfriend. Why? Is he involved?'

As I spoke, I could see her features relax. Her doll-like expression became more human – there was subtle movement in her face, her eyes were enquiring and her cheeks flushed.

'There are many who do this – my boyfriend help sometimes, but he is not a big man – there are others. But my brother is a bad man. This I have known for long time. If he goes to gaol, it's OK. He has made his own problems. I understand this. But I want you to say you can help my boyfriend,' she repeated.

'Well, I am sure we can think of something. What is his name, by the way?' I asked idly.

'Bart,' she replied without hesitation.

'I see. Yes, the Colonel did mention his name to me.'

'Khun Pongpat says you can help, as the British have good heart and have fair play. "They will understand" he told me.'

I speculated that Pongpat may have deliberately made a promise on my behalf, knowing that it was one I could not keep, just to make things difficult for me. The enforced loss of his star informant must have felt like a pointed chopstick in his side.

'Yes, of course I can help.' I changed the subject. There would be time to come back to the matter of amnesty later and I wanted to wean her away from thinking too much about Pongpat. 'Colonel Surachai tells me that your brother, Khun Bhang, works at the airport – he is a cargo manager, I understand. Colonel says he is involved in sending drugs to other countries. He says he will do a shipment for England soon.'

'I don't know. I think so. He has sent out drugs many times. I think one for England will go soon.'

'What can you tell me about it?'

'My brother gave me message today to take to my boyfriend – my brother wants to meet Bart's friend, Khun Kevin, to talk about next box to go to London. Khun Kevin is the big boss. He has big money; not my boyfriend.'

'I see. Have you given the message to Bart yet?'

'No, I have to fly to Phuket tonight to see him. I will give him message then.'

'Who is Kevin?'

'He lives in Phuket, in Patong, close to where I stay. I think he has money to give to my brother. I know my brother wants to meet him – I'm not sure why. Bhang told me that he wants to meet him in Bangkok on number twelve this month, in three days. I have to give a message to him to meet my brother at the airport hotel on Thursday, number twelve, at two o'clock.'

Everything I knew about Bart and Kevin shouted at me that Kevin was the minion, not Bart. But I would have to massage the situation for a little longer, so I disguised my surprise and said, 'Do you know Kevin's second name, Khun Lek?'

'He is from your country. Sometimes Bart calls him "Silver" – sounds like that.'

'Is he old or young?'

'He is same as Bart – about thirty-five, I think.'

'Could it be Kevin Silverstream, Lek?'

'I'm not sure – maybe.'

'OK. Can I ask you one more thing, before you go?' I glanced at my watch. 'What time is your flight, by the way?'

'I go at eight o'clock.'

'I will need to see you again soon. We have a lot more to talk about. Can I meet you in Phuket next week?'

'Yes, you can see me. We can meet in airport restaurant, if you like. I work near there.'

'Good. How can I reach you? By phone?'

'Yes, you can call me in my office.' I gave her my pen and she wrote a series of numbers on the corner of the paper menu. I watched as the tips of her elfin fingers sliced the end piece off neatly and handed it to me.

'If I do not answer, you can say you are from British Airways – I sometimes speak with them, so it will sound OK. Please do not say you are from embassy. Everyone will talk and think why is Lek speaking to a man from British Embassy?' Her cheekbones lifted upwards and her lips parted into a wide smile which took me aback.

'Of course not, Lek,' I whispered conspiratorially. 'I will be the man from BA – it sounds good to me.' She smiled delightfully again and then, as if she had glimpsed an unexpected sparkle in my eyes, she looked down self-consciously into her tea, avoiding my gaze. In a momentary reverie, I found myself staring at her smooth neck and the gold Buddha that rested against her satin skin.

'Do you go to the temple often?' I asked absently.

'Of course – I must pray to get good luck for my family.'

'Maybe you can take me sometime.'

'Maybe,' she replied. 'Maybe, one day. Why not, if you like?'

She finished her tea hastily and fussed in her handbag. My coffee had gone stone cold but I swigged it back. 'Can I give you a lift, at all? I have a car outside,' I asked stupidly, impulsively.

'No, it's OK, I can go alone. Better, I think.' Now she was telling me how to do my job. I felt foolish and she must have recognised it, but the mock disapproval on her face just made me want to see her again as soon as I could.

CHAPTER FOUR

'Are you OK?' Gill's parade-ground voice boomed across the office as I fumbled my fingers around the combination dials of my security cabinet. 'You look a bit peaky. Out too long again last night?'

'Shit! Why do these things never work when you want them to?' I started the process of turns and clicks all over again.

'I've changed the combinations,' Gill said. 'It's that time of the month again.' She scribbled down some numbers and handed them to me. We had a rule never to call out combination numbers, just in case the room was bugged. It was a standard protocol which I thought was largely unnecessary. If the Thais, or the Russians for that matter, really wanted to open my cabinets, they would have to overcome a raft of other security measures. But the fact that we went through this little charade and never spoke code numbers out loud served to remind us all that potential breaches of security were issues that needed to be taken seriously.

'It was work, Gill,' I said wearily, as I redialed the new sequence of numbers. 'I was meeting Surachai's celebrated informant, or had you forgotten?' I did my best to sound provocative.

'I thought your meeting was at three o'clock – it *must* have been an interesting one!'

'As it happens, it was. And you can read all about it, if you like. I was up all night writing the telex back to London – it's got all the gory details.'

'Fair enough, Mike – I give in,' she said, holding her arms up in mock surrender. She passed me a couple of pieces of memo paper. 'John popped his head around the door ten minutes ago

– call him when you can. And Sonny called from the Australian Embassy – he wants to know if you are free this evening.'

Sonny Yorke was the Australian Federal Police attaché in Bangkok. He was slightly older than me and had a gnarled and craggy appearance, made all the more ragged by skin that had visibly suffered the ravages of the antipodean sun. Sonny had served in Vietnam and he satirically described himself as a "sharpshooter". This meant that he had spent most of the war taking pot shots with four and a half inch cannons at the Vietcong from ten miles away in the relative comfort and safety of the deck of HMAS Vendetta. His face was partially shrouded by a short, badly-cut, white-haired beard. As the senior AFP man in town, his remit was much wider than mine, encompassing all types of serious crime that had a bearing on Australian national security. He seemed to spend hours every day talking to arrested Aussies within the confines of Klong Prem prison and even more in the equally infamous and squalid immigration gaol.

We had become firm friends over the last two years, having met at one of the Bangkok F.A.N.C. (Foreign Anti-Narcotics Community) meetings – which were really just organised piss-ups. We hit it off immediately and talked about cricket *a lot*. England's win in the '86/'87 Ashes series gave me some rare bragging rights and, naturally, I took full advantage. Sonny was a proud patriot and any chance he had to have a dig at the *old country* was grasped with both hands. His nationalistic sentiments hardened further when I teased him that he was really English, after he had ill-advisedly, and under the influence, confided in me that his father had been born in Whitby, North Yorkshire. But the main ingredient that made our relationship so successful was that he, like me, was on an unaccompanied posting. He had divorced five years previously and lived alone, about a quarter of a mile from my apartment. Although our professional paths crossed infrequently, we often found ourselves in one another's company on sticky Bangkok evenings when there was not much else better to do than to slake our thirsts and talk rubbish in one of the local bars – we enjoyed the crack hugely. I goaded him by telling him that our jobs might look much the same on paper, but they were, in fact, massively different. He was all about trying to solve crimes once they had already taken place, while my focus was to anticipate and prevent them. He was the bludgeon to my rapier. He countered by telling me that I was just a glorified tax collector and what would I know about world policing?

'Best leave these things to the pros, mate!' he would say in his New South Wales drawl.

I picked up the phone and rang the Australian Embassy.

'Sonny – it's Mike. What did you have in mind, mate? As I'm a bit tucked up, to tell you the truth.'

'I have a friend in town tonight, buddy,' he answered. 'Do you fancy a cold one later? Around nine – I thought we could take him to see Soi Cowboy, after.'

'Thanks for the invite, but it sounds like a late night. I'll have to give it a miss. I've got something on the go that I need to keep on top of.'

'What's her name, Micky?'

'Ha, ha. Yes, funny. Look, I'll give you a call in a few days and maybe we can catch up then, OK?'

'OK by me, matey – enjoy whatever her name is…'

I replaced the receiver and looked over sheepishly at Gill. She was busy typing words onto index cards – all part of keeping an efficient information retrieval system. Over the last three years, the work had generated a lot of intelligence which Gill, like a diligent village librarian, did her best to file logically. Each file had its own unique number and she maintained a cross-referenced index, which would lead us to the appropriate records. We maintained indexes on a range of topics that included people, places, vehicles, businesses, telephone numbers and bank accounts.

'Gill, could you dig out all we have on Kevin Silverstream, please. I need to check if we have a last known address for him.'

Gill prided herself on her system and would take ages to explain it to official visitors from London. This had the hidden benefit of leaving me less time to talk to them, which suited me fine.

Two minutes later, she dropped a rather slim dossier onto my desk.

'Can you also have a look at flights to Phuket? I'd like to go down there this weekend for a couple of days.'

'Gadding about again? Don't forget what Mr. West said about the budget.'

'Leave Joe West to me, Gill.' I pulled an expression like a hanged man.

I rang the number Lek had given me the night before and after a few seconds there was a voice; I recognised it immediately.

'Thai International Airways Passenger Services – can I help you?' the voice said brightly.

'Hello, Khun Lek. It's Mike – we met yesterday afternoon.'

'Oh, yes.' Her words suddenly sounded more distant.

'I was wondering if you could spare me some time on Saturday. I am coming to Phuket and I hoped we could meet. There are some more things I want to go over with you.'

'Yes, Khun Mike. I can see you after my work. I finish at six o'clock. But I cannot stay long time – my boyfriend will worry.'

We arranged to meet on Saturday evening at the *Ocean View* restaurant on Kamala Beach, a quiet, rustic settlement off the west coast of the island, between the airport and Bart's house in Patong. With the appointment made, I buried myself in the files on my desk.

After an hour, I called Wut. 'Can you bring the car down, Wut? I need to go to the BNU.'

The BNU was in a most unlikely setting for an operational police unit. As the crow flew, it was no more than three quarters of a mile from the embassy on Wireless Road, but the sheer weight of Bangkok traffic and the over-complicated one-way system meant that on a particularly bad day it could take nearly an hour to cover the distance. The office was situated along a narrow, dusty, unprepossessing soi, which branched off a busy four-lane highway. The obligatory circular route meant that we had to travel at least double the distance, but the alternative was far worse. A walk in the stinking, draining heat for fifteen minutes was not an option. I had naïvely tried the march in the sun during my first week at post and vowed never to attempt it again. It was embarrassing to shake hands on arrival with dripping fingers and sweaty palms. And the underarm shirt stains had not done a lot for my confidence, either. So, from then on, I had settled for a seat in a mobile, air-conditioned goldfish bowl.

There was never any visible security at the BNU gate – we just drove in and parked in front of the single-storey building. It sat on a piece of waste ground that resembled a grubby scrap yard; old, broken vehicles and metal junk littered the site, and discarded food containers and torn plastic bags were scattered by light puffs of air. As I stepped out of the Land Rover, I was greeted cheerily by a couple of the surveillance team, who were sitting on wooden boxes just outside the front entrance. They passed their time sipping cold jasmine tea and smoking thin cigarettes. Inside, Khun Maew was looking as cool and busy as usual. She greeted me with a polite *wai* and I reciprocated.

'Colonel is busy now – wait five minutes, OK, Khun Mike?'

I sat down on a hard stool and tried to absorb the frenetic scene. There seemed to be people coming and going everywhere. It was a large, open-plan office designed for twelve perhaps, but I could count at least twenty-five officers and assorted support staff. The noise of constant chatter intermingled with high-pitched laughter was ever-present. I always enjoyed being there to witness the hubbub. It was not like London. It was certainly not an area of studious endeavour, or an inner sanctum for composed deliberation. This place was *alive* with movement and sound. As I waited for the Colonel, some of the staff noticed me and wandered over for a chat. By the time we had agreed that Liverpool F.C. were going to be First Division champions again, Maew waved me in to see Surachai.

'*Swadi krub*, Khun Mike,' he greeted me with his famous formality. 'How did your meeting with Lek go yesterday? I hope you did not catch my staff watching you!'

'No, Colonel, they must have all hidden very well,' I laughed. 'But it's about the meeting that I want to speak to you – I need your help. I need you to keep Bart on phone intercept for the next month or so and let me have daily access to the tapes.'

'No problem, Khun Mike. I have authorised the next three months already. I can let you read the transcripts any time. But there has not been much of interest in the last few days.'

'And I need a surveillance team to help me cover a meeting on Thursday at the airport hotel. Bhang is going to meet Bart's sidekick, Kevin, and we should do all we can to be there.'

I explained the details that Lek had given me about the impending meeting and he quickly agreed to put a small observation team at my disposal. We also decided to monitor the morning flights from Phuket, in case Kevin was on one of them. If we found him on the passenger list, we would attempt to dig into any checked-in luggage he might have, although we concurred that this would be fairly unlikely; it was probably just a brief trip to Bangkok and doubtless he would be travelling light.

'Did you find Lek helpful, Khun Mike?'

'Yes. I think we can work together OK. She *did* talk a lot about wanting to help her boyfriend, as you said she would.'

'What did you tell her?'

'I told her it was out of the question, of course. That we could make no deals.'

'And what did she say when you told her there would be no deal?'

'Well, Colonel…' I paused and swallowed hard, covering my chin with my hand in an effort to disguise the giveaway twitches around my throat. 'She seemed to accept it OK. I told her it was the only way to clear this business up and get her out of the predicament she was in.'

'Good, Khun Mike,' and as he looked at me, he nodded silently.

CHAPTER FIVE

On Thursday, just before noon, I arrived in the unprepossessing police office at Don Muang's domestic terminal. Surachai had let me have a group of four surveillance officers and had nominated a Sergeant Thip as their team leader. The passenger manifest for the one fifteen flight from Phuket had come up trumps – Kevin Silverstream was on board. We found another booking for him on the four o'clock return flight. I cautioned the BNU officers to be extremely careful not to show themselves. It was early days and I didn't want to spook him.

I proposed a simple exercise: we would watch Kevin walk through controls and into the airport hotel, where we would observe proceedings discreetly, from a distance. If we could get in close, we would do so only if we could avoid any risk of being seen. Sergeant Thip, a bespectacled, gaunt, young officer agreed. He would wait unobtrusively at the exit from the aircraft and the other three would find quiet spots in the hotel lobby to await the rendezvous. I would hover independently, starting in the arrivals hall, as I was anxious to see Kevin in the flesh and get a good feel for him. For once, things went according to plan. The inbound flight was on time and it was almost empty – only three *farangs* disembarked from the aircraft. Two were young women sporting backpacks and the other was a smartly dressed, rather chubby, receding, thirty-something carrying a small, brown briefcase.

That's our Kev.

I watched as he strolled, unchallenged, through the arrivals hall and was comforted to see that Sergeant Thip had come to the same conclusion; he was following Silverstream from an inconspicuous distance of about thirty yards.

Kevin picked up his pace once he was on the main concourse, walking briskly with the gait of a man who knew where he was going. We followed him together out of the terminal into the full heat and glare of the Bangkok afternoon. He took a right turn, crossed the busy airport road via a footbridge and skipped down the steps on the other side. Within twenty minutes of leaving his seat on the aircraft, he was safely ensconced in the lobby of the hotel.

The lobby was chock-a-block with people and piles of suitcases. There were no empty seats anywhere. But Kevin was in luck – the BNU were on their game. Two of the officers assigned to the lobby had managed to find a couple of seats next to one another and as Kevin marched into the hotel, with Sergeant Thip just twenty yards behind and surreptitiously alerting his colleagues with a prearranged hand signal, one of the officers had the presence of mind to get up with a flourish, just as Kevin approached. Like a man hunting for a seat on a rush hour train, he took the bait and dived into the now vacant chair. He was visibly sweating after his short walk in the sun. He beckoned a passing attendant and ordered a coffee. The other BNU officer held onto his seat, just two feet away, and quietly sipped his coke.

At ten minutes before two o'clock, Kevin was greeted by a solid-looking Thai man in his early forties. Kevin stood up and the two shook hands warmly. The room was still crammed, so they continued talking where they stood. The adjacent BNU officer rolled an ice cube around in his mouth and looked the other way. I immediately recognised the Thai man as Lek's wayward brother, Bhang. I had seen dozens of BNU covert photos of him in a file the Colonel had copied for me. From my vantage point on the far side of the heaving lobby, I could get only occasional glimpses of the two heads chatting animatedly. After five or six minutes, the pair broke up and I saw the Englishman heading back towards the front steps of the hotel. We had agreed in advance that if the men split up, two officers would follow Kevin, while Sergeant Thip and his other colleague would tail Bhang, just in case he took him to another meeting. I decided to go with Kevin. The longer I could watch him, the better I would know my man – and now I was getting a very good look. One thing was obvious: as he checked himself in to the return flight to Phuket, he no longer had the small, brown briefcase.

And there was a bonus. The BNU officer who had been seated just inches away had taken a covert photo of the bag switch, using a camera concealed in his rucksack. He reported back that the two had spoken in English, so his understanding had not been great. The noise of the lobby had not helped, either. But he had overheard two Thai place names. They were repeated often: Chiang Mai and Mae Sae.

* * *

My flight to the island of Phuket the next day was smooth and uneventful. Gill had, by coincidence, booked me on the same four o'clock flight that Kevin had taken the day before and the circumstance brought a certain piquancy to the situation; the pursuit had started in earnest.

She had also reserved me a room at the *Meridian*, just south of Patong Beach. When I had settled into its plush embrace, I grabbed a cold beer from the mini bar and made a call to Rupert Barclay, the British Honorary Consul. John Morris had given me his name and number and suggested I give him a ring.

'He knows the ropes in the south pretty well and may be able to help – even if it's just some guidance with the geography or a recommendation for a bar or restaurant,' John had said helpfully, over a plate of spicy chicken noodles the evening before. 'I told him you might be in town sooner or later. I'm sure he'll push the boat out – he was excellent to me when I chaired the British Businessmen's Symposium down there last month.'

'You didn't tell him what I did, at all, John?' I enquired.

'No, of course not. I just mentioned that a colleague was coming down for a long weekend break – I hope that's OK.'

Honorary consuls are not professional diplomats; they do not make a living as attachés and any remuneration they receive is limited to expenses. Rupert was a few months shy of sixty-five and lived and worked in Phuket as a salesman for a well-known British glass company. He had been in Thailand for over twenty years and his current job was the latest in a long line of many others that had included real estate, ship brokering and leather importing. The embassy propaganda will tell you that what honorary consuls do, they do for love of country – but the truth is that the kudos can be, for some, the main attraction.

Rupert was terribly affable. He liked people and if he could help out a Brit in trouble he would do so. He made a point of meeting as many as he could and his networking was legendary. When the phone answered, I introduced myself. Rupert replied with a flurry of geniality and charm.

'Hello, old man,' came the singing reply. 'John said you might call. Nice chap, John. Met him at the conference last month – went down brilliantly here, you know.' He spoke as if he was rolling the Elgin Marbles around his oral cavity. 'How long are you here?'

'About three days, I think. I have some bits and pieces I must do tomorrow, but if you fancied a drink on Sunday, I'd love to buy you one.'

'Sunday is golf. I say, how are you fixed? Are you a golfer, at all, Mike?'

'Well, I do play actually, but I don't have any clubs or shoes with me,' I replied hesitantly.

'Handicap?'

'Yes – nine.'

'Not a problem, then!' he announced. 'I have a good spare set – left to me by the widow of a Brit who had a heart attack last year. Fine chap – too much sauce, I'm afraid. What size are you?'

'Eleven,' I said, hoping that would rule out any chance of him finding me shoes.

'Excellent! That was his size, too – big chap, he was. Actually, you'd be doing me a favour. I have a four-ball game booked at the country club at ten a.m. with some ex-pats and my old mucker, Jack, has pulled out – sick as a dog. So you would make up the group perfectly. What do you say? I'll pick you up at nine thirty. How about it?'

I felt cornered, but at the same time the offer of a friendly round of golf was quite appealing, so I muttered my agreement and before I knew it, we were all fixed up.

'I'll let you have his balls as well, if you want,' he announced happily.

That's the last thing I need. A dead man's balls.

I put the receiver down and tapped in Lek's airport number. She answered immediately.

'Hi, it's Mike – just to let you know I am in town. Are you still OK for tomorrow at six?'

'I can meet you tonight, if you like. My boyfriend has gone to Chiang Mai. He is back tomorrow, so maybe today is better.' She sounded upbeat.

'OK. Sounds fine. Can I buy you dinner?'

'Where are you staying?' she asked directly. My natural instinct was to lie to her, but I didn't.

We agreed to meet at seven thirty in the *Meridian* lobby and take it from there. She assured me it was just a short taxi ride from her home and, in any case, it would be easier than the *Oceanview* in Kamala.

When I exited the lift and sauntered into reception, a full five minutes before the agreed time, she was already waiting for me and looking quite stunning. She wore a crimson raw silk skirt and an ivory blouse. It was the first time I had seen her legs properly and they were, as I had secretly visualised, perfectly shaped and smooth. She greeted me with a sparkling smile that gave the appearance of genuine sincerity – but I had seen smiles like this before.

I made an effort to smarten up; a five minute shower and an extra handful of aftershave.

'You like to see some of the town?' she asked straight away. 'If you want, I can show you quiet place so we can talk.' One of the bellboys hailed a cab from the long line of waiting taxis and we jumped in.

'You want Thai tonight?' she questioned and I blinked slightly, as an improper thought angled into my brain. She said a few words in her own language to the driver and the cab rumbled off, heading north into Patong.

She has taken control already. Why not? – it feels great.'

The *Baan Rim Pa* restaurant was perched on a low cliff at the northern extremity of Patong's west coast, just before the tiny hamlet of Kalim. To my surprise, a corner table for two overlooking the expanse of beach and half a dozen anchored long-tail boats had already been booked in my name.

'I think you will like it here – it is not noisy and we can speak,' Lek announced as crisp, white napkins were being unfolded and put across our laps by two delightful, young waitresses dressed in stunning, silk outfits of peacock blue and emerald green. 'I have never been here, but my friends say it is very good. And I think maybe not a good idea to go to place where I am known.'

I grinned clumsily and deliberately averted my eyes from the gold Buddha pendant that dangled between her breasts. Lek smiled at me and looked utterly relaxed and tranquil.

She is pretty good at this clandestine stuff.

Over dinner, I found it difficult to be business-like, even though I needed to ask her some key questions. I had prepared them in advance, mentally going over them time and time again, but somehow it never seemed the right moment to talk shop. Instead, we chatted away happily about ourselves and our lives, much as two expectant, lost souls might do on a blind date. She did nothing to bring the conversation round either, although she must have known there were things we needed to discuss. I wondered if her meetings with Major Pongpat had been like this and came to the rapid conclusion that they would have been very different. Maybe she thought I was a soft touch – she would get dinner, a glass of wine and engage in meaningless small talk, without either of us confronting the issues that were so critical to both of us.

I learned some interesting things about her, all the same. She was an orphan, abandoned as a one-year-old and adopted by foster parents before she could walk properly. She never met her real mother or father but had grown to love her adoptive parents as if they were her own, especially her father, who had been very kind to her all his life. This helped to explain the fractious relationship she had with her brother. He was not a blood relation, after all. Lek told me about all the recent family problems with money and how he had dissipated what little they had.

'One time my family owned a lot of land for rice in Nong Khai. My great great grandfather had it long time before. Bhang was next in line to take the land.'

'How did things go so badly wrong?' I asked.

'About five year ago Bhang told my father to put money into Bangkok stock market. He said he could make big profit from stocks and shares. They lost badly and my brother bought more stocks to get money back. But still they lose. My father had to sell many paddy fields so now we have only our house and a little land. My father owed many people too and no money coming in from rice. Very difficult for us. I was very sad but angry too with Bhang. He did a bad thing. Now we must work to give back to my father but Bhang keep a lot for himself. It make me so unhappy.'

She looked directly at me and forced a smile, explaining brightly how much she enjoyed her airline job, but then her mood changed again as she described her enforced labours as her brother's postmistress. A deep frown told me that she was troubled every time his name was mentioned. It occurred to me that for such a naturally beautiful woman, it must have been difficult to display any hints of malice, but she managed it all the same, albeit in the briefest glimpses, when she spoke about him. It was as if the whole outline of her face, the contours of her cheekbones, were being altered by hidden torments whenever the subject came up.

I changed the subject. 'Lek is an interesting name. It means small, doesn't it?'

'Oh, Lek is not my *real* name. They gave it to me when I started work at airport. My real name is Somsri.' Her eyes flashed at me. This did not come as a surprise as I knew that it was normal for Thais to adopt nicknames, so the pseudonym did not carry with it any suggestion of intrigue.

And then she spoke about her son. For some reason, I had assumed that she had not been married – Surachai had made no mention of a husband. So I blinked a little when she told me how much she loved her only son.

'How old is he?'

'Fourteen, now. I miss him so much. Nin is in Nong Khai with my father and my aunt who take care of him. I have to send money every month, so it's better that I work in Bangkok. Anyway, my brother says I must stay to help him, so I cannot go back.'

'And your husband – where is he?'

'I never had husband, just boyfriend. My baby was mistake. My family was not happy at first, but they agree to help. Then Nin's father left me – about three months later. He met another lady. I have not seen him since then.'

'So you brought your son up on your own, Khun Lek?'

'Yes, but my family support me. Now he is doing well at school and he is growing up fast. I want to be with him – to help him before he become a man and forget me. I miss him very much.'

She mentioned Bart only once – just to confirm that he was away until Saturday night and even though I was anxious to find out more about him, I found myself letting the subject go. It was not the right time, for some reason.

She asked me about my life and I was surprisingly honest, for once.

'Are you married?' she asked suddenly, as the bananas in coconut milk arrived.

I swigged down the last drops of my *Tia Maria* and said steadily, without any emotion, 'Yes, and I have a daughter who is twenty-two – but they both live in England. They tried to live here, but it didn't work out. They have their own lives at home, now.'

'And you, Khun Mike, are you lonely?' I was startled by the directness of the question, but at the same time, entranced by its natural innocence.

'Sometimes, Khun Lek, sometimes...'

I signalled the waiter to bring me another drink.

By the time we had finished our jasmine teas, I felt I knew her pretty well, while appreciating that she had got more out of *me* than I usually cared to give. My natural ability to duck and dive had steadily, over the years, become an unwelcome friend and it felt wonderful to be free of its chains for a few hours and talk straight for a change. But for the most part, I sat back in my chair and listened. The dreamlike evening wafted through me and swirled around me as if I had been under a spell. I felt totally at ease, comfortable, calm and stress-free – it was an experience that I had not enjoyed for a very long time. And I was sure that it was not the alcohol that had brought on this sense of tranquillity; I had drunk much less than usual. It was something else. Being in the presence of this attentive, intelligent, dazzling woman, who even appeared to show a vague interest in me, was like releasing a pressure valve. I felt mellow and the sensation was delicious.

The bill came and it dawned on me that I had covered very little of the business I had wanted to discuss. It was nearly eleven, the restaurant was empty – save for us – and the silk-clad waitresses were beginning to clear the tables.

My official persona broke the spell. 'Look, I need to ask you some serious questions about Bart and your brother. Can you spare me a little more time? Can we find somewhere else to talk? We can go back to the *Meridian,* if you like, for a nightcap – you can get a taxi from there since you live so close.'

As I spoke, I realised that my invitation sounded like an old cliché – "fancy coming back for coffee, dearie?"

Lek appeared unfazed. Maybe she had not read anything untoward into my ham-fisted proposal. 'That is OK, but I cannot stay long. I have to get up early tomorrow – at six thirty.' This also sounded rather too much like the traditional, hackneyed response, but I was sure she had not intended it that way.

Fifteen minutes later, we were back in the lobby of the hotel. I had a large *Lagavulin* in my hand. Lek was clutching a glass of iced water.

I asked her first about Kevin. What was his relationship to Bart? She told me that they had been long-time friends and had been in commerce together for many years – most recently in the flower and fruit import/export business. Bart had told her that they had been doing this happily and profitably for some time, until one day Kevin had persuaded him that they should send some drugs back to Europe in a consignment of orchids. After weeks of persuasion, Bart had put aside his misgivings and had reluctantly agreed.

'It is the first time Bart did this thing,' she said and fixed me with a steady stare.

One day! The first time! If only she knew – poor maid hasn't a clue.

I convinced myself that this was just one of many lines he must have spun to this innocent girl.

How could he? And she – such a blameless beauty. How could he deceive her so viciously?

'How did you and Bart first meet?' I asked.

'My brother gave me message to take to him – something about Kevin's orchids. I think he liked me when he see me.' She explained that a few months later she had warned Bart about the London-bound mangoes and told him that the authorities in Britain had found the drugs. Bart then asked her out. 'Major Pongpat told me to do it – he wanted Bart to know. I worried at first, but Bart was good to me; he gave me many presents and then he ask if we can live together, so I move to Phuket. I like him now – he is kind to me and takes care of me.'

'But is it true that Bart is planning another shipment, Lek?' I enquired softly.

'No, not him – Kevin is doing it. Bart, he is only helping a little. Kevin went to Bangkok this week to see my brother. I told you about it, *na*?'

'Yes, I know. And they did. I was there and saw them together – what you told me was correct. It was very helpful – so I want to thank you.'

'No need to thank me. I just want you to stop all this so my brother can get locked up and Bart and I can have new life together.'

'Does Bart know you have been helping the police? Does he know about Major Pongpat?'

'For sure, no!' she exclaimed. 'He will be very angry, I think – he will not understand. I only help the police so they can catch my brother. When he is arrested, it will all finish. I want them to do it soon. They have promised me many times.'

'Do you mind if I ask you a personal question, Lek?'

'Up to you, Khun Mike – I don't mind.' Her eyes were gleaming now.

'Do you love Bart?' I asked. What a dumb question! But it spurted out all the same.

'What is love?' she fired back, her eyes blackened, showing a sign of defiance I had not seen in her before. 'I do not know what that is. I love my father, I love my son and I love my family. I think Bart can help me – he is kind and he says he will take me away so I can make a new life and support my family.'

My heart ached for her now. The pitiable girl was being deceived in the worst possible way by a callous, unfeeling parasite, who only wanted her close to him because she had the inside track on what was going on at the airport.

Bastard!

My revulsion for the man rose to a new level.

It was an uneasy moment for both of us and I saw that it was time to conclude our meeting. I felt emotionally drained, and to make matters worse, I now had a lot of writing to do. I suspected that Lek had been feeling the strain too, for she looked tired and morose all of a sudden.

'I'll call you a cab,' I announced. 'Goodness, look at the time; it's nearly one a.m.'

She stood up and flattened her skirt with her hands. The sight of her delicate fingers moving across her hips made me bite my lip and take a deep breath.

'What are you doing tomorrow?' I said absently. 'You say you have to get up early.'

'Yes, I am going to temple.' She tucked her sleek handbag under her arm and looked up at me. 'You want to come?'

CHAPTER SIX

I woke as the sun was shedding its early morning rays onto the blue vastness of the Andaman Sea. Twitching and murmuring, I had been absorbed in a vivid dream and I was still in the grip of its intensity. My eyes opened with a suddenness that made my heart thump. I fumbled around the sheets in a pointless search, feeling and hoping to find something warm and comforting beside me. But my flailing arms discovered just cool, cotton sheets; the reverie was ended, the bed was empty.

As I came gradually to my senses, I gazed out across the balcony. It had rained during the night and the *leelawadi* plants leaked droplets of moisture onto the brick-tiled floor. A tiny fishing boat chugged slowly across the bay, far in the distance. I could make out two men on the open deck, their dark skins against the rising sun, heaving nets from the placid water. Theirs was the single sign of human activity. The miniature boat bobbing and their diligent straining were the only movements that punctured the calm stillness of the postcard scene.

I opened the sliding glass doors and padded out onto the terrace. It still retained some of the coolness from the night's downpour, but the sun's furnaces were even now moving into overdrive. It would not be long before their power would make my skin glisten. As I stretched my aching limbs, I gazed casually at my wrist. The gold *Omega Seamaster* that my mother had given me when I turned twenty-one told me it was seven fifteen.

Shit! I agreed to meet Lek at half past seven. We are going to the temple. She asked and I accepted. Hadn't I? Yes, I had, for sure.

By the time I reached the ground floor, she was already sitting in the back seat of a cab, but it took me a few minutes to find her. After some scowling scans around the lobby, I emerged into the open air, where my eyes finally fell upon her lovely face. It brought back the recent memory of our first meeting, when I had lifted my hand against the sun to search for her on Sukhumvit Road. This time it had taken a high spirited shout from her for me to turn my head and see the car. I bundled myself alongside her slim frame. She looked as fresh as the golden *leelawadi* on my balcony.

'Oh, you are wearing shorts,' she said, sounding a little offhand. 'Never mind, we can get something for you.'

In contrast to my casual attire, which I had thrown on in a hurried panic after a twenty-second sluice, Lek was dressed very demurely in thin, white, cotton trousers and a long-sleeved, yellow blouse.

The Buddhist temple at Kamala is about three miles north of Patong and is situated on a quiet beach road, free from all but the most intrepid tourists and sightseers. Lek explained that it was important to conduct any religious rituals in the morning. Since my arrival in Bangkok nearly four years earlier, I had only recently found time to visit the famous Buddhist sights in the city. I had wandered around with the holidaymakers, marvelling at the gold statues, the exquisite craftsmanship and the huge, rather frightening, effigies. I had clicked away carelessly with my *Pentax* and over a couple of months I had compiled a marvellous set of photos to send home to my father in the diplomatic bag. My sister had written to me saying that Dad had developed a severe back pain and was feeling rather run down – I hoped the pictures would cheer him up and remind him of the days he had spent in the Far East.

Lek grabbed my elbow and tugged at my arm as she encouraged me towards the temple's entrance. We walked across a sandy track and under a red and gold carved arch into the sanctuary grounds. The strangest of visions came into my mind, one that brought about a pang of homesickness. I imagined the two of us strolling insouciantly into a remote Cornish churchyard on a bright, English summer's morning. As a place of worship, Kamala's solitary temple had a lot in common with a rural, English church. It was about as far removed from the vast grandeur of Bangkok's glittering and ancient sights as a quiet, Saxon chapel was from St Paul's Cathedral. We ambled into the gardens and I stumbled over a pair of rangy chickens and their babies pecking busily into the arid ground. A bell chimed softly in the background. The waves on the nearby beach crawled up the sand with a gentle rustle, and crabs, no larger than my fingernail, skated across the surface, disappearing from time to time into their tiny burrows.

'Wait here one minute, Khun Mike. I will get something to cover your legs.'

An elderly, saffron-robed monk was sitting cross-legged in the corner of a polished, wooden structure that reminded me of the stage in a village theatre. Lek approached him, bowed her head and after a brief conversation and more nods of heads, he handed her something and she hurried back to me clutching what looked like a set of multi-coloured, cotton pyjama bottoms. An unholy image of the *Elan* massage parlour came to mind briefly, but I blocked it out quickly.

'Put these over your shorts. I hope they fit – you may be too big for them.' She smiled. 'He say they are the biggest they have.'

As I struggled, wobbling and one-legged, to squeeze into the thin garment, she held my arm to steady me. After a brief skirmish, I finally succeeded in stretching the waistband over my hips and felt a warm glow of triumphant achievement. But the finished article must have made me look preposterous because Lek could not suppress a wide, amused grin.

My god! I am beginning to get used to these wonderful smiles.

'Come – we can go now.' She prodded me gently in the side.

In the centre of the wooden dais, under the low, carved ceiling, sat another monk, younger than the first, in the full lotus position. He was as motionless as the statues that surrounded him. All around were dozens of thin, amber-coloured candles and sticks of incense, most of which were burning silently, their exotic fumes tantalising my nostrils. About the stage, lotus flowers in half bud, their long stems protruding upwards, had been arranged sensitively amongst the various gold effigies of Buddha and framed photographs of old monks whose souls had presumably moved on to a better place.

The temperature must have risen five degrees within the hour. Without the electric fans that had been placed at strategic points around the room to cool the faithful, who sat on the carpeted floor, under the eye-line of the presiding monk, it would have been unbearable. As I reflected on the serenity of the scene, an upsurge of calmness and composure invaded my solar plexus. Lek had detached herself from me and was quietly writing on a slip of paper that one of the temple devotees had given her. She appeared to be in a world of her own and to have completely forgotten about me, enmeshed in her private thoughts and prayers. I decided to adopt a low profile and retreated into a remote corner from which to observe the proceedings.

Lek crossed to another part of the temple where she put a red, hundred-baht note into a bronze collection bowl and in return she was handed a wicker basket stuffed with groceries. It looked a little like a *Fortnum & Mason* Christmas hamper. With paper and hamper in hand, she joined the others on the floor, where she sat in a half kneeling position, her legs tucked neatly under her hips, looking composed and perfect. The simplicity of the scene was striking. After a few moments, the younger monk turned his head towards her. This was the cue for her to crawl forward and pass up the hamper and the handwritten note she had prepared. The monk made a sign of acknowledgement, put the proffered paper to one side and handed the hamper to another attendant. As he did, I noticed that the basket contained, amongst other useful items, a bottle of *Coca-Cola* and a roll of toilet paper. Rather like the Queen might hand over flowers given to her by a small child to a lady-in-waiting, the monk passed on his gift and then rotated with outstretched hands towards another member of his small congregation. This process continued three more times. Then he commenced a low chant and as he did, he casually, almost thoughtlessly, tossed down some printed cards into the stalls where his audience collected them. The mantra began in soothing, monotonous tones and his disciples, following the annotations on the card, chanted the incantations back. One of the small group stumbled with her words, and the monk appeared to make a little joke, which made everyone laugh in a subdued sort of way. Perhaps he said, 'Don't worry. I get it wrong too, sometimes.'

Lek poured some water into a small, metal container. The monk waved around an exotically decorated banner on the end of a long pole for a few seconds and then dipped some flaxen reeds into another gleaming, bronze bowl at his side. As he withdrew the stems, I could see they were dripping with moisture. He flicked the reeds over each of the congregation, one at a time, and the water fell on their heads like a mist of tiny raindrops. When it was Lek's turn to receive the droplets, she looked particularly serious and thoughtful, her hands clasped tightly together in a praying position, touching her forehead. Despite the obvious solemnity of the moment, I sensed a lightness too – purity, innocence, even joy.

And there was something else that tugged at my heart. The peaceful tranquillity of the temple, the ancient theatricals, the feeling of timeless continuity married with the pleasure of being in the company of this handsome but fragile-looking woman who sat cross-legged and gazing away from me, reaching for Nirvana, brought about in me a strange restlessness. A feeling of unfinished business swamped my thoughts, a yearning for something out of reach, something indefinable; something that could hurt me, if I let it.

When the formalities were over, the monk spoke to the group. I understood none of his words, but they must have been encouraging and uplifting, for the entire congregation looked placid and content, as if a great thirst had been sated. He then spent a few moments chatting to each of them individually but within earshot of the others, rather like the curate might pass the time of day at the door of the nave as the parishioners left the Sunday service. When he spoke to Lek, he seemed to be giving her advice of some kind. Whatever he said to her, it took longer to impart than his exchanges with the others. At the end of it, his gentle, avuncular frowns had turned to warm, broad-cheeked smiles and I noticed a look of relief on Lek's face. As she crawled backwards, still prone, towards the rear of the temple, she turned and now out of earshot, her cheeks puffed up and she exhaled loudly, as if she had been through a minor ordeal of some kind. When she reached the furthest edges of the room, the audience now over, she stood up and must have remembered suddenly that she had arrived with someone else, for she looked around anxiously, trying to find me.

'That was interesting,' I said once she had picked me out.

'Is this your first time?'

'Yes. There is a first time for everything,' I replied inanely. 'Tell me, Khun Lek, what did you write on that paper you gave to the monk? Was it wishes you wanted him to grant for you?' Another idiotic comment and as soon as the words left my lips, I regretted them. I detected a small ridge of disapproval forming between her eyes.

'No, not wishes,' she said gravely. 'It was prayers. I give prayers for all those who have died before me – all my family who are not here now. I pray for them.'

The taxi had been waiting for us and as we drove back towards Patong, the mood lightened a little. We chatted about her work and the problems she was having with some disgruntled passengers, but nothing more. It was a friendly but anodyne dialogue.

As the cab pulled up at the *Meridian*, I said carelessly, 'What time does Bart get back from Chiang Mai?' I knew the answer already. I had asked Khun Maew at the BNU to make some enquiries and she had found a booking for him and Kevin on the eight o'clock flight. It was an idle question designed just to give me a little peace of mind and to confirm Lek's honesty – to test her newfound loyalty.

'Oh, he is back already,' she replied swiftly. 'He came back last night.'

I tried not to look surprised. Then I heard myself saying to her, 'OK. Fine. Good. I thought you said he was coming back today?'

'Yes, but he change for some reason. He does this sometimes. He did not tell me why. He came back in a car, drive all day with Kevin. He was waiting for me after our dinner last night.'

'Did he ask why you were out so late alone?' I asked earnestly.

'Yes – I told him that I was having dinner with a British secret agent.'

For a desperate instant I believed her. Then I saw her dark eyes flicker and her lips make an exaggerated pout and I knew she was joking.

'Please don't do that, Lek. This is serious, you know. Do you really want me to help you finish all this?' I bleated. 'If you really want to get back to your happy family life and stop your brother hurting you, you have to be sincere with me.'

'Yes, I know!' she said mockingly. 'Only joking – *poot len*, as Thai people say. Don't worry. I told him I had a birthday party to

go to at work. And I wanted to see your face too, Khun Mike –
just to see if you are serious, like me. I really want you to help me.'

'And am I serious, Khun Lek?'

She looked at me purposefully. 'Yes, I think so... yes, for sure.
You are serious. I can see it. I will not joke again – promise.'

'Promise?' I said.

'Promise.'

CHAPTER SEVEN

The rest of the day passed slowly. I found myself thinking of Lek and wondering what she and Bart might be doing. I wrote up my notes, made a call to John Morris in Bangkok, sat by the hotel pool for a few hours until I felt my neck burning and by evening I found that I had nothing better to do than worry about whether I could hit the golf ball straight the next day. I watched the sun set with sombre indifference and had a couple of beers at the pool bar in an effort to lighten my mood. By seven, the bar had emptied and I was alone. A wave of melancholy enveloped me like a heavy set of sodden velvet curtains.

Maybe an outing into town might lift my spirits. A trip into Patong and the bright lights of Bangla Road.

During the daytime, Bangla Road is just another run-down thoroughfare in the middle of Patong. Electricity cables drop like bundles of black spaghetti around the torn angles of mould-infested buildings that had seen their best days thirty years ago. Rooftops are crammed with all manner of vegetation, only some of which was intentionally planted; street vendors on trishaws ply their trade of tourist tat; *tuc tucs* and motorcycles contest every inch of road as if their lives depended on it, in a dangerous, high-speed boogie. The place looks worn out and seedy – which it is.

But at night-time, Bangla Road transforms itself into a kind of *Disneyland* for grown-ups. As darkness falls, the blemishes and stains are hidden and the deprivation is temporarily shrouded. The lights come on, the party starts. Despite its squalid and immoral inner core, it feigns an "end of pier" charm – a veneer of phony gilt and glass that attracts ever-increasing numbers of happy and hapless tourists each year. The thumping noise of the bar music is complemented perfectly by the glare of neon, as is the clack of pool table balls by the laughter of drunken tourists and shrieking girls.

In Bangkok, I had visited such places rarely and always in the company of others. If we got led astray, we did it together. I always felt there was something insalubrious about stalking the sois and back alleys of Bangkok alone, but here in Phuket, I could tell myself that I was on holiday – it was Saturday night and a man needed a beer, at least. I made for the *Sexy Nine* bar, located halfway up Soi Dragon. I had stumbled across it on my first visit to Patong and had returned on a few subsequent trips. Despite my sporadic previous attendance, I felt comfortable there – I recognised the faces behind the bar and had got to know some of the girls. And that evening, I wanted to be amongst people I was familiar with, albeit very loosely. The strange feeling of unease that had swamped my thoughts since I left Lek that morning had persisted and I was in need of some lively company to cheer me up.

Besides, it's better to go straight to the Sexy Nine, rather than wasting time trolling around the other bars.

I took my usual seat at the end of the gleaming, U-shaped bar and my morale lifted instantly as the manageress greeted me like a long-lost friend. That was her job, of course – to be extra welcoming – but I persuaded myself that she had reserved her warmest smile for me. And to prove it, she had even remembered my name.

'Khun Mike, where have you been? We missed you!'

I, too, was good at recollecting names. 'Khun Aungkana,' I replied loudly so everyone could hear. 'I missed you toooo!' And we fell about in exaggerated laughter.

'Cold *Singha*, Khun Mike – yes?'

All the big cities and major towns in Thailand, especially those where foreigners visit regularly, have bars like the *Sexy Nine*. The formula is simple. The owner recruits the best looking girls he can muster and pays them a few baht to sit at the bar all night and chat to his customers. Some bar owners do not even pay their girls at all. In effect, the proprietor provides his girls with a stage on which to perform. If they play their part well, they are rewarded by the customers, who buy them drinks. "Lady drinks", as they are called, are charged at double the ordinary rate. The girl keeps half the money for every drink she gets a client to buy for her. If she gets lucky and she likes her man, and he takes a fancy to her, she may agree to go out with him. If she hits the jackpot, the fleeting encounter may lead to something more permanent... bar girls are relentlessly exchanging stories about former co-workers who are now living happily in Belgium or Sweden, or anywhere, in fact – except Thailand.

If the girl agrees to go out with him, the customer must pay the boss a fee to release her from the bar for the night. It's called a "bar fine" – and of all the fines a man may be asked to pay in his life, this must surely be the most painless. He does so voluntarily, often with a thudding heart and a shaking hand – the combined effect of too many destabilising beverages and his rising testosterone levels.

The girls usually have some props to help them catch a visitor's wayward eye. Some bars have pool tables to attract the men and all have dice games and other assorted skill- and luck-based amusements, which are designed specifically to be played one-to-one to help foster the beginnings of a transient bond, a passing connection. One such game is *Connect Four*. Losers buy the winner a drink, so the girls make sure they are well-practiced and even when they lose, a sultry smile and a squeeze of the winner's arm is usually enough to make his resolve soften; he ends up buying, all the same.

The *Sexy Nine* had all these beguiling pastimes plus one other, which had always fascinated me – the log and nail game. The idea was to knock a four-inch nail into a huge log of wood using a hammer that is just a quarter of an inch wide. It looked simple to a casual bystander, but it was not, especially with a belly full of beer. The girl and her client took turns trying to bang the nail home. It was really a game for novice customers, especially those who imagined that their brawn and muscle would enable them to outmatch the waif-like creature holding the other hammer. Most of the regulars shunned the sport and watched the novices make fools of themselves – as they had done, in their turn, before.

'You here long time, Khun Mike? On holiday?' Aungkana asked as she polished a cocktail glass.

'No, just a few days, I think.'

A cold towel arrived fresh from the freezer, along with a ramekin of salted peanuts that tasted greasy and unpleasant.

I glanced around the bar. There were only two other customers – a couple of T-shirted young men, whose red faces suggested that they had been drinking on the beach all day. In addition to the seats around the U-shaped counter, there were half a dozen tall, wooden tables with stools, some of which spilled onto the soi outside. Five girls sat around one of them, chatting animatedly amongst themselves while eating *tom yum goong*, a spicy prawn soup. It was just eight thirty and still early by bar standards. The girls looked relaxed and stress-free, giggling happily as they exchanged stories and applied lipstick. It was as if they were backstage in make-up, getting prepared, priming their minds and bodies for the night-time shift, which wouldn't end until after three. I thought of a Sunday morning football team in their rectory field changing room, greeting one another, dragging on their shirts, rubbing embrocation into their legs and talking tactics in readiness for another muddy game.

I recognised one of the girls as Noy – we had chatted about three months before and I'd let her beat me at *Connect Four* – at least, that was what I told myself. She looked up from her food, acknowledged me with a pretty nod and a coy smile and then resumed her meal and conversation. I got the feeling that it would not be long before she drifted over to renew our acquaintance.

'Khun Aungkana, how has business been?' I said loudly to catch her attention. Above my head, a huge, black speaker blared out percussion and beat music. There was no detectable melody – certainly not any that one could hum to in the bath.

'No good – it is high season now, but no customers – very no good!'

Aungkana's place was firmly behind the bar, controlling the show: watching the customers, mixing the drinks, uncapping the beers, feeding ice into glasses and above all, distributing the bills and collecting the money. Behind her welcoming smile was a hard-nosed business lady. The only two people she reported to were the bar owner himself, a tough-looking Thai with a hint of gangster about him called Khun Sat, and the local policeman who popped round for his protection money. I downed my drink and without asking, Aungkana silently took away the empty bottle and brought me another *Singha,* which she slipped effortlessly into the same foam cooler that she had brought me earlier. It wrapped itself suggestively around the fresh, cold bottle.

'Same condom, Khun Mike – OK?'

'Yes, same condom – that's fine for me!' Condom was an indelicate nickname, but it provided the girls with an oblique opportunity to bring up the subject of sex, which was never very far from their minds. It was the activity that brought in the greatest revenue. The girls in the *Sexy Nine* would have been hugely indignant to be described as prostitutes – they did not see themselves as that. Good time party girls, for sure, but not whores – that was for the street and the brothels outside. They had the power to pick and choose – go or stay. The fact that money drove most of their decisions was just an inconvenient truth.

The bar began to fill now, but not with more customers. The rest of the bar girls were arriving in dribs and drabs, one by one, joining their friends in an increasingly noisy gaggle of squeals. All looked dressed to kill: bright nail polish, dark mascara, shining hair and the tightest of short skirts. I counted a dozen girls in the small bar already. The young, inebriated, blushing travellers had just staggered away, so I was alone.

The ladies had just me to care for – what a lucky man! Perhaps not...

'How are you, Khun Mike? Not see you long time.'

I looked over my shoulder and saw that Noy had sidled up alongside, now replete and geared for action. She was about twenty-eight and had worked in the *Sexy Nine* for four years. Small, svelte and with a shock of shoulder-length, dark hair, she was wearing a bargain basement, body-hugging, white dress and a padded bra. All part of the performance. She sat down next to me, slipped her arm into mine and said something in Thai to Aungkana. The wretched *Connect Four* game appeared from under the counter. Noy obviously had a good memory, too.

'You play with me?' she said, and flicked her hair to afford me a better view of her squeezed cleavage.

I thought to say no, but did not. I was content that evening to let events take their course, however predicable that was. I just wanted to relax, forget my inner emptiness, and let her make the running, drink my beers quietly, laugh with them all, pay my bill and totter back alone to my soft, cool bed. Tonight, I just needed a pretty girl to talk to and one who would flatter me. It would make me feel good. My restlessness would eventually dissipate like mist on an October morning. The unease would just go away.

So, I agreed and we clattered into the first game. I knew the form. She would win the first two competitions, I would buy her a couple of drinks and then, to make me feel good, she would let me win the third. She would giggle at my pathetic attempts to speak

Thai and, after a while, she would rest her hand on my thigh. I would pretend not to notice and take her other hand to read her palm, telling her that she would meet a rich *farang* who would whisk her away to New York. After about six beers, when she thought my guard was down and I was feeling no pain, she would choose the right moment to say, 'I want to go with you, Khun Mike – yes?' I would blink animatedly in mock horror and decline politely.

And that's exactly how it went. Except when, at about eleven o'clock, she popped the fateful question, I stalled for time and said, 'Can I have another beer, Khun Aungkana? *Kop khun krub.*'

I had reached the top of the slippery slope and I knew it. The void beckoned tantalisingly. I mulled things over, trying to weigh up the pros and cons, having convinced myself that I was still sober. I watched her slender fingers as she stroked my arm. The bar was busy, full of intoxicated holidaymakers; two Germans had already tried to befriend me. I had been evasive and Noy had clung proprietarily to my shoulder. The last thing I wanted now was a drunken dialogue in pidgin English with a tanked-up Teutonic tourist.

'OK. I have to go. Can I have the bill, please, Aungkana,' I announced.

'I go with you – no?' pleaded Noy. She draped most of her limbs around my waist and puckered reproachfully.

I shook my head. Noy looked downcast. I exhaled with an exaggerated sigh and blew air onto my forehead.

'OK – if you must,' I said quickly. In an instant, Noy released her grip, jumped off the stool and squealed with glee. She did a little jig of joy and hurried around the counter to join Aungkana behind the bar, where she picked up a small, prettily patterned rucksack – her overnight bag, I assumed. She smiled a triumphant smile to the other girls who bobbed their approval. The bill was more than I expected, not that I had been counting. I queried a squiggle on the hastily handwritten statement – an item with two hundred baht against it.

'Bar fine,' Aungkana said shortly. 'You take girl – you pay bar fine.'

The thrall was broken in an instant.

This is a business. For all the smiles and friendly banter – this is an industry.

As we walked away arm in arm down Soi Dragon in search of a cab, I started to regret my decision.

What had I even been thinking about?

Away from the bar, the glare of the Bangla streetlights suddenly made Noy look stony and cold – no longer the warm, affectionate kitten I had been teasing for three hours. A *tuc tuc* chugged up alongside us and she jumped in. She knew the procedure. I skulked in alongside her and we sat mutely behind the driver. She opened her handbag to retrieve a small vanity mirror, which she studied as she touched up her make-up. She looked very pleased with herself, much as a fisherman might after pulling in a valuable red snapper. I wondered what she had in mind for her catch – barbecued, perhaps, or steamed with garlic? Maybe she would just take out its guts and put it aside for another day.

CHAPTER EIGHT

The bedside phone rang sharply, close to my sleeping ear. I turned over and picked up the receiver. At the same time, my vacant hand detected something smooth and snug under the sheets.

'I'm in the lobby – you ready to go?' a plummy voice bellowed into my throbbing skull.

'My god, what time is it?'

'Time you were up, my friend. It's Rupert... golf!'

'Oh, I'm sorry! I'll be down in five minutes.'

The slumbering corpse beside me whimpered as I prodded it into life. The awkward vulgarity of the situation hit me abruptly like a blast of hot air.

'Sorry, I have to go. I mean, *you* have to go. Now!'

I pulled the sheets off the bed and dragged the curtains back. It was going to be another hot day.

'Now... please, Noy. I must go.'

She tumbled off the divan and a sudden flash of sunlight blazed onto her naked body as she stretched and flaunted her soft, honey-coloured limbs. Without a word, she reached for her clothes and as she pulled on her skimpy underwear, she looked at me insolently, as if I had affronted her – which I had and I knew it. As she pulled on her little white cocktail dress, I stuffed a thousand-baht note into her patterned bag and this softened her glare slightly.

'You have to go. I have a big meeting. I forgot.'

'OK, Khun Mike. See you tonight – OK?'

'Yes, sure. See you tonight.' I pushed her out of the hotel room.

As Noy stumbled into the corridor, clutching her belongings, a passing chambermaid glanced indifferently into the room and seemed not to notice. She must have witnessed this scene many times before. Five minutes later, I lurched into the lobby – unkempt and reeking.

A good walk and some fresh air will soon take care of that.

The *Phuket Country Club* sits like a radiant, cut emerald amongst wooded groves, watered grasses and sculpted lakes, about twenty minutes' drive from the hubbub and kitsch of Patong. For expats, it's a tropical reminder of home. Its rolling fairways and neatly-cut fringes mimic the best that Surrey can offer. For Thais, it's an exclusive possession, a place to boast about, a venue for business and an outlet for ostentation. Rupert had been helpfully silent during the journey from the hotel but now, as he steered his ancient, blue Jaguar down the mile-long driveway, he piped up. 'We might have time for a spot of fried rice at the club, if you need something to sustain you, old man. What do you think?'

'Thanks, Rupert. I'm normally better organised than this – worked a bit late in Patong last night. Lost track of time.'

He winked at me annoyingly. 'Don't fret. We'll have you sorted in a jiffy. Should be a good four-ball today. They are both single-figure guys, or so they tell me. Not played with them before. In business here, so I thought I'd invite them for a round. One is a Brit, so it's a good excuse to do something for Queen and country.'

He rambled on and on but I was not paying attention. I was thinking about the night before and how much worse I felt after the experience. Lek featured heavily in my thoughts and, for some reason, her slight physique and neatly-framed face came into my mind time and time again. I just could not shake the vision out. Of course, I felt bad about getting so drunk, but I did that all the time and could keep relatively sane throughout. But there was guilt too, now. What really rankled was that I had not possessed the guts to change my mind once I realised that I was making a mistake. I had time to turn away from the abyss but had chosen to plunge in all the same. My mind wandered back to Lek and the uneasy thought came to me that she was inextricably connected to my worsening mood and this new level of heartache and despondency. It was not any worry that I might have compromised my career; nor was it a feeling that I had betrayed my family. For a wild moment, I wanted to call her and apologise.

Rupert pulled the Jag up outside the entrance to the clubhouse. Two pink-clad, female caddies were waiting as the car came to a stop and were soon dragging the golf bags out of the boot. I wished they could heave me out of my isolation, as well. Rupert parked the car and we trudged up the clubhouse steps towards an expansive bar area. About thirty yards away, in the furthest corner, I spotted a pair of European-looking men in neat, tailored shorts and bright golf shirts, sitting at a table overlooking the eighteenth green. One of them was dragging on a cigarette. Rupert shouted a hello and made a series of gestures to indicate that we would not keep them waiting much longer; we were going to change our shoes and pay our green fees.

'Those are our opponents for the day. The Brit is the chubby guy – Kevin. The other bloke is his business partner. He's Dutch – Bart is his name. I met them for the first time last week at the *Blue Canyon*. They are both members there.'

My hangover dissolved instantaneously. I looked over at the two men and gestured cheerfully, although suddenly my arms felt like concrete posts. They smiled back at us and as I nodded graciously in return, I could hear and feel the blood pumping into my chest. A cold, clammy sweat broke out on my temple as I identified the man now stubbing out his cigarette. It had been ten years, but there was no mistaking it. It was Bartholomew Vanderpool in all his smug arrogance.

Kevin's podgy presence gave me no such inner qualms.

Although I had studied him from a respectable distance at Bangkok Airport only recently, I was sure that he had not seen me then and would certainly not recognise me now. But I had actually met Bart and had a ten-minute conversation with him, albeit from the rear seat of a BMW with his back turned to me.

Would he recognise me?

It was too late to worry now. He had already seen me and my instinct told me that I could not back out. It was a time for some quiet resolve and a calm, cool approach. I was bearded then and ten years younger. The only thing I could do was to front up the situation, get to know them both, and try to learn as much as I could.

It is an opportunity, an opportunity not to shy away from.

'I need to talk to you, Rupert,' I said quickly.

'If you want to apologise for being late this morning, it's fine. We are on time – no worries,' Rupert whistled back breezily.

In the quiet of the changing room, I put my arm around his bony shoulders and said in low tones, 'Listen, Rupert, I want you to tell me what you have said to those men about me – have you told them where I work?'

Rupert looked startled. 'No, nothing. What is it? I have not even mentioned your name. I didn't even tell them you would be playing today, in fact. They never asked.'

'OK, good. Now, this is important, Rupert.'

His startled look was tinged with panic.

'You must not, on any account, tell them that I work at the embassy.' I looked him directly in the eye and paused for effect.

He nodded and his jaw dropped by half an inch.

'If they ask you about me, you must tell them that I am here on holiday. I am a friend of a friend – you hardly know me – you were asked to invite me for a round of golf as a favour to your friend. I will do the rest.'

'Which friend?'

'It doesn't matter. We can make one up – your old school friend from England – we can call him George.'

'What's this all about, Mike?'

'I'll brief you fully later, Rupert. All I'll say now is that I am working on something that is vital to national security. The protection of Britain is at stake and I have reason to think that these men could be involved.' I had deliberately overstated the situation, but it was the only way to appeal to Rupert's celebrated patriotism.

'OK, I understand, Mike. Mum's the word.' He looked resolutely back at me. I had clearly struck a chord and my confidence lifted. I was sure that Rupert would be able to play his part.

At that moment, Bart walked into the changing room. He appeared taller than I remembered. He looked fit and had gained a few pounds, which suited him. He was tanned and had lost none of his fine, blond hair. Though he smiled at us, he looked distinctly agitated. 'Hallo, Rupert. I think we must hurry – our tee time is now. Are you ready?'

'With you in a jiffy. Go ahead to the tee, if you like; we will follow.'

Bart looked at me. 'Hi, my name is Bart,' he said simply with an outstretched hand.

'Hi, I'm Mike – thanks for inviting me today. I'm sorry, it's my fault we are late. I had a few too many in Patong last night.'

He smirked and showed me a neat row of perfect, white teeth. 'OK, no worries. I have done this before, myself. It can be easy to forget the time,' he said in guttural, Dutch tones which were all too familiar. He looked at me again. 'Have we met before? Do you live here in Phuket?' We strolled out of the changing room together into the heat.

'No, I am just passing through on my way to Sydney. My daughter lives there, so I decided to break the journey here for a few days and see the sights. My friend in England gave me Rupert's number for a game of golf. And you? Do you live here?'

'Yes, I have a business in Thailand.'

'Lucky man,' I replied jauntily.

'Yes – I think so.' His reply was curt and impersonal. He changed the subject. 'What is your handicap, Mike? I am playing off three.'

'Nine.'

'Where are you from?'

'London, and you?'

'Amsterdam.'

I felt more at ease now. I thought I had detected a glint of recognition in his eyes when we had first shaken hands, but I now dismissed the idea. I persuaded myself it had been just an anxious look because we were running late.

When we arrived at the tee, Kevin was waiting, looking agitated, clutching a driver in his right hand and pulling a ball out of his pocket with his other. Rupert came puffing behind us. Kevin and I greeted one another and exchanged names. He was expressionless as he tossed a coin in the air. Rupert shouted heads – it came down tails.

The early exchanges went against us. Rupert was looking red-faced and flustered and I was out of practice and wrestling with the dead man's clubs. At least the borrowed shoes fitted well. By the fifth, we were two down and by the seventh, three down.

Bart and Kevin played solidly. Bart hit some long drives and looked a powerful opponent – as he should, off a three handicap. By the turn, when we halted briefly for cooling drinks, we had stopped the rot and prevented any more lost holes, so the score was unchanged – we were still three holes adrift. We spoke little during the walks between shots and neither of our adversaries offered up anything other than pleasantries about the heat, the condition of the course and the varying skills of the caddies.

The tenth hole at *Phuket Country Club* is a long par five, which curves one hundred and eighty degrees in a huge 'U' shape, left to right, around a large lake. The hole is well over five hundred yards long and the almost circular design means you can reach the green with three good hits by keeping to the cut fairway as it bends around the edges of the water. Bart stepped up to the tee with the steely look of a man who had confidence seeping from every pore of his suntanned body and, instead of aiming his ball straight down the fairway, he lined himself up diagonally with the tee box to shoot directly at right angles to the narrow green, which lay about two hundred and seventy yards away, across the expanse of the lake. The caddies whispered quietly to one another and then fell silent as it became obvious to all of us that Bart had decided to cut the corner by attempting to strike his ball directly over the swathe of water and the guarding palm trees, aiming at the green itself, thereby avoiding the inviting fairway altogether. It was a high risk shot, but as he and Kevin were three up, he must have felt he could go for it – and he was a big hitter. The ball left his club like a scorched rocket and soared into the sky towards the remote flag stick. The caddies gasped as the ball climbed into the blue and then disappeared over the trees close to the green.

'No water – green, *tok* green! On the green, Khun Bart! Good shot!' his young caddie shouted.

'Shit,' I murmured under my breath and then added as sincerely and audibly as I could, 'Great shot, Bart – I didn't think you could make it.'

Bart remained silent, calmly wiping the face of his driver with a towel and taking his plaudits with a face that looked like flint. Kevin and Rupert played next and decided on the conventional route, banging their balls sensibly down the fairway. Then it was my turn.

I knew I could hit a ball two hundred and seventy yards on a good day – with a following wind – but it would mean a terrific strike and the way I was playing, I was not sure it could be done. Then again, we were losing badly; Bart had laid down the gauntlet and I was in no mood to refuse it, even if I ended up looking foolish. I placed my ball on the tee, giving it a little extra height than normal, and turned to face the green. Bart had positioned himself on the tee box, assuming that I would follow the others with a simple fairway shot. As I made my intentions clear and lined up my shot over the lake, he was forced to move. He hurriedly found a new spot to stand on the tee.

Second blood to me, at least.

It is hard to know what generates a memorable golf shot. Some skill comes into it, of course, but when the pressure is on, it's really about focus and will, but not so much that the shot is forced. The recipe is an equal measure of smooth control and violent hostility. I was aware of a hushed silence as I drew the club head back and as soon as it had made contact with the ball at the bottom of its return journey, I knew it was good. My god, it was good! It came clean off the face with the satisfying thwacking sound that only a perfectly-struck ball will make. But would it make it over the lake? The ball cruised into the ether on a perfect arc, directly at the pin. After a few seconds, the caddies shouted again. Their eyesight was better than ours.

'On the green, Khun Mike! Very close to pin, Khun Mike!'

John Betjeman's famous golfing poem rushed into my mind.

> *How straight it flew, how long it flew,*
> *It clear'd the rutty track*
> *And soaring, disappeared from view*
> *Beyond the bunker's back –*
> *A glorious, sailing, bounding drive*
> *That made me glad I was alive.*

I picked up my broken tee and grinned conspiratorially at Rupert. There was a shortcut to the green, over a bridge at the side of the lake. My caddy, glad that she did not have to walk the long way round, strode off, beaming, towards the path leading to the crossing. I followed with Bart and his caddy. The others started their hot march around the side of the lake. Bart and I were alone for the first time since our walk from the clubhouse. He had remained unerringly quiet as my dream shot had speared onto the green and as we walked, he kept his head low and seemed to be deep in his thoughts.

'So what sort of business do you have, Bart?' I asked dispassionately.

'I buy and sell flowers and send them to Europe,' he replied. 'There are a lot of rare, exotic types here, orchids mostly. We can get a good price for them in the flower markets. And you, Mike, what do you do in England?'

I was waiting for this question and had prepared my response.

'I have a family property business in London. My father owns it – I work for him.'

'So one day, you will be rich!' He smiled at me.

'I suppose so.' His answer took me off guard for a moment and made me think of my ailing father. I had not contemplated my inheritance and what would happen when he died.

Would I be rich? Yes, I suppose I would – on paper, at least.

The thought unsettled me. We reached the green in time to watch the others playing their second shots towards us from about three hundred yards. We sat down, side by side, on the grass and waited. My ball had stopped just eight feet from the pin. Bart's was at least twenty-five feet away.

'So, do you enjoy living here?' I ventured. 'Do you have a wife?'

'Yes, life is good. You don't need a wife here – you can have what you want, as long as you have money. No need for a wife in Phuket, unless you are stupid.'

He leered at me in a way that expected me to nod in agreement. But I just thought of Lek and wondered how she had fallen for him. I told myself that although I was losing the day's round of golf, I held most of the shotguns in our ten-year game between poacher and gamekeeper. I knew so much about him and his plans, and was sure that he knew virtually nothing about me. That was the way I liked it, but the sudden, combined thoughts of my declining father's health and Lek's apparent innocence put me on edge.

The others arrived, panting, at the greenside. By this time, they had both played four shots each, so the destiny of the hole rested with Bart and me – and I was nearly twenty feet closer. Bart took a long time studying the line of the putt with his caddy. While they chatted, I looked across the lake and my mind drifted to thoughts of home and it made me feel lonely. The brief elation of my heroic golf shot had now completely disintegrated. My daydream was interrupted by the sound of a soft clunk and then a screech from a caddy. I looked round to see that Bart's ball had dropped into the hole – for a two. An albatross was unheard of – at least in the games that I usually played. I felt a heavy rock plunge into my stomach as I muttered my congratulations. It was my turn now – an eight-foot putt to halve the hole. I waved away my caddy disdainfully. I could see the line of the putt clearly and did not want any interference. The putter felt damp in my hands.

Rupert looked at me intently. 'Dead straight, I think, old man.'

I wished he had kept silent. I was in my own world now, in a kind of surreal trance. The putter struck the back of the ball cleanly and it sped towards the hole. It hit the back of the cup and popped up into the air. As gravity halted its brief ascent, it fell back towards the hole, but instead of being swallowed up by the void, the ball fell softly onto the tightly-cut grass, where it remained, glued, half an inch from the lip. I looked over apologetically at Rupert and he grimaced sympathetically. I had hit the ball far too hard. It was an eagle three, but we had lost another hole. We were now four down with eight to play.

I remember very little about the rest of the round. I played robotically and, apart from a couple of holes won by Rupert, we failed to make any ground. By the sixteenth, the match was over.

Bart and Kevin, who had hardly spoken a word over the last five holes, shook our hands and then Bart announced that he was sorry but they had to go. They had remembered an important meeting and, as we were now so close to the clubhouse, he hoped we would not mind if we played the last three holes alone. It was all very cordial, but I sensed something in Bart's behaviour that worried me further. Had he recollected me after all? Had he seen through my improvised story and the half-baked deceptions? Did he already know more about me than I had thought? And most ominously, I started to wonder if it was Lek who had, all along, been misleading me. We said our goodbyes and watched them tramp back towards the clubhouse.

'That's a bloody shame,' said Rupert. 'And just as we were getting on so well!'

CHAPTER NINE

Back at the hotel, there was a message waiting for me from Colonel Surachai. He wanted me to return his call as soon as possible. It was three o'clock on a Sunday afternoon and such requests were rare. Something important must have happened. I went to my room and dialled the number; it was his home telephone. He picked up the receiver almost immediately.

'Khun Mike, have you spoken with Khun Lek today?' he asked earnestly. I replied that I had talked to her the previous day, but not since.

'Oh, I see.' He sounded dismayed. 'Well, she has come to Bangkok. We think to meet her brother. Maybe he has a new message for her. Did she tell you about it yesterday?'

'No, Colonel, not a word, but I have been out of contact for most of the morning; maybe she tried but could not reach me.' I hoped I was right. 'When did she get into Bangkok?' I decided, for simplicity's sake, not to advise him straight away about my unforeseen meeting with our main target that morning.

'She arrived just one hour ago. We picked up a message on the line. I sent one of the surveillance team to the airport. He saw her come through the terminal. We are watching the return flight to see if she goes back to Phuket tonight. The flight leaves at seven o'clock.'

'OK, I'll wait here on this number. If she leaves on that flight, let me know immediately; I'll go up to the airport and try to see her when she arrives.' I put the phone down and lay back pensively on the bed. Time for some sleep. I felt so weary.

Surachai woke me from a deep slumber at six thirty and told

me that Lek was about to board the plane for the return leg. I called reception for a cab and within five minutes I had started the hour-long journey north to Phuket Airport. As long as there were no traffic jams, I'd be there to see her walk through the concourse. Even then, I was not sure what to do, or say, when I saw her. Maybe she did not want me to know that she had been to see her brother. Maybe it would be risky to intervene now. I decided to leave my options open and play it by ear when the time came.

The airport terminal looked deserted when I stepped out of the cab. There was a small café just outside the domestic arrival channel and I found a seat, concealed behind a few stray travellers, ordered a coffee and waited. The flight landed ten minutes early and quickly the passengers started to come through in ones and twos. Lek was the tenth person to walk past the sliding doors onto the main concourse. She appeared to be alone, but I needed to be sure.

I watched her approach the airport taxi desk, where she spoke fleetingly to the supervisor. She handed over some folded baht notes and, in return, received a pink slip and some directions to go outside into the warm evening air. I followed, about fifteen yards behind, and observed quietly as she waited for the cab. She looked calm and unhurried, as if nothing untoward had happened. A taxi pulled up and she handed the slip to the driver. I was just yards behind her now. They exchanged a couple of sentences and then I heard him laughing; she was smiling, too. Then she got into the rear seat.

By the time she had closed the door, I was alongside the cab and quickly grabbed the handle and pressed its button. The door flew open and I leapt in beside her. The taxi driver said nothing and started to drive away, presumably because he thought I was part of his fare. At first, Lek looked horrified, but then, when she recognised me, her face changed swiftly to one of genuine warmth and openness.

'Khun Mike, what are you doing here? Why did you not

answer my call this morning? I worried where you were.'

'I was playing golf. Why did you not leave a message at reception?'

'I rang three times to your room and got no reply,' she said. 'Then I had to rush to airport.' She looked at me quizzically. 'And why are you here now? How did you know I would be here?'

'You were seen in Bangkok by one of the Colonel's men and they called me. Lek, tell me – why did you want to speak to me?'

'My brother, he telephoned me. I had to go to see him today. He gave me a message to give to Bart and Khun Kevin. I am going to take it to him now. It is here. I write it in English so he can read it. Do you want to see it?' She showed me a small piece of paper containing lines of letters and numbers.

'Did Bhang tell you what it means?' I asked, suddenly aware that the taxi driver appeared to be taking a keen interest in our conversation. Before she could reply, I leaned forward. 'Can you stop at the next police station, please,' I called to him. He turned his head and the car swerved dangerously into the middle of the road. He said something loud in Thai, doubtless cursing me. 'He does not speak English. Why do you want to go to police station, Khun Mike?'

'I don't. I just wanted to make sure he couldn't understand us.'

'Oh no!' she laughed. 'He is from Isan – from my hometown, Nong Khai. He cannot speak English, only Isan and Thai. I speak to him in my language.' She paused and knitted her brow. 'Now, do you want to know what my brother said to me?'

I nodded. 'But can we stop first? I'd like to find somewhere quieter to talk. The *Oceanview* in Kamala is just twenty minutes from here. I'll pay him the full fare to Patong and we can get separate cabs when we have finished.'

She spoke to the driver and he made a vague head movement, which apparently meant he understood. The *Oceanview* was very busy when we arrived, its restaurant lights glittering at the water's edge. We managed to find a table away from the most of the congestion. It was Vietnamese buffet night and people were jostling round a huge table groaning with food. Lek fished into her bag and retrieved the note again. It had become crumpled, but the numbers and letters she had written on it were still very clear. She pointed to the markings on the paper.

'This is flight number of Thai Airways flight from Chiang Mai to Bangkok every Wednesday and this is connecting flight from Bangkok to Phuket. You can see it leaves two hours later.'

Against the flight numbers, there were some times written in the twenty-four hour clock system plus some other numbers. She pressed a scarlet fingernail against the scribbles. 'This says, "$2T \times 2 = 4T$," she said. 'It means four tons – it is the weight and this is a figure for money.'

I deciphered the numbers myself: *THB 500,000 X 2 = 1 million – 50,000 = 950,000.*

'But there is no date,' I said.

'No, Khun Kevin has to choose date. My brother can do his business, but only on special flights – only on Wednesdays. Kevin must choose the dates he wants and give him the money and he will do it for him.'

'Did your brother tell you any more about this?' I asked hopefully.

'No more, but I think I understand it OK. It means he can send two shipments for Kevin – from Chiang Mai to Bangkok and then to Phuket. Each one is two tons weight and Bhang says he can do this only on Wednesday. But first, he wants the remainder of the money to be delivered. Kevin already give him 50,000 for expenses; he wants the balance – that is 950,000. And he needs to know the dates – then he will do it.'

'But why is it two shipments? Not just one of four tons?'

'That is easy. These shipments are done without paperwork, so no one knows – not even captain of plane. It is dangerous to put on too many heavy weights without him knowing. So Bhang can do only two tons maximum. Kevin has ordered four tons, so it has to be done two times.'

It certainly made sense – even two tons of un-manifested cargo was pushing things to the limit. 'Any reason why just Wednesday?' I asked.

'Yes – it is quietest day, so plane is lighter. Also my brother's friend is on duty in Chiang Mai on Wednesdays to load plane. Bhang will arrange for another man in Phuket to unload. He will do exchange in Bangkok by himself.'

We discussed the details in as much depth as possible, but little more of interest emerged. Lek told me she would be delivering the message to Bart that evening, but made the point again that it was really for Kevin. She repeated that Bart was hardly involved. Although I knew better, I acquiesced, as I did not want to upset her.

'Look, Lek, there is something I must ask you – do you trust me?'

'Yes, of course. What do you want to know?'

'I know that Bart is not really involved – just Kevin,' I lied, 'but I want you to help me by telling me what Bart says to you. The messages he gets from your brother are a great help, but I need to know more. It will help me to end all this – to catch Kevin and Bhang.'

She looked at me disapprovingly.

'I know it is difficult,' I persevered, 'but if you trust me to protect Bart, you need to help me a little more.'

'What do you need to know?'

'Anything that Bart tells you about his business. If he is travelling or meeting anyone, I need to know.'

She put her hand on her forehead and ran her fingers through the fringe of her hair. 'He is going to England after Christmas, in New Year. And Kevin is going to Australia at the same time. I do not know dates – just that it will be January, I think. Bart says they will be away for two weeks, maybe more.'

'Do you know why they are going away?'

'No, he just said it was for business and when he comes back everything will be OK – and we will go to Amsterdam together.'

We ordered some Vietnamese salad rolls and a couple of drinks from a passing waiter. For once, I decided to have a lime soda and as I sipped on the straw, I thought about Christmas. I would be alone again this year. Maureen and Caroline had decided, once more, to stay in England.

'Lek, will you be sure to tell me when they are going.'

'Yes,' she said simply. 'I will.'

'Good. And next time, if you cannot reach me, leave a message with someone you trust, please. You can call the Colonel or Major Pongpat, if you like. I was worried about you tonight. That's why I came straight out to find you.'

She slid her right hand into the middle of the table and the gold ring on her little finger glinted under the soft lights. Instinctively, I put my hand over hers and squeezed gently. I stared at her.

'It's true, Lek. I missed you today. I was concerned for you.'

She pressed her fingers against mine, but as I tried to look into her face again she gazed away.

'Khun Mike,' she sighed and turned her eyes back in line with mine. A drop of moisture fell onto her cheek from her long eyelashes. 'Will you help me, please? I am so tired of this, I want it to stop. I cannot go on like this. Please, help me.'

CHAPTER TEN

I took the early morning flight back to Bangkok. Wut picked me up and took me straight to my office. After an hour with Gill, going through a raft of dull messages from London, I called Sonny Yorke at the Australian Embassy.

'G'day, matey. Where have you been this weekend? Up to no good, I'll bet!' His cheerful tones, despite the undercurrent of lively sarcasm, always had the ability to raise my spirits.

'Can you meet me at the BNU in about an hour, Sonny? Something has come up which I think will interest you. I think it could be big.'

'An hour? Make it thirty minutes, Micky – I'm on my way!'

I rang Wut to bring the car round, grabbed a few papers and hurried out of the office.

Sonny was already waiting outside Colonel Surachai's office when I reached the BNU. Khun Maew told us that the Colonel would be able to see us in about twenty minutes and asked if we wanted some pad thai – the street food vendor has just arrived and the BNU were ordering their lunch.

'Can we have one prawn and one chicken? Thank you, Khun Maew,' and I gave her forty baht.

'I'll treat you to lunch, Sonny, to show how much I love you.'

'It was never in any doubt, Micky,' he snorted.

As we waited, I explained why I had invited him over for the meeting. I needed his help to get the AFP to put a surveillance team on Kevin Silverstream when he flew to Australia in January. I told him about the imminent drugs shipment destined for the UK and that recent intelligence suggested a strong Australian connection. I wanted to do a joint case with him and offered to share all my intelligence, if he agreed. I crammed in as much information as I could in the limited time available and promised him a proper briefing after we had met Colonel Surachai.

'Are you finished, mate? You haven't stopped for breath in five minutes.'

I blinked back at him. 'Yes, Sonny – sorry, but this is going to be big. I can feel it in my gut.'

'No worries, Micky. You can count on my support – even though you are a Pommy bastard most of the time!'

Surachai arrived and I informed him that Sonny and I were now working on the Vanderpool case together. He seemed pleased. I could tell that he liked Sonny and he readily agreed to share his own intelligence with us both – but true to form, he made the point that our joint cooperation would be restricted, for the time being, to the boundaries of this particular investigation.

'Has anything of interest come over the wiretaps recently, Colonel?'

'Actually, it has,' he said and reached over to pick up a folder of neatly-typed sheets, which he passed to me. 'Khun Maew transcribed this today. It's the conversations over the weekend. You will see that Bart and Kevin have been to Chiang Mai and they plan to go again soon.'

'Yes,' I said. 'I knew that. Is there anything else?'

'Yes – Mr. Rupert Barclay called Bart. We checked – he is the British Honorary Consul in Phuket. They arranged to play golf together. Maybe this is something we need to be careful about, Khun Mike.'

I explained what had happened at the *Phuket Country Club* the day before and Colonel Surachai nearly fell off his chair laughing. Sonny looked a little bemused – he still had a lot of catching up to do, and had not fully understood the implications of my fortuitous but stressful round of golf.

I scanned the transcripts and passed them back to the Colonel. We chatted through the options for about half an hour and I briefed him on the information Lek had given me that Bart and Kevin were planning trips abroad.

'We now have to watch and wait. Christmas is next week – we only have a short time to prepare. Colonel, can you use your intelligence team to search the airline passenger lists for flights for Bart and Kevin?'

He nodded his assent.

'I will arrange for London to put Bart under surveillance when he arrives in Britain and Sonny will do the same for Kevin when he goes to Australia. It is essential that we know who they are meeting. It could make all the difference to the investigation. In the meantime, we must keep the intercepts going. If I could have twice daily updates, it would be really helpful. I plan to base myself in Phuket in the New Year and if you agree, I'll use the BNU sub-office as a base. Is that OK, Colonel?'

'Yes, Khun Mike. I will speak to Major Jirapat. He is in charge in Phuket. He is a good man – you can trust him. And Khun Lek?' Colonel Surachai asked. 'What about Khun Lek?'

I had not had any time to give Sonny the background about my postmistress informant and was reluctant to speak openly about her now. 'The situation is fine there – it's under control. It will help to be close to the source when I am in Phuket.'

'Yes,' he said simply, and then gave me one of those eyebrow-lifting, "I hope you know what you are doing" looks. I understood him completely.

I invited Sonny back to my office and we went through the case in detail. I gave him as much information as he needed about Lek – she was my informant. Sensibly, like a true professional, he did not ask any pointless questions about her. As we chatted, I found some relief at being able to assign part of my burden to a like-minded and likeable soul.

I meant what I had said, but knew there were boundaries to our cooperation. He said nothing; he knew the ropes too. As friends, our collaboration would take us a long way, but we both knew that as intelligence partners, there would be some red lines. I just hoped there would not be too many.

Sonny returned to his embassy to cable a message back to Canberra and I settled down to work through some long-outstanding expense claims. Gill had been strangely quiet while I had been talking to Sonny and now I glimpsed her out of the corner of my eye, hovering next to my desk.

'Mike…,' she said in faltering tones, 'I have some news for you. Your sister rang about an hour ago.'

I stopped my scrawling and looked up. I could see her face clearly now and she looked as if she was going to be sick.

'Are you OK, Gill? You look awful.'

'It's your father – you have to call your sister straight away.'

'Did she say anything?'

'Better you call and speak to her.'

'Gill, please tell me – what did my sister say?'

She gulped and I could see her hand trembling. 'I'm afraid your father died last night. Your sister was so upset – she wants you to call her as soon as possible. You looked so happy when you came in with Sonny; I thought it best to let you have your meeting and speak to you when he had gone.'

I stood up and put my arm around her.

'You did right, Gill, thank you. I'll call her straight away. Look, could you pop down to the canteen and bring me some hot tea.'

'I can make some here, if you like.'

'No, the canteen tea is so much better, don't you think?'

She smiled half-heartedly. I could see tears in her eyes. She understood. She quietly padded down the corridor toward the stairs. I crumpled onto my desk, held my head in my hands and wept.

CHAPTER ELEVEN

London Airport at six o'clock on a foggy, late December morning is a friendless place. I had hurriedly packed a few warm clothes, not really knowing what I was doing. There were no business class seats left on the midnight flight to Heathrow, but Gill had rung Joe West in New Fetter Lane and he agreed to stump up for the last remaining place in first class. I had slept for most of the thirteen-hour journey.

When I called to give Maureen my arrival time, she said she couldn't be there to meet me – it was just too early and she had a host of other things to do. 'Better you get a cab. The Department will pay anyway,' she told me. She was right, of course, but somehow she had missed the point. I would have appreciated a welcoming face at the airport – someone to embrace, someone with whom to shed a tear. Instead, I took a taxi for the thirty-mile trip to Purley and by seven forty-five I was turning the key in my front door. It was barely light.

The dog came rattling down the stairs to greet me and I made a big fuss of him. He jumped and jiggled and sniffed and wagged his tail like an unstable windmill. At least someone was pleased to see me. I stood in the hall amongst the Christmas decorations with my bulging bags, listening for any other movement in the house. Evidently, everyone else was still sleeping, so I wandered into the kitchen, put the kettle on and gave the dog a biscuit.

I expected the next few days to be the worst of my life but, in fact, they were not. I had lost my father without saying goodbye to him and without ever really saying that I loved him. But despite the grief, a surprising inner calm enveloped me like a goose down quilt and enabled me to get through the funeral, the desperate meetings with long-lost relatives and, of course, Christmas itself. I kept my private sorrows to myself; I wanted it that way. The funeral took place two days after Boxing Day and was well-attended. My father had been a much-liked man. My mother came up from her pink cottage on the Isle of Wight and cried as if she had lost a baby. I did not cry. I had done my weeping unaided and alone, and to the assembled relations I must have appeared like an impassive chalk cliff.

Maureen did her best to be attentive and sensitive, but despite her efforts, I began to realise that the gulf between us was just too wide. It was easy to delude myself that the relationship still had substance from six thousand miles away, but here, close at hand, the cracks were all too evident. I could see that she had made a life for herself without me and was happy in it – the round of coffee mornings and trips to *Debenhams* were enough to satisfy her. It was pretty obvious that she no longer needed me to make her life a contented one – my salary was supporting her and that's where it ended.

A few days after our muted New Year's celebrations, I announced that I planned to fly back to Thailand soon. I still had a lot of unfinished business, I explained. Maureen was fiddling with the controls of the TV and video recorder when I broached the subject, trying to replay the *Morecombe & Wise Christmas Show*. She hardly looked up.

'What about your birthday tomorrow? Will you be here for that?'

I sensed a degree of suppressed venom in her voice. I had completely forgotten that I would be starting my forty-ninth year the following day. I said quickly, 'Yes, of course. I plan to leave the day after.' The silence that followed hung in the air like a huge, inflatable elephant.

The festive streamers seemed to droop around the hallway

cornices as the car came to take me to the airport, two days later. I had made farewell calls to my sister and mother and kissed Maureen and Caroline as they rubbed their shoulders, shivering on the steps of the front porch. Our embraces felt like a performance – a dull, domestic ritual.

As the taxi rounded the corner onto the Brighton Road, I felt a huge sense of relief. I had been in England for just ten days and was already desperate to take back charge of my life. The unfinished business I had been agonising over for so long was within my grasp – all mine to control, if I dared.

In stark contrast to the outward journey, I immersed myself in the first class flight service on my way back to Bangkok, taking full advantage of every scrap of sustenance and glassful of beverage the cabin staff generously offered. I had called Joe West a couple of days earlier to thank him for authorising the costs. He sounded his normal, stuffy self and mumbled a few words of embarrassed condolence. 'There is no need to come into the office,' he explained. 'I know you have a lot on your plate and we are all waiting anxiously for news about your new investigation – so the best place for you is at your desk. Just call me when you are back in harness.'

It cheered me to find that Wut was waiting for me and, despite a mounting sensation of fatigue, I asked him to drive me straight to the BNU. It was just eight a.m. and the air was pleasant as we pulled up outside. I could see that Colonel Surachai's car was already parked in its reserved place. He greeted me without any fuss and handed me the latest file of telephone transcripts and assorted reports that had accumulated over the last ten days.

'Khun Mike, better if you read these first – then we can talk.'

As I sat down to read the bundle of documents, Khun Maew came in with some coffee and a glossy Danish pastry. 'So sorry about your father,' she said softly and I could see she was genuinely touched.

The paperwork told me that Bart and Kevin had been

busy while I had been away and had not allowed Christmas to interfere with their planning. The telephone transcripts were full of innuendo and guarded conversations and sometimes it was difficult to understand their full meaning. It helped that I knew already that they were planning a shipment of drugs and with this as context, the task became easier. The subject of orchids surfaced from time to time and it was a simple assumption to conclude that this was code for something else. Lek featured in the transcripts, too – usually telling Bart when she would be back from work and asking if she could bring anything for him. I asked Khun Maew to get me some of the original tapes so I could listen first-hand and analyse them myself.

After a few short conversations, I found that I was as fascinated with their small talk as I was with the main business at hand. I knew I was eavesdropping on irrelevant domestic chatter and while I felt some tinges of discomfort, I convinced myself that it was important to the case and the job had to be done. The mere sound of Lek's voice, however, gave me twinges of melancholy and I found myself replaying the tapes over and over again just to hear her speak.

Amongst the transcripts there were two surveillance reports. Using a clue from the wiretap, the BNU had followed Bart and Kevin one morning to the *Shangri La* hotel, where they had met a thickset man sporting a dark ponytail, in the coffee shop. The surveillance team identified him as Christopher James Manton, a forty-five year old Australian. He was from the Sydney suburb of Rushcutters Bay and had been staying at the *Shangri La* for the last two days. Later that afternoon, the BNU followed Manton to a specialist marine shop near the port, where he purchased five walkie-talkie radios, a portable radio base station, a box of batteries and two maritime maps covering an area off the east coast of Phuket, in Phang Nga Bay. The reports were dated the day before and my heartbeat accelerated as I read them. It was all beginning to come together.

'Have you discussed any of this with Khun Sonny, yet?' I

asked Colonel Surachai.

'I rang him just now while you were reading the files – he is on his way here. I thought it would be good if we all had a meeting.'

'Is this Australian man, Manton, still in the hotel? I asked.

'No, he checked out early this morning. We are watching him at the airport now. There is a flight to Jakarta at eleven and he is on the passenger list.'

'Great work, Colonel – your boys have done you proud. I think this is very important information indeed.'

'And this has just come in, Khun Mike.' He handed me a sheet of formatted transcript paper timed today at nine thirty a.m. – just twenty minutes previously. There were only seven lines on it. Bart had called Lek at her office at the airport. The typed message read:

Male voice (T1): Hi, teelak. Look, I have to go north with Kev today. I'll be away about two days. Sorry it's so sudden. I'll see you when I get back.
Female voice (KL): No worries, Bart. I will wait for your call. Take care, teelak.
Male voice (T1): OK, bye. I have to go – Kevin is waiting.
Female voice (KL): Bye, teelak.

The repeated use of the word *teelak* grated. It made me think again about Lek's relationship with Bart and my increasing anguish about how things might turn out in the end. I buried the lingering forebodings and looked at Surachai. 'They must be going back to Chiang Mai. Can we check the flights?'

'Already checking, Khun Mike,' he replied.

At that moment, Sonny strolled in, looking a little bloated and more unkempt than usual.

He must have really enjoyed his New Year celebrations!

'Great to see you, matey. Sorry about your Dad and all that. Hope everything is good now.'

'Yes, fine. Look, you need to read these reports quickly.' I thrust the two surveillance reports at him and the latest transcript that I had just been given.

His reaction was swift. 'Blimey, mate – we could be in business. I'll get the verifications done straight away. Can I use your phone, Colonel?' And with that he shunted off to a vacant desk and rang his office. When he was finished, Khun Maew came over to us.

'Khun Bart and Khun Kevin are both on the four o'clock Thai Airways flight from Bangkok to Chiang Mai,' she said. 'They arrive in Bangkok from Phuket just after two o'clock.'

I looked at Sonny and he read my thoughts.

'Khun Maew, I think there is an earlier flight up to Chiang Mai – a one fifteen, I recall. We have time to make it, if you can find a way to get us both a seat.'

'I can do that for you – no problem. I will speak to my friend at the airport and let you know in five minutes.'

After a hasty exchange with Sonny, I told Colonel Surachai that we planned only to meet the flight in Chiang Mai – no more – just so we could see who the two men encountered. He knew I was being untruthful and that our surveillance would almost certainly go beyond that. He looked serious for a few seconds, as if in deep contemplation, and then asked if we wanted him to arrange some support from the Chiang Mai police. He already knew what my answer would be. When I declined graciously, he did not act surprised, and judging by the sideways look in his eye, it was clear he appreciated that such an approach might compromise the situation. He could not trust his counterparts in Chiang Mai, either.

'OK,' he said reluctantly. 'You are on your own – but please keep me fully informed, Khun Mike. Can you ring me tonight at my home to tell me any news?'

I was grateful for his trust and for his good sense. He knew better than me that involving the locals in Chiang Mai posed some significant operational risks. He was too proud to admit it openly, but he knew it all the same, and his practical approach was hugely welcome. I just hoped he would keep his word.

I hastily rearranged the London luggage that still sat in the back of the official car and made up an overnight bag that would support Sonny and me for a day, or until we could find some more supplies.

Sonny rang his office again and after a brief conversation put the phone down with a broad grin. Our new suspect, Christopher Manton, had a conviction for cannabis possession in 1980. He was also the part-owner of a sixty-foot ketch called *Guiding Lights*, which operated from Darwin in northern Australia. The boat had not been seen for over three weeks and had last signed out to Bali, Indonesia. We were beginning to put the pieces together. Manton's flight to Jakarta and his boat's last known destination *must* be connected. The implications were obvious. The owner and his vessel were going to be reunited – this was going to be a yacht smuggle and we high-fived each other in exuberant anticipation. I rang Gill to let her know my movements. And just before we left the BNU, I rang Lek, as well. I needed to know whether she would volunteer any information about Bart's new travel plans.

'Oh, it's you, Khun Mike.' She sounded happy. 'Are you back in Bangkok now?'

'Yes – everything is fine. Has anything happened while I have been away?'

'No, nothing. It's been very busy with Christmas.'

The phone went quiet and my heart sank, my incipient doubts about her hardening with every silent second. And then she said brightly, 'But Bart called me this morning – he is going to the north today with Kevin. You said you want me to tell you if he is travelling. I think he is going to Chiang Mai.' She stopped talking and I could find no words to respond. 'Khun Mike can you hear me?'

'Yes, Lek… that's great,' I stuttered. 'I'll call you later. I'll try to come down to Phuket soon. I'll let you know.'

'Is everything OK, Khun Mike? You sound strange.'

'Yes, everything is perfect now, Lek. Everything is just perfect.'

CHAPTER TWELVE

Chiang Mai is the largest and most culturally significant city in northern Thailand, and one of the most beautiful in the country. With over three hundred temples, an ancient history and rolling countryside, its climate is fresher than the steamy cities of the south. During the winter months, there is an English summer's day feel about the place. Strawberries are cultivated and the region is famous for its food and the welcome it gives to visitors.

But Chiang Mai has a darker side. Its proximity to the eastern borders of Burma, with its warlord-controlled mountainous terrain, where effective law enforcement is nigh on impossible, has meant that over the years, the region had developed into an important transit point for the illegal traffic in contraband. By the mid-70s, the production and smuggling of both heroin and cannabis had become a major breadwinner for many of its indigenous frontiers people. Sonny and I had both visited the border region before on official trips, so we knew the basics: the difficult geography and jungle topography, the structure of the prominent local tribes, the challenging political backdrop and the UN estimates for opium production. But our official contacts there were untested and, for the most part, distrusted.

On the flight up, we did a little planning. We agreed that we would take as few surveillance risks as possible and spend only as much time in the area as was absolutely necessary. We were confident that the strands of the investigation were tightening and the last thing we needed was to show our hand. Sonny asked about my unexpected encounter with Bart on the golf course, and although the details amused him enormously, the story further

FRANK HURST

confirmed that we needed to take care. We agreed that if any close surveillance was required, Sonny would do it. They would not recognise him.

'Always happy to be at the front of the charge, Micky. Don't fret, mate – you can hang back and let the Aussies do all the dangerous work; just like Gallipoli.'

At Chiang Mai Airport, we hired a car and I parked it at a point where I could see the exit clearly. We had some time, so we grabbed something to eat and waited for the Tannoy to call the arrival of the four o'clock flight from Bangkok – it was due down at twenty past five. Severe fatigue and jet lag had set in now and I was regretting my decision not to sleep on the London flight. The six glasses of *Gevrey-Chambertin* that I had guzzled may have had something to do with my general lethargy, too – not to mention the scotch and sodas that had preceded them.

We had no proper means of communicating with one another and wild hand signals would be too showy, so we decided to keep things simple. Sonny would carry our overnight bag as cover and find a discreet place to wait inside the terminal. He would follow Bart and Kevin, from a distance, when they appeared on the concourse and then jump into our hire car to tail them away. I gave him their descriptions. Hopefully, there would be only a few *farangs* on the aircraft, so Sonny was confident he would identify them. We calculated that they would either rent a car, grab a taxi or be met. The last option was the preferred one for us, as it would give us an early clue who they were contacting.

At five thirty, Bart and Kevin sauntered casually out of the airport building. Bart was sporting a pair of reflecting sunglasses that glinted blue under the sun. He wore white, tight-fitting, cotton trousers, a dark leather belt and a black silk shirt. On his head was a large, cream Panama hat.

Very Miami Vice. What a prat!

My dislike of him intensified – it was getting personal.

Kevin lagged a few yards behind, pulling a small bag. It looked like he was wearing the same outfit as on the golf course two weeks previously – green shorts and a yellow T-shirt. There was no mistaking who the boss was between these two. Despite the crush of cars, taxis and people milling around the entrance, I had found a good spot to watch them and was relieved when I saw Sonny meandering along behind, looking for all the world like a lost tourist on his first trip abroad. The two men halted on the pavement and panned their eyes down the stream of arriving and departing vehicles. Clearly, they were expecting to be met.

My passenger door opened and Sonny chucked the bag in the back and stepped in, perspiring from his brisk walk to the car. 'Piece of cake, matey. Your guy dresses well, doesn't he?' he chuckled.

No one came. The other passengers dispersed in cars and taxis or went to the bus stand on the other side of the road. Bart and Kevin looked increasingly isolated as they stood in the baking sun. Their only bag was the one Kevin was dragging. Bart looked at his watch.

'It's a *Patek Philippe*,' Sonny announced. 'I got a good view of it as he came through. And an expensive, gold one, at that.'

Then things started to happen.

'They're on the move, Sonny.' We watched as the two walked towards the hire car office in front of the taxi rank. Bart approached the desk and started to speak to the young man behind the counter. At that moment, a black Mercedes sedan with darkened windows pulled up alongside them and I saw Kevin tugging at Bart's silk shirt. A man got out of the driver's seat, wearing a dark grey-brown uniform with gold shoulder straps and gleaming buttons. He looked like a soldier. He beckoned the two towards the rear of the car and as we watched, a gloved hand extended through the open car window from the back seat. Only the sleeve showed and it was the same grey-brown colour. Bart shook the proffered hand and the rear door opened. He stepped in and the uniformed driver held the front door open for Kevin. I strained to read the car's number plate. I could just make out that there were a couple of black Thai letters and four black numbers against a blue background.

'Sonny, while they are fussing around, any chance you can get close enough to read the plate?'

'I'm on it, Mike.' And in a flash, he was out of the car and walking unobtrusively towards the Mercedes. Kevin had just settled into the front passenger seat and the driver was walking round the bonnet to regain his position behind the wheel. The car started then began to pull away. I fired up the engine of the hire car. As they exited the ramp, I picked Sonny up from the pavement.

'Any luck?' I barked unnecessarily.

'Yes, Micky – I think I've got it, but there were some Thai squiggles. I'll write them down on my hand, but they may not be accurate. I have the numbers – 6769 – for sure.'

We followed them onto the airport approach road, where they headed north at a sedate pace. I allowed a couple of cars to get between us, knowing that if the Mercedes made any quick manoeuvres, we would have very little chance of tracking them, but every minute the car drove north gave us a better idea about their destination. So, I was content to hang back and take things steadily. The sedan took the ring road around the city and came off at a sign for Doi Saket on route 118. It continued to head north and soon we started picking up signs for Wiang Pa Po and Chiang Rai.

We had been following for thirty-five minutes and had covered twenty-five kilometres. Sonny had found a very basic tourist road map in the glove compartment of the car and was doing his best to read it.

'This is the road to Chiang Rai and the northern border.

Trouble is, it's nearly another two hundred kilometres. What do you reckon, Micky? Do we stick with it?'

Just as he spoke, the Mercedes started to slow and, without indicating, it pulled into a petrol filling station.

'I'm going to follow them in, Sonny, but I'll keep as far back as I can.'

Surprisingly, the car did not stop at a petrol pump. Instead, it halted just outside the forecourt shop. Kevin went in; Sonny followed. Four minutes later, Kevin re-emerged, holding bottles of water and as the Mercedes door opened, Sonny brushed past, just a few feet away, also carrying water. I was thankful for that, as I was dehydrated and my throat was as dry as a piece of emery paper. The black saloon pulled away again and resumed its journey north. A mosquito dive-bombed into the foot well of the car. I waggled my legs and flicked my hands over my feet – but it disappeared around my ankles.

'Bingo, Mike!' Sonny said as he got back in alongside me, pushing a freezing bottle into my groin. 'They are going to Mae Sae – Kevin bought a map and asked the man in the shop to point it out for him. Evidently, he was worried how long the trip was taking, too.'

I glugged down the refreshing liquid.

'And another thing – the guy in the back looks like a fucking general or something. He appears to be seriously important – at least, his uniform looks the part!'

Damn!

The mosquito had clearly found its target. My skin began to itch and I leant down for a scratch. My fingernails drew blood and I thought of Bart.

'I think we'll call it quits for the day, Sonny. We have pushed our luck enough. What do you say we find ourselves a proper drink?'

'Micky, I always said you were a decent bloke – even for a Pom.'

Back in Bangkok, I spent the next two weeks writing up reports for London and going through the twice daily transcripts from the BNU, which Wut brought me each morning and evening. Sonny and I held regular update and intelligence-sharing meetings, alternating the venues between our offices. Behind closed doors, in Colonel Surachai's office, I went through the details of the Chiang Mai surveillance and the possible links to the military. I gave Surachai the car registration number and descriptions to check. It was highly sensitive stuff, but I felt I could trust the Colonel. I knew the police had a fractious relationship with the Thai Army and Surachai was no exception. I had heard him many times moaning about interference and corruption within the armed forces. He gave me a stern look when he heard the news. He asked me to sit down, while he made a call to an anonymous recipient. Speaking in low tones, in his own language, with his hands wrapped around the receiver, he looked distinctly troubled. Within five minutes, he confirmed to me that the black Mercedes was indeed a military vehicle, assigned to a Thai Army major-general. He would give me no names and no more information, but agreed to hold off any action until our case had been made.

The scenario was well-trodden and the implications were obvious. Corrupt officers in the Thai Army at the Burmese border had been organising safe passage for shipments of drugs for many years. This was a well-known piece of intelligence, so notorious in fact that it was almost a cliché. But it was knowledge that the law-abiding authorities felt powerless to exploit effectively. The hierarchy was just too well-connected and the backhanders too lucrative.

Surachai promised to investigate the matter, as best he could, after we had made our own arrests. Until then, we agreed to bury the information. I was content with the arrangement. There was no sense in shaking the tree now, and anyway, all I needed was confirmation that Bart was moving ever closer to organising his shipment and this connection proved the point. We could deal with the other issue later.

Joe West called me a couple of times and we discussed the case on the scramble phone. He told me that he had his best surveillance team waiting for Bart's arrival in Britain. We were both frustrated; we had still had no clue as to his arrival date. The only intelligence we possessed that the trip was imminent was my single conversation with Lek – that's all we had to go on. The wiretaps told us nothing and the passenger manifests were equally devoid of any useful information. I called Lek from time to time, but she told me nothing that I did not already know. She was working; Bart and Kevin were in Phuket; everything had gone quiet. All we could do was wait.

Joe sanctioned my move down to Phuket so I could be closer to the action when things became more critical. Gill had rented an inconspicuous, serviced apartment for me in Kalim, a quiet, beachfront neighbourhood, a few miles north of Patong.

During the lull, John Morris and I had time to catch up. Although he had no direct involvement in the case, I shared some of the details with him. As an ex-colleague, I knew I could trust him and he would understand the dynamics of the investigation as it unfolded. It was useful to have a sounding board and there was no way I was going to trust Jim Gallow and his Station guys. John seemed particularly interested in my relationship with Lek and asked a few direct questions about the liaison, which made me slightly defensive and uncomfortable.

'This bird – your informant – what is she like, Mike?'

'Well,' I hesitated, 'she's a cracking informant, and I am sure she holds the key to the case.'

'Yes, Mike – but what is she *like*?' he repeated.

I stalled again. 'Like? As I said, John, she has been A1 up to now. I have been able to corroborate everything she has told me. I don't think I could finish the case without her input. She is that important.'

'Mike, look at me!' He flourished his hands, like a conjurer offering up his sleeves. 'You fancy her, don't you?' he said.

I exhaled. 'She is a looker, I must admit, but you know I can't mix business with pleasure. The whole thing would go to rat shit.'

'Christ, you *do* fancy her – that look in your eyes! You can't fool me; I have known you too long.'

'OK. I admit that I have become quite fond of her. This guy, Bart, is just towing her along to suit himself, and her brother is another complete bastard. I would like to help her, if I could. Poor girl is lost in this whole mess and can't find a way out.'

John looked at me gravely. 'You know you can't get involved – business is business. What would the blokes back home think if they knew you had gone soft on one of your snouts? They would laugh you out of court.'

'I know, John. I just have to get through the next few weeks and try not to get in too deep with her. With a bit of luck, the case will be knocked in a month or so.' Then I added, 'John, please don't breathe a word of this to anyone – I am dancing on coals as it is. Trust me; I can manage this.'

He could see that I was feeling distraught.

'Of course, I won't say a thing.' He put his hand on my shoulder. 'But if you need someone to talk to – to give you some untainted advice – call me. Anytime. Call me and I'll come over.'

By the beginning of February, Sonny and I were beginning to get nervous. We had two surveillance teams on standby in London and Sydney and no new intelligence. And worse, I was desperate to see Lek. I missed her dreadfully. In my heart, I knew she would not be able to add anything useful, but the more my churning emotions took hold, the more I convinced myself that an assignation with her was essential.

'Sonny, I am fed up with this!' I exclaimed at one of our fruitless case meetings. 'I am going down to Phuket. I'll see if a change of scene can make a difference. And I'll have a chance to meet the informant again. It could be useful to dig a little deeper, in case she has something that might help.'

With Sonny, I always tried to avoid using Lek's name. I was anxious to present the relationship as impersonally and professionally as I could, although sometimes I suspected he had guessed that I had an ever-growing, hidden agenda. Thankfully, he said nothing, and his silence seemed to confirm that he wanted to keep out of this part of the operation altogether, in case it all went belly-up. The last thing he needed was to be tainted by an improper informant/handler relationship.

'OK, matey, seems a good plan. I'll hold the reins here. Go down and enjoy yourself and leave me with the BNU and Surachai!' I was grateful for his discretion. He was turning into a true friend.

I called Lek at her office as soon as I had unpacked my bags. The apartment Gill had found for me was tiny. It had two bedrooms, but the second had barely enough space for a single bed. There was a poky cooking area and small, open terrace, which compensated for the cramped conditions by providing a wonderful view over the bay of Patong and the palm trees that fringed its beaches.

'Can I see you after work, Lek? It would be good to catch up – the case is going too slowly for my liking.'

She agreed, sounding a little reluctant, and gave an excuse that it would have to be brief, as she was having dinner later with Bart. We met just after six o'clock at the *Ocean View*. I had already settled into my second scotch by the time she arrived. I watched her wistfully as she parked her car and skipped up the steps into the restaurant. This time she was in uniform, and she looked fabulous. She gave me a striking smile as soon as she spied me, and for a moment I thought she was going to embrace me, but she just touched my arm lightly as she sat down opposite. We chatted easily for about five minutes. It was wonderful to see her again – she looked as radiant as a full moon on a stellar night. She had nothing official to report, however, and was anxious not to be late for her dinner with Bart. I gave her my new contact number and felt a growing sense of loss as the meeting sped to its inevitable conclusion.

'I'll call you in a couple of days. Let's see if we can have lunch or something,' she shouted out as she hurried away to her car.

I ordered some Thai green curry and another whisky.

CHAPTER THIRTEEN

Lek rang me three days later. It was a little before nine in the morning and she had just arrived at her desk. 'Khun Mike, I have some news for you.'

I straightened my back and waited.

'Bart has packed his bags – he is going to London today. And Kevin is going to Australia, like I said before. They are leaving the house at about ten this morning. Bart has said goodbye to me already.'

I couldn't understand it. We had been checking the Bangkok flights to Heathrow and Gatwick for the last six weeks and had picked up nothing. 'Are you sure, Lek? It's today?'

'Yes, for sure. He has big suitcase. He says he will be away for two weeks, maybe more.'

'OK. Look, I'll call you tonight, all right?'

'Yes, please call me, Khun Mike.'

'And, thank you, Lek – you're a star!'

I rang the embassy, but Gill had not arrived yet. I called Khun Maew – she always started early – and asked her to check the London and Sydney flights again. I dragged a clean shirt over my shoulders, hauled on the nearest pair of trousers and within fifty minutes, I was at the airport. The departure board gave me no real clues, as there were no direct flights to Europe or Australia from Phuket. All the aircraft routed via Bangkok. There was a noon flight to Don Muang and I determined that this was probably the flight Bart and Kevin were going to take. I found a pay phone and called the BNU. Maew told me that all the London and Sydney flights were negative – we still had no trace of either of them. I was perplexed.

The departure hall at Phuket Airport is above arrivals, on the second floor. The third floor is reserved for airline offices, which are situated in a gallery around an open walkway. Risking exposure to Bart or Kevin by lurking behind them in the queue was not an option, so I took the lift to the third floor. From this elevated vantage point, it was possible to observe, reasonably covertly, the whole expanse of the check-in area. There was nowhere to sit, so I hung around the railings, watching the long queues of passengers from on high. I paid particular attention to the Bangkok check-in desks and waited.

An eternal hour passed and then I saw them. Bart was instantly recognisable, as he approached the Thai Airways first class counter, in a stylish, black suit and an expensive-looking, pale pink, open-necked shirt. Kevin, as usual, was skulking behind him. They checked in separately. Both had large, hard-sided, black suitcases and after brief exchanges with the elegant staff, they were walking together towards the airside immigration counters. I lost sight of them as they rounded a corner and cursed under my breath in frustration. I was none the wiser – I *still* did not know their final destinations. As I weighed up the risks of approaching the airline to ask for the information, I heard a soft voice calling my name. It was Lek, standing just three feet away. I froze, as much in pleasure as in surprise.

'I think I have what you need,' she said simply. She must have been watching me, unobserved, for many minutes. She gave me a single page of a Thai Airways computerised printout. It was full of abbreviations and airline jargon which revealed dates, flight numbers, times, weights, classes of travel and the airport codes for origin and destination. Against the name Bartholomew Vanderpool, it read, "CDG".

'Charles de Gaulle – Paris!' I hissed. 'Bloody Paris!'

'And Khun Kevin is going to Jakarta after Bangkok – see.' She pointed out the letters "CGK" – Soekarno-Hatta International.

I put my hands onto her pretty shoulders. 'Thank you, Lek. This is great. I could kiss you!'

She looked coy and offered up a cheek. I leant forward and held her face in my hands – the scent of her perfume was overwhelming and her skin felt smooth and warm. As I kissed her, my fingers enfolded her neck and I felt her body give way slightly as she inclined towards me. It was as if she wanted to linger in the embrace. I stood back slowly and looked at her, my hand loitering briefly on her shoulders.

'Thank you,Lek. I can't say how much this helps.'

She flushed slightly and said, 'Will you call me tonight? We can have dinner, if you like. I am free.'

'Yes, I will call you,' I said and backed away deliberately. I turned and hurried down the steps towards the exit.

I rang my London desk officer shortly after I got back to the apartment. I had a portable encrypted phone for urgent, confidential calls. It was nearly seven a.m. in New Fetter Lane and I hoped Bill would be in the office. He had to work to my timings, as best he could, which meant arriving early, but it allowed him the luxury of an occasional early pop, as events seven hours ahead of him started to slow.

To my relief, he was already at his work and we examined the options. The Paris to London connection caused us some problems. If Bart's final destination was indeed London, he was doing his best to cover his tracks and the travel choices at his disposal for the leg from Charles de Gaulle were almost endless. We would have to cover a host of airports, as well as the Channel ports – and obtaining accurate passenger manifests from Channel ferry companies was always problematic. Bart could just turn up and walk on. I had little inclination to seek any assistance from France. They always seemed to overcomplicate things. They had a host of competing agencies; the police, customs, gendarmerie and intelligence services were always squabbling and whichever one we chose to help us would inevitably try to find a French angle to justify them taking control of the case. So, the French were dismissed as allies almost immediately.

If Bart was really clever, he would cross the border into Belgium or Holland and find a way into Britain from there. If he did that, it would be very difficult for us. We would not be able to post viable surveillance teams at all the potential border crossings. But my gut feeling, knowing Bart better than any of my colleagues, was that he would not go to all the trouble – he would simply take a connecting flight to one of London's airports, probably one of the smaller ones – Stanstead or Luton.

We agreed to notify all port and airport intelligence teams anyway… and wait. If we had enough notice, we might be able to get a full team out to meet him. If not, we would have to think again. It would be another fifteen hours before Bart arrived in Paris, so we had time to tee things up, at least. I called Sonny and left the problem of Kevin with him. His only option was to notify the AFP's Jakarta office and ask Canberra to monitor all the flights from Indonesia.

At about five o'clock, I decided to ring Lek. I had been thinking about her for most of the day and wondering whether dinner that evening would be such a good idea, after all. She had said she was keen to meet me and I certainly wanted to see her, but my longing to be with her again had become almost unbearable and I knew that my motives were becoming seriously blurred. She was very upbeat and talkative when I called and asked where my new apartment was. The reasons why I should have prevaricated were endless, but I blurted out my address almost immediately. She suggested she came round at eight and we could find somewhere local to eat. It did not take much for me to give her my submissive agreement. I felt tired again – a helpless, beached dolphin waiting for a kind soul to drag it back into the sea.

Despite my misgivings, I did my best to remain calm. I slept a couple of hours, showered, shaved and put on a half-decent shirt. I found the rest of my aftershave in the bottom of my wash bag and doused my neck. For no apparent reason, I tidied the bed and plumped up the pillows. The apartment was on the fourth floor of a small block serviced by a tiny lift. At five to eight, I took the lift down to the ground floor and waited. It seemed more respectable somehow, to meet her outside rather than in the doorway of what was, in effect, my bedroom. I did not have to wait long. When she appeared, she was wearing the same silk blouse that she had worn when I had seen her for the first time in the lobby of the *President*. As before, the gold Buddha pendant hung provocatively from a chain around her slender neck. There was one difference, however – the pair of cream slacks had been replaced by a slim-fitting, black, knee-length, cotton skirt. I shook her hand awkwardly and mumbled a few words of cheerful greeting. We walked, side by side, to my hire car.

'How did you get here tonight?' I asked nonchalantly.

'I took a taxi,' she replied and seized hold of my arm as she spoke. 'Do you want to drive tonight?' she asked. 'The rain has made everything cool and it feels so lovely now. I know small place to eat, very close – we can walk.' There must have been a deluge while I slept.

'Lead the way, Lek. You are in charge tonight!' It was indeed a gorgeous evening. A fragrant breeze blew in gently from the west and walking was no effort. Lek steered me to a tiny, open-air restaurant on the fringes of the ocean. *Unpretentious* would have been a kind description. It did not have a name, but there was a small bar and some simple tables and wooden chairs, arranged under a rustic palm leaf roof at the water's edge. It was no more than a cute, bamboo shack really, but thoroughly enchanting, all the same.

We removed our shoes and wiggled our toes into the sand. I tried to start a conversation about the investigation, but it quickly fizzled out. There was nothing to discuss. Bart and Kevin were away; she had heard nothing from her brother for nearly a month. It was the nth week in my long waiting game. No doubt, I would learn something from London in the morning, but for now, I just wanted to enjoy the food, the sky and her company. She talked about taking a trip to Nong Khai. She missed her son and her father and when she asked me how I felt about my own father's death, my reply seemed to make her all the more anxious to go back home as soon as she could. I spoke very little and listened. Her English had improved significantly over the last four months and I complimented her for it.

'It is you – you helped me. I speak better because I met you!'

'*Bhag wan!*' I exclaimed jokingly. It was a Thai expression for a flatterer. Directly translated, it means "sweet mouth".

She giggled back, 'Not *bhag wan* – true!'

I gazed at her and watched her lips purse, then break into another glorious smile.

How appropriate – bhag wan.

'Can I ask you another personal question, Lek?' I said as the remnants of the rice and fish were carried away.

'Of course – you can ask me anything.'

'What would you say if I told you that I had become very fond of you and that our meetings are much more to me than just this wretched work?'

'I would say I believed you. In fact, I am feeling the same about you.' Her reply stopped me in my tracks for a few seconds.

Did she really say that?

'You know I am married.'

'Yes, you told me a long time ago – but you never talk about your wife. I think maybe you do not love her anymore.' Lek could still surprise me with her candour.

'You have a boyfriend,' I said, trying to match her directness.

'Yes.' She paused as if she wanted to say something more.

I interrupted her train of thought with another question. 'What do you think of me, Lek? Do you think I am a good man?'

She studied me, then, in a very quiet voice, she said, 'Yes, you are a good man, for sure. But you are also a lonely man.' She reached out and gently caressed my forearm. 'I think you are scared of something, sometimes. I'm not sure what. But I like you – you make me laugh and I feel safe when I am with you.'

'I make you feel safe?'

'Yes, I know I am protected when I am with you. It's as if no one can hurt me anymore.'

Those words had never been said to me before, not in all my nearly fifty years of gasping for air. It rendered me temporarily speechless.

Then, in a sudden rush of emotion, 'Would you come back to my room tonight, Lek? It would make me very happy, if you did.'

She tightened her grip on my hand and leant towards me. I could feel her soft breath on my cheek. 'If you want me to come with you, I will,' she whispered.

The lift was out of order when we returned to the apartment, so we had to walk up the four flights of stairs. I fumbled with the damn lock and as the door gave way suddenly, we fell into the tiny hall. Once inside, she put her arm around my waist and I was conscious that my shirt was moist with the unplanned, uphill exercise. I groped unsuccessfully to find the light switch and turned to face her; we were standing in the gloom, the only light was from the half-open door. She raised her head and offered up her wonderful face. As I kissed her full lips, her hands travelled up my back to my shoulder blades. She gently pulled me closer still.

'Let me find the AC – or we will boil.' I banged the front door shut.

I took her hand and led her into the bedroom. The cooling rush of the AC started to permeate the room as we tumbled onto the bed. I made a vain effort to pull off my shirt, trying to lock my lips on hers at the same time. Her hands went to my face and held it as I kissed her again. We released the embrace for a few seconds, as we ripped away the rest of our clothes. I watched as Lek deftly unclipped her bra and dropped it onto the floor. Her small breasts were perfect. I glimpsed her generous, brown nipples, now silhouetted against the dim light from the window. She stretched out towards me and I enveloped her mesmerising body in my arms. Her figure was sublime; her skin was taut and soft to touch and felt unbelievably smooth – like fragrant satin or warm polished marble – to my caressing fingers. I kissed her again, our lips and tongues now exploring each other's open mouths. Her eyes were barely closed, the lids flickered; I glanced at her dark eyebrows and marvelled at their exquisite symmetry.

My arousal was bulging and palpable. She grasped me in her small hand and guided me, quivering, into her. The explosion, when it came, was precipitate. It was an eruption of energy and release, such as I had never experienced. My limbs trembled and shook, as if whole rivers of submerged torment were being pumped out of my system. Lek let out a low moan and I cried out, suddenly unashamed, unconfined. I held her and buried my face in her neck. She released her hands from my shoulders and turned my face towards hers. Her eyes were wide open and I could see tenderness in their dark pupils. She grazed her lips against mine and we fell into a slumbering embrace that was to take us both into a contented, soothing, dreamless sleep.

The insistent ringing of a phone woke me from my yawning unconsciousness. Lek stirred and dragged the bed sheet around her ochre-coloured body. The AC was still whirring and the room felt cold.

'Mike, sorry, it must be early for you.' It was Joe West, burning the London midnight oil again. 'But I thought you should know straight away...'

I looked at my *Omega* – it was six a.m. I grunted an acknowledgement.

'It's not a safe line, so I'll rocker it up,' Joe said.

Rocker was the term we used for speaking in an oblique language to disguise the message. It was not secure, but it was better than nothing.

'We've found a seat for Tango One. He is on an Alpha Foxtrot flight into Lima Golf Whisky, arriving at transpose six-five tomorrow morning. I have got the Deltas primed – they will be on the plot in strength to do the business.' He sounded very upbeat. I wondered if he had fortified himself before the call with the bottle of gin I knew he kept in his cabinet.

'Great,' I said, still struggling to wake up. Joe's attempts at coded speech made me cringe. If the Thais, or anyone else, were listening, it would not take them long to work out that Bart was booked on an Air France flight, arriving at ten a.m. at Gatwick Airport.

Joe carried on talking. He *would* be to the point: 'Your girl has done wonders again. Give her a kiss from me, would you?!' It was very unlike Joe to make a joke like that and for a bizarre moment, I looked around the room for a hidden camera.

'Yes, sure Joe. I'll make sure I do that.' I glanced over at Lek's sleeping curves and laid my hand gently on her naked back.

'I'll get the boys to give you regular updates. I have got someone reviewing all the BNU material, as well – the stuff you send us each week, just in case we have missed anything.' He was referring to the tapes of conversations from Bart's home that I sent to Bill, my desk officer, each week. They served as a backup and allowed London to conduct their own analysis. Most of the material, up to now, had been unhelpful. Bart knew better than to conduct his main business on the phone.

'Anyway, I am off home, now,' he said cheerfully. 'It's after eleven here, but I'll be in first thing, as usual. I am watching this one very closely – there's a lot riding on it. I briefed the Chief yesterday and he told me to give you his best wishes, and hopes you are keeping out of trouble.' He blathered on for a few more minutes and then there was a blessed pause.

'Thanks, Joe. Goodnight. Thanks for the call. Safe journey home,' I said in soft tones and replaced the receiver.

Lek was still sleeping soundly; I was now fully awake, so I walked out onto the terrace and sat down quietly with my own thoughts. There was a yellow luminosity above the eastern hills as the sun, still hidden from view, climbed into the morning sky. I was filled with an infinite feeling of warmth as I studied her sleeping form, half covered by the ruffled sheets, with the room slowly brightening. Then a wistful sadness engulfed me as if I knew that this brief moment in time would be lost for ever once it had passed me by.

CHAPTER FOURTEEN

The next three weeks spent with Lek were the happiest of my life. The enthusiasm for my work returned and my energy levels soared, as I busied myself contentedly with the tasks at hand. I provided daily reporting to London, as usual, visited the local BNU office for an hour each day to get the updates from Maew and Surachai and spoke to Sonny most afternoons to chew the fat.

The AFP had found no trace of Kevin, so we presumed he was still in Indonesia, somewhere. I came to the conclusion that when Lek told me Kevin was going to Australia, she had misheard. It seemed more likely that he was going to meet the *Australian* Chris Manton, the yacht skipper of the *Guiding Lights,* in Bali.

I rang Gill every day and she assured me that she was running the office better alone, now that I was not fussing around her.

I spent nearly every night with Lek. Our relationship blossomed and, for the first time in many years, I felt free from conventional ties and prying eyes. Hardly anyone knew me in Phuket and Lek's work friends were just that. It dawned on me that she had no real life, outside her routine at the office, and she confided in me that living with Bart was an isolating experience. His house was secluded and he had discouraged shared acquaintances.

We spent the evenings and some free afternoons exploring the island and found some delightful, out-of-the-way spots to while away the hours. Most nights, she stayed with me and we made love. We slept with our arms and legs intertwined in a soft and sensual embrace and when I woke in the mornings, her cosy, inviting form would be lying next to me, my hand nestling between her velvet thighs and my face against her neck.

I was hungry for her body and she gave it to me eagerly: she made love with a passion that I had never before encountered. It was simultaneously a deep, fulfilling salsa of physicality and a delightful, dreamy encirclement of tenderness.

The enchantment was forcibly broken from time to time, as we agreed that she would have to return to Bart's house, in case there were messages to collect and to keep up appearances. I missed her terribly when she was away and thought of her incessantly, finding it nearly impossible to contemplate my work. Our personal bond had transcended our professional relationship, which had fractured beyond repair. But the awkward reality was that I still needed her to help me in my work and there were uneasy moments when I was obliged to raise the difficult subjects of Bart, Kevin and Bhang. Although I made an effort to maintain whatever vestiges of our official liaison remained, day by day, this task became increasingly distasteful. I reminded her constantly that on no account should she call me from Bart's house. I was misleadingly vague about the reasons and I felt guilty not telling her that Bart's telephone was being tapped by the BNU. But she seemed content to call me from her office. I was walking a tightrope and knew it.

The Deltas had done a magnificent job during Bart's three days in England. They had stuck to his tail throughout and by the time he had boarded a return flight to Amsterdam, they had amassed a pile of significant intelligence. They had covered a lot of miles, too and I smiled when I thought of their huge expense claims. Joe would grumble, of course, but the reward for their endeavours was plain for all to see.

Bart had walked off the Paris flight and headed straight into London, booking himself a suite at the *Dorchester* in Park Lane. This was a stroke of luck for the Deltas, as they had a good contact there – the security manager was an ex-Flying Squad inspector. He gave us a complete breakdown of Bart's one-night stay: every penny spent, every call made, every taxi used. Amongst his outgoing calls, Bart made one which was traced to the *Admiral Hawke* public house in Polperro, a small fishing village on the south coast of Cornwall. He also made a call to Amsterdam, which was pinned down by the Dutch to a flat rented by Alicia Duykers, his old girlfriend who had gone to gaol for him ten years previously.

My, my... they are still in touch. Bart's deception is deeper than I thought.

When Bart checked out of the *Dorchester*, the Deltas followed him to Paddington, where he took the train, first class, to Plymouth. He was met at the station and driven into Polperro. There, he spent two nights at the *Admiral Hawke* with the man who had collected him from the London train – Nathanial Fletcher, co-owner of the pub. This is where it got really interesting. Fletcher was not just a publican, he was a sailor – a qualified yacht master. In fact, he had a part share in a seventy-foot, steel-hulled schooner, built just after the Second World War – the *Cornish Lady*. The harbour master's records showed that she had not been seen in Polperro since Christmas. She had signed out to the Mediterranean on 2 January with a crew of four. The skipper was Fletcher's best mate, business partner, newly-certified ocean yacht master and none other than my old adversary, Conrad Duncan. When I read the report, my heart missed a beat. The connections to Bart were amassing fast. There could only be one reason why the *Cornish Lady* was not lolling at her berth in sleepy southern Cornwall. She must be on her way to the Far East to collect Bart's drugs shipment – it was the near inescapable conclusion – but I needed more information before I could be sure.

I presumed that Bart's visit to Polperro had been to deliver money and check on the progress of the boat. He and Fletcher were seen in nearby Talland Bay on a couple of occasions, patrolling the coastal path and gazing out to sea. After two days, Bart boarded the return train to Paddington, took a taxi to Heathrow and a KLM flight to Amsterdam's Schiphol Airport. The Delta's job was over, for the time being, but their work had put nearly all the jigsaw pieces onto the table. Now, all we had to do was put them together.

'Have you heard anything from Bart?' I asked Lek one evening as we came out of the local cinema. It was her birthday and we had been to see Bruce Willis and Alan Rickman in *Die Hard*. I had hated the film – it seemed so unrealistic to me. But Lek had loved it and was full of chatter when we emerged into the heat. Earlier in the evening, I had taken her to a jewellery shop in one of the backstreets of Patong and bought her a gold bracelet. She had taken ages to select it, but her choice was now glimmering on her wrist and complemented her necklace perfectly.

'No – he never calls me. He will ring when he wants to,' she said, taking my hand as we crossed the beach road. I found the car and began the drive back to Kalim. We dodged through the traffic and I did my best to avoid the multitude of motorcycles that kept trying to overtake us on the inside. Driving in Thailand was like a video game – you never knew from where the next missile was going to come.

'Bart and I never sleep together, you know, Khun Mike,' she said unexpectedly. The sudden statement made my head turn involuntarily towards her and as it twisted, I narrowly missed an unlit cycle rickshaw which was lumbering along in the shadows.

'I wish you would just call me Mike, now,' I responded, trying to change the subject. Her sexual relationship with Bart was too painful to contemplate. 'Khun Mike sounds so formal.'

She ignored me. 'It's true, Khun Mike. He doesn't really love me, I think. Sometimes, I think he has another lady.'

I poured a glass of brandy when we got back to the apartment and took it onto the terrace. I gazed at the flickering candles on

Patong beach. I could see the bright lights of the town beyond and the cars advancing up the beach road. The air was balmy, the cicadas started up a racket in the bushes below and as I sipped my drink, I felt an arm envelop my waist, and then another. The two hands interlocked over my stomach and rocked my body gently from side to side.

'Thank you, Khun Mike. I had a lovely evening,' Lek purred in my ear.

'Just Mike – Mike is better now, don't you think?'

'Yes, Khun Mike – of course,' and she squeezed me and we fell giggling into the room and onto the sofa.

The following morning, I received two pieces of news. Both were welcome in their ways, but both also brought pangs of anxiety. The BNU informed me that Kevin was back at his house in Patong. He had arrived the night before from Singapore. My desk officer then sent me a telex to tell me that the Dutch had seen Bart leaving Amsterdam on the non-stop flight to Bangkok. He was due into Phuket later that evening. He had been in Holland for nearly three weeks and it was now early March. I had been expecting the news of Bart's return for a week or so and Lek and I had discussed its implications. I pledged that I would be as good as my word and do all I could to protect him, when the moment came. She became tearful from time to time and it distressed me to the point of breaking. I told myself that all I had to do was hold my nerve. But when the intelligence arrived that Bart would be home in a matter of hours, I disintegrated.

I pulled myself together enough to call Lek and assure her, as cheerfully as I could, that we would meet from time to time and hinted at the unfinished business that still needed her help. She fell silent at the mention of returning to Bart and as I broke the news to her, I felt the most desperate pangs of guilt, fear and sadness all rolled up into one. The situation was simply awful, but the choice we had made was the only sensible one. She would get her wishes for a secure future fulfilled; I would get closure on an investigation that had plagued me for over ten years. However, the idea of losing Lek and allowing Bart to get away scot-free was troubling me more with every passing hour. I consoled myself with the knowledge that my abject feelings for Lek and my subsequent promise to her had given me a chance to do the decent thing, for once in my life. So, I resolved to honour my pledge to protect him, even if the decision poisoned the rest of my career. It was the right thing to do and I owed it to her.

I wondered if she would throw in her lot with me and abandon Bart, if I asked her. She, too, was torn. I knew it was her family's future that drove her, not a passing affair like ours – not even if it was true love. She would set aside passion, love, if it meant a better future for herself and her son. Although the mercenary objectives that ruled her life chafed with me, deep down I knew they made sense. And anyway, she had no life to look forward to with me. My existence was way too complicated, too fraught with insoluble problems. My office would not countenance a relationship with an informant, declared or concealed, and I would be shown the door in double quick time, if they found out. My marriage, however hollow and unfulfilling, would be over. I would be an outcast. No; her future lay elsewhere, even if it meant that Bart would slip the net, yet again.

There was another niggling factor that teased my waking thoughts. Did Bart really love her, or was he using her? Would he merely abandon her, once her value to him had ended? I knew she had her own doubts, but she had set aside her qualms when the jackpot prize of a comfortable life in Europe beckoned. From there, she could support her family honestly and maybe even become a lady of stature. If that's what she wanted, I was not going to stand in her way. She may be deluding herself, but I was not going to argue.

There was an aggressive knock on the apartment door. It was ten p.m. and I rolled my head in surprise, staying silently on the bed for a few moments. Then another knock. It was firm and assured – not the knock of a woman.

'Look, are you going to open this bloody door or not?' came a strident voice that I recognised instantly. I hurried to the entrance and swung the door open.

'John! What the fuck are you doing here?' The tall figure and broad, welcoming face of John Morris greeted me.

'I'm down for another of those business seminars with that old tosser, Rupert. Didn't Gill tell you? No, I suppose not – as I never told her!' he guffawed. 'Anyway, I wanted to surprise you!'

'Well, you have succeeded, mate! Come in and grab a pew!' John's arrival was the perfect tonic. I was wallowing in self-pity and I needed someone to jerk me back to reality.

'Look,' he said, 'I'm not on parade until tomorrow afternoon. What say you and I hit the town tonight? I bet you know a few good places – you have been down here long enough. Everyone in the office is talking about it, you know. They think you must have found another woman. Ha, ha!'

My mood brightened instantly. 'Yes, John – let's do that!'

I showered while he watched the local TV channel and then I drove him into Patong to the *Sexy Nine* bar. There were others that I had been frequenting of late, but I thought the place would suit him and I was looking forward to seeing Aungkana again and catching up on the gossip. The minute we arrived in the bar, I spotted Noy sitting close to an elderly fellow with pink cheeks. They were building a tower of bricks together with small pieces of oblong-shaped wood. While he was focussing on his next move, she glanced over at me, flicked her hair and smiled. The implication was that she would dump the old guy if I bought her a drink. I disregarded the hidden message and sat down with John.

From behind the bar, Aungkana handed us some frozen

towels and screeched, 'Khun Mike! Where have you been? I missed you!'

'I missed you, tooo!' I yelled back gleefully. John looked a little bemused but seemed to realise we were playing a game of some sort.

'Condoms with your beer, Khun Mike?'

'Yes, condoms, Aungkana. Thank you.'

By two a.m., we had visited six bars and had introduced ourselves to half a dozen different Aungkanas and a score of Noys. We had nattered happily above the din and bang of the music and now it was time to go home – but only if I could remember where I had left the car.

'Let's take a *tuc tuc*. We can come back in the morning for the car. You can stay at my place, if you like. I have a huge spare room going begging,' I fibbed.

The lift was out of order again and as we started the long trudge up the stairs, my mind flooded back to that first night with Lek, and the uplifting effects of the evening's alcohol began to reverse. By the time we had reached the fourth floor, I was back in the nadirs of gloom.

'One for the road?' John said, as I switched on the lights. I went to fetch the glasses. 'Now, I want you to tell me everything about this snout of yours,' he said loudly. 'Have you been behaving yourself? That's what I want to know.'

I poured a couple of beers. 'Look, John, I'm not really in the mood for it now – maybe we can talk about her tomorrow.'

'Tomorrow we may both be dead!' he said with mock solemnity. 'I reckon you have had your evil way with her in this very room, you dirty bastard,' he laughed.

'Well, now's not the time, John. Can we leave it for another day?'

'My god, you look positively glum, all of a sudden.' He looked at me closely and I could see he was doing his best to sober up. 'Look, old man, I can tell she has got to you. It's as plain as the cheeks of your arse – or even the dick in your pants,' he said, reverting back to his alcoholic one-liners. He put his arm around my neck. 'I don't want to pry. Only joshing. You know me – all mouth and trousers. But if you do want someone to confess to – now's your chance. I may be a bit pissed, but I'll listen and help, if I can.'

I started a faltering reply. My speech was slow and painstaking. 'John, the thing is, I am in a bit of a pickle – I think I love her and it's really killing me.'

'I see,' he said calmly. 'Bring us another beer and tell me all about it.'

I sat opposite him, clutching my bottle and the whole sorry tale poured out. He listened attentively and never touched his beer. By the time I had finished, the bottle he gripped must have felt as hot in his hands as the one in mine did.

'So, you see, I'm in a right spot. But I'm pretty sure that if I can get through the next few weeks, everything will sort itself out.' I tried my best to look optimistic.

'You say you love her, Mike. Are you sure it's not just a passing fascination?'

I wondered why he had chosen the word *fascination* – polite for lust, perhaps. 'I know I must seem like a fool to you – an old fool, at that – but I know I want her and I am scared of losing her. I am not getting any younger and the thought of the next ten years or so petrifies me. It's as if I have been given a chance to find a happiness I never knew I wanted. And in case you are thinking it's just the sex, it's not.' I halted for effect. 'It never was really – the sex, I mean; and, in any case, it's gone beyond that now. The trouble is – I cannot see how it will end. Something has to give soon.'

'My god, Mike, you look like a nervous wreck. This girl, Lek, has she told you that she loves you?'

'Not in so many words,' I replied. 'But it doesn't work like that with women over here. You will get to understand that once you have been around the block a few times. I don't think she understands love like we do. For her, it's a sense of warmth, of security. If I am kind to her, comfort her and give her the things she wants in life, she will be happy. If I am unfair, mean and cruel she will be miserable and leave me. It's her future she wants to secure and if I could help her do that, she would stay with me – she would love me for it.'

'But what about Bart? Bloody hell, man! She is living with him, Mike! Can't you see this will end in tears? He is your main target, for Christ's sake, and there's a good chance that he'll be locked up soon!'

'I know!' I cried. 'I know. I just think he is using her and I suppose she is him, in her way, too. I just think I could give her more.'

'And how do you propose to do that, Mike? Leave your wife, leave your family, quit your job? If the office knew about this, they would tear you to pieces. And where would you live? What about money? What about your friends? My god, Mike, you're not thinking straight.' He pointed at the other side of the room, where a painting of Buddha stared impassively back at us. 'See that wall, Mike? You are about to crash into it head first and there will be no survivors.'

There was a long silence.

'Look, mate, all I can say is that I think you're deluding yourself if you think this woman loves you. My advice would be to finish the affair and finish the case – *in that order!* Resume your professional relationship with her, by all means, if it's crucial to the investigation, but get out as soon as you can. And I hope, for your sake, you can, because this looks like a crock of shit to me, Mike.'

He was right, of course; I knew I was conning myself. How had it come to this? But he was speaking from a point of pure logic and common sense. He did not have the turmoil of infatuation with which to contend. The body chemistry that drove these uninvited emotions was now unstoppable and I was struggling to cope with the consequences. I felt whacked and wanted to lie down, but an inner voice told me I had to pull myself together – I had too much riding on it.

I showed John to his room and he tried to make a little joke about the old days, presumably in an effort to relieve the tension. I crept onto my bed, slumped on the mattress and scrutinised the slowly turning ceiling fan. The phrase "tired and emotional" came to mind and gave me a brief moment of amused respite. It was three thirty in the morning and I found I could not sleep. Words and ideas were spinning in my head and I tried to liberate my anguish by forming some sentences that would express my condition. For some reason, I felt an all-consuming need to write them down. Maybe it would exorcise the demons. I grabbed some paper and started to scribble. By the time I had finished, a weight had been lifted and I settled exhausted onto my bed, still fully clothed.

These days, I feel quite lost…like a shuttlecock in a stream.
 Is it love? PLEASE, not at my age – so undignified, so unnecessary…
It crept up on me like a snake under the picnic blanket.
A chaos of my own making.
This wonderful folly could have passed me by.
So, I welcome it: though the pain is difficult sometimes – well most times…
I wonder what it is that I crave so much.
 Tenderness, passion, spoken love in return; a soft hand to hold?
Or is it just condescending kindness I thirst for; or worse, is it the danger that goads me?

No, not that please... tenderness, I think.
I want so much to protect and nurture my new-found
agony.
But I cannot.
It will destroy me...

I turned in my bed as a gust from the fan rustled the manuscript, raising its edges from the side table. For a second it lifted gently into the air and then floated downwards onto the floor. I stretched out to catch it but it eluded my despairing grasp.

CHAPTER FIFTEEN

Mid-morning, John drove me to my parked car and I wished him luck with Rupert and his British League of Tradesmen – or whatever they were called. We had hardly spoken on the way over, as much a product of our hangovers as of our evident discomfort about the revelations of the previous night. John gave me an encouraging wink as he left and we promised to hook up in Bangkok when I next returned. I continued on to the local BNU office.

I had got to know the BNU's point man in Phuket, Major Jirapat, quite well by now. Although he came highly recommended by Colonel Surachai, I found him hard to take seriously. About fifty, he was possessed of a huge gut that overflowed his belt by at least three inches. He wobbled, rather than walked and seemed to do very little work. He was always chewing on something and I wondered how he managed to pass his annual medical. His posting in Phuket was as comfortable as it was sought after; presumably, there would have been a lot of competition for his job. I concluded that he must have friends in high places and left it at that. After all, this was just a transitory assignment for me and I did not need to slog hard at building a relationship.

Over the next few weeks, I settled into a steady pattern of work. I wrote my reports in the morning and drove to Major Jirapat's office just before noon. Every day, his rather frightening-looking secretary, Khun Nok, handed me a yellow dossier. Nok meant bird in Thai and I reflected that her remarkable resemblance to a carrion crow may have had something to do with the nickname. I sifted through the dossier, read the papers, made a few notes and used the BNU phone to call Maew and Sonny in Bangkok, if I needed any clarification. About two o'clock, I wandered around the corner for a plate of steamed chicken and crispy pork rice at a nearby stall. I had become quite a celebrity there and the staff always looked happy to see me; I felt wanted. I would then drive unhurriedly back to my apartment, drag out the scramble phone, insert the codes and call Gill for messages. By four o'clock, I was ready for my daily report to London. This had to be done on the phone scrambler too, as I had no access to secure telex equipment where I was. The daily BNU reports merely confirmed that Bart and Kevin were in residence and not much else, so most days I had little of interest for London. We had resumed the normal listening and waiting game.

I thought of Lek constantly and every time the phone rang I rushed to it, expecting it to be her. It never was. I called her office twice; each time she was out. I left messages, using the British Airways cover that we had agreed, but the calls were not returned. There was a limit to how many times I could ring her like this before arousing the suspicion of her colleagues, so after the second failed attempt, I desisted. I told myself that if she had any information for me, she would ring me, but as time passed without any contact, I began to wonder if the whole case was collapsing around me. The misgivings about Lek's trustworthiness resurfaced – and I suffered periods of self-doubt. I was in a spiritual vacuum, where my cause and all I stood for appeared futile and worthless.

The days passed like this, in a combination of tedium and distress, for the next three weeks. I conducted my round of visits dutifully, made my calls, wrote my reports and waited. Sleep brought some reprieve from my misery and at daybreak, during the first few seconds of consciousness, my mind was blissfully uncluttered and I felt a dreamy, balanced calm. Then, as I awoke and my awareness gradually returned, all the negative thoughts flooded back to me like a gigantic wave striking an exposed cliff at dawn. The nauseating anxiety of another day without her stretched hopelessly ahead of me. I waited for the phone to ring and to hear her voice again. I spent many evenings drowning my sorrows in the bars in Patong and, on occasion, I even flirted with the idea of hooking up with Noy again – or anyone, for that matter, that might relieve my loneliness. I resisted; it was drink that sent me to sleep each night, not the tender embrace of a warm and willing body.

Then one morning, as I was shaving, the phone rang. The tones sounded insistent for some reason. I grabbed a towel, tiptoed hastily across the floor and lunged for the handset. It slipped out of my soapy grasp and thudded onto the tiled floor. By the time I picked it up, the line had gone dead.

'Blast the damn thing!' I yelled and slammed the receiver down with such force that it cracked the casing. I turned to resume my shave and it rang again. This time I grabbed it cleanly.

'Yes?' I bellowed, hoping to sound as irritated as I felt.

'Khun Mike, it's me – Lek. Can I see you today? I have a message for you.'

'You can tell me now,' I said icily, assuming she was going to say that our relationship was over and that she had decided she could no longer see me, let alone help me with the investigation.

'No – I mean I have a message for my brother from Kevin. I have to take it to him tonight. Do you want to see it?'

I mumbled my assent and my stomach churned at the thought of seeing her again. We arranged to meet in the airport coffee shop in an hour. She was waiting for me when I arrived and without speaking, she passed me another of her handwritten notes. I peered at it closely. It was a further series of numbers and letters.

2T x 2 = 4T – OK; TG – OK; ETA HKT 1900 5/4 and 12/4 – OK; 950k – 2/4, 1100 – OK

'I think I can work this out,' I said. 'Kevin wants Bhang to arrange two shipments on Thai Airways flights arriving in Phuket at seven p.m. on the fifth and the twelfth of April. He will send the money on the second of April at eleven o'clock.'

'Yes,' she declared. 'That is what it means. I have to tell Bhang that Kevin will bring the money as before – they will meet at the airport hotel on Sunday.'

'OK – this gives us a few days to prepare,' I said, as I copied the details into my pocket notebook. 'Tell me, did Bart say anything about this to you?'

'No, he gave me the message. He just said it was from Kevin.'

She looked as wonderful as ever; the smart airline uniform with its pinks and purples looked as if it had been specifically designed for her. 'I have missed you, Lek. I have missed you very much. Why did you not return my calls?'

'I had nothing to tell you and I needed time to think – time for my heart.'

I was not exactly sure what she meant.

'I missed you too, Khun Mike. I cried a lot. I wanted to see you, but you said I could not. I have been thinking about everything – you and me, me and Bart.'

'And what did you think?' I asked her tenderly.

'I think that I love you, Khun Mike,' she started to whimper. 'I feel very bad when I am alone with Bart. I think about you every day and I am so sad.' She sat upright in her seat, pulled her shoulders back and mopped a tear from her cheek. 'But he is kind to me – he wants to take me to Holland and that will be good for me. So I have decided to go with him.' She said it with an air of finality, as if it was an announcement.

'You know I love you, Lek.' There, I had said it. Lek just looked at me dolefully.

I tried to lighten the mood. 'I have missed you so much I have been lovesick; look, I have lost three kilos.' I patted my flatter stomach and saw a tiny smile appear around the edges of her mouth. 'I am serious, Lek – you mean the world to me, but I understand why you have to go. I can do nothing for you. If you stay with me, it will be bad for everyone. It's not an option; we both know that.'

She wiped away a trickle of moisture from her cheek, doing her best to disguise her mood.

'And I'll keep my promise – I will take care that Bart is not arrested. If he stays away from the drugs, I will see he comes to no harm. You will be free to go where you want. But if he gets too close to the consignment, I cannot guarantee what might happen.'

'Why do you do this for me, Khun Mike?'

'It's because I love you and I want you to be happy. My life is so complicated. It would never work out for us. If you are happy, I will be happy. I will always love you – always think of that.'

'But I am not happy to go with Bart. I want you!' she pleaded. And then her head bowed slightly as she whispered, 'But I know you have a wife and so I cannot – so that is why I have agreed to go with him. He is my chance for the future.' She said the words deliberately, pronouncing each syllable slowly and carefully.

I was feeling more tension than I thought I could endure, but I knew I had to change the subject and press on with a few more official questions. 'Lek, listen to me carefully. I think Kevin is arranging a boat to collect the drugs that Bhang will send him. If you hear anything about a boat you must let me know – promise?'

'I promise, Khun Mike.'

'What time is your flight to Bangkok?' I asked.

'I leave after my work, on the six o'clock flight.'

'OK. I'll see you back here just after five. I am coming with you.'

CHAPTER SIXTEEN

I drove back to my room at breakneck speed, narrowly missing an elephant trudging along the coast road outside Kamala. Its mahout swore and gesticulated at me as I swerved past the poor creature on a tight bend. There was no reason to drive so fast – there was plenty of time to make the arrangements. But I was seized with the urgency of the moment and the sense that *at last* I had made a major breakthrough. I desperately wanted to tell someone about it.

Safely back in my room, I pulled out the scrambler phone, loaded the cipher and called Gill. I repeated the codes and numbers that Lek had given me, explained their meaning and told her to get a telex off to London immediately. They would be sleeping now, but I knew that Control would get the message onto Joe West's desk by the time he arrived for work in a few hours and the thought of him reading it gave me a kick. I told Gill to get Wut to meet me at Don Muang off the Phuket flight and then I rang Sonny. I could not use the scrambler for this call as he had no compatible receiving equipment, so I kept the message simple and we arranged to meet later in one of our favourite Sukhumvit bars, which I selected because it was more intimate than most and would give us a chance to share a few guarded words.

The rest of the day was spent trying to work out all the angles and planning for as many eventualities as I could. It soon became obvious there were too many uncertainties to construct a foolproof strategy. Critically, I needed to persuade Colonel Surachai that seizing the air freight shipments in Chiang Mai, Bangkok or Phuket was a waste of time – I wanted to track them as far as possible. Raiding the cargo shed at Don Muang was the easy option and would, almost certainly, have resulted in Bhang's arrest. But we needed to roll the whole case up, not just one corner of it.

The new yacht intelligence identifying *Guiding Lights* and *Cornish Lady* was uppermost in my mind. I knew we could take this case a lot further. We had no firm information about the vessels' whereabouts, but my strong guess was that, with each passing hour, their passage was bringing them ever closer to an ocean rendezvous in the tropical waters that encircled Phuket. I conjectured that Bart and Kevin would split the four tons: some for the Australian market and the rest for the UK. Two tons of Thai sticks would fetch A$8 million in Australia which, at two dollars to the pound, translated to a cool £4 million. The same drugs would fetch even more on the streets of Britain. Assuming the load was to be divided evenly between the yachts, two tons each, the all-up value of Bart's four-ton load was approaching £10 million. To make the most of our intelligence advantage, we needed to be audacious. We had to start our surveillance when the air freight consignments arrived in Phuket and then follow the packages until they reached the two foreign yachts. That would be the time to strike.

Keeping our nerve was critical – if we could sustain covert observations until the drugs were unloaded onto the yachts, a fantastic opportunity to capture both the UK and Australian transport syndicates would be handed to us. We would use the local maritime police patrol boats to pounce on the yachts in the act of delivery and then sweep up Bhang's corrupt airport team in the second phase. The arrests of so many would have a genuine impact. It would send signals around the smuggling community that British Customs were capable of more than just intercepting couriers at airports. The plan was bold and full of risk; it would take much skill and daring to pull it off, but the rewards would be epic.

The first hurdle was to persuade Sonny that the idea would work and then there was the much more challenging obstacle of convincing Colonel Surachai. By the time we landed in Bangkok, I felt drained. From my aisle seat, I had been able to watch Lek sitting quietly, four rows in front of me. We had decided not to make any contact on the flight, so I just gazed at her neatly-cut hair, the turn of her leg and her left hand that sometimes came into view, still glittering with my golden birthday present. It was a distraction I could have done without; I should have been focussing on what I was going to communicate to Sonny later that evening.

I had told Lek before we left that I would call her at her office first thing the next day. She was returning to Phuket on the night's last flight, after delivering the message to Bhang, and there would almost certainly be a return missive. I would need to ask her about it.

Sonny was in rousing form when I walked into the bar and stood up to greet me like a long lost relative.

'Hi, cuz!' I called. I had been telling him for ages that we were related – he was really just a Brit in an *Akubra*. He hated the teasing, but it made the banter even more entertaining. We huddled together to discuss business. Sonny had no more news on the whereabouts of *Guiding Lights* or its skipper, Chris Manton. Discreet checks in Bali had shown the vessel had left with a crew of five, including Manton, on 15 March, but we were still no further forward in locating her. Our best calculation was that *Guiding Lights* would take three or four weeks to reach Thai waters and the departure of *Cornish Lady* from Polperro on 2 January, with an estimated three-month easterly passage, would put both vessels in the same area by mid-April. Bart's game plan was taking shape – surely the idea was to deliver the drugs to these yachts. There seemed to be no other scenario that fitted the intelligence. The timings of the two Chiang Mai air consignments, scheduled for 5 and 12 April, also fitted neatly into the plan. Bart would have all four tons in Phuket by the second week of April – bang in the middle of Songkran, the Thai New Year; right at a time when the country went mad with celebration; precisely when the authorities' guard would be down. The police would be using their resources to control the crowds and police patrol boats would be tied up in harbour, their crews enjoying the drunken festivities.

I had to hand it to Bart; this took a lot of planning and soon we would see the next stage take shape – the delivery of the final payment to Bhang. It was an episode we had to observe and the increasing importance of invisibility in our work was self-evident. It was not a time for faint hearts and we had to trust one another. Sonny and I talked into the small hours, plotting. We spurned the intermittent attentions of a gaggle of bar hostesses, who did their best to catch our eye. By two a.m., we had agreed a plan of action. We would approach Surachai with it the following day and hoped we could sway him to our position. Until then, there was just time for one more beer.

The next morning, I rang Lek, as arranged. She had more to tell me. Bhang had read Kevin's message, absorbed it and agreed to meet him at the airport hotel the following day. He also gave Lek a name – Pisak. This was his cargo contact in Phuket. He told her that Bart or Kevin would need to meet Pisak at the airport in the next few days to fix up the next stage.

'But there is something else,' she said. 'Bart has been very angry recently. He and Kevin had a big fight two days ago. I don't know why but now they do not talk. Bart will not call him on the phone – he says it is not safe. Last night, he told me to take a message to Kevin. It was late, but he said I must go, so I went to his house in a taxi.'

'Did he write the message down?' I asked.

'No, but it was easy to remember. He told me to tell Kevin to book into the *On On Hotel* in Phuket Town today and wait for instructions. He would send me with more information later, but he wanted Kevin to wait there until he contacted him. He said it was the safest way.'

'What was Kevin's reaction?' I asked.

'Nothing – he said to tell Bart it was OK.'

I could not resist asking Lek an obvious question. 'I don't understand,' I muttered, trying to sound naïve. 'If Kevin is the boss, how can Bart tell him what to do?' There was silence for a few seconds.

'I know – it has made me very worried. But I just do what Bart asks. He wants me to take messages for him too, now. He says there will be more. In two weeks, he says, we will be together in Holland.'

To say anything in response would have only complicated matters. Maybe this episode had opened Lek's eyes to Bart's deception. Perhaps she had resolved to stick it out all the same. It was too late now to try and change things, so I made no comment.

Later at the BNU, things went surprisingly well. Surachai dispatched two of his staff to the airport hotel to watch the encounter between Kevin and Bhang and by midday they had returned grinning happily. The little reunion had gone down as scheduled and a leather briefcase, larger than the one exchanged before, had been passed to Bhang. The whole thing had lasted just thirty seconds and then Kevin was on his way back to Phuket. It was a sensible assumption that the money transfer had taken place. Now, it was up to Bhang to deliver on his side of the bargain and get both shipments from Chiang Mai to Phuket within the next ten days.

Colonel Surachai had listened to us attentively and had nodded encouragingly when I proposed that we let the drugs through Bangkok without interference. I suggested we commenced the surveillance at Phuket Airport and asked him to send his best officers to watch the consignments arrive. I promised we would pay all the costs: airfares, hotel bills, expenses – the lot. Sonny joked that Queen Elizabeth would stump up personally and we laughed contentedly at the thought. Then we started to encounter resistance.

I briefed him about the two *farang* yachts and as I outlined our plan for the takedown and explained the interception role expected of local marine police and coastguard assets, his demeanour changed.

'This is not a good idea, Khun Mike,' he announced, interrupting me. 'I do not know what they do down there. I do not understand how their operations work, so I cannot trust them.'

'Do you worry that you cannot trust them because they are corrupt, like the army general in Mae Sae?' I asked, deliberately reminding him of the embarrassing reality of provincial cross-border operations.

He looked exasperated. 'No, I don't think they are corrupt. But I would not be sure if they could do the job properly – follow instructions and carry out their duty.'

I persevered. 'I have met the commanding officer. Major Jirapat introduced us. He was delighted to meet me. His name is Bamroong. The marine police have a substantial presence on the island and a base near Chalong, on the southeast coast. Major Jirapat knows Bamroong very well – they go fishing together. He seems like a decent man to me.'

With the mention of Jirapat's name, his face softened a little. 'You say Jirapat knows him well?'

'Yes, they are good friends. I always think good men choose their friends carefully and I know we both think Jirapat is a good man,' I lied. I had never been impressed by his lethargic manner, but I knew he and Surachai were close, for some reason.

'Yes, Major Jirapat is my cousin. He is a respectable man – a bit lazy, but no monkey business.'

'I'm sure it's the best way to close this case, Colonel. Can I suggest something else that might help? I am closely connected to my own maritime service, back in Britain. They have done excellent work for us over the years: patrolling the coast, intercepting boats and trapping yachts like the ones we are after now. I could ask London to send us their best cutter commander to work with Bamroong. It might help him make the best decisions. What do you think, Colonel?'

He tugged at his chin. 'And you, Khun Sonny – what do you think?'

My suggestion to introduce a Customs Maritime Commander to mentor the Thais was completely off the cuff – I had just thought of the idea and was not sure if I could deliver on it. I looked hopefully at Sonny. He never blinked as he said to Surachai, 'Mike and I have discussed this at length and the idea has the full support of the Australian Federal Police, Colonel.'

'That is good,' Colonel Surachai said solemnly. 'OK, maybe it will work. We should start to make our plans. What do you both think we should do first?'

'Let's select the surveillance team,' I said.

CHAPTER SEVENTEEN

The first shipment into Phuket was just three days away and Surachai honoured his promise. By two o'clock, I was briefing six of his best investigators and making arrangements to move them down to the south. Sonny and I commandeered three unmarked BNU cars fitted with mobile communications radios, essential kit for the forthcoming surveillance. Gill found a discreet hotel, tucked away about three miles from Phuket Airport, with rooms for all eight of us. If we needed more help, we could call on Major Jirapat, but for the time being we had enough officers for the task at hand.

Our initial undertaking was to monitor the arrival and watch the subsequent movements of the first consignment. We all agreed that Bhang's contact, Pisak, would not want to sit on two tons of drugs for very long. It was a domestic flight so customs would not be in attendance and I guessed that as soon as the consignment was offloaded, it would be carted away. It was our job to find out where it went. If things went to form – according to the *last on, first off* principle – the first set of boxes unloaded from the aircraft would be the dirty ones.

The surveillance team started the long drive from Bangkok the following morning, all looking very happy that they would be enjoying two weeks in sunny Phuket at our expense. Later that day, I told Colonel Surachai that London had agreed to send us the commander of Her Majesty's Cutter *Vigilant*; James Breach from Boscastle, Cornwall was on his way to join us. The net was tightening, minute by minute, hour by hour. All we could do now was make our preparations and try to anticipate Bart's next move.

For the time being, his fate remained in his own hands, although, without knowing it, his grip was loosening imperceptibly as each day passed.

5 April dawned through thick clouds and hammering rain – an early taste, perhaps, of the southwest monsoon. By lunchtime, the clouds had assumed a stolid, leaden appearance, which brought with it an uncomfortable mixture of heat and humidity. The leader of the surveillance team was my old friend, Sergeant Thip, who was now fully accomplished in this role and carried the respect of his small group of men, most of whom were considerably older than him. The flight from Bangkok was due on the ground at seven p.m. By six thirty, the light was fading fast and it had started to rain again. I wondered if the choice of flight was deliberate – landing just as darkness set in; it made our job that much more difficult. But we were ready; the days before had been spent rehearsing – conducting covert observations of the arrivals and departures of all the Thai Airways flights from Bangkok. This proved to be an incredibly useful exercise, as we found that the inbound aircraft always went to the same stand. Just as the light was fading, Thip positioned an officer about sixty yards from the stand, concealed in a low run of bushes that snaked around the perimeter of the airfield, where he could see the plane unload. The apron was well-lit and in the drills all had gone well, communications had worked fine. It was a piece of cake, really.

The wheels of TG452 made their controlled impact with the runway bang on time; a squeal went up and a cloud of spray spattered into the cooling damp air as the tyres momentarily skidded and bounced on the wet tarmac surface. The Boeing turned at the end of the runway and started to lumber its way back to the now-familiar stand at the northern edge of the apron. I had found a quiet spot on the airport's small observation deck with a full view of the apron and runway. As the aircraft approached the stand, I gave a running commentary to Corporal Thaksin, lying doggo in his soggy hedge, and the others, sweating in their cars.

James Breach had arrived the previous evening bearing gifts from London: a set of the latest covert radios with earpieces and hidden microphones. I had distributed these marvellous bits of kit to the surveillance team earlier that day. We had been practising all afternoon and had become quite adept, so I felt confident that we could bring them into use immediately. My view of TG452 was blocked for a few seconds as it taxied behind a hangar. When, after ten seconds, the plane's nose failed to reappear, I radioed Corporal Thaksin, asking if he had sight of the jetliner.

'India Mike One – negative,' came his staccato reply. 'I have no eyeball of the aircraft.'

Thirty seconds went by.

'Shit!' I said under my breath. 'All mobiles, this is India Mike One – we have a loss of eyeball. I am moving my position to regain eyeball – all mobiles stand by.'

The radios clicked in acknowledgement.

'India Mike Six – Mike One, receive.' I was calling Corporal Thaksin. 'Can you move your location to see if you can get eyeball? The aircraft was last seen behind the green hangar at the southern end of the apron.'

'Roger, India Mike One. On my way.'

I was perturbed but not unduly worried. The plane had changed its normal stand for some reason, but we had all the exits covered, so it would just be a question of time before we regained control of the situation. I walked briskly to the far side of the observation rooftop, hoping I would get an obscured view, at least. From my new vantage point, I could just see the tail fin and part of the rear fuselage – no more. A motorised flight of steps moved past the tail towards the front of the plane. Clearly the passenger disembarkation had started. A few seconds later, I glimpsed a bulky, black, open-sided pick-up approach the side of the aircraft. It was followed by a larger white truck, with a Thai Airways emblem on its doors. Both quickly went out of view.

However hard I strained and leant, I could see precious little else. I reported the two vehicles to the others.

After a further five excruciating minutes, Thaksin came on the radio. 'All mobiles, I have full view of the aircraft now.'

Good boy!

'There is a dark pick-up at the rear and a large white truck at the side. Bags are being offloaded.' There was a pause. Then a minute later, 'From India Mike Six, the pick-up is moving – heading into the hangar. I can see a lot of large sacks in the back. Mobiles – acknowledge.' Before the others could reply, Thaksin was on the radio again. 'The pick-up has just gone past me onto the perimeter road. It came out of the back of the hangar through a metal rear door. The door is closed again. The pick-up is heading north – black Toyota. Two men on board, looks fully loaded.'

'From Mike One – can anyone respond? Acknowledge.' I knew the answer before I made the call. The pick-up had joined the main road from a concealed exit – one which we had not covered. A couple of cars went off in pursuit but the vehicle was a quarter of a mile ahead and after twenty minutes of fruitless driving, I called off the surveillance and we returned, chastened, to the hotel for a debrief and autopsy.

Thaksin told us that the pick-up had emerged suddenly and absconded through the perimeter fence via an old access gate that had hitherto been padlocked. Pisak and his team of corrupt cargo workers had done their job well. It was a slick operation that had caught us off guard. The implications for Pisak's collusion with air traffic control were all too clear. *He* could not have arranged for the aircraft to unload away from its normal stand. ATC were responsible for directing the aircraft and that meant that they were being paid off, too. The bottom line was that we had screwed up. Sonny and I felt utterly dejected.

But I had one more shot at it, if Colonel Surachai would just let me take it. The temptation to seize the second load in Bangkok was huge, but it had to be resisted. I called Surachai and explained my thoughts, assuring him that we could cover all the bases next time. We had come so far, we were so close, but I knew it was his call. He could return the surveillance team to Bangkok at any time and I knew the future of the case now lay in his hands. He listened without speaking then told me to rest. He would give me his answer the next day.

CHAPTER EIGHTEEN

Sonny suggested he take the early bird Bangkok flight next morning to speak to Surachai personally and I readily agreed. Sergeant Thip would go with him for the hour-long journey north. The following day I waited impatiently and tried to busy myself with the remainder of the surveillance team, going through some other potential scenarios. In quiet, confused moments I wondered sullenly if Lek and Bart were together and the hollow ache resumed. When Sonny and Thip returned – bizarrely enough on TG452 – with the news that Colonel Surachai had authorised the rest of the operation, my anxiety lightened a little. At least we could continue as planned.

'I owe you one, Sonny,' I told him. 'How the hell did you manage it?'

'Not me, matey – Sergeant Thip did all the talking,' he said. 'It was all in gobbledygook, but from what I gathered, Thip took the blame personally and assured Surachai that it would not happen again. And it might have helped a bit that I invited Surachai to spend two weeks in Sydney next month on a familiarisation and liaison visit.' He winked at me. 'The Colonel gave me an update on the latest wire intelligence, too. Apparently, Bart made a very quick call to the airport yesterday at six and arranged to meet someone thirty minutes later. The BNU never informed us because they could not identify him and, anyway, we were in the middle of our surveillance. They traced the guy this morning.' Sonny paused for effect. 'His name is Pisak Cholyut and he is the cargo supervisor at Phuket Airport.'

'Are you thinking what I am thinking, Sonny?'

'Yes, Micky. I reckon the second man in the truck last night was our friend, Bart. He was riding shotgun and directing the driver to the stash.'

'Exactly,' I said. 'It must have been a calculated risk for him. Maybe Kevin's current indisposition has forced him into the open. He must have thought he got away with it, too.' We both smiled.

It was too risky to put the surveillance team on Bart while we waited for the second consignment to arrive, so we used the time to familiarise ourselves with the local landscape and the network of roads that surrounded the airport. We knew that the truck had been heading north when we lost it, so we concentrated on the routes in and out of the area. North led towards the Sarasin Bridge, which connected Phuket Island to the mainland, but it was also the direction to the yacht marina and the east coast. We detached two men to the *On On Hotel* in Phuket Town, close to the eastern coastline.

The *On On* was Phuket's oldest guesthouse and tiny by the standards of the modern hotels sprouting up on the island's opposite west coast. It had an old-fashioned, Portuguese colonial air about it – all shutters and ancient blue-tiled floors – a charming throwback to the last century. It was a surprising choice in some ways, but it was tucked away and quiet and relatively close to the east coast marinas – an ideal place for Kevin to wait. The news that Bart and Kevin had fallen out was intriguing; maybe it was over money or maybe they had disagreed about the way the operation was running. It was also possible that Kevin had compromised himself in some way and Bart wanted him hidden. Whatever the reason, it was clear that Kevin had been banished to the hotel and told to cool his heels.

I rang Lek a couple of times but she reported that all was quiet. There was little reason for her involvement now. The business between Bart and Bhang had almost concluded – the last messages had been exchanged, the money had been handed over and the first load had been successfully delivered. It helped to know that Bart had made contact with Pisak. It meant the two were self-sufficient and would only revert back to Bhang if something went horribly wrong. The *On On* surveillance team confirmed that Kevin and his girlfriend had booked into a room on the second floor. She went out only occasionally and Kevin looked moody and restless when he appeared briefly at breakfast. I hoped Bart would break his silence and dispatch Lek with another message for Kevin. Clearly, he still needed him to implement the plan, although I suspected Kevin knew pretty much what he had to do already.

In Marine Police HQ, I introduced James Breach to Commander Bamroong. They hit it off immediately. James was a bluff but incredibly likable man, broad-chested and loud. I worried slightly that Bamroong might react defensively to him – why did he need a whiskered Brit to tell him his job? But I was way off the mark. After a short summary of our objectives, I was abruptly sidelined, as the two men started yakking and cracking jokes with one another. It seemed their maritime backgrounds and the mysterious language of the sea transcended mere landlubber conversation. I left them to it – sharing their sea dog stories and swinging the lamp. By the end of the week, James informed me that the Phuket Marine Branch was a fine collection of men and all very capable – even if they had some idiosyncratic ways and habits which he found difficult to fathom.

'They're a bit trigger-happy,' he commented. When I asked him to explain, he told me that Bamroong ordered a lot of gun drills at sea and that his men were constantly cleaning and checking their weapons, as if they were itching for a scrap. Daily firearm training was mandatory and most of it was aimed at harmless chunks of assorted flotsam. HM Customs' cutters in Britain had not been armed for over a hundred years, which meant that the whole business was alien to James. So, he just watched them practicing and blocked his ears while they blasted away happily. When they were not shooting, James had time to run some boarding exercises, talk tactics, test their radios and by the time he had finished, he understood their capabilities and those of their vessels. He gave them a hearty "thumbs up". I was relieved James had fitted in so well and made a mental note to thank Joe West for supporting me again.

On Wednesday, 12 April, we plotted up around the airport in a slightly different formation from the previous week and waited for TG452 to land. We had ensured the hanger exit was observed properly and cars were positioned to follow the truck north. We knew we could not mess up this time and I felt nervously confident. I had wanted to put a tracking beacon on the load – it would have made our job so much easier – but we concluded that there was no time or place to secrete a device. We would rely on good, old-fashioned surveillance instead – "Mark One Eyeball", as we called it.

'And, anyway, it will be more fun this way!' I told the team, tongue firmly lodged inside my cheek.

The second delivery was a carbon copy of the first. At seven fifteen, the black pick-up emerged like a greyhound out of its trap from the back of the airport hangar, through the un-padlocked gate and started to head north. Only one thing had changed – the vehicle had just a single driver on board this time. Sonny and the surveillance team followed. A few minutes before eight, the pick-up clattered down a narrow turning towards Kung Bay, on the north-eastern shores of the island. Our earlier reconnaissance told us it was a one-way track which led to a tiny settlement nestling under the trees and dripping mangroves of the shoreline. The team stopped their cars. As the truck disappeared into the darkness, they held back. Any unfamiliar car lights would have attracted attention. Sergeant Thip dispatched two men, on foot, down the trail to see what they could see. Sonny and the rest dispersed soundlessly into the shadows. He told me later that it had been eerily quiet, so they had maintained strict radio silence as they waited. Forty minutes later, the footmen re-joined their cars, mud-spattered and dishevelled. They reported that the pick-up driver and three other men had unloaded a lot of heavy sacks into a decaying shack perched at the side of an unsteady-looking, wooden jetty. They had counted forty bags. By dragging himself on his hands and knees through the vegetation, one of the footmen had got close enough to observe similar sacks already stacked in the back of the old shed, lit in the murk by a burning taper. He estimated at least another forty. We did the sums: about eighty sacks in all, each one, we speculated, weighing in at fifty kilos.

The officers had another piece of vital information to add to the growing mix. Fifty feet from the boat shed, lying alongside the jetty in shallow water, was a weather-beaten fishing boat, about forty feet in length, with an open deck and a covered wheelhouse at the stern. It was too dark to identify, but a surreptitious return visit in daylight would soon rectify that.

Colonel Surachai greeted the news that we had wrested back control of the operation with palpable relief. He had risked his neck and had been rewarded for his courage. To have located the stash of drugs was a huge step forward, but there were still many gaps in our intelligence. Critical, was the date and time the drugs would be moved; we agreed they would not remain there for long.

The destination of the packages was easier to guess. My experience told me that the scruffy fishing boat held the key. The gang must be awaiting the arrival of another boat, or boats, capable of making a long sea passage through international waters. The fishing boat would be used to rendezvous with the larger craft a few miles offshore, where the cargo would be transferred. Months later, the process would be repeated in reverse: the drugs offloaded onto smaller inshore vessels for their final landing. We called this smuggling scenario a "mother ship/daughter ship operation" or "coopering". The latter term came into use in eighteenth century Britain when Dutch boats used to sit off the east coast of England, at the three-mile territorial limit, passing contraband to English buyers across the maritime border. A Dutch word for selling or trading sounded to the English like "cooper" and the name stuck.

In this case, of course, we had two mother ships over the horizon – *Guiding Lights* and *Cornish Lady*. But we still did not know when and where the cooper would take place. Without these crucial pieces of information, we needed to take a few more operational risks. One option was to put a tracker beacon onto the fishing boat and follow it when it left the shade of the mangroves. After a long discussion with James, we ruled that out – we had neither the time nor the resources to conduct a covert boarding and attach the beacon. But he was optimistic about his new friends in Commander Bamroong's little navy. His advice was to position one of the police patrol boats about a mile offshore and monitor the movement of the fishing vessel using on-board radar. He assured me that it would work and his encouraging noises gave me some renewed confidence.

Eventually, we reached a consensus and it was agreed that I would have to brief the embassy. If it all went badly, the Ambassador would get one of those unwanted surprises that he had warned me so often about.

I called Lek the following morning and we exchanged a few strained words. She confirmed that Bart had been at home all night and there was still no sign of Kevin. Sonny drove me to the airport, after a snatched plate of fried noodles, and I took the next flight up to Bangkok. At four o'clock, I was sitting in Bernard Norman-Smith's plush office. Jim Gallow had joined us at the Ambo's insistence and I tried not to let his presence unsettle me. I went steadily through the details and both men listened attentively. Jim looked hostile, but I was accustomed to that – he was merely aggravated that his own band of loners had not come up with something half as interesting.

'I assume you have briefed your people in London, Mike?' the Ambassador drawled.

'Yes, they have been involved every step of the way.'

Gallow glowered at me, doubtless resentful that I had not kept him equally well-informed.

'Good. And they support you in your proposed action?'

'Yes, one hundred percent. They know how important it is to pull out the roots – not just the flower tops. We have a terrific chance to dig up some very deep roots, some that have been frustrating us for many years.' As I spoke, I reflected that the most entrenched root of all, Bart, would not be one of them, but they did not need to know that I had my own private plan for him. The case would still be a massive success, even if Bart slipped away into the night again.

The Ambassador said, 'Well, I suggest you hold a proper briefing tomorrow, if you can. I'll invite some of the Mission, just in case your plans have an impact on their work. I suggest you bring along a couple of your Thai friends so we have a balanced mix.' He turned to Jim Gallow, who had remained silent throughout.

'Any thoughts, Jim? Sound OK to you?'

'Just one thing.' Jim leered at me like a cat that had cornered a defenceless field mouse. 'This agent of yours; what do you know of her? Is she reliable? A lot seems to rest on her shoulders – quite a burden, if you ask me.'

'I know her very well, Jim. And it's a good question,' I said, trying to flatter him. 'She has been flawless up to now.' I paused as I cogitated on my choice of words. 'I am waiting for one final piece of intelligence from her before I pull the trigger.'

'And what might that be, Mike?' Jim glared.

What a question! You simply do not ask questions like that and you know it, you bastard.

But the Ambassador grunted approvingly. 'Yes, Mike,' he said, 'what do you hope to learn from this Lek person next?'

The two of them looked at me without blinking.

'She is going to tell me where the drop will be,' I said slowly and deliberately to maximise the impact. I knew it was not true – all I expected from Lek was a little information about Kevin and Bart's movements on the day – but I was pleased with the effect the outright falsehood had on my audience.

As he stood up, the Ambassador said, 'Well, shall we say eleven tomorrow, Mike? – for your meeting, that is. I'll ask Joan to make up a list. I won't be able to come, as I'm having lunch with the American Ambassador, but I'll ask Head of Chancery to attend. Better invite some of our antipodean cousins, too – I don't want to upset Bruce. You can use the conference room and I'm sure everyone will be most interested to hear your plans in detail.'

After I left Norman-Smith's office, I rang Sonny. 'You had better get on the next flight up here. We have some more talking to do,' I said wearily.

CHAPTER NINETEEN

Phuket, Thailand – 14 April 1988

Twenty-four hours later, I was back in Phuket. The briefing of the masses had concluded and despite some irritating moments, I had got the green light to proceed. I flew south immediately for a final meeting with Lek, which had been decidedly fraught. We had come together in the *Blue Lotus*, said our goodbyes and held hands for the final time. She had cried and I had left abruptly to avoid doing the same.

The information she had shared at this, our last meeting, was stunning. The previous day, I had lied to the Ambassador about my expectation of obtaining the coordinates for the handover. Now, with my feelings in utter chaos, I believed I had them. And the date and time of the RV, too! Lek had shown me a tatty tourist map with an "x" marked in the middle of Phang Nga Bay. She also gave me some coded numbers that Bart had told her to take to Kevin. The figures had made me gasp. The assignation with Lek had been traumatic in the extreme – but when I had collected myself, I called James Breach to my apartment and asked him to bring his assemblage of local maritime charts. Together, we transposed the code and plotted the numbers. Transpose code is incredibly simple. To crack it, you just add five to each digit up to ten. Hence, one becomes six, three becomes eight. It works in reverse also, so nine becomes four, not fourteen, seven becomes two, and so on.

The numbers Lek had given me were:

535543955855609

Transposed they read:

080098400300154

In other words, the message from Bart to Kevin was giving him a latitude and longitude position, as well as a time and a date: *0800 North, 9840 East, 0300, 15 April.*

When we plotted the position on one of James' Admiralty charts, the spot coincided with my memory of the rough biro cross I had seen on Lek's tourist map. The information was startling: the RV was going to happen at three a.m. tomorrow morning in Phang Nga Bay. It was now a few minutes after eight – we had less than seven hours to pull things together.

My best guess was that Kevin, armed with the information given to him by Bart, would drive to the stash in Kung Bay and give the RV position and timings to the awaiting fishing boat crew. They would load the daughter ship with the eighty sacks and motor out the twenty-odd miles towards *Guiding Lights* and *Cornish Lady,* which I presumed were now loitering somewhere in the darkness of Phang Nga Bay. We estimated that at between seven and ten knots, the fishing boat's journey would take two to three hours. To make the crossing in time, it would need to leave Kung Bay at around midnight.

I wondered where Bart would be at that time. If Lek's intelligence was accurate, he would be keeping his head down, awaiting news of a successful loading. He and Kevin must have set up some ship-to-shore communications. I remembered the walkie-talkies that Chris Manton had purchased in Bangkok and the picture got clearer. It would be a simple task to communicate with a vessel at sea from the coastline, as long as there was line of sight and both parties used the same frequency. We contemplated the position on the chart again. The island of Koh Yao Yai had the shape of a dumbbell and appeared to block line of sight radio between Phuket and the sea to the east.

'Hang on,' said James. 'Look! The RV spot is quite close to that low-lying isthmus that joins the two parts of the island together. That is very low land indeed. There should be line of sight, after all. And by the look of things, the best place to send and receive messages is from that promontory, just to the north of the boat lagoon.' He jabbed his finger on the map. 'Mind you, if he has a scanner, he could eavesdrop other messages, too,' he added, trying to be helpful. He watched the expression change on my face, as I worked out the implications. 'Don't worry, Mike. I've set up an encrypted system for us. I brought some brand new kit with me from Marine Branch – thought it might come in useful.'

'Are there no ends to your talents?'

'My wife says so, in some areas…,' he sniggered.

'I bet that's where that bugger, Bart, is going to wait tonight – on that bloody headland and we have no spare men to cover it. We are stretched to the limit as it is,' I said.

'It's where I would sit if I wanted to keep in touch with the action,' he replied. 'But don't fret Mike, it's only a guess – he might even go out to meet the boats himself and anyway you know where he lives. We can always kick his door down in the morning!'

'Yes, we'll just have to see how things pan out,' I said thoughtfully.

James telephoned Commander Bamroong and after a high spirited conversation, scuttled off to the marine base in Chalong, where he had set up a control room. We agreed to meet again at ten for a final briefing. As he hurried out the door, the phone rang. It was Sonny; he had just arrived back at the hotel.

'Hi, Sonny. Listen, it's hit the fan – at least, it will do in a few hours. I am going to brief Surachai. Can you gather the surveillance team and meet me for a briefing at Marine HQ, Chalong, at ten p.m.?' He needed no further explanation and replaced the phone. I was grateful to have him alongside.

I drove the forty minutes to Chalong alone. The relative

tranquility made it hard for me not to think about the corner into which I had painted myself. I was an optimist; the operation, despite the potential setbacks and possible disappointments, would somehow work out OK. But I knew in my core that this time it was going to be different. This investigation was special to me, obviously, and it would be a professional test, of course, but I could cope with that. However, I had a more intimate struggle to endure, involving my deepest personal demons and my seemingly countless human insecurities. Invisible forces were lining up against me, ones that were immune to my well-drilled and practiced skill sets. There were private battles to fight, if I was to survive. The thought of them made me retch. I was scared.

We assembled at Marine Police Headquarters at the allotted hour. Sonny had arrived with Sergeant Thip and his surveillance team; Commander Bamroong and his sailors were seated in a conspiratorial huddle in one corner; and I could see the half-dozen of Jirapat's men that Surachai had purloined on my behalf in another. Our strategy was simple. The surveillance team would be quickly dispatched to Kung Bay with three of Jirapat's group as muscle backup. Their job was to dig themselves into covert positions around the small jetty, within sight of the fishing vessel. Sergeant Thip had already done the ground work and knew where to place his men. When the bags were being loaded, they would report events, watch the fishing boat depart and await its return. On a signal from us, they would storm the boat when it reappeared, hopefully unburdened of its cargo, arrest the crew and anyone else foolish enough to be hanging around.

We had three police vessels at our disposal: one fifty-foot, steel-hulled patrol boat and two nine-metre, offshore, rigid-hulled, inflatable boats or RHIBs, as the specialists called them. Each of the RHIBs had a tiny cabin, open to all the elements, from which it was controlled. The large patrol boat had a top speed of twenty knots, but the RHIBs were capable of over forty and could perform tight turns, even on a moderate sea. In terms of pace and manoeuvrability, we were more than a match for an ancient Thai fishing boat and a couple of large yachts. All the vessels and each of the crew were armed to the gunwales and the array of weaponry was scary. James reminded me that the men were not short of shooting practice, either.

We decided to deploy the patrol boat and one of the RHIBs about two miles to the north and east of the known RV point. If the crews of *Guiding Lights* and *Cornish Lady* were keeping a radar watch, the signals given by the police boats should not cause them much alarm. To a standard yacht radar, the vessels would look like small fishing boats. The police's radar was powerful and could detect other craft around them across a wide ring of open ocean. In addition, each boat carried the latest night imaging equipment – another gift from James, courtesy of Auntie Betty. This allowed the crew to see in the dark, literally. It should not be difficult to identify our three targets by their speed, direction and, ultimately, by their interaction with one another. Anyway, we knew the latitude and longitude of their meeting place, so any pings in the vicinity would attract our attention. We decided to keep one RHIB at the marine base in reserve, as a southerly backstop to cover the route into the wide expanse of the Andaman Sea.

'How do you think the RV will pan out, James?' I asked as we pored over the charts.

'I reckon the fishing boat will not want to mix it with both yachts at the same time – too dangerous. They will want to offload one at a time.' Commander Bamroong concurred – the two like-minded, aquatic animals in full agreement again. 'With the speed we have at our disposal, we will be down on them like a pod of dolphins and give them the shock of their lives,' James added gleefully.

We agreed to observe the first transfer from a safe distance and then strike the second as it was taking place. If the fishing boat had already detached from the two yachts, we could scoop it up later, either using the reserve boat to intercept it or simply by allowing it to return to its swampy base where Sergeant Thip's reception committee waited. Sonny offered to go with James in the patrol boat and I could not object. *He* would see some of the action, at least, unlike Commander Bamroong and I, who were forced to remain in the control room in an insane attempt to orchestrate things from there.

James gave us the weather forecast; the rain had stopped and we were in for a clear, still night. There was no moon so it would be dark. Frequencies and call signs were exchanged, ammunition distributed and I wished everyone the best of luck. The briefing had taken less than ten minutes. The team shuffled out of the room noisily and then all of a sudden it was as quiet as solitary confinement. I had done all I could – it was up to the others now.

'Would you like some jasmine tea?' Bamroong popped his head into the room. It was a harmless question that evoked despondent memories of my first meeting with Lek in *Filomena's* coffee shop all those months ago.

'Yes, please, Commander. That would be excellent.'

Just before eleven, the first radio messages of any importance began to crackle into the control room. Sergeant Thip reported that they had taken up their dug-in positions; all was quiet. They could see a few locals congregating near the jetty, eating barbecued food around a blazing fire and drinking from the necks of cheap Thai whisky bottles. Importantly, the fishing boat was still alongside, gently rocking on her lines and the doors to the jetty shack were tightly shut. The skippers of the two deployed police vessels had logged three radar hits each on their way out to their allotted points and this gave me some encouragement that someone else was out there, under the stars of the cloud-free night.

At half past eleven, I punched the air when I heard the welcome news that there had been an arrival in Kung Bay. A car had pulled up and a rotund *farang* had joined the barbecue. The flames from the campfire lit his face enough for a positive identification. It was Kevin Silverstream. Within minutes, the locals had gulped down the remnants of their whisky and were loading the fishing boat. I knew we were in business and I could feel my adrenaline levels start to rise.

By midnight, the loading had been completed and a muffled bang, accompanied by a cloud of acrid black soot, announced that the old boat's engines had come to life. The surveillance team had counted eighty sacks being lifted onto the open deck of the tattered little vessel – just as we had predicted. Each bag had taken two men to shift and I wondered how easy it would be to do the same, in the dark, on a rolling ship. At least it was calm tonight but visibility without a moon could be a problem for them. It meant they could see us less easily, too. Maybe the weather was in our favour, after all.

The likeable Commander Bamroong called for more tea and this time some sticky cake came with it. As we waited, we chatted about our respective careers and found we had a lot in common. Outside our work, there was more that bonded us – we both had twenty-two-year-old daughters, a passion for golf and a liking for *Singha* beer. Within an hour, we had become the best of friends. When the conversation slackened, we listened to the intermittent clicks and scratches of the radio.

I began to feel very tired and my thoughts turned to Bart and my pledge to Lek that I would protect him. I wondered again where he was – I assumed he would be on the eastern coastline by now, monitoring a radio frequency, waiting to get the all-clear from Kevin. I knew that once he heard that things had gone badly, he would make a run for it. One unsettling thought came back to me repeatedly: Lek's story about a fast boat Bart had chartered to take him the two hundred miles to Langkawi and the safety of Malaysian jurisdiction. It would be an eight-hour trip, at least – and a difficult one. I lifted my head from my pineapple sponge.

'Commander Bamroong, tell me, do you know of any Thai men who own a speedboat around here?'

'Oh, there are many, Khun Mike. Many people have fast boats for fishing and things like that.'

'But what about a bigger craft – one that could get to Langkawi in a single night?'

He thought for a moment.

'Maybe a boat based in Rawai, right down in the south?' I added.

'Well, Khun Mike, there is only one like that in Rawai – the *Golden Bua*. It does trips to the islands for rich tourists. The owner is a Thai man. He used to work for the Marine Police. I know him well.'

I didn't know whether to pursue the subject, in the light of this interesting revelation, but I had now got Bamroong's interest. 'Oh, a policeman,' I said coolly. 'That's OK. I was thinking about someone who might be a criminal.' I watched his reaction carefully.

'Oh my Buddha, Khun Mike, I said I knew him, but I did not say I liked him. We have been trying to catch him for years, but he is too smart.'

'Why, what does he do?' I tried to look surprised.

'He is a smuggler, Khun Mike! And a thief! A very big, dangerous crook, if you ask me. He bought his speedboat last year and we don't know where he got the money. But, for sure, he is up to monkey business.'

'What's his name, Commander? It's possible that he might be involved in this case.'

'His name is Natthapat Pakbeekit – but everyone calls him Khun Bee,' he replied, looking triumphant.

I frowned a little but said nothing. Instead, I took another chunk of cake. Bamroong must have seen something in my reaction because he followed up with a question. 'Khun Mike, if you know anything about this man, you must tell me.'

I looked at him innocently and could see urgency in his eyes. 'Oh, it's not much more than a hunch, really,' I responded. 'It's just a vague idea we have that one of the *farangs* may try to use a speedboat to escape to Malaysia if the night goes badly for him.' As I spoke, I could see his interest mounting.

'I know where the *Golden Bua* is,' Bamroong said abruptly. 'Maybe we should send the reserve RHIB down to cover it. If the *farang* leaves tonight, it would be best if we were closer to him, I think.'

'What is this *Golden Bua* boat capable of?' I asked.

'Oh, about thirty-five knots. The RHIB is faster, for sure, but if he gets too far away, we would not have the range to catch him.'

Just then, the radio sparked into life. It was Sonny reporting from the patrol boat. 'We have located two possibles – about half a mile from the RV. They are about a mile apart and approaching the target location.'

I looked at the control room clock; it was three minutes past two. 'Looking good,' I said to Bamroong, changing the subject. I was hoping he would not resurrect the conversation about sending the spare RHIB to cover Bart's potential means of escape. I wished I could pour myself a stiff drink – maybe it would make me think straighter. My enforced sobriety was preventing me from keeping all the helpless thoughts about Lek from eating into my consciousness. A couple of whiskies would dull the heartache and put me back on track. 'Commander – I don't suppose you have a drink anywhere around here, do you?'

'Yes, of course, Khun Mike.' He clapped his hands. 'Bring some more tea – warm tea!' he shouted.

I wondered how I had got myself into this hopeless situation. I wanted to keep Lek so badly, but knew it was wrong. It was wrong every way I looked at it. Wrong each time I counted the reasons. Wrong from every imaginable angle. Just plain wrong. I could not and must not have her. And yet, I yearned to hold her in my arms again and see her electric smile and the intensity in her eyes. It was almost too much to bear and still the damn radio went chattering on noisily, annoyingly. The growing awareness that I would never see her again was wounding me so deeply I thought I would start to weep. By the morning, Bart would be in Malaysia, waiting for her, and there was nothing I could do about it.

'The RHIB, Khun Mike.' It was the Commander's voice. 'Do you want me to send the RHIB out towards Rawai? It may be your only chance to catch this *farang*.' His voice sounded as distant as a dream.

Your only chance to catch Bart! Your only *chance.*

'I'm sorry, Commander – what was that?'

The fugue cleared slightly. Bamroong was staring at me with bulging eyes. 'I think we should send out the RHIB. All three boats are on the radar screens now – they are just metres apart. It will be over very soon. We must send the boat now, if you want us to catch him.'

My *Seamaster* told me it was ten minutes to three. 'How long will it take the RHIB to get down to Rawai?'

'About thirty minutes,' Bamroong replied quickly.

'OK, but I want to be on board, Commander. Is that OK? I will recognise this man. I know what he looks like.'

'It will be bumpy – I'll get you a life jacket.'

Another message sputtered over the system, sounding tinny and synthetic. It was James this time. 'It's a knock! It's a knock!' came the strident voice. 'All units acknowledge.' This was the familiar Customs code word for a strike, but it sounded strange to hear it six thousand miles away from New Fetter Lane, under the whirring fans of a maritime control room in southern Thailand.

I could only imagine the drama and noise of the unfolding ocean scene, sitting helplessly as I did, surrounded by the protecting walls of our antiseptic, white-washed cell. Whatever was happening, it was happening fast and our master plan, the one that involved boarding one vessel at a time, had obviously gone right out of the window. One thing was plain – all three target vessels had converged on the same position at the same time and were now in the process of simultaneous unloading and loading. It must have been mayhem. James would not have called the knock unless his vessels were within striking range. So it seemed clear the two police patrol boats had arrived out of the darkness and surprised the fishing vessel and its attendant yachts in the middle of their coopering.

Minutes passed in stillness for us. By now, they must be alongside and trying to board. I imagined bright searchlights illuminating the scene and guns trained on *Guiding Lights,* warning shots being fired at *Cornish Lady,* coarse words exchanged between the police and cowering crew members. An image came to mind of Conrad Duncan standing on the rolling deck of *Cornish Lady,* hands held in surrender and I visualised Kevin Silverstream cursing as the handcuffs were wrapped around his wrists. We sat wordlessly, picking our teeth as we waited for further news. Nearly ten anxious minutes elapsed. And then the silence was broken abruptly. 'Control, Control – India Mike Two.' It was James again. 'We have all three vessels in custody. Drugs on board, repeat, drugs on board. We have ten persons under arrest. Only minor injuries. Making for Chalong Port now. ETA three hours.'

The police radio operator acknowledged the message in a professional monotone, but the mood in the control room had changed from one of dull foreboding and finger-pulling apprehension to soaring triumph and blessed release. Bamroong did a little jig and clapped his hands over and over again. I simply slumped in my chair – I had no energy for high fives or shrieks of delight. It was over, at last, and I just wanted to go to my bed.

Bamroong screamed something into the radio; there was a long exchange in Thai as he barked out orders and instructions. I sat silently and watched the show, as if I had been suddenly transported from the front row of the stalls to the most distant perch in the gods, far away from the action around me.

CHAPTER TWENTY

My trance was punctured by a jarring tug of my arm and a bright red life jacket being thrust into my chest.

'We must go now, Khun Mike,' came a low, urgent voice from one of Bamroong's men. 'I know where to find the boat,' he whispered. 'Come, we must go.'

He dragged me up before I could resist and I followed him, trying to gather my thoughts. We moved out into the balmy air and onto a rocking pontoon. Three marine policemen were already on board the RHIB. I stumbled over the gunwales and climbed into a sculpted seat. One of the crew strapped me in. The engines erupted and their enormous power shot us away from the pier; in seconds, we were careering between the dark shadows of Phang Nga Bay's tiny islands and heading south towards Rawai.

The craft bumped and crashed across the surface of the sea; it was lucky I hadn't eaten anything except fruit cake in the last twelve hours. At first, the feeling of speed was exhilarating and my head cleared enough for me to enjoy the ride. But after twenty minutes of continual slamming into the waves, I began to feel distinctly uncomfortable. I looked over at my shipmates. Their faces were resolute against the rushing sea air. They wore no expression, save a look of quiet determination and solid, driven purpose. It was far too noisy for conversation, especially in Thai, so I grimaced into the wind and tried to look at the horizon, to prevent me heaving up the bile that was now creeping towards my oesophagus.

By three forty, we reached a point off the most southerly tip of Phuket Island that commanded an excellent view of the tiny harbour in Rawai. The RHIB slowed to a stop and we wallowed in the lapping water. I was drenched, but at least my brain was now buzzing. The crew smiled and nodded approvingly at me, presumably understanding what I had just gone through. One of them pulled out a pair of James' night vision goggles and peered at the shoreline.

'Can you see Khun Bee's boat?' I asked in a whisper, which was curious, as there was no one else around for at least half a mile. The crew did not reply, taking it in turns to stare into the goggles.

Finally, one of them spoke. It was the policeman who had escorted me to the RHIB and he must have been the one in charge. 'This man you want to find – does he have a gun?' he asked impassively.

The question had huge ramifications and I needed time to think my answer through carefully. If I said yes, I knew it would be a licence for the police to shoot first. If I said no, it would make their job more difficult and potentially more dangerous; if indeed there was a firearm on board, their lives would be at risk. I knew in my heart that the answer was no. Nowhere in the files, nowhere in any of the intelligence that we had collected on him for the last ten years was there any suggestion that Bart had ever carried a gun. I knew that he was not that type of man – a nasty, bloodsucking, drug smuggling criminal who used and abused the woman I longed for, but definitely not a killer. The officer looked at me and repeated the question. I answered it with another.

'This man, Khun Bee, you know him well. Does *he* have a gun?' I hoped that the reply would be yes – and that the question of Bart's firearms history would become irrelevant.

'No, never. He never had a gun – we have boarded him many times, we never found a gun. He has never fired at us before.'

As he spoke, one of his team passed him the night vision goggles and pointed at the beach, about four hundred yards distant. A few excited words were exchanged by the crew in Thai and the engines of the RHIB fired up again. We were on the move, but not fast. We were merely ticking over – almost in idle – as we crawled closer to the shore. The officer nudged my shoulder and pointed at a light moving from left to right in front of us, only a quarter of a mile away.

'That is Khun Bee!' he cried. 'You were right, Khun Mike – he is going out in his boat tonight.' The crew looked pleased and as the RHIB picked up speed, they started to check their weapons – clicking and flicking, ratcheting and rattling.

'Khun Mike, you did not say if this *farang* is armed or not.' He repeated the question for a third time.

The vessel crossing our path was now heading directly south and appeared to be picking up momentum. It was difficult to judge from the single light and the vaguest silhouette, but it looked like the boat was accelerating away, increasing the distance between us with every second. The officer in charge grabbed the radio and shouted into the microphone. I could not understand most of the words, but it was evident that he was ordering the vessel to stop. It did not. After twenty seconds, he bellowed the message again, virtually screaming down the mike. I could make out the words, '*Golden Bua, Golden Bua!* Police! Police!'

The RHIB skipper stared down at me, awaiting an answer to his question. In that desperate moment, I grasped that I was being offered a chance to change the future – to scupper Bart's plans, to prevent his escape, to win Lek back. Maybe I possessed more power than I thought. Conceivably, I could do something to alter the course of events. But at what cost?

The coxswain opened the throttle of the RHIB and we leapt forward. We began to make ground on the fleeing speedboat, but it was slow progress. Bee's boat was clearly quicker than they had thought and its driver was evidently aware we were in pursuit, for he showed us that it was manoeuvrable, too. *Golden Bua* started to weave and roll, dart and dive, changing course every few seconds, in its attempts to elude us. The chase went on like this for ten more grinding, bouncing minutes with us gaining ground, inch by slamming inch and then I glimpsed the RHIB coxswain yanking at the skipper's elbow and pointing towards the control panel. I tilted my head and saw he was indicating the fuel gauge – we were running low. There was a heated, incomprehensible exchange and an infuriated look on the skipper's face. I speculated that whoever was responsible for fueling the boat had not done his job properly and the long, fast trip down from Chalong must have done the rest. Heads would roll if this meant the difference between capture and escape – someone would have to take the blame for his idleness. I wondered how long we could maintain this earsplitting pace and the skipper appeared to be thinking the same. He was making some hurried calculations on the back of his hand. *Golden Bua* continued to thunder south, rocking and zigzagging across the bay. The RHIB flew past Coral Island and then, minutes later, Racha Island disappeared behind us. We were nearly twenty miles offshore, but now we were making noticeable progress. As we gained on them, I began to see the speedboat in greater detail. She was just a hundred yards from us now. The skipper kept up his frantic calls for it to stop.

The coxswain shouted something, the skipper turned to me. 'We cannot continue – we have no fuel.' He pointed at his greased weapon. 'Does he have a gun? Yes or no, Khun Mike?' His face was inches from mine. We thudded into another wave; the engine screamed at me.

'Yes, he has a gun!' I yelled. 'Yes, he is armed.'

'He will fire first, you think?' I could hardly hear him above the noise and splattering of sea water. But I knew exactly what he meant. The combination of sheer adrenalin and my foul mood made the decision for me.

'Yes, he may fire first. Take care,' I bawled.

The skipper nodded expressively to his small team. The RHIB slowed to a dead stop. The crew crouched against the hull and took deliberate aim with their automatic weapons. I wondered if they would fire warning shots first; within seconds the answer came. In a series of cracks and fizzes, each man fired two, maybe three shots directly at the stern of *Golden Bua*. The bullets flew off into the night and I could see them raking the superstructure of the boat, one after another, in quick succession. Still she sped away from us.

One of the projectiles must have hit something combustible, as a small fire broke out just above the water line. Within seconds, the flames had licked around the stern, enveloping the area over the rudder and propellers. Despite the damage, the boat seemed not to lose any speed. Indeed, she was further away from us now than before; our enforced slowing, to enable the crew to take aim, had put greater distance between us. The blaze grew larger and I could make out a man on board spraying extinguisher onto it.

The three policemen took aim again. I covered my ears as the bullets flashed past the bow of the RHIB. *Golden Bua* was now over three hundred yards away. It was to be our last volley. The coxswain turned the RHIB to starboard and we lay dead in the water for a few moments, contemplating the fleeing, smoking powerboat.

And then something sickening happened. As the five of us gazed at the vanishing ball of fire, even now receding rapidly away from us, there was a flash, followed almost immediately by the blast of a huge explosion. The speedboat had quite simply erupted, like a comet spewing its contents into the clear night air, the red and white dazzle of its pyrotechnics reflecting on the dark glass of the flat sea. A black-topped cloud formed above the orange glare as pieces of debris – wood, steel, bone – slapped into the water around us.

'It's the fuel!' cried the skipper. 'She has extra tanks on the deck for the long trip – we must have hit one of them.'

The sea set alight as acrid smoke and flame combined; the inferno appeared to float both in and on top of the water simultaneously. Through the crimson light, I caught sight of the bow of the *Golden Bua* pointing vertically out of the sea like a jagged rock. As I watched, transfixed, it slid silently backwards under the waves and disappeared in a churning cauldron of oil, steam and water.

Even for the hardened policemen around me, the shock and horror of the scene was hard to digest. We watched helplessly as the sea enveloped the vessel like a python consuming a rodent. As the water flattened, an unnatural calm descended on the tableau as the eerie, silver luminosity of the stars replaced the fiery, red glow and night was restored. The coxswain steered the RHIB toward the spot where the vessel had gone down and we shone torches vainly into the gloom and listened for noises. But all was stillness. The skipper broke the silence by yelling a few words in Thai and the RHIB turned back towards the shore at a sedate pace.

'We have marked the spot on the chart,' he said to me. 'We need to make for the base. We have very little fuel. We will return at first light.'

We tied up against the jetty as dawn was breaking over the east coast. In the distance, across the bay to the north, I could make out the tiny silhouettes of five boats moving slowly towards us – a small Thai fishing boat, two large yachts and their escort. Within an hour, a fresh team had been assembled and was heading south to search for wreckage and survivors of the *Golden Bua*, but all of us who had witnessed that huge ball of fire knew that it was pointless. By midday, we had secured the seized vessels, unloaded the eighty sacks of Thai sticks and the interviews of the ten arrested men had commenced; Major Jirapat and Commander Bamroong orchestrated the interrogations.

Sonny was euphoric. 'Shit, Micky, that's the best fun I've had since the night my wife walked! We are all bloody heroes, mate, bloody champions!' he bellowed.

By the end of the day, as I collapsed onto my bed in complete and utter exhaustion, the news of the bust had made the press – and not just the *Phuket Gazette*; the *Bangkok Post* had already dispatched reporters to Chalong and even the BBC was screaming for information. I woke the following morning to headlines in the Thai national papers.

"Police Seize Drugs – Farangs Arrested."
"Massive Haul of Weed – Two Men Feared Dead."
"Shoot-out at Sea!"

CHAPTER TWENTY-ONE

While I was reading the papers and rubbing cream into a new set of lines that had formed around my eyes, the bedside phone rang. I was not expecting another call from London, so I assumed it was Major Jirapat.

But it was a soft, female voice that spoke to me. It was Lek.

'Khun Mike – what has happened? I have seen the news and Bart has not called me. I have been waiting for his call, but no one has rung.'

'I have some bad news, I'm afraid, Lek. Look, it's difficult to explain on the phone, but I will not be able to meet you for a few days—'

'You can tell me, Khun Mike. Please tell me what has happened to Bart!'

I sat on the bed and tried to collect my thoughts. 'There was an accident early yesterday morning,' I said, trying hard to sound calm and reassuring, 'on the boat Bart was using to go to Malaysia. I was there – I saw it all.'

'What happened, Khun Mike?'

'There was some gunfire and Bart's boat was hit. I'm sorry, Lek – Bart is dead.' There was a horrible silence. I pressed the phone deeper into my ear, craning to hear her voice.

'But you promised me you would protect him.' She sounded very distressed. 'You said it would be fine – he would be OK. You would let him go.'

'Look, *teelak*, things got out of control. I did my best to look after him, but the police fired some shots and the boat just caught fire and sank right in front of me. There was nothing I could do.'

'But you promised me, Khun Mike. You gave me your word.'

'I know I did and, if it had been up to me, he would be in Kuala Lumpur now, waiting for you. But the fact is things did not go to my plan. Look, I need to talk to you, Lek. I have something important to tell you.'

I could hear a whimpering noise on the line. Lek was more upset than I had expected. 'What do you want to say? You can tell me now.'

I took a deep breath. 'Lek, I want to see you again. I want to help you.' I paused. 'I love you, Lek. I want to be with you.'

There was another dreadful hush. I repeated my words. 'I want to be with you, Lek. You and me. I will do anything for you,' I implored.

In a muted voice she said, 'Really? But you told me we could not work out – you and me. You had too many complications in your life.'

'I know, but I have been thinking about you every second and I really want things to work out for us. I want to be with you – I always wanted this, but I was too scared to admit it. Please tell me you will meet me. We can have a good life together – together we can help your family. Do you love me, Lek?'

'I feel sad about Bart,' she sniffled. 'But I have missed you very much. I would feel happy if we could be together, if that is what you want. It would be good for me. I miss you, Mike, for sure. Can I come to see you now?'

'Do you want to? Are you sure?' I muttered, hardly able to contain my emotions.

'Yes – for sure. I feel sad about Bart, but I know you can help me. I want you to help me.'

'Lek, I have a lot of things to do now. I have much to organise and arrange. I must go back to Bangkok today and then I have to go to London for a while. Look, I have an idea. Why don't I meet you in the lobby of the *President* exactly two weeks from today – on the last day of the month at eleven o'clock in the morning? I will be back by then. It's a Saturday, so we can make a day of it. Do you remember? That was the place where we first met?'

'Can I not see you now?'

'No, Lek, it is too dangerous for us. It's better if we do not speak until then. If you want us to be together, I'll have to sort out a lot of things. My office will want to talk to me. I have to go home to speak to my wife. Please give me some time. We can meet at the end of the month and we can start a new life together.'

'If that's what you want, Mike, I am happy. But we met in a coffee shop – not the *President*.'

'Yes – I forgot. But you went first to the *President* and the receptionist gave you a message to go to the café – do you remember?'

'Yes, I remember. OK, I will see you in the lobby, two weeks from today.'

'Until then, we must have no contact. Do you understand?'

After a little gentle cajoling, she agreed. As we spoke, I sensed her mood change from the initial despair on hearing about Bart's fate to excited anticipation, as a new vista had opened up for her. I had made my decision and I would stick with it, despite the obvious consequences. This was one promise I meant to keep. I would not let her down again. I would divorce Maureen and persuade the ID to give me another eighteen months in Bangkok. After the success of the investigation, how could they refuse? That would buy some time to work out a proper future for us. One day, we would be married; maybe children would follow – a son and heir for me, perhaps. The simple fact that I had ended months of anguished indecision was sufficient to send an awesome serenity through my whole system. My future now appeared crystal clear, so full of promise and adventure. The thought of it made me tingle. I felt like a newly freed man.

The world looked wonderful from every angle. My long-running investigation had ended – it had been a huge success; my reputation was made – I was a champion amongst my peers and all my detractors were left scurrying for cover; and most important, Lek and I were going to be together.

'Look, I have to go now,' I said, 'and you have your work, too!'

'No, I am not going to work today. I am too tired. I am going to call in and tell them. I just need time to think about everything. I'll go in tomorrow.'

The next week flew past in a haze of meetings and long-distance telephone calls. As expected, London wanted me to fly back to debrief them and Gill had booked me some tickets. A meeting with the Chief had been scheduled and the Treasury Minister for Customs wanted me to call on him in his Whitehall office. It had been one of the ID's greatest successes and everyone wanted to be a part of it.

All ten men arrested in Phang Nga Bay that night had been charged, plus four others found hiding in the makeshift jetty warehouse in Kung Bay. Christopher Manton, the Australian skipper, confessed after only an hour of questioning and implicated everyone else. That suited me. A few years' discount on his prison sentence in exchange for damning testimony against the rest was a good bargain. Kevin Silverstream stubbornly refused to answer any questions for two days, much as we had anticipated – the old lag knew the ropes and did not want to add any further evidential fuel to the fire. But just as we began to feel a quiet respect for his stolid self-defence, he made the desperate mistake of trying to pay off one of the Thai police officers. In some circumstances, this might have worked, but not under the full glare of world publicity. It backfired badly and he ended up facing further charges for attempted bribery. Poor Conrad Duncan, ham-fisted as ever, tried to lie his way out of things and made valiant but contradictory bids to explain what he was doing in charge of a Cornish yacht in the Andaman Sea at three in the morning. His network of stories combined to trap him like a wayward fly in a black widow's web. We wrapped him up in the silk of his own deception. Realising too late that his errant strategy was just tying him up in knots, he shut down completely for the last two hours of his interview, but the damage was done. Surachai had sent a gang of his strongest boys to arrest Bhang and his cargo cohorts at Don Muang Airport. It was just as well, apparently, as Bhang had put up a violent struggle and attacked Major Pongpat with a long screwdriver. It took five of the BNU to hold him down and handcuff his writhing wrists. I learned later that Pongpat had chosen to interview him personally, behind closed doors. Blood had been spilt in the fight to arrest him, so a little more would not be noticed; Pongpat wanted to make the most of the opportunity. Bhang folded after three hours of blunt, behind the scenes interrogation and when I saw his mugshot, taken when he was charged, he was barely recognisable.

After two and a half days, there were eighteen men on remand awaiting trial. The evidence against them appeared to be irrefutable, whichever way we looked at it. Things could not have been better – or so I thought. One afternoon, the day before I was due to fly to London as the conquering hero, I was going through the backlog of intercept tapes at the BNU. These had been largely neglected, due to the fast-moving events of recent days, but I needed to be sure that we had not missed anything useful before we closed the case. With earphones attached, I had listened to four thirty-minute cassettes and dismissed the content as mundane and irrelevant. The last one in the box was dated 16 April, which I thought strange, as it was a day *after* the knock had gone down. So, as I slipped it into the replay machine, I did not expect to hear anything of interest. There were the normal outgoing ringing tones (they went on longer than usual, I thought), the noise of the receiver being picked up, a muffled sound and then the voice of a woman:

'Klun Mike – *what has happened? I have seen the news and*

Bart has not called me. I have been waiting for his call, but no one has rung.'

I felt a cold bead of sweat form between my eyes. I lifted the collar from my neck – it was sticking to my skin. Then things got worse.

'I have some bad news, I'm afraid, Lek. Look, it's difficult to explain—'

The comprehension of what had happened hit me in the solar plexus like a fifty-kilo sack of hashish smashing against the hull of a fibreglass yacht.

My god! The lines on Bart's house have not been cut yet. When Lek called me, she rang from his home – just what I had told her not to do! Why had I not worked it out at the time? It had been too early for her to be at work. I should have twigged!

My complacency had cost me. I had let my guard down and unless I could do something about it quickly, I would pay for it. I listened to the rest of the tape – it was excruciating. There was her sobbing, my attempts at gallant reassurance, my emotional invocation of love, the appalling acknowledgement of our illicit pact to protect Bart and our heart-rending talk about forging a new life together. It was unbearable to overhear each and every syllable. I was eavesdropping on my own folly. And this, of all conversations, was the one that I had yearned to have for so long. Now, I just wished I could bury it in the deepest waters of Phang Nga Bay, along with the wreckage of Bart's boat. This would sink *me* if it got out.

I tried to pull myself together.

Maybe the BNU had not heard the call yet – yes, there was a good chance of that.

I was alone in the room, so I surreptitiously put the tape in my pocket. But what about the copies Gill and I sent to London every week in the diplomatic bag? Had they gone? Or were they still here somewhere? I struggled to think when the dip bag last went out, but my mind was trying to compute too much already. So I rang Gill at the embassy and asked her.

'Hi, Mike. Oh yes, don't worry. I know you've been busy. Wut collected them yesterday – they went out in last night's bag. Oh, and the Ambassador wants you to go with him to see the Minister for National Security tomorrow. Khun Chavalit, I think his name is. He says it's a good news story. I have put it in your diary. You'll have time before your flight to London…'

I was not listening anymore.

CHAPTER TWENTY-TWO

On the fifth floor of the ID's New Fetter Lane bureau, the Chief Investigation Officer, Ralph Skinner, was waiting for me. Joe West was already seated when I entered, presumably there to corroborate the next few minutes – my painful execution. On the long flight into Heathrow, I had half convinced myself that the incriminating tape would be lurking, unheard, somewhere in the bottom of my desk officer's cupboard. But it took only seconds to work out that this had been a false hope. The Chief looked more like a schoolmaster than ever – positively aggressive, in fact. On his desk was a small cassette tape and he picked it up as soon as I sat in front of him. Joe shuffled in his chair uncomfortably. At the end of a twenty-minute, bile-filled monologue, during which the recording was played back to me in all its toe-curling glory, I was told my fate.

'I am short-touring you, Mike. It's as simple as that. I want you back in London in ten days. I cannot trust you anywhere overseas anymore. Go back to Bangkok, pack your things and return here by...' he looked at Joe for assistance.

'First of May, Chief,' Joe said calmly.

'Precisely. Back before the end of the month. I will have selected your replacement by then. I spoke personally to the Ambassador first thing this morning – charming man, I might add – and he is as disappointed in you as I am. And you can thank your lucky stars that this was not a case for us to prosecute in this jurisdiction. The Thais have assured me that they can convict on what they have and that your foolhardiness is immaterial under Thai law. If it were here, you'd be out of the door in a flash with a prosecution for malfeasance in a public office hot on your heels. I am going to assign you a desk job somewhere in personnel, you will lose your vetting and I'll be watching your every step. This will be the last time you venture abroad for Her Majesty. Do you understand? Now you can leave us.'

I decided to take the train straight back to the Purley suburbs, rather than face the wrath and ridicule of my colleagues. It was strange, sitting in a practically empty carriage at one o'clock on a Wednesday afternoon, without the barging, perspiring crowds to struggle against. I wished I had something at which to rail. Instead, there was just me and quiet reflection to cope with, as the wheels clattered rhythmically over the tracks past Thornton Heath.

It could have been much worse. I had fully expected a much harsher penalty for what I had done – a reversion of rank, at least. A quiet job in the backwaters of administration was generous, in fact, despite the loss of face and reduction in pay. But maybe the Chief was playing his own game and wanted to diffuse the whole affair. He was a consummate politician, after all. Any dramatic punishment would have attracted more attention than was welcome. At least he could still brief ministers positively about the case; he would not have wanted to take the gloss off that, especially as all the follow-up court work was out of his hands, yet to be carried out by others, over six thousand miles away. There would be no long-winded trial at the Old Bailey to open wounds and expose the frailties of the case. He would get the glory for a brilliant piece of international law enforcement without the potential damage of an embarrassing prosecution. In any event, within weeks, the matter would probably be forgotten and everyone would move on. Except me, it seemed.

As I gazed out of the rain-stained carriage window, my mind wandered across the open fields of South Croydon towards the eastern sky and I wondered what Lek was doing. She would be home from work, making plans to see me, perhaps. I was not sure. But one thing was certain – I still wanted her. I craved her so much it hurt. I would go back to her and all would be well. The job could stick itself!

My brief stay with the family confirmed my decision. There was no welcome for me there either, even though Maureen was unaware of my official predicament or why I had returned home unexpectedly. The fact that I been to see the Chief had not interested her. She did not ask about the progress of my investigation or question me when I told her that I was returning to Bangkok in a few days. Caroline was away at university. Even the dog looked decidedly underwhelmed this time. I decided not to tell Maureen that I had been ordered back to London at the end of the month. I had other plans anyway – and the news might spoil her chili con carne.

The next day, I visited the bank and made some international money transfers. I spoke to a kind cashier who gave me some tips about moving currency around and he generously helped me to do it – for a commission, of course. By the time we had finished, I had found enough money for me to exist in the Far East without work for twelve months, more if I was careful. I would need to find an apartment and a job in due course, but that could wait for the time being.

I knew I was being a coward when the time came for me to leave for the airport. I had not hinted at anything to Maureen; she had not asked either, so that made my behaviour feel more reasonable. I did not want a scene. I would call her from Bangkok to break the news about my new life and that I would not be coming back. I persuaded myself that she would have wanted it that way.

Back at the British Embassy, the Ambassador called me in for another humiliating dressing-down. I was getting used to them now and a weary fog seemed to envelop me as he droned on, his voice changing pitch inexplicably from time to time. I could cope with his ugly rhetoric, but what I found hard to endure was the sight of Jim Gallow perched at his side like a smirking velociraptor. I said very little and assured him that I would complete my exit arrangements within the next few days.

It was more difficult to explain to Gill what had happened. I could tell she was upset and from her tone, I detected that her innocent part in my downfall had not eluded her. I apologised to no one, packed my things, sorted out my lease and said goodbye to Wut. I arranged for various bits and pieces to be shipped back to England and collected all my essential belongings for transportation to a warehouse on the outskirts of Bangkok, where they would remain until I furnished my new apartment. I handed my keys to the security officer, left the embassy a full day ahead of schedule and booked myself into the *President Hotel*. I thought it would be a wonderful surprise for Lek. When we met, I could take her to my room, so we could talk about our future in privacy. I thought about calling her, but I worried that her phones might now be tapped and I did not want to exacerbate an already sensitive situation.

So I settled in for the night, drank a few more whiskies than usual and slept soundly for ten hours.

The lobby of the *President* was just as I remembered it when I had first met Lek. It was hard to believe it was that short a time – it felt now that I had known her all my life. My mind went back to that bright December day when I had watched her arrive in a *tuc tuc* and make her way gracefully into the hotel; her poise and her beauty had nearly taken my breath away. On that day, I had lurked like an assassin in the shadows, worried that she was being followed, wanting to size her up properly before making a move. But today it would be different. There could be no secrets now and the thought of a future existence without ambiguity or deception felt like a huge release of pent-up stress.

I came down from my room ten minutes before our arranged time. I wanted to ensure that the red leather sofa where I had first seen her sit was vacant. It seemed appropriate to greet her from there. It added a degree of poignancy and I was sure she would remember. I had vigorously scrubbed every inch of my body and in the process, I noticed that there were some areas that were less streamlined than I had imagined – a few sags and curves – but nothing a bout of proper exercise would not cure. I shaved as close as I dared and splashed some newly purchased, expensive aftershave on my neck. My hair had been cut the day before by the hotel barber. I put on a crisp, white, cotton shirt. I wanted so much to look good for her.

The red sofa was empty, so I spread myself across it, hoping to deter anyone else from joining me. I looked around the lobby and watched the holidaymakers with tight shorts and cotton dresses, the bellboys hurrying about with piles of suitcases. At precisely eleven, I looked towards the lobby entrance, but a large party of American tourists had just arrived from the airport and I could not see over the comic hats that the middle-aged men were wearing. I thought about standing up and half got to my feet but then thought better of it and sat down again. No point in looking apprehensive; she would be here any minute now.

'Mr. Rawlin?' a voice spoke gently next to my ear. 'Mr. Michael Rawlin, from the British Embassy?'

I looked up to see the pretty receptionist in her tight, emerald green skirt, hovering over me. I recognised her as the girl who had delivered my first message to Lek – the one that Gill had phoned through. I smiled cheerily as I recalled her face.

'Yes, I'm Mike Rawlin.'

'I have a message for you,' she said, handing me an envelope.

'It was left this morning by someone with an instruction for me to deliver it to you at eleven.'

I looked at her offering but did not take it. 'Was it a lady who came?' I asked.

'No, it was a man, a pilot from Thai Airways. He just gave it to me and asked me to give it to you.' She dangled the envelope ever closer and, hesitating, I took it from her hand. It had my name on it and the handwriting was unmistakably Lek's. As I tore it open, I wondered if she had been called into work for some reason.

There was no letter inside – just a single, colour photograph. I put it closer to the light; my eyesight seemed to have got worse in the last few months and I made a mental note to get some decent reading glasses.

There were two people in the picture. One was Lek, smiling and with her hand raised, as if in greeting. She looked as beautiful as ever and my heart started to thump. She was standing close to a blond-haired young man, who had his arm around her waist and was holding her close to his side. I peered intently at the picture again. It was Bart. It was Bart! Behind the happy couple was a low building on the corner of a city street. A notice above the door displayed the unmistakable words *Black Sun Coffee Shop*. The street sign was legible, too – *Prinsengracht*. It was Amsterdam and the photograph had been automatically dated by the camera – 27 April 1988. Three days ago.

I gawped at the picture, not knowing what to do or what to say. I opened my mouth to ask a question, but there was no one to hear me. So I just stared, bewildered, speechless and utterly confused. Bart was alive. Lek was with him. They were together. Had they started their new life? I looked around helplessly into the bustle of the hotel lobby. Was this some sort of cruel joke? I wanted someone to help me. A passing waitress smiled sweetly as she glided by, but the gesture passed through me like a drifting apparition. Nearly a hundred cheerful, noisy people gabbled to one another in the crowded foyer – excited, waving, laughing. But my world was perfectly silent. I felt completely alone, more so than ever before. The picture slipped out of my numb fingers and fluttered towards the floor. The two jubilant faces stared heartlessly back at me, as it settled gently onto the heavy carpet.

ACKNOWLEDGEMENTS

I would like to extend my thanks to my Editor Lauren Dennington (www.LCDediting.com) for her terrific advice, technical nouse and stalwart encouragement throughout the whole process, to Jason Bevan for the eye catching cover design and to the kind and supportive staff at the Indochine Resort in Phuket where most of the writing was done.